MURDER AT THE PTA

3 8043 26825801 5

Knowsl@y Council

KNOWSLEY LIBRARY SERVICE

Please return this book on or before the date shown below

WHITE KB S   Hannah KB3

1 4 OCT 2013
29 Oct

Doland

2 3 MAY 2014

1 6 JUN 2017

-7 SEP 2018

MURDER AT THE PTA

LAURA ALDEN

THORNDIKE
CHIVERS

This Large Print edition is published by Thorndike Press, Waterville, Maine, USA and by AudioGO Ltd, Bath, England.
Thorndike Press, a part of Gale, Cengage Learning.
Copyright © Penguin Group(USA) Inc., 2010.
The moral right of the author has been asserted.

LIBRARY OF CONGRESS CATALOGING-IN-PUBLICATION DATA

Alden, Laura.
   Murder at the PTA / by Laura Alden.
     p. cm. — (Thorndike Press large print clean reads)
   ISBN-13: 978-1-4104-3644-3 (hardcover)
   ISBN-10: 1-4104-3644-6 (hardcover)
   1. School principals—Crimes against—Fiction. 2. Parents' and teachers' associations—Fiction. 3. Divorced mothers—Fiction. 4. Murder—Investigation—Fiction. 5. City and town life—Wisconsin—Fiction. 6. Large type books. I. Title.
PS3601.L3448M87 2011
813'.6—dc22   2011001441

BRITISH LIBRARY CATALOGUING-IN-PUBLICATION DATA AVAILABLE

Published in 2011 in the U.S. by arrangement with NAL Signet, a member of Penguin Group (USA) Inc.
Published in 2011 in the U.K. by arrangement with NAL Signet, a division of Penguin Group (USA) Inc.

U.K. Hardcover: 978 1 445 83742 0 (Chivers Large Print)
U.K. Softcover: 978 1 445 83743 7 (Camden Large Print)

Printed in the United States of America
1 2 3 4 5 6 7 15 14 13 12 11

To my parents, who gave me life, love, a college education, and a voracious appetite for reading. Thanks, Mom. Thanks, Dad.

ACKNOWLEDGMENTS

No book is written in a vacuum, and this book is no exception. My heartfelt gratitude goes to about a zillion people, but I'd like to mention a few by name. Thanks go to Lorraine Bartlett (aka Lorna Barrett) for poking and prodding, and to Peg Herring for Thai lunches and writerly conversation. To my fantastic editor, Jessica Wade, and to my intrepid agent, Jessica Faust. To the Guppies chapter of Sisters in Crime, because if it weren't for the Guppies, I wouldn't have persevered. To the Plot Hatchers for plotting and hatching, and to Julie Sitzema for her knowledge of Girl Stuff. To my husband for his expertise in All Things Sports (and for a few other things that I'd list except I don't want to be responsible for the deaths of so many trees). Thanks, everyone!

CHAPTER 1

"You need to get out more," Marina said.

As I was in her backyard, my best friend's comment was obviously incorrect. "I am out."

"Don't be a putz." Without turning, she spoke to a five-year-old playing in the nearby sandbox. "Andrew, don't whack your sister on the head. It's not good for you, her, or that piece of processed petroleum stamped into a plastic toy shape in China by underpaid employees and brought to this country on a containership undoubtedly carrying illegal aliens."

Marina and I stood in the late-September sunshine of Rynwood, Wisconsin, enjoying the warm weather. There wouldn't be many more days like this before the cold of winter set in, and Marina was a big believer in outside play for the children in her home day care.

"You know what I mean, Beth," she said

to me. "Socially out."

On the inside I was shrieking, *No! It hasn't been long enough! The kids aren't ready!* I'm *not ready!* On the outside, my lips tightened an infinitesimal fraction of an inch.

"Now, don't look like that." Marina shook her finger at me; she was the only person outside of a sitcom I'd ever seen actually do such a thing. "It's been a year since the divorce."

A year and eight days of sleeping alone, but who was counting?

"Which makes this a perfect time to get back into action." A wisp of Marina's light red hair fell out of her ponytail and across her plump cheek. We looked across the yard to where my ten-year-old daughter, Jenna, had barricaded herself in a tree fort and was dropping bits of maple leaf onto the head of my seven-year-old son. Oliver was red faced and grunting from the effort of trying to reach the lowest branch of the tree.

Ripping apart their young lives with divorce had been the hardest thing I'd ever done. Jenna had taken it on the chin, but Oliver had started sleeping with a pile of stuffed animals big enough to smother him, and every single one had to be given a kiss good night. Bedtime took forever in our house. I knew I should start weaning him off the animals, just as I knew I should start talking to Jenna about the "wonders of womanhood." After Christmas, I thought. Why rush things?

"Know what?" Marina pushed back the stray hairs. More, and then more, would fall out of the ponytail without her noticing, and finally the full glory of her reddish locks would cascade over her shoulders. The hair scrunchie would be on the floor, or in the yard, or in the car, or on the kitchen counter. Marina dropped hair scrunchies like Hansel and Gretel dropped bread crumbs. "I ran into Dave Patterson the other day —" Her extrasensory powers reasserted themselves. "Nathan! Don't climb the fence."

"But my mom's here!" Young Nathan jumped, trying to swing his legs over the white picket fence.

"Wait for your mother to open the gate."

Nathan jumped again.

"Gate!" Marina's sharp command was like a whip. The boy dropped to the ground.

"Hey, Marina." A slim blond woman walked up the side yard's stone path and stood at the gate. "Wonderful day. Oh, hi, Beth. Got a new name for that bookstore yet?" Debra-don't-call-me-Debbie O'Conner grinned at me.

11

If I'd been blessed with quick wit instead of quick alphabetizing skills, I would have come up with something clever enough to silence Nathan's overly perfect mother. But since I hadn't come up with anything better than the current "Children's Bookshelf" since I'd bought the store two years ago, I just shrugged. "Not yet."

Debra opened the childproof latch with one hand, a task that took me two hands and a considerable amount of sotto voce cursing. "Let's go, kiddo," she said to her son. "See you ladies later. I'd love to stop and chat, but the book club is at our house tonight, and I need to fill the cream puffs I baked last night. Bye!"

Cream puffs? No one *made* cream puffs. You bought them from the bakery or thawed them after getting a box out of the grocery store's freezer. I climbed the stairs to the deck and sat in a plastic green chair, feeling inadequate. Cooking I could do, but baking? The last thing I'd baked from scratch had been cupcakes for Jenna's birthday — her eighth. It hadn't gone well.

"Quit that." The deck stairs squeaked under Marina's weight.

"What?"

"You have that comparing-apples-and-oranges look. Speaking of which, did you know Debra can't swim?"

"Please. Everyone knows how to swim."

Marina shook her head. "Can't swim a stroke. She's so scared of water, she wears a life jacket around a pool."

My childhood bulletin board had been crowded with hockey photos and blue ribbons from summer swim meets. I could do something better than Debra? Inconceivable. She was my opposite in a thousand ways — blond, where I was mousy brown; slim, which I hadn't been in years; elegant in a way I only dreamed about. "Why didn't you ever tell me?"

"Didn't know until the other day. Which was the same day I ran into Dave Patterson. We were at the community pool for the ducky swim class, see, and —" Her smile was a little too wide, and she was talking a little too fast, clear indications she was trying to convince me to do something I didn't want to do.

"I'm not going to date Dave Patterson." I didn't want to date anyone. All I wanted was to raise my children and to run my store. I wanted everything and everyone safe and sound: no traumas; no tragedies; no upsets or upheavals — a peaceful *Goodnight Moon* existence.

"He's not bad looking." Marina waggled

her eyebrows.

"I don't care if he's Apollo reincarnated. I'm not ready to date anyone. Not yet." Or ever. Men left the toilet seat up and complained about mowing the lawn. Why bother with them?

"How about —"

"No," I said as firmly as I could, which must not have been firmly enough, because she looked ready to offer up another victim. "Maybe in the spring," I said.

She looked thoughtful, and I was sorry I hadn't said a year. Marina's circle of friends was larger and more varied than mine. We overlapped solely because we'd been neighbors years ago, before Richard had decided to move us into a brand-new pseudo-Victorian house more suitable for his status as CFO of a large insurance company. Maybe living in a ranch house three blocks away from the elementary school didn't fit Richard's image, but it worked wonderfully for Marina's home-day-care business. She watched two children during the day, and three more walked to her house after school.

"Okay," she said. "No dating."

I slid down a little in my chair. Safe and sound. No pressure. Just the peace and warmth of early fall. Leaves turning yellow, orange, and red against the bright blue sky.

14

A tangy earthy smell in the air — that special autumnal scent that summoned memories of high school football games, trick-or-treating, and scooping wet stringy seeds out of pumpkins. I closed my eyes and breathed in fading images of Jenna in a princess costume and Oliver dressed as his favorite stuffed animal.

"Then how about being the secretary of the school's Parent Teacher Association?" Marina ran the words together as fast as an auctioneer trying to unload a box of moldy books.

I opened my eyes and sat up straight. She couldn't possibly have said what I thought she'd said.

"You'd make a great committee secretary. You're organized. You do what you say you will. You know how to do things. You're reliable. Responsible. People trust you." Her smile stretched two feet wide.

"What makes you think I know how to do things?"

"You don't give yourself enough credit. You own a business, for crying out loud. Doing this little secretary thing would be a piece of cake."

"If it's so little, you do it."

"My darling," — "daah-ling" it came out — "think about what you just said."

I did. I thought about it, visualized it, and rejected it. Marina, with her big heart and cheer and love and flamboyance, was not what you'd call efficient. Her husband and youngest son got fed on time, and her college-aged children got regular care packages in the mail, but her desk looked like a horizontal wastebasket. Paperwork was not her strength.

"What happened to the old secretary?" I asked. Though I was a member of the Tarver Elementary PTA, I'd skipped most of last year's meetings. Raising money for handicapped playground equipment was important, as were most of the causes, but my children had needed me more than the PTA did.

"You'll make a great secretary," Marina repeated. "And you need more social interaction. Running that bookstore doesn't count."

"The kids —"

"PTA meetings are on Wednesday, and Richard has the kids that night, yes? I bet you're not doing anything fun with that free time. I bet you do laundry. Maybe sometimes you go wild and balance your checkbook."

Chores weren't my typical Wednesday night, but I wasn't going to tell even my best friend what I did do.

Jenna dropped out of the tree and tore across the yard. Oliver gave up his attempt to climb Tree Everest and tore after her, his shrieks joining hers. Marina's surprise child, nine-year-old Zach, abandoned his pogo stick and followed. In seconds the yard was full of children playing a bizarre variety of tag. My flesh and blood didn't look at me once.

A tiny piece of my silly sentimental heart shredded into pieces. My babies were growing up. Maybe it was time for me to grow up, too. "Okay," I said, sighing. "I'll run. For secretary. I probably won't win, but I'll run."

"Hallelujah!" Marina clapped her hands, leaped out of her chair, and pulled me into a hard hug. "Bet you dinner and a movie that you win."

"You're on."

A few days later I stopped at Tarver to drop off a box of special orders. Delivering to the local schools was one of the services the Children's Bookshelf offered. I wasn't sure it was cost-effective, but it generated a lot of goodwill, and that alone made it worthwhile.

I handed the box to the school secretary,

then turned and almost ran into the wide body of Paul Richey, Jenna's teacher. Paul was often at the store buying books and stickers for the kids in his classroom. All the purchases were out of his own pocket. Many teachers did the same, and I gave them what discount I could.

"So you're going to be the new PTA secretary." He grinned. "Who talked you into volunteering?"

Volunteering? I was getting a bad feeling about this. "I'm running, that's all."

"Gotcha." He nodded sagely. "And because sitting on the PTA committee is such a coveted position, you'll be competing against dozens of candidates."

"There's bound to be a couple." I zipped up my coat. "Aren't there?"

Paul's grin got a little bigger. "In a perfect world, sure. But we're in Rynwood." He sketched a salute and walked toward his classroom.

Mother that I am, I desperately wanted to follow him, to peek in the door and see my daughter. Then I wanted to check on Oliver; I wanted to see his tongue stick out in concentration as he worked out math problems.

But since I also didn't want to see their faces flush with embarrassment — "Mom, I can't *believe* you waved to me in front of my friends!" — I headed back to work and left my children behind.

Two weeks after Marina's not-so-subtle push, I sat at a table near the front of a Tarver Elementary classroom. A PTA-approved tape recorder and blank legal pad sat in front of me, a two-page agenda lurked to my right, and a bright blue portable filing system was on the floor next to my feet.

"Beef Wellington," Marina said. She sat in the front row of the audience, her grin as bright as a shiny shoe. "And *Halloween Two.*"

That dinner-and-a-movie bet wasn't going away. "*The Lion King* and pizza from Sabatini's."

She made a gagging motion. "The owner's connected. You know, the mob? I wouldn't trust any meat he serves. Grilled steaks and *Blazing Saddles.*"

In June I'd blown off my eyebrows trying to light the grill. I hadn't started the evil thing since, and Marina knew it. She also knew I wasn't a Mel Brooks fan. "Peanut butter and jelly and *Dr. Zhivago.*"

As Marina crossed her eyes and stuck out her tongue, a gavel banged down. I jumped and started the tape recorder.

19

"This meeting will come to order." Erica Hale, the PTA's silver-haired president, peered out at the audience over half glasses. "I'd like everyone to welcome our newly installed secretary, Beth Kennedy." Polite applause sprinkled through the room, punctuated by Marina's fist thrust and earsplitting whistle. My cheeks flamed hot, and I shuffled papers that didn't need shuffling.

Erica went on. "As some of you might remember, our former secretary and her family moved to Belize, and Beth has graciously agreed to donate her time and services."

I blinked and mouthed the word to Marina. "Belize?" I'd heard of people vacationing in and retiring to Belize, but moving there? With young children? That was far outside my comfort zone — about two thousand miles outside.

Marina shrugged.

"With the committee's permission," Erica said, "I'd like to rearrange tonight's agenda. We have a guest who has another commitment, and I'd like to move action item number one to the beginning of the meeting."

I glanced at the agenda, but before I could locate the action items, Erica requested a voice vote approving the change. "Ayes?"

Erica asked. The other committee members said aye. "Nays?"

I found the action items. Number three was putting allergy warnings on bake sale goods. Number two was buying an automated snow-day notification system. Number one was . . . "Uh-oh," I said.

"Was that a nay vote?" Erica frowned at me.

"Uh, no." I picked up a pen, circled the pertinent item, drew an arcing line up to the top of the agenda, and ended it with an arrow. "I'm fine with the change. Sorry."

Erica nodded and looked at the back of the room. "Agnes? You have the floor."

Twenty-odd members of the PTA were in the audience, and every one of them twitched as Erica said the name "Agnes." As if choreographed, all heads turned to watch the fiftyish Agnes Mephisto, principal of Tarver Elementary, walk to the front of the room. Topped by a haircut that even I knew had gone out of style years ago, Agnes's body had an unfortunate resemblance to a fire hydrant. She walked with solid steps and planted herself directly in front of me. I had an excellent view of her back and her long, overpermed hair.

"Good evening, PTA members!" Agnes's voice was piercing at a distance. At point-blank range, it was all I could do not to cover my ears. "I have outstanding news for you, for our community, but most of all for the wonderful students of Tarver Elementary." There was a smile in her voice, and I was just as glad not to see it. Agnes had a weasel-like cast to her face, a resemblance that grew even more pronounced when she smiled. Luckily, that didn't happen often. "I'm sure," she said, "that everyone will be as excited about this project as I am."

I leaned to the left to look around Agnes. Excitement wasn't the word I would have used to describe the crowd's emotions, not if the crossed arms and stone faces were any indication. In the ten years she'd been principal at Tarver, Agnes had alienated a host of parents and encouraged more than one teacher to take early retirement. Only the school board seemed to like her. "Test scores are up," Mack Vogel, the superintendent, had said when he'd stopped by the store the day before. He also said he hoped that, as the new PTA secretary, I'd ease tensions with Agnes. "You're the conciliatory sort, Beth. Calm and peaceful." He'd given me a hearty handshake. "You'll do a great job of cooling tempers."

Right. I raised my eyebrows and tried to catch Marina's eye, but she was too busy scowling.

"We're entering a new age," Agnes said, "and I can't stand by and see Tarver Elementary left behind. I can see exactly what we need, and I know you'll agree with me."

Not a head nodded. I sneaked a look down the committee table. No one there was nodding, either.

"This school needs better facilities," Agnes said. "I want our children to have a larger library. I want more computers and more books. And our children need more exposure to music. Have any of your kids ever seen an opera?" She looked at the cold expressions. "I didn't think so. Children need artistic stimulation. They need to play instruments. They need to paint and draw and sing. And they need pets. They need to —"

"Agnes." Erica drummed her arthritic fingertips on the table. In years past, PTAs had consisted of parents and teachers, but the Tarver PTA had conceded the need to expand its membership and had allowed grandparents to join. "A well-rounded education is one of Tarver's missions," Erica said. "That isn't up for debate. Could you please get to the point?" She gave the clock hanging over the classroom door a hard look.

23

The female fireplug swelled in all directions, and I shrank back. Stories of a shouting and sputtering Agnes were legendary, but I had no wish to see or hear the reality. The swelling went down, and Agnes settled back on the balls of her feet. "Of course, Erica." Her shoulders rose and fell slightly. "I've been notified that a benefactor is willing to make a large donation to Tarver Elementary."

Agnes talked over the low buzz of conversation that circled the room. "The benefactor, who wishes to remain anonymous, is happy with my suggestion for an addition to the school building."

The buzz grew to a dull roar.

"Who is it?" called a woman from the back of the room.

"Anonymous means anonymous, Cee-Cee," Agnes said. "The benefactor's name won't be made public. Our secret donor is eager to get started, so I've hired an architect to —"

"You did what?" A young father in the back row tried to stand, but his wife dragged him back down.

"I've hired an architect," Agnes repeated. "With my guidance, this addition should —"

"*Your* guidance?" A blowsy woman

grabbed the back of the chair in front of her and heaved herself up. "What about our guidance?"

Another woman stood. "What about the taxpayers?"

"Since this is a donation," Agnes said smoothly, "there will be no bond issue. The taxpayers needn't be consulted."

The room exploded into sudden sound.

"You can't —"

"Of all the high-handed —"

"Just because you're principal doesn't mean you can —"

I laid down my pen. How does a secretary take minutes of a free-for-all? I watched the wheels of the recorder spin and hoped there'd be enough tape.

"Where on earth have you been?"

"Ahh!" Everything I was carrying cascaded to the kitchen floor. "Richard!" I put a hand to my chest. Yes, my heart was still beating. "What are you doing here?"

"Waiting for you to get home so my children wouldn't be left unattended."

I took a deep breath — then another. Frights like that couldn't be good for you. "Why isn't your car in the driveway?"

"Since I don't know which side of the garage you use, I parked in front."

The house was on a corner lot. "A choice corner lot," the real estate agent had said when we'd toured the place. Choice of what? I'd asked. Richard had chuckled, but I hadn't been trying to be funny.

"What are you doing here?" I asked. "The kids sleep at your place on Wednesdays."

"I have to leave at six for an emergency meeting in Chicago." He looked at his watch. "That's in six and a half hours. I left messages at your store and here and on your cell phone. Why you didn't call me back, I can't imagine."

I could, but imagination wasn't one of Richard's strong suits. "Are you going to be back for the weekend?" I asked. "The kids are looking forward to carving pumpkins."

"Yes, I know." He picked his coat up from a kitchen chair. "What's all this?" He gestured at the floor, now covered with PTA paraphernalia. I explained my new role and he chuckled, using the same patronizing frequency that had incited divorce proceedings. "Marina talked you into it, didn't she? Not a bad idea. You need to get out more."

Please, I begged the universe, send me a witty retort.

"I'll pick the kids up from school on Friday." Richard jangled his car keys. "You will be home on Sunday at seven, won't you? I don't want to have to wait like this again."

When he'd left, I took off my shoes and padded in stocking feet up the hardwood stairway. The doors to Jenna's and Oliver's rooms were ajar. Jenna was flat on her stomach, arms spread wide across a rumpled blanket, our black cat curled up between her feet. I kissed the top of her head and straightened the sheets.

In Oliver's room, stuffed animals were dropping off the bed like fleas from a swimming dog. I picked up a bear, a lion, a dog, a hippopotamus, and lined them up on the desk so that Oliver would see them when he woke. I kissed my baby boy and headed to the kitchen with one thought in my head.

In the back of the supremely unreachable cabinet above the refrigerator, there might, just might, have been a bag of Hershey's kisses. I dragged over a chair, clambered up, opened the cabinet door, and spied the unmistakable sheen of aluminum-covered chocolate. "Found you." This would be medicinal. I'd eat one or two. Three, at most. Four would be too many, but —

"Mom? Mommy?"

Jenna. I jumped to the floor and ran up to her room. "What's the matter, sweetheart?" I went to my knees beside her bed. "Another nightmare?"

"I — I think so." She sat up. In the dim glow shed by a night-light, I could see hot sleep creases on her face. "Someone was chasing me and I tried to run, but I kept falling down and getting up and falling down." Her strong chin trembled.

"It was just a silly dream. Slide over, sweetie." She made room, and I pulled my daughter onto my lap. "Just a dream. Mommy's here. Nothing's going to hurt you. Just a silly old dream." In time, my nonsense words calmed her. When she was soundly into the land of Wynken, Blynken, and Nod, I tucked her back into bed and gave her one more kiss.

The kitchen clock showed an ugly time when I came back to collect my PTA notes — half past midnight. A sensible person would have left the chore of typing the meeting minutes until the next day. Until the weekend, even. I took the files into the study, turned on the computer, and started typing. Heroically, I took only one chocolate break.

Well, maybe two.

Three, tops.

CHAPTER 2

The next morning it took me three tries to punch in the correct code for the store's alarm system. Five hours of sleep just wasn't enough. Once upon a time I'd pulled all-nighters with ease, but my last collegiate exam had been a long time ago.

While I turned on lights, I did the math and came up with eighteen years since I graduated from Northwestern, journalism degree in hand. As it turned out, I'd hardly needed that degree with my only newspaper job being the circulation editor for the Rynwood paper, published twice weekly. Richard and I had married straight out of college, and he hadn't wanted me to work for the big paper in nearby Madison. "You'll be safer here in Rynwood," he'd said.

He was probably right, and when I paused to think about things, I realized I was content with my life. I'd answered an ad for a part-time bookstore clerk when Oliver started preschool and had progressed to store ownership. Funny how things turned out, sometimes. I loved Rynwood's downtown with its quirky collection of stores and store owners, and I loved my brick walls, tin ceiling, and faded carpet. But most of all I loved the intoxicating scent of new books.

Once the store was bright with halogen lights, I headed to my minuscule office at the back. I dropped my purse into a desk drawer and picked up the report my manager had left last night. Clerks came and went with seasonal frequency, but Lois, the last holdover from the previous regime, was forever. For that, I was grateful — almost all of the time.

"Less two percent," she'd written on the monthly financial figures. "Party?" This meant our September sales were down two percent from the previous year and Lois's idea for spurring sales was a Halloween party. Which meant decorations and costumes for the staff, and cookies and cider and spooky music — probably a machine to make fog, too. Lois didn't do things in a small way.

As I sat heavily in the scratched wooden chair, also a holdover from the last owner, the wheels squeaked. They squeaked again as I stood. Teatime — I had to make decisions, and no way could I do that without a mug of tea.

"Good morning, Beth!" Lois breezed into the tiny kitchenette. She was twenty years older than I was, three inches taller, ten pounds lighter, and, since the death of her husband, infinitely more adventurous in her clothing choices. My idea of cutting-edge fashion was adding a paisley scarf to a navy blue blazer. Today, Lois wore canvas high-top tennis shoes, a plaid kilt kept closed by a brass pin, a pink ruffled blouse that miraculously managed to go with the kilt, and noisy metal bracelets. She twirled a black velvet cape from her shoulders and pulled off her red beret, hanging them both on hooks. "Got that tea water going?" she asked. "I have a new kind of chai. Vanilla peach spice." She waved a small box.

"Lois, about a Halloween party. I'm not sure —"

"We can afford it? Don't worry. It'll cost hardly a penny. We'll print a few posters and hang them around town. We'll make some flyers and stuff them in bags. Half sheets, to save paper." She talked with one hand on the handle of the almost-hot teakettle. "We'll get the staff to bring a treat each, and I have boxes and boxes of decorations at home."

The whistle began its throaty chirping. Lois snatched it off the electric hot plate and poured water into two mugs. The tea bags steeped as she talked. "I checked the attic last night, and I have oodles of orange lights. Only things we'll have to buy are cider and plastic cups."

"I have cups." The words were out before I knew I was going to say anything.

"Excellent." Lois dunked the tea bags a few times and dropped them onto a cracked Peter Rabbit dish. The store carried child-sized dinnerware of Peter and his sisters. Breakages happened on occasion, and I had a varied collection of repaired dishes at home. The kids considered themselves too old for such babyish things, but I didn't mind eating toast with Flopsy, Mopsy, and Cottontail.

"I'll bring in my special Halloween CDs." Lois wrapped her hands around the mug. "And my sister has a neighbor who has a friend who bought a fog machine for his last Halloween party. I bet I could borrow it."

Sometimes I wondered if Lois knew whose store this was. Sometimes I wondered if I knew.

"Hello? Is anyone here? Beth?"

I put down my tea and hurried out. "Good

32

morning . . . Oh. Hi, Debra."

Nathan's mother, dressed in a skirt-and-jacket set two shades darker than her pale blue eyes, put her hands on her hips. Light glinted off her multicarat engagement ring. "Is it true?" she demanded.

"Umm . . ." I tried to like Debra. She was pleasant. She watched her son's soccer games and didn't scream at him. She attended church every Sunday and held hands with her husband on walks. I'd even seen her brush snow off an elderly woman's windshield, but I just couldn't like her. Marina said it was my inferiority complex rearing its butt-ugly head. Maybe knowing Debra was afraid of water would give me an edge. Not that we were in competition.

"I couldn't make it last night," Debra said. "What is Agnes Mephisto doing now?"

Last night's PTA meeting came back to me in a rush — Agnes and her anonymous donor. And since for every action there is an equal and opposite reaction, there also came the remembered instant opposition to Agnes's proposal. "Would you like a copy of the meeting minutes?" I asked.

"Just tell me what that woman is trying to do to our school this time."

I gave her a summary, then said, "I'll send out minutes tonight. Is your e-mail address still debra at rynwood dot com?"

She ignored my attempt to slide away from the subject of Agnes. "She's trying to railroad us into this addition."

"Well —"

"Anonymous donor, my aunt Fanny. We have a right to know who's putting up the money. What if it's some kind of drug lord? We don't want dirty cash in our school."

"I suppose you're —"

"And how can that woman bypass getting a taxpayer vote? I don't care where the money is coming from. The parents of Tarver Elementary should be at the table for this issue."

Her voice was stern but not strident. She was being assertive but not aggressive. The perfect balance. So of course I couldn't help myself. "It would be nice to have a bigger library."

Debra's expertly made-up eyes thinned. "You're in favor of this?"

I shrugged. "There are positives."

"That's not the point. None of her plans has had public approval. She can't just forge ahead making decisions without a consensus. This is the United States." She stood tall in her outrage. "This is Madison!"

It was Rynwood, five miles away from the hotbed of liberalism in Madison, but I didn't say so.

"I'll be at the next PTA meeting," Debra said, "and I intend to speak up." Her blond hair bounced like something out of a television commercial as she strode outside and down the sidewalk to the bank where she was a vice president. The bells hanging on the door had barely stopped jangling when CeeCee Daniels came in. "Can you believe that woman?" she asked.

"Debra?" Maybe if I paid seventy-five dollars for a haircut, my hair would bounce like that. Not that I was ever likely to find out.

"No, Agnes! She's shoving that project down our throats. She can't do this!" Cee-Cee put her hands on her hips and leaned forward. I had a premonition about the rest of my day. Tarver parent after Tarver parent would march into my store, ask about last night's meeting, complain about Agnes, and leave without buying anything. If I were more like Debra, I'd tell people I had a business to run and could they please contact me after hours. But I was Beth Kennedy, and I'd been raised to be a Nice Girl.

"How can she do this without taxpayer approval?" CeeCee's face was turning pink. "It's *our* school, not hers!"

I nodded sympathetically and prepared

35

myself for a long, long day.

The only customer who didn't complain about Agnes was Randy Jarvis. Randy was one of the few male members of the PTA. He was also the committee treasurer. Why, no one seemed to know. Randy owned a gas station and convenience store two blocks away from the Children's Bookshelf, and I spotted him parking his SUV in front of the store. He heaved his three-hundred-pound bulk down from the driver's seat, and I opened the front door for him.

"Afternoon, Randy. How are you?"

"Middlin', middlin'. I was passing by, so I decided to stop and chat instead of calling." The short walk from vehicle to store interior had him out of breath.

"Have a seat." I pushed a chair out from behind the counter.

"Hot out there," he huffed. Sweat beaded on his forehead and dripped down his temples as he sat. From his shirt pocket he withdrew a handkerchief, which he used and replaced. He smoothed his flyaway white hair with sweat-damp hands. "Winter can't come fast enough. Nothing like a nice cold blast from Canada to set things right."

The bell jingled and I nodded at a customer. "What can I do for you, Randy? If you're after the meeting minutes, I'm going to mass e-mail them tonight."

"Fine, fine." He unbuttoned his cuffs and rolled up the sleeves. "Good to have them out before Monday."

"Why?"

"Erica is calling a special meeting. Monday at seven o'clock. Add that to the minutes." He held out his hands and made a typing motion. "Won't take but a minute." He tilted his head. "A minute? Get it?"

"Good one," I said. "Why do we need to meet on Monday?"

Randy's bushy eyebrows went high, putting deep wrinkles into his forehead. "The addition." Duh, his expression said.

It was hard to believe I'd first heard about the addition less than twenty-four hours ago. I'd liked life better back then. "Can't it wait?" I heard the whine in my voice and summoned my inner Debra. "We don't want to rush into this. Big projects take time to plan properly."

"Agnes wants to start construction in November."

"*This* November?" My jaw dropped and stayed open long enough that my tongue started drying out. "The less-than-thirty-days-from-now November?"

"No time like the present. And no rest for

the weary." He grabbed the chair arms and pulled himself up. "See you Monday night." He headed out with the lumbering gait of a bear fattened for winter.

I slumped against the counter. Another meeting. More rancor, more insults and accusations, more anger. "Thanks a lot, Marina," I muttered.

"Beth?" Lois stood in front of me, arms full of picture books. "Are you all right?"

Not hardly. "Fine, thanks. But I could use another cup of that tea."

Friday night there was a double knock on the kitchen door, and Marina stuck her head inside. "Can I come in?"

"No."

She laughed, sending forth a bubbling stream of cheer, and came inside with the smell of outside air clinging to her clothes. "Would it help if I promised never to talk you into doing anything ever again?"

"Wouldn't be worth the breath it would take to say it. You'd break a promise like that inside of two weeks." I went back to slicing up carrots. The firm noise of knife hitting cutting board echoed around the room.

"It's not like I knew Agnes was going to pull a stunt like that."

"My brain believes you, but the rest of me isn't so sure." I started in on the broccoli.

"Is this my punishment?" She waved a hand at the vegetables. "Rabbit food for dinner? And then I'll be forced to watch *Bambi*." With her fingers spread wide, she fake-choked herself.

Marina was a big believer in meat, potatoes, and action movies. Part of my mission in life was to get her to appreciate vegetables and epic historical sagas. So far her reaction had been the same as Jenna's and Oliver's — lots of face scrunching accompanied by a considerable amount of whining. "No better than you deserve," I said.

"Do you realize what that could do to my digestive system? And I have it on good authority that watching *Bambi* after the age of forty turns your hair white."

"Do you realize how many Tarver parents came through the store in the last two days?"

She dropped to her knees, hands clasped and raised high. "Please, forgive me. You're my best friend, and I would never ever wish an Agnes project on you."

"Get up, you goofball."

"Not until you say I'm forgiven. I will stay on this floor until the crows pick me clean.

I will stay until my bones are bleached. I will —"

"Okay, okay. Forgiveness is bestowed."

She pushed herself to her feet. "Good. My knees were killing me. What are we eating, anyway?"

"Vegetarian stew." Her eyes stretched open enough for white to be seen all around the hazel irises. I laughed. "Gotcha. We're having chicken stir-fry, and I rented *Rear Window*."

"Weenie." She socked me on the arm. "Maybe we should call Agnes and invite her over."

"Maybe you should keep your ideas to yourself."

"Oh, I don't know. Poooor Agnes." Marina hitched herself onto a stool at the butcher block–topped kitchen island. "She looked all alone tonight. No cars in the driveway, no lights on except in the kitchen. She's probably going to eat a frozen dinner and watch bad television."

Agnes lived across the street and one door down from Marina. "This interest in Agnes's personal habits is becoming un-healthy."

"Any interest in Agnes is unhealthy." She picked chocolate chips from a bowl of trail mix I'd set out. "Maybe she just needs a friend."

"She's been in Rynwood ten years." I opened a box of chicken broth.

"Meaning what? That if she doesn't have friends by now, there's something wrong with her?" Marina popped a handful of chocolate in her mouth.

"Don't eat any more of that. You'll spoil your dinner. I'm saying maybe Agnes likes to be alone. I would after a week with a school full of people."

"Hmm." Marina reached for the bowl. I yanked it away. "Some nights," she said, "there's a car in the driveway until the wee hours."

"Then she doesn't need an invitation from us," I said. Not that Marina had been serious. She and Agnes went toe-to-toe at full volume the first year Agnes had been principal — something about the color Agnes wanted to repaint the cafeteria, if I remembered correctly. A decade later, neither one had a kind word to say about the other.

"Why the sudden concern about Agnes?" I asked. She made a grab for the bowl, but I held it out of her reach. "You can't stand the woman. What's the deal?"

"No deal."

"Hah." I held the bowl a scant inch from

41

her stretching fingers. "Tell," I said, making the bowl dance tantalizingly. She lunged, but with a mother's instinct I anticipated her move and whisked it to a safe distance. "Tell!"

"Meanie."

"Yes, I'm the meanest mom in the whole wide world. What's your interest in Agnes?"

She slumped back and crossed her arms. "I want to know who the anonymous donor is."

I stared at her, then started laughing. "And you think Agnes is going to just let that slip?"

"It could happen."

"Oh, sure. And I could win the lottery. Agnes is as secretive as the CIA." I relented and put the bowl back on the counter.

"She can't be the only one who knows who made the donation." Marina spoke around a mouthful of chocolate-chipless trail mix. She'd already picked out the good stuff.

"It's probably no one we've ever heard of."

"I have a theory." She leaned forward, smiling in the special way that meant she had the tastiest tidbits of gossip to share.

I turned away and opened the refrigerator door. Inside was a dish of chicken I'd cut

42

up into small bits and set to marinating an hour earlier. "Don't want to hear it."

"Ooo, all grumpy tonight, are we?"

"Yes. I've had my fill of Agnes and the Addition. That's all I've heard about for two days. New subject, please." I sloshed some oil in the bottom of the wok.

"Have you heard my theory that Joe Sabatini is mobbed up?"

"Yes, and I don't believe you. Just because the guy owns a pizza place and has an Italian name doesn't make him a member of the Mafia."

"Spoilsport." She kicked her toes against the island, just like Jenna and Oliver did. "Say, have you heard the latest about Rhonda, my next-door neighbor?"

"The one with the —" I made a big curvy motion in front of my chest.

"That's her." Marina nodded. "All real."

"How do you know?" I'd always assumed Rhonda Tracy's endowment had some assistance.

"Can't you tell?"

"No. Why can you?"

"Reality TV," Marina said promptly. "You find out all sorts of interesting things, and quit making faces at me. Anyway, Rhonda keeps getting home delivery of dry cleaning."

"Oh?" I dropped the chicken into the wok. The instant sizzle sent small drops of oil bouncing high.

"The truck says 'Lakeside Dry Cleaning.' "

I grabbed tongs out of a drawer and tossed the chicken around. "Since when does Lakeside deliver?"

"They don't."

"If they don't deliver, what is the truck doing at Rhonda's house?"

Marina raised one eyebrow. "You tell me."

Light dawned. "Marina Neff, do you mean . . . ?"

"Yep. Rhonda and Don the dry cleaner. Same Don whose wife took off on him a few years ago for parts unknown. Not that I blame her," Marina said. "Don's weenie-ness has grown amazingly since he lost his hair." She tipped the last of the trail mix out of the bowl and into her mouth. "All those chemicals can't be good for you."

"No one in the history of the world has had an affair with a dry cleaner," I said. "Doctors, lawyers, health club instructors. But a dry cleaner?"

Marina and I looked at each other and started laughing. It was a good, long laugh, one that almost made me forget about the upcoming Monday meeting — almost.

■ ■ ■ ■

Monday night at six forty-five we moved the PTA meeting from classroom to gym, and even then the place was packed from stem to stern. Occasional snatches of conversation reached the committee table, and every scrap carried the scent of mutiny. A revolution was in the offing, and all I wanted was to keep my head down, take notes, and get home before ten o'clock. After ten on a weeknight my babysitter charged double.

Erica pounded the table with her gavel, and the room quieted. "Thank you for attending this special meeting of the Tarver Elementary PTA. I am aware of the charged emotions regarding tonight's topic." She scanned the audience, studying the faces. "If anyone gets carried away, he or she will be removed." She nodded at Harry, the school's janitor, who doubled as a security guard. He stood at the back of the room, six feet tall and Ichabod Crane thin. "Everyone who wishes to speak," Erica said, "will get an opportunity to voice her or his opinion."

Rats. There went the babysitting budget.

"But with this many attendees, I will be

strictly enforcing a speaking limit of three minutes."

I counted heads and multiplied. Midnight, easy.

"Let's begin," Erica said. "The first and only item on the agenda is the Tarver Elementary addition." She sat back. "Agnes, you have the floor."

Out in the audience, dozens of arms crossed simultaneously. Agnes, who had been standing next to Harry, waded through a thick silence to the front of the gym. She turned and faced a wall of opposition. To her credit, she smiled. "Good evening, everyone. I'm delighted to have this opportunity to show my presentation to so many people. Harry?"

The janitor flicked switches, and we sat in a red glow cast by exit lights.

Agnes's disembodied voice came out of the dark. "Start it, please."

A click, and a PowerPoint presentation sprang up on the screen that had unrolled behind the head table. The committee hopped their chairs one hundred eighty degrees. Well, most of us hopped. Randy Jarvis hadn't done any hopping in years.

A blast of pretentious music sequenced with the appearance of the title images. *Browne and Browne Architects presents . . .*

The Tarver Elementary School Addition.

"Oh, my," I whispered. Agnes had hired an architect weeks ago. Months ago. She'd spent money that wasn't hers on an unpopular project. She'd made plans without the input of teachers, staff, or parents.

I glanced down the table. Erica's frown was visible in the glow of the pale green lettering. Randy looked jovial, but then, he always did. Julie Reed, the vice president, looked asleep. Though since she had a set of six-year-old twins and an advanced pregnancy, it was understandable that a dark room would send her nodding.

"This is our future." Agnes spoke loudly enough to be heard over the music. "A wonderful future for us all."

The title dissolved into a three-dimensional rotating image of the school.

"This is our current structure," Agnes said. "Watch and wait."

The familiar single-story brick building started to change. It sprouted oddly shaped boxes. It changed color, and the brick disappeared. Landscaping evolved from juniper bushes to grasses that waved in an unfelt breeze. The main entrance vanished and grew back in a different place. Large banks of windows morphed into triangle shapes. And, in the center of the building's face to

47

the world, the existing front door grew into a great expanse of shiny mirrored glass.

"This," Agnes said, pride ringing through her voice, "is the new face of Tarver Elementary."

It was, without a doubt, the ugliest building I'd ever seen in my life.

There was silence. No one moved; no one spoke. Then, with a noise that started low and rose with a rush to a pounding height, the room erupted in anger.

CHAPTER 3

I ran as fast as I could, but my pursuer's footsteps came closer and closer. I fell, rolling in a tumbling somersault. "Hah!" he shouted. "Now I'll brrrring!"

I rolled the other way, desperate to escape his cold grasp.

"Mrrrr!"

I opened my eyes. Our cat, George, gazed at me disapprovingly.

The phone rang again. I tried to sit up, but the sheets and comforter had wrapped tightly around me in my nightmare struggles. I jabbed with my elbows and picked up the phone.

"Beth? This is Heather Kingsley. Listen, I wanted to catch you before you left the house."

I rubbed at the sleep seeds in the corners of my eyes. Somebody's mother. Emma. "Um, hi, Heather."

"We need to do something about Agnes,"

Heather said in her breathy voice. "And we need to do it fast. I already talked to Erica and Julie about my husband. You know Mitch? He's a lawyer, and he says that Agnes doesn't need the PTA's permission to build, but —"

I gasped. "Oh, no."

Heather paused. "He's a good lawyer. Not one of those ambulance chasers."

I gave the sheets a kick and jumped out of bed. "Sorry, Heather, but I can't talk now. I'll call you later." If the clock on my nightstand was right, I had fifteen minutes to get the kids dressed, fed, and delivered to school. How could I have slept so late?

"Oliver!" I charged into his room and slapped on the overhead light. "Up! We're late!" A small hand pushed a stuffed tiger to the side, and Oliver's head peeked out of the covers. "Jammies off. Here, wear this." I opened drawers and piled clothes onto his dresser. "Put the fire on, kiddo. Downstairs in three minutes."

I hurried to Jenna's room, but she wasn't there. Her bed, however, was neatly made up and her pajamas were on the hook behind her door. I smiled. Typical Jenna.

No time for a shower. I rushed into the nearest clothing available and hurried downstairs. Jenna sat at the kitchen island, eating a bowl of cold cereal and watching the Weather Channel.

"How long have you been awake? Why didn't you get me up?" I grabbed a bowl and poured cereal. "Oliver! Your breakfast is ready!" The phone rang.

"Beth!" The voice was so loud that I winced and held the receiver away from my ear. "Kirk Olsen here."

I opened the refrigerator door and got the milk. Neal and Avery's father. "Good morning, Kirk. I'm running late, so if you don't mind —"

He ran roughshod over my words. "It's That Woman. This addition is a hundred times worse than the time she changed the bus routes. A thousand times worse than the time she changed the school mascot from a golden retriever to a bulldog."

I poured milk on Oliver's cereal and put my hand over the receiver. "Oliver! Now! Sorry, Kirk. You were saying?"

Kirk Olsen had reached the middle of last night's meeting when Oliver finished eating. "Kirk? Sorry, but I really have to go. Talk to you later." I hung up the phone and looked at my children. "There's no time to make sandwiches. I'll give you money for hot lunch."

Jenna's face brightened; Oliver's soured.

51

My son had never been big on change. I kissed the top of his head. "Get your backpacks, you two. Time to scoot."

I was reaching for my purse when the phone rang again. All my Nice Girl instincts screamed at me to answer. I took one step toward the phone and saw the kitchen clock. No. Couldn't be done. I grabbed my purse and headed for the garage, ignoring a ringing telephone for the first time in my life.

"Alexander Graham Bell has a lot to answer for." I pushed the OFF button on the store's cordless phone and was sincerely glad the store had only two phone lines.

Lois laughed and got out her pen. "Fourteen." She'd started a tally when the third anti-Agnes call came in. "Bet we hit thirty before closing." Lois held out her hand. "Five bucks." She'd barely finished the sentence when the phone rang again.

"No bets." I handed the receiver to Lois. "If it's the president of the United States, tell him I'm in the bathroom and I'll call back. Anyone else, say I'm dead."

Lois answered the phone and looked at me, eyebrows raised. "Hi, Marina. No, I'm afraid you can't talk to her."

I held out my hand.

"She's here, but she says she's dead."

I wrestled the phone away. "I'm not dead yet."

"You will be soon," Marina said, chuckling.

I held the phone away from my ear, stared at it, then put it back. "Sorry?"

Marina's sigh whistled in my ear. "Movie quote."

"Oh." I tried to think back through the movies we'd watched. "*Young Frankenstein?*"

"Good guess, but no. Speaking of which, I'd guess your day has been busy."

"Not with bookselling, it hasn't. If one more person talks to me about the addition, my eardrums will shatter."

"Well, we don't want that. How would you be able to hear my latest news? Want to guess at today's news flash?"

"Your neighbor's black Lab has been seeing a poodle."

"Better."

"Your sister is quitting her stockbroker job and moving to Mexico City to teach orphans."

"Better."

"Um . . ." I scratched my cheek and suddenly remembered I hadn't had a shower this morning. Ick. "I can't think of anything better than that."

"Think of Randy Jarvis."

"Okay." Nice guy, would probably fool the doctors and outlive us all.

"Randy." She paused dramatically. "And Agnes Mephisto."

"No." I winced away from the idea of the three-hundred-pound Randy getting cozy with Agnes.

"Oh, yes." Marina chuckled. "Give me another reason Randy's car would be parked in Agnes's driveway last Saturday night."

I fished around for an explanation. "Randy's good with car stuff. Maybe Agnes had something wrong with . . . with one of her tires. Randy was helping."

"At two in the morning?"

"Why not? Agnes didn't want to risk hurting her tire, so it had to be done as soon as she saw it, which was after she'd come home from a late movie. And car places put lug nuts on really tight these days." I was liking this theory. A lot. "Randy was going to take the tire in and get it fixed —"

Marina started laughing. "Beth, with an imagination like that, you should write a book. You probably know where Randy was going to take this imaginary tire."

Rynwood Auto, I thought. "Well, it could be true."

"Ooo, Ms. Defensive. Only problem is it's happened more than once. Kendra, put that down. Kendra, I said —" There was a crash and a child's wail. "Uh-oh. Gotta go."

I opened the top drawer of the under-counter filing cabinet, put the phone inside, and shut the drawer. "Lois, is Paoze here? I'm ready for a long lunch."

Her gray head popped above a rack of young adult paperbacks. "He just came in."

For part-time help I'd hired two University of Wisconsin college students, Sara and Paoze. Sara was as German-looking as you could get: tall, blond, blue-eyed, and pale of face. Paoze, a young Hmong immigrant from Laos, was her reverse image with short black hair, black eyes, and dark-toned skin. He stuck out in Rynwood like a snowball in a coal bin.

Paoze materialized in front of me. "Good morning, Mrs. Kennedy. I hope I am not late." Until he'd started high school, Paoze hadn't spoken much English beyond "yes," "no," and "I need bathroom." Now a literature major, he yearned to write a novel based on his family's struggles.

"No, Paoze, you're not late. How was the bike ride?"

"Fine, thank you." He nodded, almost bowing.

I opened the drawer and removed the phone. "It's all yours. I'm going to lunch."

55

The phone rang, and I practically sprinted to my office for purse, coat, and gloves. The weather had turned in the last couple of weeks; Indian summer was a thing of the past. That morning I'd seen a skin of ice on a pond and there'd be snow before we knew it.

"Good morning, the Children's Bookshelf," Paoze said. "How may I help you?"

I pulled on my coat and headed for the front of the store. "Not here," I stage-whispered.

"I am sorry, madam, but Mrs. Kennedy has stepped out." Paoze smiled, showing brilliantly white teeth. "Would you care to leave a message?"

The kid deserved a raise. Too bad I couldn't afford to give him one. I pushed the front door open, rushing into fresh air and freedom. No phones, my heart sang. An hour with no talk of Agnes or the Addition or — "Ooomph!" I banged into an immovable object that had suddenly appeared in the middle of the sidewalk. The impact sent me staggering.

"Oomph, yourself," the object said. I felt a grasp on my arms, and my lurch for balance ended. "Are you all right?"

It was a male object. Straight ahead of me were white buttons on a blue denim shirt. I looked up and saw an attractively muscled neck — higher, a wide, clean-shaven chin. Higher yet there were firm lips, straight nose, blue eyes, wide forehead, and curly blond hair with the lightest touch of white at the temples.

"You look a little stunned," he said.

"Yes. I mean, no. I'm fine." The heat from his hands was burrowing through my clothes and into my skin. "Sorry. Usually I look where I'm going." I stepped out of his grip.

"But not always?" He lifted one side of his mouth in a devastatingly attractive lopsided grin.

"Afraid not. I'm often in a hurry, and once I almost ran right into Auntie May's wheel-chair."

"Auntie May?"

"She's not my real aunt. She's everybody's aunt. Everybody in Rynwood, anyway." I was babbling, but couldn't stop myself. Happened every time I was embarrassed. If I didn't turn bright red, I babbled. In bad cases, I did both. "She's about a hundred and fifty years old and lives in Sunny Rest Assisted Living. It's a couple blocks over, and on warm days she gets a nurse's aide to wheel her downtown."

"She sounds like a nice lady."

"She's a holy terror." *Stop,* I told myself.

Stop. "That day I almost ran into her, she screamed bloody murder and started whacking me with her umbrella. If the wheelchair hadn't started rolling away, she might have killed me."

He laughed and held out his hand. "Evan Garrett."

Tentatively, I put my hand in a palm twice the size of mine. "Beth Kennedy." He must have had experience shaking hands with normal-sized humans; his grip didn't even make me wince.

"You own the bookstore," he stated.

My neck was getting sore from looking up at him. I took a step back. My chiropractor would give me a gold star. "Yes, but —"

"How did I know?" He did that half-grin thing. "Spies."

I glanced up and down the sidewalk.

"Or," he said, "it could be that I saw your name on the Chamber of Commerce members list."

"The spy story is better."

"But we don't want our relationship to get started on a lie, do we?"

His gaze was on my face, and I felt the familiar heat moving up my neck. "You're new in Rynwood?" I blurted.

"Signed the papers on the hardware store last week."

"I thought . . ." The heat continued up my neck and onto my face.

"That Stanley was trying to unload it on some unsuspecting moron? That's me," he said cheerfully, "the new moron in town."

"Oh." I couldn't think of a thing to say. The best-looking man ever seen in Rynwood was standing in front of me and my mind was empty. I'd never known what to say to Beautiful People. They belonged in a different solar system and lived by different rules. Mr. Evan Garrett was too good-looking not to know he was good-looking, and I knew what that meant: He was most likely a jerk. Yup, a jerk. As soon as I passed judgment, my tongue loosened and my voice returned. "Even morons can run a business. Look at me." I took another step back and rubbed my neck. "It's been nice meeting you, Mr. Garrett. I'm sure I'll see you around."

"Evan," he said. "And I say there's no time like the present. What do you say to lunch? I could use some advice on restaurants."

"Oh." I glanced at my store. At my watch. At the copy of *Breaking Dawn* I'd picked up on my way out the door. At anywhere but at this stunningly good-looking man, who was no doubt trying to suck local knowledge out of my brain and leave me a spent husk. "Thanks, but I have some errands to run."

Just then I saw a nightmare marching toward me: Claudia Wolff, mother of Tyler, Taylor, and Taynor, and her compatriot-in-arms, Tina Heller, mother of Brytny and Tyfanni.

"Beth!" Claudia shouted. "Beth, is that you? I want to talk to you about Agnes."

"On second thought," I said, looking up into eyes the color of a summer sky, "I *am* hungry. Have you eaten at the Grill? No? Then you have a treat coming."

With a quick "Call me tonight" to Claudia, I made my escape.

"This isn't what I expected from a place called the Grill."

I turned to see Evan ducking under an accordion that dangled from the ceiling. With a quick step left and back right again, he avoided both a tray-laden waitress and a collection of skis stacked into a tepee shape.

"Well," I said, "the proper name is Fred's Eclectic Collections and Food from the Grill, but no one ever calls it that."

The hostess waved us to a table underneath a shelf of toasters, laid out our silverware and napkins on the paper place mats, and hurried off.

60

"She forgot our menus." Evan started to rise. "I'll go get a couple."

I pointed at his place mat. "She didn't forget."

He sat and ran his finger down the short list. "Hamburgers. Hot dogs. Brats."

Hmm. He'd pronounced "brats" the Midwestern way, rhyming it with "hots." So much for my just-formed theory that he was a transplanted New Yorker trying to bring life back to a small town.

"And French fries." He looked up at me. "That's it?"

"Yup. Fred sticks to what he knows."

"Hello, my dear." Flossie Untermayer, who was eighty if she was a day, pulled off a multicolored knit hat and shook out her silvery hair with the grace of the ballet dancer she'd once been. "Ask me to sit, will you, please? I'm aching to know about last night's PTA meeting. Hello, young man." She turned to Evan, who'd stood as she approached. "You're the new owner of the hardware, aren't you?"

"Yes, ma'am. Evan Garrett."

He blinked as they shook hands, and I tried not to smile. Flossie's grip could wring tears out of a weight lifter. "First impressions count," she'd once told me. "And I want a man's first impression of me to be

61

strength. You lose that first chance and it's a steep uphill climb to prove yourself."

"Flossie Untermayer," she said, lowering herself onto the chair next to him. "I run the grocery store, and some years I almost make a living. Do you think you can make that place work? No one has in twenty years."

Evan helped scoot her chair forward. "Time will tell."

She gave him a long look as he seated himself. "Yes, it will." She quirked an eyebrow at me, that questioning look so easy for another woman to interpret, even if the women in question were forty years and almost two generations apart.

I shrugged, shorthand for *He's just this guy I met half an hour ago. Sure, he's gorgeous, but he's probably a jerk, and I'm not ready to date anybody, anyway.*

Flossie nodded. "Tell me about the meeting last night. Dan Daniels stopped by for milk early this morning, and he looked ready to take on the whole school board. And when Kirk Olsen came in for doughnuts, I had the phone in my hand in case of a stroke. His face was that red."

Dan was CeeCee's husband. He was a nurse at Sunny Rest Assisted Living and worked the afternoon shift, so he rarely made meetings, but clearly his wife had passed on the news. Too bad. Dan was one of those people who changed personality in and out of the workplace. As a nurse, he was caring and considerate and kindness itself. As a PTA member, he fought against any idea he hadn't conceived himself.

And Kirk Olsen had certainly been busy. Kirk was often out of his office on errands unrelated to his insurance business, and it was a mystery to all how he managed to keep his company afloat.

"It's an Agnes Project," I said sadly.

"Oh, great, merciful heavens," Flossie said. "Is there any chance for us? Is there any chance for Agnes?"

We laughed, Evan looked politely puzzled, and we ordered our meals.

"I had macaroni and cheese for lunch," Jenna announced. "I could eat mac and cheese every day and not get tired of it."

"What did you have, Oliver?" I started the car and backed down Marina's driveway. In the rearview mirror I saw his small form slide into a slouch.

"Hamburger," he muttered.

"Was it good?"

"No. It was gross."

Jenna and I exchanged looks. Oliver loved

hamburgers. "Did you tell Mrs. Krenz you don't like mustard?" I asked.

"Yeah."

"Did it come without mustard?"

"Yeah." He slouched so low that I couldn't see him any longer.

"Then what was wrong with it?"

"Nothing."

Jenna rolled her eyes. "So why was it gross?"

"It just was." He sounded three steps away from tears.

"What's the matter, Oliver?" I asked softly. "Is Toby Stillson picking on the little kids again?" There was nothing but silence from the backseat. "Did you have a spelling test?"

"No."

At least he was talking. "What is it, Ollster?"

Either the pet name got to him, or he was ready to crack, anyway. "They wouldn't let us play!" Tones of outrage rounded out every vowel.

I looked at Jenna. She shrugged.

"Who wouldn't let you play?" I asked.

"It's the place we always play every single recess, and they wouldn't let us!"

They? I immediately had a picture of a cabal of fifth graders standing shoulder to shoulder, forcing Oliver and his friends to slink away. "Did you tell your teacher?"

"Yes!" he shouted. "She said they were right and we couldn't play there again. Ever."

This didn't make sense. "Who?"

"The men."

Trying to get a story out of this kid was like sweeping sand with a bad broom. "What men?"

"I don't know. They were mean. They had hammers and colored hats and big papers." He stretched his hands wide.

My foot moved from gas pedal to brake. "Show me."

Five minutes later, Oliver was trudging across the playground. "See? Robert and I always play marbles there. And now we can't." His lower lip trembled and I pulled him close.

The back side of Tarver Elementary was similar to many primary schools, with swing sets and slides and dirt packed hard by hordes of children. But tonight there was something new — a small forest of fresh wood stakes. Bright pink plastic tape fluttered from the tops of waist-high strips of wood, cryptic handwritten lettering marking each one. Things like "10' off NE B Cor," and "12″ WM," and "10' off SW B

Cor." The pink ribbons flapped noisily in a sudden north wind, and I shivered.

"Mommy?" Oliver pressed against me. "Can you fix it?"

Oh, how I wanted to say yes. Oh, how I wanted to fix everything that had and ever would go wrong for my children.

I pulled out my cell phone and started dialing.

The playground had never seen so many adults. I'd called Marina and Erica. They'd each called four people. Each of those people had called four more. Within minutes of my red alert, parents started arriving. Claudia Wolff had brought her friend Tina, who had brought her husband, Tony, who had brought Don the dry cleaner, who had brought Kirk Olsen. Instead of six degrees of separation, Rynwood had more like three.

"Did we miss anything?" Claudia Wolff charged up. "Hey, who was that handsome hunk we saw you with this noon? You sly cat, you. Do your children know?" She winked at Jenna.

"I'm pulling out these stakes!" a burly man shouted. "Every time she puts them in, we'll pull them out."

A murmur of assent ran through the group; I was suddenly sorry I'd called anyone. They called Madison "Mad City" for a reason, and Rynwood was close enough to Madison for the city's history of civil disobedience to be contagious. "Um . . ."

No one paid attention to me. The crowd was turning nasty, and I sincerely hoped Agnes didn't make an appearance. These people were ready for a witch hunt. Give them pitchforks and torches and they'd set upon Agnes even if she lacked the black dress and pointed hat.

"Pull them out!" Claudia yelled. "We'll pile them on her front porch."

Jenna tugged on my coat sleeve. "Mom, I'm hungry." I looked at her face and knew the tightness had nothing to do with a delayed dinner.

"Me, too." Oliver ducked his head under my arm and snuggled close.

It was past time I took the kids away from this. "Me, three," I said. Jenna smiled, and I felt Oliver's giggle against my hip bone. "How about a treat tonight? What do you say to Hot Dog Heaven?"

A single shout became a chant. "Pull them out! Pull them out!" Mob rule took hold, and the pack surged forward.

My children and I went in the opposite direction, hand in hand in hand.

"My tummy is all happy now," Oliver said as I was starting the animal good nights.

"I'm glad."

"Mom?"

"Yes, sweetheart?"

"Will Robert's dad get into trouble for taking out those little poles? The men who put them in said to leave them alone or the police will put us in jail."

"Robert's dad isn't going to jail." I supposed the surveyors had been trying to keep their stakes intact, but scaring children was a poor way of going about it. "I promise." And one day soon I'd have to figure out who Robert's dad was. "Time to sleep. It's way past your bedtime."

"I know." He grinned, and my heart went mushy around the edges. "But you made us go out to eat."

"That's right." I picked up an armful of stuffed animals and started the routine. "Good night, Rex. Good night, Fred. Good night, Dancer." By the time I'd finished, Oliver's eyes were drooping. "Good night, Oliver." I kissed my son's forehead. "Sweet dreams and may tomorrow be your best day ever."

"Okay," he said sleepily.

Jenna was already out. I took away her *Sports Illustrated* and clicked off the bedside light. "Night, sweetheart," I whispered, and kissed her lightly.

I went downstairs as quietly as I could. After half an hour, Oliver slept like a rock, but for the first thirty minutes a cough two floors away would wake him. I flicked on the desk light in the study and turned on the computer. Good little secretary that I was, I wanted to finish the minutes of last night's meeting before falling into bed.

The first pages of my handwritten notes were filled with quotes from concerned parents. Each succeeding page had an increasing number of doodles. Every person talking had said the same thing, over and over, the same things I'd heard on the phone all day. And I'd probably had dozens of e-mails on the subject, too.

My own eyes were drooping when I reached the proofreading stage at one in the morning. Yawning, I printed a hard copy and decided to look at e-mail. After subject lines such as "Tarver Addition," "Agnes Must Go," and "Legal Action Called For," there was a series of e-mails from Marina. "Call me," said the first one. Then, "Call me — urgent." There were more with increasing numbers of capital letters and exclamation points. The last message had been sent less than five minutes ago.

CALL ME!! URGENT!!!!

"Why didn't you call me yourself?" Grumbling, I picked up the phone, but there was no dial tone. "Oh . . ."

Thirty seconds after walking in the door, the phone had rung. Carly, mother of Thomas and Victoria, had wanted to know how we were going to stop Agnes. After I'd finished with her, I'd pulled the cord out of the phone jack. Voilà, no more calls.

I went into the kitchen and dialed Marina. "Sorry. I unplugged the phone. You wouldn't believe how many people have called. What's so important?"

"Sit down."

"Why?"

"Sit!"

Marina never yelled at me. She scolded, cajoled, and occasionally henpecked, but she never shouted. I sat on a bar stool with a thump. "Something's happened." To Marina's kids. To her husband. Her parents. Her sister. "Tell me." My heart pushed blood through my neck in thick clumps.

"It's Agnes."

My fear vanished. Annoyance replaced it. "Oh, geez. What's she done now?"

Marina breathed into the phone. Short, tension-filled puffs. "She's dead."

"Dead?" That couldn't be right. People as obnoxious as Agnes lived forever and turned into Auntie Mays. "As in *dead* dead?"

"Yes."

The stool cut into the backs of my thighs. Agnes, dead? It couldn't be.

"And . . . Beth?" Marina's voice was so quiet I had to press the phone hard against my head. "She was murdered."

CHAPTER 4

The morning after Agnes was killed, I woke early and wondered how to break the news to Jenna and Oliver. "Good morning, kids! Your principal was murdered last night. How about some cereal?"

No, that wouldn't work. How about: "Mrs. Mephisto's head had a bad accident with a blunt object." Or "Last night, Mrs. Neff's neighbor noticed the back door of Mrs. Mephisto's house was open and went inside and saw . . ."

Ick.

I flung back the covers and decided to cook the children's favorite breakfast. This meant two breakfasts, because naturally they couldn't both like the same thing. For Jenna I cooked bacon and scrambled eggs; for Oliver I made blueberry pancakes and sausage. By the time we sat down to eat, the kitchen was piled high with dishes I didn't have time to wash.

"Cool!" Jenna slid into her place at the kitchen table. "It's like a birthday breakfast."

"We both have birthdays today," Oliver said.

"Don't be stu—" She glanced at me and made a sudden revision. "My birthday is in June and yours is in May. No one has a birthday in October."

"Robert does."

Jenna heaved a giant sigh. "No one in this family."

"Then why are we having birthday breakfast?" he asked.

"Because . . ." Jenna, frowning, realized she had no clue why I'd cooked a real meal on a weekday. "You're going to tell us something, aren't you?" She stabbed her fork into a piece of bacon.

I leaned over and cut up Oliver's sausage into quarter-inch pieces.

"You are, aren't you?" Jenna shoved a piece of bacon into her mouth. "I bet it's about what Mrs. Wolff said last night."

"What?" Oliver moved his head to look at his sister around my arm. "What did Mrs. Wolff say?"

I was glad he'd asked, because I couldn't remember myself.

"She said you were with some man yesterday. She said you were a sly cat. She said

73

—" Jenna blinked, her eyes flashing fast. "She asked if Oliver and me knew."

My first instinct was to correct her grammar, but I decided to let it go for once.

"Knew what?" Oliver asked.

With a rush, I remembered why I didn't care much for Claudia Wolff.

"You're getting married, aren't you?" Jenna dropped her silverware on the table in a metallic crash. "You're going to marry some guy we don't know."

"No!" Oliver shrieked. "You can't! I'll run away. I'll lock myself in my room. I'll —"

I made my thumb and middle finger into a circle, put them in my mouth and blew a loud whistle. The kids went silent, albeit with mutinous expressions.

"Number one," I said, "I am not about to marry anyone."

Oliver's face cleared immediately. He speared a piece of sausage and popped it in his mouth with a flourish.

Jenna wasn't so easily pacified. "But who was that man?"

"A business acquaintance."

"Then why did Mrs. Wolff say what she did?"

"I'm not sure." The alternative answer had a lot to do with a word rhyming with ditch. "Jenna." I reached across the table and held my daughter's hand. "Do you really think I'd marry anyone without making sure you loved him, too?"

She used the heel of her other hand to push away her unshed tears. "I guess not."

"You and Oliver are the most important people in my life." My own eyes started blinking. "No one else comes close. No one ever will."

"Okay."

I reached out to give her a hug, but she leaned sideways and picked up another piece of bacon.

"Why are we having birthday breakfasts?" Oliver asked.

I looked from one young face to the other. When I'd woken up so early, the idea of cooking a nice meal had seemed like a great one. But maybe I'd done it more for me than for them. "I'm afraid I have some bad news for you."

"Dad!" Jenna shot to her feet. "What's wrong with Dad?"

"Nothing," I soothed. "He's fine. Your grandparents are fine, all your friends are fine."

"How do you know for sure?" Jenna's voice went shrill. "Maybe there was a car accident or something."

"Someone would have called. Everyone's

fine. Sit down, Jenna." As she eased herself into the chair, I asked, "Remember Mr. Stoltz?"

Oliver poured maple syrup over his pancakes. "The outside train."

Norman Stoltz had lived two blocks away and had built a magnificent garden train. The place was a kid magnet. If a child put in the requisite number of hours of weeding, he (or she) got to wear an engineer's hat and run the controls. Sadly, Norman Stoltz had collapsed the year before from a massive heart attack.

"He's dead." Jenna eyed me.

"Yes." I looked at my untouched plate. Cold poached eggs on a piece of cold toast. "I'm afraid Mrs. Mephisto is, too."

"Our principal?" Oliver asked.

"She died last night." I watched my children carefully, waiting for an emotional response, waiting for a tumultuous reaction, waiting for tears.

"Like Mr. Stoltz?" Jenna asked. "Her heart gave out?"

The adult phrase sounded strange coming from such young lips. "No, I'm afraid not."

"She was pretty old." A drop of maple syrup dripped onto Oliver's shirt. "Maybe she just got tired."

"People don't die because they're tired,"

Jenna said.

"Paoze said that's why his grandmother died. She was tired and went to sleep and never woke up."

"Maybe where he came from they die because they're tired, but not in Wisconsin."

They both turned to me, each of them looking to be supported as being correct. I sidestepped the referee job. "Mrs. Mephisto was killed," I said quietly.

"Like car crash killed?" Jenna asked.

"No, she died at home." Last night, Marina had said an EMT had said the back of her skull had been bashed in. I shied away from the image. My poached eggs, now congealed to the consistency of soft plastic, looked up at me with wide eyes. I pushed the plate away. "The police will find who did it and put him in jail for a long, long time."

"Mrs. Mephisto was murdered?" Jenna's eyes went wide.

I wondered how many fictionalized murders my ten-year-old had watched via television and movies. But this time the victim was someone she knew. "I'm sorry, sweetheart. Yes, she was murdered." I searched for words of comfort — words that would help them through the stages of grief; words they could carry the rest of their lives.

Before I came up with the perfect phrase, Jenna jumped up.

"Where are you going?" I asked.

"To call Bailey," she flung over her shoulder. "Bet she doesn't know. I can be first!"

When I dropped the children off at school, Lauren Atchinson, Oliver's teacher, was standing on the sidewalk. She caught my eye and made I-need-to-talk-to-you motions. I pushed the DOWN button for the passenger window, and she leaned in.

"Does Oliver know?" she asked softly. Which was the only way I'd ever heard her talk. How this quiet woman controlled twenty-six seven-year-olds, I hadn't a clue. She pushed curly blond hair behind her ears.

"They both know," I said.

She nodded. "Good. Gary called the teachers last night. We're to tell the kids first thing. A grief counselor Gary knows is coming later on this morning."

Gary Kemmerer was Tarver's assistant principal, browbeaten by Agnes for too many years. If the reactions of my children were any indication, the counselor wouldn't have a lot to do. "That was smart of Gary," I said.

"Do you think he'll be principal?" Lauren's eyes darted left and right. "I shouldn't be thinking about it at a time like this, but you're a friend of the superintendent. Gary would make a perfect principal, don't you think?"

"It'll take a while before things get sorted out."

"Mack Vogel couldn't do better than Gary. You think so, don't you?" Her face was flushed with an emotion that didn't look at all like sorrow.

"It's the children who are most important right now," I said. "Everything else can wait."

"He's perfect for the job." Lauren kept on track, and I got a glimpse of how she ran a classroom successfully. "He deserves to be principal." A silver SUV braked to a stop behind my car, and Lauren moved away to speak to another parent.

Thoughtfully, I watched her go. Yet another person not prostrate with grief. Maybe I should start a tally.

"Did you hear?" Lois stood in my office doorway. This morning her hair was spiked and gelled. She wore a white tuxedo-style shirt, a silk paisley vest, and a blue skirt made of a crinkly fabric that made a swishy sound when she walked.

"Please be more specific," I said. "Did I hear the weather forecast? Did I hear the Jonas Brothers' latest release? Did I hear the Dow Jones report?"

She sniffed. "No tea for you. And today I brought in a box of your favorite."

"Indian spice chai?"

"And milk."

I caved instantly. "Marina called me last night. She lives almost across the street from Agnes."

Last night, strong, confident, I-know-what's-best-for-you Marina had needed my comfort, something that had never happened before. Sure, Marina hadn't liked Agnes, but who had? It didn't mean she wanted her dead. I chewed on my lower lip and thought about life and death and just deserts.

Lois made a rolling motion with her hand. "And? Details. I must have details!"

"All I have is thirdhand knowledge," I cautioned. "Accuracy is questionable."

"Perfect. Let me get the kettle on."

Fifteen minutes later, I'd finished a mug of tea and come to the end of the story.

"No suspects?"

"She was killed less than twelve hours ago. There's hardly been time."

Lois made a snorting noise. "Especially

with our police force. Last time someone in this town was killed was twenty years ago. Harvey Knotton." Lois had lived in Rynwood all her life and was better than the newspaper archives for what really went on.

"Who was Harvey Knotton?" I asked.

"Dairy farmer south of town."

"What happened?"

"Harvey and his brother Matt were in the barn arguing about something. Matt had a temper — always did. He grabbed a pitchfork and" — she made a fist and thumped her chest — "blammo."

"How horrible!"

"Matt called the ambulance, but it was too late. When he got out of prison, he moved to Wyoming. Or was it Montana? One of those. I hear he's a hospital janitor, cleaning up people messes instead of cow messes."

"How on earth do you know this stuff?"

"Harvey and Matt's big sister used to date my little brother," she said matter-of-factly, as if maintaining bonds from the offshoots of a high school romance forty years ago were an everyday occurrence. And for Lois, they probably were.

"Mrs. Kennedy!" Paoze rushed into the back room. "There was a murder in this town! Mrs. Mephisto is dead!" His large brown eyes were filled with empathy. "Your children must be sorrowful."

"Um." I pictured Jenna's face, alive with the excitement of being the bearer of bad tidings. I saw Oliver's empty breakfast plate, and like that other Oliver, his small hands picking it up and asking for more, please. "They're young and resilient."

"How did you know about the murder?" Lois asked. "The Rynwood paper doesn't come out today, the Madison paper hasn't shown up yet, and I'm pretty sure you don't have a car radio on that ratty bicycle of yours."

"No, I do not," Paoze said. "How can a rat be on a bicycle, please?"

Lois had an evil gleam in her eye. "Rats have long tails, right? Kids around here train barn rats to sit on the handlebars and wrap their tails around them for balance. But you need to start them when they're young. A tricycle is best."

One of Lois's favorite pastimes was to test Paoze's gullibility. He'd called her on the cow tipping, but had swallowed the snipe-hunting story hook, line, and sinker. He was starting to nod as she patiently told him that rats preferred green bicycles because green was the color of garbage totes and everybody knew rats were smart about food sources.

I took pity on him. "Paoze, she's doing it again."

His dark skin flushed, and Lois said I'd ruined her fun.

"Hey, did you guys see?" Sara poked her head into the room. The store was at full complement today, thanks to the need to get the Halloween decorating done before Halloween. The two youngsters had afternoon classes, but had agreed to come in this morning.

"See what?" I ran more water into the teakettle.

"WisconSINs."

"Wisconsin's?" I asked. "Wisconsin's what?"

"What? No, WisconSINs. You know, the blog."

"Yes." Paoze nodded vigorously. "This is where I read about the murder. This blog is about the people of Rynwood."

"Is this part of the newspaper?" Though it had been years since I'd been on the *Gazette*'s staff, I often had lunch with Jean, the editor, who kept me up-to-date with tales of staffing woes and horror stories of computer failures. She'd never once mentioned the paper had started a blog.

Sara shook her head, and blond hair

whisked from side to side. "No, it's anonymous. It's been up at least a month. I can't believe you don't know about it."

Lois sniffed. "I prefer to get my gossip the old-fashioned way."

"Did you know about Don Hatcher?" Sara asked.

"Don the dry cleaner with the horrible jokes?" Lois rolled her eyes. "His wife was always whining about the cold winters, and a while back she just took off. Vamoose!"

"Yeah, but did you know Don's getting a hair transplant?"

"A hair . . ."

There was a small stampede to the closest computer. I stayed behind to brew tea and brought a laden tray to the front of the store.

A short chorus of thank-yous was interrupted by Lois's exclamation. "Did you see this? It says here that an S.W. drives to Chicago every other weekend to get her roots done. That's got to be Stephanie Waldruss. She told me she was visiting her mother in assisted living!"

I blew across the top of my mug. "Maybe she does both," I said, and got a withering look in response.

"Go to the entry about Mrs. Mephisto." Sara pointed. "There it is. 'Too Many Suspects to Count.' "

I watched the steam on my tea drift upward and thought the phrase had the ring of a mean-spirited epitaph.

Sara read on. " 'The heinous crime of murder was committed in Rynwood last night with the death of Agnes Mephisto, principal of Tarver Elementary. Her reign was marked by brouhaha after brouhaha, each of which created enemies for the aging woman.' "

Ouch.

"What is brouhaha?" Paoze asked.

"Look it up," Sara said, and continued reading. " 'After ten years of Mrs. Mephisto, even eternally patient teachers could be seen marching away from meetings with clenched fists and a cloud of rage. Parents, with the welfare of their children on the line, were even more easily riled. Who's to say one of these tormented individuals didn't snap last night? Who's to say the affair of the school buses wasn't enough to drive some poor soul to murder? Who's to deny the furor wrought by the elimination of Fish Fry Friday? Stay tuned to Wisconsins for the latest developments in the murder of Agnes Mephisto.' "

Lois turned. "You're on the PTA. Could Agnes have been killed because of something at the school?"

My first reaction was to say, Don't be silly. But then I remembered the hot anger on the playground last night and the fear that had snaked around my neck.

"What do you think?" Sara asked.

"That we need to get to work." I picked up a spray can from the counter. "Cobwebs, anyone?"

CHAPTER 5

Police Chief Gus Eiseley offered me a mug of coffee. "Strong enough to pull your socks off."

I demurred and sat in the proffered chair. The morning sun lit a metal desk, originally painted brown, but chipped down to bare metal at the corners and edges. Orderly stacks of paper covered the entire surface.

Gus and I had mutually attended countless church choir practices. His tenor section sat behind my alto contingent and, thanks to the Latin he'd taken in high school, I knew exactly how to pronounce *Sanctus, Te Deum* and *excelsis Deo.* I still didn't know what they meant, but Presbyterians don't have to.

"So, Beth." Gus set his coffee mug atop a bloated three-ring binder. "What can I do for you this morning?" He glanced at his wrist. Reflexively, I did, too. In any group larger than one, if one person looks at his watch, everyone will. Pavlov in action — or something. In this case it was still morning by forty-five minutes.

"I suppose," Gus said, "that you want to know if the murderer of Agnes Mephisto has been apprehended and brought to justice. If we've been doing the job for which we're being paid. If the marble bookend with blood on it was, in fact, the murder weapon. If we've gotten results on the DNA samples. If we have the slightest clue what we're doing."

"Um, no." The Gus I knew was as mild mannered as Clark Kent and as patient as Mother Teresa. To hear him wax sarcastic was similar to hearing my very proper grandmother swear like a sailor.

"Sorry." He slid his glasses up with his index finger and pinched the bridge of his nose. With a face unlined by aging or sun, he'd always looked about my age. Today, I believed he was the fifty he claimed to be.

I looked closer. "Did you get any sleep last night?"

"No. Winnie says it's the first time since that big pileup on the highway five years ago." His wife, Winnie, round and red as he was skinny and white, was constitutionally incapable of passing a garage sale. I loved her dearly and didn't get to see her nearly enough.

"You're tired." I started to rise. "This can wait. It's probably not that important."

"If it's about Agnes, I need to hear it."

I thumped back into the chair. "I don't know if it is or not." I fidgeted with my purse. It had taken me all morning to gird up enough gumption to make the short walk to city hall. Twenty minutes ago, my information had seemed as if it might be useful. Now, I wasn't so sure.

"Spill it," Gus said.

I blew out my cheeks. "Yesterday evening, about six thirty . . ." The story of the stakes on the playground came out bit by gory bit. Gus, far from dismissing the incident, started taking notes almost immediately.

"And you don't know the name of Robert's father?" Gus asked, pen poised.

"Oliver might." Or not. Last names weren't nearly as important as how high you could jump your bike. "I'll ask him tonight."

"No need." Gus kept scrawling. "I'll call the school. Claudia Wolff and who else?"

My older sister's accusations from years past came back with a slap. *You're nothing but a whiny little tattletale!*

"Beth?"

I bounced forward thirty years. "Sorry.

89

You're not going to tell anyone I told, are you?"

"This is a police investigation."

"And that means what?"

"That privacy isn't as important as finding a murderer." Gus sat back, moving into a slanting beam of sunlight.

I saw, in addition to reddened eyes, weary circles under them. "Right. Of course." Quickly, I gave him all the names I could remember. "There were a few others I didn't know." I fiddled with my coat zipper. "It's all my fault."

"You killed Agnes?"

I looked up and saw the corners of his mouth twitching. "I thought law-enforcement officers weren't supposed to have a sense of humor."

"Don't believe everything you read. And if you're blaming yourself for inciting a riot by making that phone call last night, don't. If it hadn't been you, it would have been someone else."

"Okay." I'd never bought that kind of argument. It sat side by side with the but-all-my-friends-are-doing-it   reasoning. "Thanks."

"Thank you for doing your civic duty. It's people like you who make our job easier."

I shook hands and left, feeling worse than

when I'd arrived.

Tattletale!

I nodded to the officer at the front desk and walked out. I was head down, which was not the way to play the puck and not the way to walk down a downtown sidewalk, even if the sidewalk in question was in sleepy little Rynwood.

"Gotcha!" Firm hands gripped my shoulders, and my momentum carried us around in a small circle. "Sorry for grabbing, but you were about to walk straight into that barricade." Evan Garrett looked down at me, blue eyes bright in a face still summer-tanned.

Jerk, I reminded myself. Too-handsome men are always jerks. I looked at the orange sawhorses and the gaping hole beyond. "They were supposed to be done with that storm sewer two weeks ago," I said, "and still there's a trench that's deep enough to hide small children."

I suddenly realized his hands were warm on my shoulders. "Thanks for saving me." I stepped back. "I'll try to keep my head up from now on."

"You're welcome. How about lunch again?"

"What?"

91

"Lunch. The meal traditionally eaten at noon." He smiled. "You are eating lunch today, aren't you?"

"I did yesterday." What a dumb thing to say. Not that it mattered. He was a jerk, and saying dumb things to jerks didn't matter.

"How about now?"

A "thanks, but no, thanks" was on my lips. I had customers to cajole, invoices to pay, and Christmas books to order. I'd packed a peanut-butter-and-strawberry-freezer-jam sandwich for lunch and had intended to eat it while filling out order forms. And if I didn't eat the sandwich today, I wouldn't eat it at all. I hated waste, but I hated soggy PB&J even more.

As my mouth opened to say no, I noticed how fast the veins at his neck were pulsing. Either Evan Garrett had serious medical issues, or . . . or he was nervous. Which didn't make any sense, because Beautiful People didn't get nervous.

"You're busy." His mouth turned down at one corner. "I understand. Maybe some other time."

"Wait." I put out a hand and grabbed the sleeve of his jacket. "Lunch is a great idea. I was just deciding where to go."

He flashed a brilliant smile, and I smiled back in return, my heart suddenly and unaccountably light.

This is not a date, I told myself.

Evan and I slid into a booth at the Green Tractor — he on one side, I on the other. The waitress started to hand us menus.

"Thanks, Dorrie, but I don't need one," I said. "I'll have my usual."

"How about you, sir?" Dorrie put her pad on the table and leaned down to write my order, giving Evan an excellent view of her cleavage. Dorrie's claim to fame was that she'd married and divorced the same man multiple times. I wasn't sure of the current Dorrie/Jim status, but since I'd never seen her write down my order this way before, I'd say if Jim hadn't been kicked out of the house yet, he was halfway through the door.

"What are you having?" Evan asked me. He didn't even glance at the displayed skin.

"Fish sandwich with coleslaw." I was in a rut, but it was a nice rut.

"Is it good?"

"All our food is good," Dorrie said. "You look like a hamburger guy to me. We have a half-pound burger that can't be beat."

"You talked me into it," Evan said. "And fries, too, please."

"I'll get you a big mound of 'em." With a wink and a swish of her hips, Dorrie sauntered away.

I straightened the packets of sugar in the wire rack. "How's it going at the store?"

"You mean, have I figured out a way to make it turn a profit for the first time in ten years?"

I started in on the fake sugar packets and tried to think of something to say that wouldn't be inappropriate. "No one in his right mind would have bought that place" wasn't going to work. "It's a nice store," I said.

Evan laughed.

"No, I mean it." I centered the salt and pepper shakers. "Really. The wood floors and the tin ceiling, and those metal trays filled with nails you buy by the pound, and the smell . . ."

I was babbling again. What an idiot. I stopped talking and hoped Dorrie would show up with our drinks so I could bury my embarrassment in a mug of bad tea.

"The smell?" Evan asked, but he didn't seem to be making fun of me. His voice was quiet and kind. "You mean that multilayered scent of raw wood and machine oil and fresh-cut metal and maybe . . ." He looked at his hands, and I could have sworn I saw a flush over those high cheekbones.

"The aroma of tradition?" I suggested.

94

"Of wisdom?"

My palms tingled with an excitement I hadn't known I could still feel. If I'd said something like that to Richard, he would have said my imagination was going to land me in trouble someday. But this gorgeous man was smiling at me, and I didn't want him to ever, ever stop.

"Here you go!" With a double thud, Dorrie plopped tea and soda on the table. "Your food'll be up in a sec."

As mood-breakers go, this one worked like a champ. I remembered that I had two young children, who had been threatened by the mere mention of another man in my life, and I busied myself with dunking the tea bag.

"Did you hear about last night's murder?" I asked.

Evan sat back against the booth's cracking vinyl. "All morning," he said, peeling the paper off the straw Dorrie had left. "Didn't sound as if anyone was very sorry she was dead."

"Well . . ." I held the tea bag above the mug and let it drip.

He grinned, and my heart did a quick tattoo against my rib cage. "You're operating under the 'if you don't have anything nice to say, don't say anything' theory, aren't you?"

"Is there something wrong with being nice?" I asked.

"Cutting sarcasm is the trend."

"Once I was trendy," I said, "but it was an accident."

His laugh made my breaths flutter fast. Oh, my. Oh, my, my. "It was paint," I said. "Thanks to my daughter's artistic talents, I needed to repaint the living room the day before a dinner party. I didn't have time to go to the paint store, so I mixed up some different cans and slapped it up. Turned out to be the hip color of the month on HGTV." It was the only time Debra O'Conner had ever given me a look of approval. Not that I cared.

Dorrie put our plates down. "Can I get you anything else?" She looked at Evan and, I swear, she batted her eyelashes.

"All set, thanks," he said.

"Let me know if you need anything." A couple more bats, and then she put her hand on her hip and waltzed off.

Evan reached for the ketchup. "Did you know the woman who was killed?"

"Not well. She was principal at the elementary school. My daughter and son both

96

go there, but Agnes and I didn't cross paths much."

"Murder makes it different, though."

I paused, a forkful of coleslaw halfway to my mouth. "That sounds like the voice of experience."

"Just an overactive imagination. My ex-wife always told me it would get me into trouble someday."

I wasn't going to ask, but out it came. "How long have you been divorced?"

Dorrie returned and did the leaning thing again. "Dessert?" When the answer was no, she slid the bill on the table and winked at Evan. "Have a nice day."

Over my protests, Evan placed his big hand over the bill and put it in his shirt pocket. "Five years divorced," he said. "I waited to leave Chicago until my girls got out of high school. The younger one's a freshman at Wisconsin." He jerked a thumb in the direction of Madison. "The older one is in the army, jumping out of perfectly good airplanes."

That made the army daughter at least ten years ahead of my Jenna. Maybe he was older than he looked.

"I married my high school sweetheart a month after graduation," he said. "I'd say it was one of the dumbest things I've ever done, but I ended up with two top-notch daughters, so I don't regret a minute of it."

What I needed was a mood-breaking topic. "What did you do in Chicago?" Perfect. No one could talk about their jobs without being boring.

"Corporate. Talk about boring." He made a face. "Want the last of these fries?"

"No, thanks. So you just chucked the whole rat race and came up here?"

"Pretty much," he said cheerfully.

Ah-ha. I *knew* he was a jerk. Big-time Chicago lawyer playing at being a small-town store owner. He probably saw himself sweeping the sidewalk every morning, popping the awning with a broom handle after a rainstorm to let the water whoosh to the sidewalk. So idyllic. So quaint. Sooo unrealistic.

"My dad ran a men's clothing store up in Green Bay," he said. "It won't be easy, but I have some ideas that might make it work."

I wanted so badly to dislike this man, and he wasn't making it easy. Clearly, I was going to have to try harder.

Up at the cash register, Ruthie greeted us. "How was everything?" Her thin face was a map of wrinkles — one for each year she'd run the restaurant, she always said.

"Excellent." Evan laid down an unusual

credit card that, after a moment, I recognized. No plebeian applications could get you a card like that. For that card you had to receive an invitation from the credit card company. "Best burger I've had in a long time," he said.

Ruthie lowered her voice and leaned toward us. Our three heads drew together in a conspiratorial huddle. "Sorry about Dorrie," she said. "Did you hear about Jim? I think it's really over this time. He left Dorrie for Viv Reilly's youngest."

"Nicole?" I gasped. "You can't be serious. She's barely out of high school."

Ruthie's lips firmed, and she shut the cash register drawer with a slam. "Young and pretty and not a brain in her head. Not that Dorrie is going to win a MacArthur Fellowship anytime soon, but she doesn't deserve that."

Poor Dorrie. I instantly felt guilty for my uncharitable thoughts. At least she was fighting back for her self-esteem instead of crawling into a dark closet and crying. Since I had no cleavage to speak of, if something like that happened to me, I was a candidate for the closet.

Ruthie stood straight, breaking us out of whisper mode. "I assume you heard about Agnes?"

"Gus says the investigation is proceeding," I said.

She made a rude noise in the back of her throat. "Gus Eiseley is a nice man, but running a murder investigation?" Shaking her head she said, "Agnes had a lot of enemies in this town. Did you know her?" She shot a look up at Evan.

"No. She sounds . . . as if she must have been an interesting woman."

Ruthie chuckled. "The man has tact."

"Just taking the lessons of my kindergarten teacher to heart," he said. "Mrs. Pelton-Banes always said, 'If you don't have anything nice to say —' " He broke off as he noted the expression on my face. "What's the matter?" he asked.

"Mrs. — Mrs. Pelton-Banes?" I stuttered.

"I don't think she had a first name."

"Mrs. Pelton-Banes, the kindergarten teacher at Alice A. Black Elementary School? In Illinois? In *Peoria,* Illinois?"

He frowned. "How did you know that?"

"You're not Evan Garrett. You're Evan Hill!"

CHAPTER 6

Evan stared at me, his face slack with surprise.

"You're Evan Hill," I repeated. "You made fun of me for reading instead of playing tag. You said I wasn't old enough to read and to quit acting big." The ancient insult came back fresh. "Even when I read the book out loud, you didn't believe me."

Evan's mouth dropped open. He didn't look like a movie god any longer; he looked like a bigmouthed bass. "Beth Emmerling. You're Beth Emmerling." He repeated my name over and over and might have gone on for hours except Ruthie started braying with laughter.

"You two look like Moses just came down from the mountain. Kindergarten pals, eh? This is a small-world story to beat the band."

Evan looked at Ruthie. "I think she's still angry."

They considered me. My hands were on my hips, and my chin was jutting forward.

"Sure looks like it," Ruthie said. "You'd think the statute of limitations on things that happened in kindergarten would have expired by now."

"Do you think an apology would help?"

Ruthie pursed her lips, making tiny lines radiate around her mouth. "Couldn't hurt."

"How about if I tell her I just wanted to play with the prettiest girl in class?"

"Probably not a good idea," Ruthie said. "She's not big on flattery."

"Stop talking as if I weren't here." I took a deep breath, willing away the flashback to a childhood pain. "I was never the prettiest girl in any class, anywhere."

"To me you were," Evan said softly. My gaze met his bright blue one, and the electricity that had connected us over lunch sprang back to life. He took hold of my elbow and ushered me toward the front door. "Come on. There's a park bench down the street that's waiting for us. Let's go talk."

Lois glanced up as I paused in the retelling of my luncheon events. "So how'd he end up Evan Garrett if his name was Evan Hill? He's not hiding from the law, is he?"

I smiled, but she was serious. "Evan's birth father abandoned his mother when Evan was four."

"Oh, the poor woman." Lois clutched a stack of graphic novels to her chest. "That poor little boy."

"She waited a year, then ran out of money and moved back to her parents' up in Green Bay. She married Ed Garrett two years later."

"And Evan's birth father let Garrett adopt him," Lois said.

"Not such a mystery, after all." As a first grader, I'd wondered why Evan wasn't in school. The day after kindergarten let out, his mother had packed up the station wagon and driven north to Green Bay, but I hadn't known that until fifteen minutes ago.

"Hmm." Lois shelved the graphic novels. Bendis, Dini, Eisner, Yang. "Seems like fate might be taking a hand in someone's romantic life."

"Don't be silly," I said. "I've been divorced only a year. The kids aren't ready."

"Ready for what?" Lois's smile would have been appropriate on a cat who'd just sneaked her tongue into a bowl of milky cereal. "Jenna could use some help with soccer. And it wouldn't hurt Oliver to have a strong male presence in the house."

"Don't be silly." This time I said it so sharply that a blue-haired customer looked up from the rack of stickers. "My children need a stable home environment."

"And what could be better than a rich stepfather who has loved their mother since sandbox days?" Lois's smirk disappeared behind a cardboard display of Stephenie Meyer books, and a flush of embarrassment engulfed me from collarbone to hairline.

"Hot, are you?" the blue-haired lady inquired kindly.

"Um, yes." I fanned my face with the stack of invoices I held. "How are you today, Mrs. Tolliver?"

"I'd be better if I wasn't afraid of being murdered in my bed. I saw you coming out of the police station earlier. Has young Gus arrested anyone for killing that Agnes Mephisto?"

"Not yet."

"Well, the DNA evidence will tell the tale." She handed me a small pile of twenty-five-cent stickers. "These are for my granddaughter. I'd like them wrapped individually, please. Each in different paper."

I pasted on a smile. "No problem." As I cut small squares of wrapping paper off the rolls under the counter, Mrs. Tolliver went on at length about the shortcomings of our local law-enforcement officers. I nodded at the appropriate places, but my mind was far away. Would DNA evidence really help find the killer? If there were no suspects, could a stray hair mean much? Okay, if the stray hair was identified in some police database as belonging to a serial killer, it meant a lot, but how likely was that?

Mrs. Tolliver moved on to new topics, but I continued to think about tracking down a killer.

"I hate spaghetti," Oliver announced. As I'd just put a plate of steaming hot pasta in front of him, his statement wasn't welcome news.

"You love spaghetti," Jenna said. "Last week you said you could eat spaghetti for supper every night the rest of your life."

I sat down. "Jenna, your turn for grace."

She bounced a little. "Rub-a-dub-dub, thanks for the grub. Go, God!"

Oliver giggled and I shot them both a mom look. "Jenna, would you like to try again?"

A dramatic sigh.

I held out my hands, left hand to my daughter, right hand to my son. The soft touch of their palms at this quiet second of the day filled me to overflowing with love.

"Bless us, O Lord," Jenna said, "for these thy gifts which we are about to receive from thy bounty, through Christ our Lord. Amen."

My silent prayer was similar, but not identical. *Bless them, O Lord, for they are the bounty you have bestowed upon me and for which I will always be grateful. Amen.* I gave their hands a gentle squeeze before releasing them, before letting go of the moment of grace.

"I hate spaghetti." Oliver crossed his arms harder and higher.

Ah, yes.

"You said that already." Jenna tucked a paper napkin into her sweatshirt's collar. "How can you love something one week and hate it the next?"

"I told you. That was before." He pouted. Clearly, we weren't listening.

"Before what?" I passed Jenna the green cardboard canister. "Go easy on the Parmesan, okay? It's supposed to enhance flavors, not eliminate them. Before what, Oliver?"

"Before Robert told me about spaghetti."

A born storyteller, Oliver was not. Or maybe he was. He'd be a master at end-of-chapter cliff-hangers. Jenna had paused in her fork-twirling and was looking at her plate with cautious interest. I put my fork down. "What did Robert say?"

"That spaghetti is . . ." He slid down in his chair.

I leaned forward. "Is what?"

"Is . . ." His chin trembled.

I *hadn't* been listening to him, not really. The poor kid was upset, and I should have realized it earlier. I scooted my chair sideways and put my arm around him. "Tell me, Ollster. What did Robert tell you?"

"That spaghetti is dried *worms!* I've been eating worms my whole *life!*" Tears sprang from his eyes. "Robert said grown-ups won't tell you what spaghetti really is because it's a pirate thing. He says if you eat too many spaghetti worms, they'll come alive in your stomach and grow out your ears."

Oh, eww. My own stomach felt a lurch. Robert must have older siblings, to come up with a story like that.

"That's gross. Good thing I like worms." Jenna shoved a monstrous bite of spaghetti into her mouth and chewed hugely.

"Jenna," I said.

"What?" All innocence.

"I don't like worms!" Tears were double-streaming down Oliver's face. "I don't want to eat worms!"

Without saying a thing, I gathered him up and onto my lap. I held him tight and

touched my cheek to his silky-smooth forehead.

"Who am I?" I asked.

Oliver snuffled into my chest.

"C'mon, Ollster, who am I?"

"Elizabeth Anne Kennedy," came the
muffled words.

"Who am I?"

"Grandma Emmerling's daughter."

The time-honored litany continued. "Who
am I?"

"Aunt Darlene and Aunt Kathy and Uncle
Tim's sister."

"Who am I?"

"Um . . ." Oliver wiped his face with the
shoulder that wasn't burrowed into my
armpit. "You're somebody's cousin."

"Bill," Jenna said.

"And Bill." Oliver looked up at me, his
small face stained with wetness. "You have
two cousin Bills. A hockey Bill and a doctor
Bill."

"That's right." I hugged him. "And who
else am I?"

"Mommy." He dove against my chest,
thumping me hard enough to drive air out
of my lungs. "You're my mommy!"

And always would be. "That's right. And
would Mommy give you worms for dinner?"

"Nooo." But he didn't sound convinced.

"Don't move." I plopped him into my seat and went into the kitchen. "No moving!" Both kids giggled. I opened the cabinet door under the sink and extracted a long, skinny box from the trash. I brought it back to the table and reinstalled Oliver on my lap. "See this? It says 'Ingredients.' This is a list of everything inside this box of spaghetti. Semolina, durum flour, niacin, iron, also known as ferrous sulfate, thiamine mononitrate, and riboflavin." I left off the folic acid in case the acid part scared him. "Not a single worm."

His index finger ran over the unfamiliar words. "No pirate thing?"

"You mean conspiracy?" He nodded. "No pirate thing," I said. "No conspiracy here. If the spaghetti company doesn't write down exactly what's inside the box, they'll get in big trouble with all the mommies in the country."

"That's a lot of mommies," Oliver said.

"A force to be reckoned with," I agreed. "Now, are you hungry? Do you want me to put your plate in the microwave?"

"Yes!" He slid off my lap with the speed of a seal and was soon slurping down pasta. I blew out an invisible sigh of relief. Not only relief that Oliver had recovered, but also relief that I'd divorced Richard. Oliver's father wouldn't have comforted him and explained the mysteries of ingredients; he would have told him to eat what was on his plate.

"Um, Mom?" Jenna took a piece of garlic toast.

"Hmm?" My lovely daughter was growing. The top of her head obscured the bottom of the wall calendar. In June I'd been able to see all the way to the end of the month.

"Mom?" Though she hadn't taken a bite of toast, Jenna took another from the pile. "Can we get a dog?"

Jenna's request hung in the air. I got the feeling that if I squinted the right way, I'd see the words spelled out in light and dark furry shadows. But maybe I'd heard wrong. Maybe Jenna had asked about getting something that only sounded like dog. A bog, perhaps. There was room for a little bog in the backyard, tucked between the garage and the sandbox.

Or maybe she'd said hog. That was easy to turn down. We were zoned residential; no agricultural animals allowed. Sorry, kids. It's out of my hands. Or maybe she'd said log. Or maybe —

"Mom?"

"Yes, sweetie." I wiped away my imaginings. "Did you ask about — ?"

"A dog." Oliver sat up straight. "A puppy. With big paws and a pink tongue." He dangled his own tongue out of his mouth.

This was not good. I looked from one child to the other. "Didn't we have this same discussion last year? The reasons we couldn't get a dog then are the same reasons we can't get a dog now."

"But it's different now." Oliver wiped his mouth of dog drool.

"How so?"

"You said we weren't big enough to take care of a dog, but now we're a year bigger."

"That's true, but —"

"And we've been taking care of George all by ourselves for months," Jenna said. "Litter box and food and water and brushing and everything. That shows we're responsible enough to have a dog."

"It helps, but —"

"And we'd be safer with a dog in the house," Oliver said. "He'd bark if anyone broke in. Really loud, like this!" My son the dog let out a series of yips, more poodle than guard dog.

"If Mrs. Mephisto had had a dog," Jenna said, "maybe she wouldn't be dead."

Her simple words hit me like a physical

111

blow. "Oh, sweetheart." I reached for her hand, but she pulled away. I stifled a sigh.

Gus had told me there'd been no signs of forced entry at Agnes's house, so it was likely she'd let the killer inside, and given that the time was late, it was likely she knew the killer. That knowledge wasn't very helpful, though, as Agnes knew hundreds of people. But since only the killer knew exactly what had happened, in theory Jenna could be right.

"So can we get a dog?" Oliver clasped his hands together and aimed them at me, elbows tight together. "Pretty, pretty please, please, please?"

"Please, Mom?" Jenna did the hand-clasp thing, too. "We'll walk him and brush him and clean up his poop with those little plastic bags."

"We'll teach him to get the newspaper," Oliver said.

"We'll give him baths."

"We'll teach him to roll over."

I did not want a dog. I especially did not want a puppy. Puppies had a knack for chewing up the most expensive shoes you owned. Puppies left puddles in the middle of the night. Puppies with great big paws grew up into great big dogs. I looked from one child to the other.

"Please?" they chorused.

I did not want a dog, but they'd lost so much in the last year, and now their principal had been murdered. Having the care of a dog might be good for them. But still . . . I didn't want a dog. No matter what the kids said, I'd end up on dog duty. I pinched the bridge of my nose. If Richard were here, he'd say no and that would be the end of it. But there was no Richard, and the decision was up to me.

"I'll think about it," I said.

Jenna and Oliver grinned at each other, and I got the feeling I'd lost the first battle.

As soon as Richard had moved out of the house, the standard pattern of visitation rights had begun. The first Wednesday night I sat on the couch and made a gap in the curtains so I could see the kids the instant Richard dropped them off. The second Wednesday I made a pot of coffee and brought it with me to the couch.

When I found myself putting together a tray of coffee and snacks for the third Wednesday, I knew I was in serious trouble. Ignoring the fact that it was dark, raining, and cold, I went for a long walk. When I got home, I was drenched and shivering, but an idea was banging around in my brain.

I needed a hobby.

In the months since that walk, I'd gone through knitting (too much counting), scrapbooking (too many options), and baking (too much weight gain). I'd settled into journaling. My writing sessions had seen me through the worst of the effects of the separation and the post-divorce aftermath. In writing to myself, I took my share of the blame for the marriage's failure. Through writing, I calmed my fears for the children and my fears for myself. I wrote about coming to grips with my status as a divorced mom, and I wrote about my high hopes for the future.

Jenna and Oliver and I were a family, and Richard was a good father, even if he did live on the other side of town. Together, we'd make this work.

But would it work with a dog?

On this Wednesday night, the four board members of the PTA met in Erica's kitchen.

"Are you sure this is legal?" Randy Jarvis asked around a chocolate-chip cookie. His concern about PTA proprieties didn't extend to ignoring the plate of treats Erica offered.

"I checked the bylaws," said Julie. Our vice president had lowered herself onto a ladder-back chair, eschewing the padded window seat on the grounds that the bump wouldn't fit behind the table. "We can call special meetings without the rest of the members as long as we publish minutes afterward." Even when discussing murder at the PTA, Erica was bound and determined that we would follow all bylaws.

She put down a china cup and saucer of decaf in front of me. Cream, no sugar. "Beth, you ready to start taking notes?"

"On it." I extracted a spiral notebook and pen from my voluminous purse.

Erica slid into the window seat next to Randy. Julie and I sat in chairs facing the window. Even on a dark October evening and only partially illuminated by floodlights, Erica's garden was beautiful.

"This special meeting of the Tarver Elementary PTA is now called to order." Erica lifted the half glasses that hung from a chain around her neck and put them on the end of her nose. I called the roll.

"As this is a special meeting," Erica said, "we can dispense with a reading of the minutes and committee reports and move on to the topic of the night."

"Agnes," Julie breathed. "Oh, it's so horrible."

I remembered Marina's fairy tale of Randy

being involved with Agnes. If he and Agnes had had a relationship, surely he'd be distraught. On the verge of tears. Full of sorrow and grief. But as far as I could tell, the only thing Randy was, was hungry. He was already chewing on his third cookie, and I guessed he'd go for a fourth any second.

"Yes, we must decide what to do." Erica put down the very short agenda and looked at us over her glasses. "Now, Agnes was born and raised up in Superior."

"Really?" Julie's eyebrows went up. "I didn't know that."

Neither had I. Superior lay due north an amazing number of miles, about as far north as you could get and not be in Lake Superior. You heard stories about life up there. That you knew it was cold when the keg of beer on the porch froze solid. That if you milked a cow in January, you got ice cream. That in spring they didn't spring clean the house — they defrosted it. And so on. People from that far north usually made fun of us down-staters for complaining about a long winter. That Agnes had never once mentioned her hometown seemed odd.

"Did you know she was from Superior?" I asked Randy.

He shrugged and took another cookie.

"Considering the distance," Erica said, "I don't think the PTA needs to send a representative to the funeral. It's too far, and we don't have the budget. But there are two things we can and should do. One, we'll all sign this card." She handed me a sympathy card. "Two, the PTA should phone Agnes's family with a condolence call."

"Good idea," Julie said.

"Appropriate," Randy agreed.

Only then did I realize my three committee comembers were looking straight at me. My pen made a sudden, deep mark on the legal pad. "Um . . ."

"Thank you for volunteering." Erica smiled. "Call tomorrow, please." She pushed a small piece of paper across the table. "Here's the phone number for Gloria Kuri, Agnes's sister. Please convey our deepest regrets."

She nodded; Julie nodded; Randy nodded. I took a cookie.

Well, two.

At the store the next day, the shock of Agnes's murder had evolved into speculation and sidelong glances at strangers. Lois and I unpacked books and checked the contents against the packing list. Between boxes, she told me about the comments posted on the WisconSINs blog.

"No one's signing their real names, but I'm sure 28in68 is Bruce Yahrmatter and I *know* flower girl is Colleen Emery."

"How?"

She gave me an "Oh, please" look. "Have you seen what Donna drives?"

"You know I don't notice cars much."

"You must have noticed the VW Beetle around town, the one with the flowers painted all over?"

Even my car-impaired brain had noticed the purple vintage Beetle with the big daisies. "Okay, but how do you know about Bruce?"

Lois flicked out the blade on the utility knife. "He graduated from high school in 1968 and wore number twenty-eight on every team he played: football, basketball, and baseball."

So simple, once you knew.

Lois sliced open a box and stood there, clicking the blade in and out, in and out. "Who do you think killed Agnes?"

"Me?" I reached inside the box for the contents list. "How would I know?"

"You must have a theory. Everybody does, and you're much smarter than the average yahoo."

"If I'm so smart, why did I forget to order

that new Thanksgiving book?"

"C'mon, tell Aunt Lois your guess for the killer."

"I really haven't thought about it." I fastened the contents list to a clipboard. "Ready?"

She cocked her eyebrows. "Puh-lease. You can't pull that one on me. You're a mom and you're scared for your kids. Of course you've thought about it."

"Well . . ."

"Ah-hah! I knew it!"

Truth be told, I'd thought about the killer's identity on and off ever since Marina's phone call. How could I not wonder? There was a murderer running free, and it was only natural to imagine yourself inside an episode of *Columbo* or *Magnum, P.I.* or *NYPD Blue*. Though I didn't think I was overly smart, neither did I think myself completely stupid. So it was disquieting that I couldn't come up with a single person who might have killed Agnes. Sure, a lot of people didn't get along with her, but it was a long way from anger over school cafeteria offerings to murder.

"Do you think Gus is reading that blog?" I asked.

"Gus has handed over the investigation to the county sheriff, so I can't imagine it matters if he reads it or not."

I gaped at her. "He didn't say anything when I talked to him yesterday."

"Not sure it was voluntary." She snicked the utility knife closed. "Cindy said the sheriff called just after lunch." Cindy did the landscaping at the police department and had a knack for being around for breaking events. "Forty-five minutes later," Lois said, "the parking lot was jammed with county vehicles and the conference-room door was shut tight for two hours." She tossed her head. "Looks as though the county folks think Gus couldn't figure this out himself."

Yesterday, it had seemed most of Rynwood thought the same way, but that was before the big guns had muscled in. We could scoff at Gus and his staff, but no outsider had better do so.

"I'm sure the sheriff and his deputies have had a lot of experience with murder." I unfolded the packing list.

"But they don't know *us*." Lois pulled books out of the box, scattering foam peanuts everywhere. "They may have fancy investigating techniques, but they don't know Rynwood."

And to that there was no rejoinder.

CHAPTER 7

Procrastination can be a useful tool. Sometimes, if you delay long enough, the need to do a task evaporates completely, and you can joyfully feel justified in your procrastination. Of course, there are times when the job hangs over your head and clouds your days, making you miserable with stomach-tightening anxiety. You *know* you should get on with the task; you *know* that delaying the icky job isn't going to make things any easier. You *know* all that, but you still find reasons to put it off.

So it was Friday, the day after I was asked to call Agnes's sister, that I tacked Erica's slip of paper to the bulletin board over the bookstore's teapot.

"Who's Gloria Kuri?" Lois peered at the handwriting. "That's the area code for the great white north. Is she a new writer?"

Since I'd purchased the store, I'd done my best to have events promoting any author who happened to wander by. We also had reading groups where we gave gift certificates to any child who read a book a month. We'd had poetry parties where each child read a poem aloud. Last summer the employees had dressed up as children's book characters and given a prize to everyone who guessed all of them correctly. Lois's costume was the hardest to figure, but then not many people dress up as Mike Mulligan's steam shovel.

"Gloria Kuri is Agnes Mephisto's sister," I said. "I was volunteered by the PTA to make a condolence call."

"And you haven't yet, have you?" Lois turned, arms crossed over her bright yellow corduroy blazer. "You don't want to do it, and you're putting it off."

"I'll call today," I said vaguely. "It's early. She could still be asleep."

"It's ten thirty in the morning." Lois tapped her watch. "The only day this could be considered early is the first of January."

"Maybe she works third shift somewhere and she's sleeping." Desperation makes you say stupid things. I hated calls like this. I never said the right thing, could never come up with any words of comfort, and had never once felt as if calling did any good.

"Then I'm sure she turns the ringer off

while she sleeps. Here." Lois plucked the slip of paper from the board and handed it to me. "Go call."

"Now?" I backed away from the fluttering paper. "I can't. I have to —"

"This will take all of five minutes." Lois put the slip in my hand and closed my fingers over it. "Go into your office, shut the door, and dial the number."

"What if it gets busy?" I glanced at the empty store. "I'll call later this afternoon, when Paoze gets here."

"You're worse than a teenager with a term paper." She took hold of my shoulders and turned me around. "Go." The push she gave me wasn't exactly gentle.

We both knew I'd tacked the phone number on the board to get her to goad me into action. I couldn't be angry at her high-handedness — irritated, maybe, but not angry.

I shut my office door and sat at my desk. I looked at the piles of catalogs. I put out one hand, but jerked it back. Lois was right. This wouldn't take long. And besides, she was probably listening at the door.

I picked up the receiver and pushed buttons. "Dialing!" I called.

"About time," came the muffled response.

As the phone rang, I tried to think of the

123

right words to say to the sister of someone who was murdered. By the second ring, I'd come to the conclusion there weren't any.

"Hello?" The voice was raspy and low, but decidedly female.

"Is this Gloria Kuri?" I asked. Maybe it would be someone else. Maybe I could leave a message. It'd be cheating and my grandmother would spin in her grave, but it would still count.

"Yah, this is Gloria."

So much for cheating. "My name is Beth Kennedy. I'm secretary of the Tarver Elementary PTA, and I called to say how sorry I am about the death of your sister." Instantly, I wanted to kick myself. Why had I said *I* was sorry? I was speaking for the PTA and should've said *we* were sorry. I really wasn't any good at this stuff.

"Oh. Well, thanks, I guess."

Her near-rudeness gave me a boost. She wasn't any good at this stuff, either.

"She was an outstanding principal."

"Yeah?"

There was a pause. "I'm sorry for your loss," I said. "I'm sure it was the worst phone call you've ever taken."

"Who would've guessed that ol' Agnes would end up murdered?" Gloria mused. "Of all of us, I'd have figured her last for something like this."

"You have a lot of siblings?"

"Oh, yah. Seven of us. Agnes was the oldest, and I was smack in the middle." She ran off the names of the five other siblings. I should've been taking notes. "If I had to make a stab at a murder victim," she said, "I'd pick Luke. You meet some bad people in jail, you know?"

Whether she meant Luke was bad, or that Luke met bad people, I wasn't sure.

"Or J.T.," Gloria added. "She's got Pop's temper. Wouldn't be surprised if she'd started one fight too many with that slacker husband of hers and he finally got guts enough to fight back," she said. "Yah, that I could've seen. But Agnes? Who would've figured that?"

"I'm so sorry," I whispered. "This must be very difficult for you."

"It's been hard for years, with Agnes. You know, I can't think of the last time I saw her."

"Have you ever been down here to Rynwood?"

"Nah."

Agnes had been principal for ten years, and her sister hadn't managed to find the time even once to drive down? But I knew how the years could speed by. You always

thought there would be time to do everything, until suddenly there was no time left
at all. My father had died young from a
heart attack and left behind a shelf full of
travel books for the places he and Mom
planned to visit after he retired. I yearned
to make Gloria feel better but knew I
couldn't. "If there's anything I can do," I
said, "please ask."

"Actually," Gloria said slowly, "there is
one thing. I wouldn't ask, except that you
and Agnes were such good friends."

"Um . . ." This was what I got for saying *I*
instead of the PTA *we*. Maybe they were
going to bury Agnes down here and she was
going to ask me to visit the cemetery and
plant flowers. Or maybe she wanted me to
speak at the funeral. I could cheat and write
a note to be read aloud at the service. I had
the letter half written by the time Gloria
spoke again.

"See, it's such a long ways and I'd have to
take time off work, and the boss hates when
I do that. You'd think being a clerk in an
auto-parts store was like a general in the
army for how he goes on when I want a day
off. I got to be there by noon today, dead
sister or no."

"Um . . ."

"So if I send you a key, you'd take care of

126

things, right? Seeing as how you and Agnes were close."

"Things?"

"At her house. Clean out the refrigerator, change the mail, do something with the plants, if she has any."

"I'm not —"

"I'll call the cops down there and tell them it's all good with me. You're a peach for doing this. Beth, right? What's your address, honey?"

Thirty seconds later, I'd given Gloria my address, agreed to forward any important mail, and promised to keep an eye on the shuttered house until spring, when Gloria or another sibling would come down for house sale arrangements. "None of us goes far in winter," she said.

Again I spoke before I thought. "Who's going to make the house payments? Pay the utility bills?"

"That's not a problem," Gloria said, and there was a deep sense of bitterness in her tone.

I said good-bye, hung up, and stared into space. What had I done this time? But on the plus side, at least I didn't have Marina shaking her head and telling me I needed to learn how to stand up for myself.

Cheered, I got up and went to tell Lois to

break out the chocolate. Even if I'd been guilted into a job I didn't want to do, at least I'd made the dreaded phone call and survived — a chocolate-worthy day if there ever was one.

"Mom?"

"Yes, Oliver? Jenna, you're not wearing flip-flops to school."

"But, Mom —"

"No whining. I don't care how trendy they are. A pair of flip-flops is not suitable footgear for forty-five degrees and rain."

"It won't *stay* this cold." Her lip started to jut out. "And it might get sunny."

"And it might not. Go change."

A mutinous ogre took over my heretofore cheerful daughter. The friendly face of yore was replaced by a squatted chin, crossed arms, and slitted eyes. "Bailey's mom lets her wear flip-flops all winter long."

"How nice for her doctor."

"Huh?"

"Unsuitable footwear can lead to colds and flu and bronchitis and pneumonia." Or at least it might. I was going on instinct; that's what moms do. "Go change. Now." I pointed in the direction of the stairs, and she began the long trudge to her bedroom.

"Mom?"

I looked past the empty cereal bowls I was still holding and focused on my son. "Yes, Oliver. What is it?" And please don't bring up the subject of the dog. Not on a Monday.

Oliver tugged at the collar of his shirt and didn't meet my eye.

Uh-oh. I put the cereal bowls in the dishwasher, then sat on an island stool. I patted the seat next to me. "What's the matter, sweetheart?" I asked in a bad Jimmy Cagney imitation.

His thin shoulders rose and fell.

"Did I forget to kiss Polly the Hippopotamus last night?"

He shook his head.

"Did you forget something?" Oliver often forgot things the minute he walked out the classroom door. While I appreciated his ability to compartmentalize, it meant numerous mornings scrambling to finish projects and find permission slips.

"Oliver?" I glanced toward the stairs. When Jenna came down, we had to leave. "Okeydokey, kid." I gave him a hug and laid my forehead on top of his soft hair. "We can talk tonight. Right now —"

"I did it," he said to the floor. "I was bad and now we'll never get a dog and it'll all be my fault. I'm sorry, I'm sorry, I'm —"

"Oliver." I spoke sharply. It seemed harsh,

but it was the best way to handle the boy when he edged into inanity. "Oliver!"

He dragged a hand across his face and his palm came away wet. My heart crumpled, and it took a superhuman feat of strength not to pull him tight against my heart. I had to be both mother and father to my children now, and this was a time for Dad to show up. "Tell me what you did."

"I haven't, not for a long time. I haven't!"

"Okay." I had no clue what he was talking about — none whatsoever.

"Please don't be mad."

How I hated when the kids said that.

"Oliver, just tell me."

"It's the . . ."

"The what?"

"The bed." Jenna thudded into the kitchen. "He wet the bed again last night. Are *these* okay for me to wear?" She lifted her leg and thumped her hiking boot onto the kitchen table.

"Jenna! Get that boot off the table!"

She dragged her heel across the glossy wood, leaving a dark trail.

"Oh, Jenna. Why did you do that?"

Her face took on that dreaded stubborn look. "All you care about is the furniture and what we wear. You don't care anything about us. Especially me!" She ran across the room and opened the door to the garage.

"Don't —"

Too late. She was already out the door, slamming it shut behind her. I winced. I recognized it all: the sulks, the slams. At long last, my mother's curse was coming true. I had a daughter just like me.

"Mommy?" Oliver asked.

"Yes, sweetheart."

"Are you mad?" His big, round eyes looked up at me.

I abandoned the father mode and ran straight back to being Mom. The hug I gave him was as full of love and reassurance as it was possible for a hug to be. "Don't be silly," I said. "It's not your fault you wet the bed. These things happen."

"They do?" He squirmed out of my embrace. "Did you do it when you were little?"

I decided to fictionalize my childhood. "No, but I had a friend who did."

"What happened?" A small line appeared between his eyebrows. "Is she okay?"

"She's fine. She's a. . . ." I thought through the friends of my youth and came up empty-handed. Back to fiction. "A police officer."

"What's her name?"

The short story was becoming a novella. "Sharon."

"Here? In Rynwood? Has she found out

who killed Mrs. Mephisto yet?"

The garage door opened six inches. "We're going to be *late*," Jenna wailed.

"Get your coat, Oliver," I said. "We'll talk about this tonight."

I backed down the driveway, thinking hard. Oliver hadn't wet the bed in months. Jenna hadn't had a shouting sulk like that in . . . well, ever. To have the two incidents occur simultaneously made me think there was a single cause. And there was only one way to fix it.

I dropped the kids off at school, made a short stop back home to toss Oliver's pajamas and bedding into the wash and to put some vinegar on the mattress, then headed to the store and the privacy of my office. Any other time I might have been nervous dialing this particular phone number, but today my fingers didn't quiver at all.

"Dane County Sheriff's Department," said a calm female. "How may I direct your call?"

"I'd like to speak to the officer in charge of the murder of Agnes Mephisto. She was killed in Rynwood two days ago."

"The sheriff oversees all murder investigations, ma'am, but the deputy in charge of that case is Deputy Wheeler. I'll transfer you now."

There was a click, a hum, and then a ring and a half. "Deputy Sharon Wheeler."

I gasped loud enough for her to hear.

"Hello? Ma'am? Are you all right?"

Her name was Sharon. What were the odds? My multidegreed brother could probably tell me, but then I'd have to feign interest in how he got the answer. "I'm fine. Just a . . . a little frog in my throat."

"How can I help you?" The deputy sounded busy but helpful. I knew the tone well; I used it myself every Saturday afternoon I worked at the store.

"My name is Beth Kennedy," I said, "from Rynwood. My children attend Tarver Elementary, the school where Agnes Mephisto was principal. I was just wondering if you're close to finding her murderer."

"The investigation is proceeding. The local media will be notified when we have solid information."

"Do you have *anything?*" I asked. "My son and daughter aren't sleeping well, and I'm worried about them. If I could tell them the police are close to finding the killer, I'm sure it would make a big difference."

"I'm sorry about your kids," Deputy

Wheeler said. "We're doing everything we can."

"Thank you." As if a seven-year-old would care about "everything we can." I squinched my nose at the phone. "Gloria Kuri, Agnes's sister, is sending me the key to the house. She wants me to clean out the refrigerator. I should have the key by Saturday. Will it be okay to get into the house?"

"The house is no longer a crime scene," Deputy Wheeler said. "If you have lawful right, you may enter at any time."

"What if I find something important? To finding the killer, I mean. Should I call?"

"At any time," the deputy said, and I realized I must have sounded like an idiot. Crime-scene people had probably gone over the house with all sorts of fancy equipment. What was I going to find that they already hadn't?

"Is there anything else, ma'am?"

Embarrassment heated my face. "Thanks for taking my call."

"Not a problem. Hope those kids of yours are okay."

I hung up, thinking that she was just busy, not unfeeling. She probably had children of her own and knew what it was like.

Still, it sounded to me as if this evening's

first chore would be to haul out the vinyl mattress pad.

CHAPTER 8

Friday night, Richard picked up the kids.
While Jenna and Oliver were fastening their
seat belts, I told my ex about the wish for a
dog and the bed-wetting incident and their
reaction to the death of their principal.

"But they hardly knew Agnes Mephisto."
He glanced at the car. "They can't possibly
be that upset."

"They saw her every day at school. And
it's not as if she died from cancer or a car
accident. She was murdered."

"I think you're overreacting."

This was Richard's standard response to
anything he wished to avoid. It covered
everything from worry about finding the
perfect Christmas present to panic over
blood gushing from a child's nose.

"Could be." I waved good-bye to the kids.
"But if you have to buy a new mattress on
Monday, don't say I didn't warn you."

Saturday morning I was at Marina's bright

and early. I knocked and let myself in. The lady of the house sashayed into the kitchen wearing Capri pants and a fitted blouse with a scarf tied flat around her neck. Another scarf was tied around most of her hair, the ends of her light red mop sticking out the top and flopping around in all directions.

"You look as if you stepped out of a 1950s *Good Housekeeping* magazine," I said.

"How perceptive of you, daahling."

"Why the fifties?"

"Don't you read the obituaries? That's when Agnes was born."

My own clothing was well-worn running shoes, jeans unfit to be worn in public, and an aged Northwestern sweatshirt. The purple had faded to a light plum, and half the letters had peeled off, proclaiming that I was now an alumna of NOR WE ERN. "One of us," I said, "is dressed inappropriately. Wonder who it is?"

"Only time will tell." Marina smiled grandly. "Shall we?"

I'd parked my car in Agnes's driveway and walked to Marina's house. Now we made the journey in reverse. Marina chattered about the Saturday activities of her husband and youngest son, Zach. I half listened to the hiking plans, but most of my attention was on the ranch house in front of us. Beige vinyl siding; brown shutters; juniper bushes in front; maple trees and a fence in back — so average it was hard to believe it actually existed.

We climbed the concrete steps to the front door. I took Gloria's key from my purse, inserted it into the dead bolt, and stopped.

"What's the matter?" Marina leaned close. "Is it stuck?"

I'd always wondered if I could sense where a murder had taken place. Was anything left behind? Maybe a piece of tormented soul would chill my blood. Maybe there'd be a silent cry of anguish that only certain ears could hear. Or maybe —

"Let me try." Marina brushed my hand away and unlocked the door easily. "You must have been turning it the wrong way, silly."

We stepped inside and into a dusky gloom. "Eww." Marina blew out a breath. "Stinks in here."

Marina marched to the nearest window, unlocked it, and pushed the frame high. "I don't care if it is twenty degrees colder outside than in. This stink has got to go." She circled the room, opening drapes and windows.

I flipped on the light, flooding the room with a wash of light, and stood transfixed.

Marina opened another window and brushed her hands. "There. Hey, what's the matter?"

I stared at an amoebalike stain on the carpet. The stain and its accompanying smell were organic; a cloying odor that made the back of the throat feel as if it were coated with gunk. Agnes had died right there, leaving behind a spot made up of things I really didn't want to think about.

"Oh, ick." Marina wrinkled her nose. "That's where this ranky stink is coming from. Why on earth didn't Agnes clean it up?" Marina's thoughts caught up with her words. "Oh," she said, and sat down hard on the couch. We stared in silence at the spot where Agnes had breathed her last breath, where she'd left her last mark — literally.

I supposed I'd been in hospital rooms where people had died and I'd passed crosses on roadsides put up to mark the location of fatal traffic accidents, but those were different, somehow. This had been someone I'd known. The last beat of her heart had faded away on the very floor at my feet. I stared at a single marble bookend that sat on the coffee table; its mate was in the hands of the police.

"Well." Marina rocked herself forward and

to her feet. "This isn't getting the eggs fried. You want I should clean this up?"

I gave her a grateful look. "You don't mind?"

"Don't be a goose." She gave my shoulder a squeeze. "Now. Where do you think Agnes kept her vacuum cleaner?"

We went from living room to dining room to kitchen, both of us skirting the stain with as wide a berth as possible. Next to the garage door, we found a closet full of cleaning supplies.

"I'll vacuum the . . . the living room," Marina said. "And there's some carpet spot cleaner. You clear out the fridge. We'll be done with the nasty chores in a tick." She trundled the upright vacuum cleaner across the linoleum and soon had it running at full volume, sucking up the last pieces of . . .

I rubbed my eyes. Sometimes a vivid imagination was a curse. I took a deep breath. We had three hours; I needed to get to the store by eleven. Standing here being creeped out from what had happened to Agnes wasn't very productive. I rolled my shoulders to loosen the tension in my neck and got to work.

The closet was stocked with cleaning supplies, but there was something funny about it. I stood there, looking at the cans of

140

powdered cleanser, the toilet bowl cleaner, and the furniture polish, trying to figure it out. Only when I saw the aging can of Glass Wax did I catch on. There was nothing new. Agnes didn't stock anything in her closet that had been put on the market in the last thirty years. No plug-in air fresheners, no premoistened cleaning cloths, no dryer sheets.

Weird.

I found a box of garbage bags and pulled one off the roll, wondering what I'd find in the refrigerator. I tried and failed not to think about the B horror movies Marina had forced upon me. Eyes mostly shut, I opened the door.

A quart of milk, a carton of sour cream, a bag of lettuce, eggs, and assorted condiments. I let out a breath I hadn't known I was holding. There was no reason for severed hands to be in Agnes's refrigerator, but you never knew.

I dumped the liquids and near-liquids down the drain, ran the disposal, and was filling the garbage bag when Marina reappeared, pushing the vacuum cleaner ahead of her. "I sprayed the spot remover," she said. "It needs to set for a while. Need some help?"

In my hands were jars of mayonnaise and

pickle relish. "It seems a waste to throw away perfectly good food." I looked at the jars, considering options.

"Well, I don't want them. People who live alone double-dip."

I dropped the jars into the bag and reached for the ketchup bottle.

When you don't have to make any keep-or-pitch decisions, emptying a refrigerator doesn't take long. Marina hauled the bag over to her house and I wiped down the shelves with a mixture of baking soda and water. Agnes would have approved, I was sure.

With grunts of effort, we wrestled the fridge a few inches away from the wall. I squeezed my arm into the gap and unplugged the cord; then we found blocks of wood in the garage to hold the fridge and freezer doors open.

Marina went back to the living room and sponged up the spot remover while I checked the kitchen cupboards for perishables. Potatoes, onions, and open bags of flour and sugar went into another garbage bag.

"Done!" Marina announced. She emptied her bucket of water into the sink and rinsed out the sponge. "We'll get Don the dry cleaner to take those drapes. There're some spots on that one that won't come out." She dried her hands on a kitchen towel hanging from a cabinet knob and grinned. "Now for the fun part."

"Didn't know we were here to have fun."

"That's the problem with you, Beth." My best friend looked at me sadly. "You still haven't learned that every moment is an opportunity to have fun."

We'd had this conversation before, and it always ended the same way — with my agreeing to whatever Marina was planning. I still didn't know if it was because I lacked a backbone, or if it was because she was right.

Due to time constraints, I didn't bother arguing. "Whatever you have in mind had better not take more than half an hour. I need to get to the store."

She huffed. "Not nearly enough time. But" — she held up a traffic hand — "we'll make it work. Despite the rumors, I can be efficient, especially regarding this particular task."

"Which would be what?"

Marina's hair was beginning to escape the scarf, and dirt smudged her forehead, but her cheeks had a youthful glow. "Snooping!"

"You can't do that."

"Why not?"

"Because." The idea of going through Agnes's personal belongings gave me the willies.

"That's not a reason."

"What about privacy? She's dead, but does that give us the right to poke through her private possessions? How would you feel if someone rooted through your belongings?"

Marina tapped her lips with her index finger. "You're right. I wouldn't like it."

"No one would. I'm glad —"

"Which gives me real incentive to clean out my underwear drawer. Come along, my dear."

I trailed along in Marina's wake. The living room was filled with October air. I shut windows while Marina flipped through the stack of magazines on the coffee table.

"*American Educator, National Geographic, Smithsonian.*" She tossed the magazines one by one onto a new pile as she read the titles. "No *Good Housekeeping,* no cooking magazines, not even a *People.*" She made a humph noise.

"You make it sound as if there's something wrong with learning."

"All learning and no fun makes Agnes — and Beth if she's not careful — a dull girl." She put her hands on her hips. "Speaking of dull, this furniture defines the word."

The couch and armchairs were covered with the beige-est of beige fabrics. The material was the velvety stuff that parents of young children avoided due to its amazing ability to attract food and drink stains. The oak coffee table, end tables, and entertainment center were stained a medium honey shade. The drapes looked as if they'd come from a midpriced motel room.

Marina opened the entertainment center. "Take a look at this. Can you get more boring than Frank Sinatra, the Andrews Sisters, and Perry Como? The newest singer she had in here is Paul Anka."

"Just like her cleaning closet," I said, then had to explain.

Marina hunkered down to look at the videocassette titles. "Same thing here. No movie made after 1975. The woman was frozen in time."

"The magazines are current."

"Bet she read new stuff only so she wouldn't come across like a freak." She pushed herself to her feet and grinned. "Didn't work."

"Oh, Marina."

"Yeah, yeah. Don't speak ill of the dead. But why? We didn't like her when she was alive, so why should we go all hypocritical

145

and pretend we like her now?"

"It's unkind. The poor woman was murdered. She deserves better."

Marina didn't look convinced. "You're afraid, aren't you?"

"Of what?"

"That her ghost is going to haunt us for saying bad things about her." She lifted her hands, wriggled her fingers, and made Hollywood ghost noises. "OooooOOOoo."

"Quit that."

"OoooOOoo . . . Boo!"

I jumped back from her shout.

"Gotcha." She laughed.

"Funny. Fifteen minutes and I have to leave. Are you going to spend it playing Casper?"

"You could leave me the key." She put on a wheedling tone. "Pretty please?"

"No. Gloria told the police I'd have the key. If I leave and you're here without me, you could get in trouble."

"Oh, please."

"Fourteen and a half minutes."

"You're such a worrywart."

"It's what makes me such a fine secretary for the PTA."

"Zing!" She licked her finger and made a sizzling noise as she set the finger on an invisible iron. "Good one. Now, let's go."

146

She hustled out of the room and down the hallway. Another tendril of hair popped out and bobbed alongside the brightly colored scarf. Marina didn't notice; she was on a mission.

First door on the right was a bathroom. Marina flicked on the overhead light. "Holy cats," she said. "Would you look at this?"

"If you'd move, I would."

She moved aside and made Vanna White moves. "And here, ladies and gentlemen, you have an incredibly hideous bathroom. The idea that anyone paid money for this makes you doubt that the world will ever spin the right way."

"Oh, my," I said. While the fixtures weren't of the harvest gold or avocado green vintages, they must have been born in a related era. "This is really . . ."

"Pink?" Marina suggested.

"Pink," I agreed.

The sink, toilet, toilet paper holder, and bathtub were that light pink favored by grandmothers of infant girls. The shower curtain was cloth and patterned with pink flowers; the soap was pink. Agnes had even found pink toilet paper.

Marina started to open the medicine cabinet. "Ten minutes," I said.

"Well, drat." Her hand hovered. I'd never

known how many women sneaked looks into other people's medicine cabinets until Marina and I had taken a quiet poll of friends and relatives. I'd bet dinner and a movie that only one out of ten peeked. Marina had bet nine out of ten. I still had occasional nightmares about the fate of the rabbit in *Fatal Attraction.*

She sighed and let her hand drop to her side. Though I was glad she'd given up on the medicine cabinet, I was also a little sorry. Maybe, just maybe, we would have seen something that would have helped. Silly, of course, when the police had been through the whole house, but wasn't it possible that two eagle-eyed women could reach conclusions that law enforcement wouldn't see?

Marina tried to tuck her hair back into the scarf. "Let's keep moving. I want to see how many interior design faux pas one house can hold."

The guest room was as bland as the living room: beige carpet, medium oak nightstand, and dresser. The white chenille bedspread was as much of a statement as the room made.

We trooped down the hallway to the master bedroom. "What do you think?" Marina asked. "More pink? More beige? Or, be still my heart, do you think there might be a *third* color?" She put the back of her hand to her forehead. "I'm not sure I can take the shock."

"You'd better. I don't have time to administer first aid."

Agnes's bedroom was mild mannered and polite with a quilted bedspread in an inoffensive paisley print, pale yellow dresser, mirror, and nightstand. Marina poked her head into the small bathroom. "White. Whew!"

I looked at the books on the nightstand — the Bible and a set of specifications for the Tarver Elementary School addition. "I wonder. . . ."

"What?"

"Well, if the addition had anything to do with the murder."

"Don't be silly. People don't kill each other over buildings," Marina said. "Time?"

"Seven minutes." But what was worth killing over? Nothing, as far as I was concerned, but then I was the kind of person who carried spiders outside rather than squishing them.

She pushed past me. The last door off the hallway was to a small study. Crowded bookshelves filled three walls, and a desk filled a fourth. An opaque curtain kept any sunshine at a distance. The room, covered with dark wood paneling, felt too tight for two people. Especially when one of them was a bigger-than-life redhead.

"Holy camoley. Do you see what I see?" Marina's voice was full of wonder. She picked up a piece of paper from the desk. She held one corner with her index finger and thumb, pinching her nose shut with the other hand. "I think I need to bathe in disinfectant," she said nasally.

I took the paper from her and read aloud. " 'Dear Mrs. Mephisto: Thank you for your very generous donation —' "

"You're the world's worst detective." Marina flicked the top of the sheet. "Look at the letterhead."

" 'The National' " — I stopped and looked at my friend — " 'Republican Party.' "

"Agnes," Marina said solemnly, "was a closet conservative."

We stared at each other. This was Rynwood, one of two towns in Wisconsin that voted overwhelmingly liberal in every election. Asking about a political stance couldn't be legally part of a job interview, but everyone knew there were ways to sneak in questions. Though Agnes had been smart enough to keep her politics private, if enough influential parents had known she was Republican, her job could have been in jeopardy.

"No wonder she was killed," breathed Marina.

I put the letter back on the desk. "No one would kill Agnes because she's right instead of left."

"She was principal of our elementary school," Marina said darkly. "Who knows what she was doing to the minds of our children?"

"Get a grip." I banged off the light and headed down the hall. Politics was the one thing we were agreed never to discuss. If you weren't with Marina, you were against her, but I'd declared myself a noncombatant long ago. What the politicians did in St. Paul and Washington, D.C., might affect me, but what I did in Rynwood would have little effect on them, so I paid them about as much attention as I did the time of high tide in the Bay of Fundy.

"Do you think they know?" Marina followed me. "The police, I mean?"

"About Agnes and the Republicans?" It sounded like the name of a bad garage band. "The letter was on her desk. Just a guess, but I'd say the police can read."

"Maybe you should call and tell them the

implications." Marina tugged at my elbow. "It might be important."

"Me?" I stopped. "Because I talked to the deputy in charge of the investigation for thirty seconds, I should be the Rynwood contact person?"

"You've established a rapport."

"Hah. It's been nice, but I have to get to work." Since Agnes's house was closer to the store than my house was, I'd packed a bag with a change of clothes.

"We haven't seen the basement," Marina said. "Down, a look around, and back up. Less than five minutes."

I glanced at my watch. "I'm barely going to make it on time as it is."

"What's a few minutes? Lois will be there, and I bet Sara will stay to cover."

"Paoze." It was Sara's Saturday off.

"Paoze, then. He has such a crush on you that he'll hang around the rest of the day, anyway."

With a wave I dismissed her oft-repeated theory and looked around for my purse. "I'm the owner. If I'm late, it sets a bad example." The purse sat on the end of the counter and I grabbed it up. As I turned around, I caught sight of what had to be the basement door.

And I stopped.

"Gotcha!" Marina crowed. She grabbed the knob of the door and pulled it open with a flourish. "Down we go!" Her feet clattered on wood steps, and the top of her head disappeared from view.

"I'm going to be late," I said, and followed her.

"Would you look at this?" Marina stood in the middle of a large room.

We'd found the color in Agnes's house, and it was all thanks to hockey. Other than a small corner with laundry appliances and a tool bench, Agnes's basement was a floor-to-ceiling shrine to the Minnesota Wild and the North Stars. Wisconsin doesn't and never has had an NHL team, but Minnesota does, and Minnesota is directly west of Wisconsin.

The floor was covered with a glaringly red carpet. The walls were painted a darkish shade of green. The floor molding and window frames were painted in a white bright enough to hurt the eyes.

I circled the room, staring with disbelief at the memorabilia. Signed jerseys of Wild players — Brunette #15; Gaborik #10. Signed green-and-yellow jerseys of North Star players, the team that left town in the early nineties and became the Dallas Stars — Broten #7; Bellows #23. Signed hockey

153

sticks. Photos of Agnes with coaches and players and general managers.

"So Agnes was a hockey fan." Marina slipped off her scarf, and her hair came tumbling down. "Weird. Don't think I once heard her talk about hockey."

I studied a framed set of used tickets; Agnes must have had two season passes. It was almost a five-hour drive from Rynwood to the Xcel Energy Center in St. Paul. How on earth had Agnes managed to attend all those midweek games and make it to school the next morning? No wonder she'd been cranky all the time.

"Look." Marina stuck a hockey helmet over her head. "This year's new fashion accessory."

I gaped at a framed photo of Agnes with a man wearing the longish hair of the early 1980s. He wore a yellowish beige jacket, light blue shirt, and dark blue tie. "That's Agnes with Herb Brooks. Herb Brooks! Look at that ice rink. She must have been there. The Miracle on Ice! Marina, Agnes saw it!"

"What is it with you and hockey, anyway?"

I couldn't believe it. Agnes had seen the 1980 U.S. Olympic hockey team win the gold medal.

Marina dragged the helmet off and shook

out her hair. "Do you realize what time it is?"

"Uh-huh." My gaze was locked on to the photo. Agnes and Herb Brooks. Agnes and —

"You're going to be late," Marina said.

"What?" I looked at my watch and shrieked. "I'm late! Put that down, Marina. There's no time for you to play slot hockey. It's not a toy, anyway; it's a collector's item." I shooed her up the stairs and drove to the store, pushing the speed limit all the way.

"Sorry I'm late." I rushed in, my bag of clothes in hand. "Paoze, you can go. Thanks for hanging around."

"There is no problem to stay, Mrs. Kennedy." Paoze smiled at me. "I will wait until you are ready."

I said hello to Marcia, my other part-time worker, as I hurried back to my office. In three minutes or less, I was dressed in mostly wrinkle-free polyester and ready to help customers, if, that is, I could stop thinking about the veritable Who's Who of Minnesota hockey in Agnes's basement. A hot shot of emotion ran through me — one I'd never in a hundred million years expected to feel in regard to Agnes.

Envy.

I shook it away as best I could and found Paoze. "All set. Thanks again."

"I was glad to stay." He gave another blinding smile, slipped on his jacket, and left.

Marcia, a fiftyish emphatic blonde, patted her heart. "What a cutie. Those white teeth!"

"He's a nice kid." The bells on the door jangled, and a young family walked in. I gave them the owner-of-the-store nod.

"Do you think he has a girlfriend?" Marcia asked.

"Paoze?" The rolls of stickers were already showing signs of Saturday abuse and the swags of orange and black crepe paper hanging above the rolls weren't helping. I moved to start the Sisyphean task of tidying. "I don't know. He doesn't talk about himself much."

"Polite. Clean-cut. Well educated, or going to be. Smart." She ticked off Paoze's characteristics and giggled. "If I weren't almost old enough to be his grandmother, I'd get him to ask me out."

"Your husband might object to that."

"My kids, too. Say, did you hear about the school?"

"Tarver?"

She nodded vigorously. "I heard about it

from Cindy. She takes care of the flowers at city hall? She says the guys — that's what she calls the police officers — had a call last night from someone across the street who saw some lights on that weren't supposed to be on. By the time the guys got there, the burglar was gone, but there was a big mess all over the offices. Papers everywhere. Books tossed all over." Her face glowed with the excitement of the tale. "I bet it has something to do with that principal's murder. I mean, how could it not?"

The school? I put my hand to my throat. The building where my children spent almost eight hours a day? Tarver wasn't safe? I breathed in and out, in and out. "What rooms? Do you know?" Not room 16, I begged. Not room 37.

"Just the offices," Marcia said.

"Offices," I repeated, and felt my pulse rate drop down toward normal.

"At least that's what Cindy told me. The principal's office, mainly. Hey, do you feel okay? You look a little pale."

The front bell tinkled and a gray-haired couple came in. A small cloud of leaves came in with them and puddled on the floor. Sweeping the floor in October was a never-ending chore. "Hello," I said, smiling. "My name is Beth. Let me know if you have any questions."

The woman asked about our selection of Little House books. "We have the full set," I told her. "In hardcover and paperback. Let me show —"

Someone tugged on my sleeve. "Mrs. Kennedy?"

I turned and gasped. "Paoze! What happened?"

CHAPTER 9

Paoze's formerly white shirt was streaked with grime and had a large gash down one sleeve. One bony knee was exposed where his dark blue dress pants had ripped, and blood oozed out of a scrape on his cheek.

"My — my bicycle," he stammered. "It is — is gone."

"Oh, no." I waved Marcia over and asked her to help the customers. "Come with me," I told Paoze, and practically dragged him back to my office. "Sit." I pushed him toward a chair.

"I must —"

"Sit!"

We kept a first-aid kit in the cupboard above the teapot and, after pushing around mugs and cheap flower vases and ancient ketchup packets, I found the white plastic box. Inside were all the medical supplies a mother could want. I flipped past adhesive bandages, white tape, and gauze, and found the antiseptic wipes.

"Hold still. This might sting a little." I held his chin steady with one hand and dabbed his cheek with the other. "The scrape isn't deep, just messy. But it needs to be cleaned up so it doesn't get infected." The wipe was turning pink with blood. Inside the medical kit was a small box of latex gloves; in a perfect world I would have remembered about those before I started playing EMT.

"What happened?" I dabbed at his wound. Dirt and small bits of gravel were embedded in his skin. If I couldn't get them out, I'd need to take him to an emergency room. And Paoze didn't have health insurance, so I'd have to pay the bill myself. I dabbed a little harder.

"Each time I lock my bicycle. Each time."

His jaw muscles flexed against my efforts. "I know you do. You're very careful." He was so careful that Lois had taken to calling him the oldest young man in Wisconsin.

"My father teaches me these things. I purchased the lock the same day I purchased the bicycle." He pronounced it as two separate words. By. Cycle. "The lock I use each time." His voice cracked. "Each time," he repeated.

I didn't know what to say. You do the right

thing; you try to protect yourself, but life has a way of beating you up no matter what. "How did you get this?" I indicated his scrape and his torn clothing.

He put his fingers through the hole in his sleeve and fidgeted with the frayed edges. "My bicycle is locked in back."

I nodded. The storefronts of downtown Rynwood had alleys for shipping and receiving. Lucky buildings had Bilco-type doors that went straight to basements. Buildings like mine had back doors that got propped open with a wedge of wood during deliveries.

"I always lock the bicycle to the fence. Always."

His forceful insistence bounced him half out of the chair. "I know you do. Now sit down and stay down. You're still bleeding." I opened another wipe. "You looked at the fence and saw the bike was gone. What did you do then?"

"My eyes must be wrong, I think. I rubbed them" — he demonstrated — "but the bicycle is still not there. I look around but see nothing. Then I hear." He tipped his head to the right, affecting a listening pose, and messing up my medical administrations. Florence Nightingale probably never had problems like this.

Paoze went on. "Someone is laughing on the other side of the fence. Two boys, I think, laughing and trying not to be heard."

"Oh, Paoze," I said, dismayed. "You didn't." The fence he spoke of was eight feet high and wooden, old and full of splinters and rusty nails. It had been built long ago to keep people from tossing garbage into an empty lot.

"I jumped high and grabbed on to the top. Put my leg over" — he indicated the pant leg with the torn-out knee — "and dropped to the ground. But I could see no one." He bit his lower lip. "No one is there, and my bicycle is gone."

To most people, a stolen bicycle was annoying, and a violation of sorts, but not more than that. For Paoze, it was nearly a tragedy. The boy didn't have a driver's license, and he depended on his ancient bike for transportation to work. If it rained, he brought a change of clothes in his backpack. When I'd asked him about what he'd do in winter, he'd given me that smile and said, "I will be on time every day." And I'd believed him.

I studied the woebegone look on his face. Never once had I heard him complain about anything. Never once had he been less than cheerful. To see him like this made my heart ache. I picked up the phone and dialed. "Lois? Are you busy?"

Fifteen minutes later, Lois was ensconced behind the cash register, Marcia was helping customers, and I was pushing Paoze out the front door. "It'll be fine," I said. "What are you worried about?"

"I am not worried," he said, but we both knew it was a lie. Unworried people don't frown hard enough to crease their foreheads, nor do they constantly push down their cuticles with their thumbnails. More than once I yanked Paoze toward the middle of the sidewalk, out of harm's way of people or lampposts because he was so engrossed in the ends of his fingers.

"Hello, Cindy," I said, greeting the woman on her hands and knees in front of the brick building. She was weeding the mums, though it was hard to believe many weeds were growing in mid-October. I hoped the city wasn't paying her by the hour.

The uniformed man behind the long counter greeted us. His dark blue pants and long-sleeved shirt were crisp, and his badge gleamed bright. "Hi, Mrs. Kennedy. Not another murder, I hope."

"Not today," I said. "I know it's Saturday, but is Gus here?"

"Where else would I be?" Gus stood in the doorway of his office and beckoned us in. "Winnie is off touring the county on the last good garage sales weekend of the year, and I'd rather finish up the paperwork on the school breaking and entering than paint the living room ceiling." He winked, and we all settled into chairs. "So. How can I help?"

I bumped Paoze with my elbow, but he kept his head down and didn't say a word. I bumped him again. Still nothing. Well, maybe he'd join in on the chorus. "Paoze here just had his bike stolen."

"I'm sorry, son," Gus said. Not where was it stolen, or when, or how old was it, or was it locked — no, Gus's first comment was one of sympathy. I could have kissed him.

"Thank you, sir," Paoze said to his knees. "It is not nice to have something stolen."

"No, it isn't." Gus opened a drawer, pulled out a form, and uncapped a pen. As he wrote down Paoze's hushed answers, I tried to remember if I'd ever had anything stolen. My brother's playing keep-away with my Barbie doll probably didn't count.

"Sir?" Paoze lifted his head and looked at Gus. "Will my bicycle come back?"

Gus capped the pen and folded his hands on his desk. "I won't lie to you, son. We don't recover many stolen bicycles."

Paoze's perfect posture slumped into a curve. "Yes, sir," he whispered. "Thank you."

"Most bikes are stolen for parts. Stripped down and sold, bit by bit. Your bike . . . Well, I doubt there's much of a market for parts to a twenty-year-old department store ride."

I squinted at Gus. "Do you know who took it?"

"Let's just say the chances of recovering this particular bike are slightly better than average." Gus smiled, but it wasn't the kind smile he'd shown earlier. "Don't get your hopes up, Paoze, but there's a slim chance you and your bike will be reunited."

Paoze bit his lip. "Thank you, sir."

We were almost out of Gus's office when I had a thought. "Paoze, go back to the store and wait for me, okay? Gus, do you have another minute? And do you mind if I shut the door?"

When we were seated again, I pushed at my cuticles. "The sheriff's department is investigating Agnes's murder."

"That's right." His voice was neutral. "They have the equipment, experience, and manpower."

"But they don't know Rynwood like you do." I'd have to tell Lois I'd used her line.

She'd be so proud.

"It's out of my hands."

"How about the break-in at the school?" I asked. "Is it true the only room broken into was the principal's office?"

He looked at me curiously. "Where did you hear that?"

"Around." I wasn't about to tell him I'd heard it from Marcia who'd heard it from Cindy who'd probably overheard it by listening at open windows. "Were any of the classrooms disturbed?"

"Not a one. And if you're worrying about the safety of your children, quit. There's an officer at the school the whole school day, and he'll stay that way until things calm down."

"Thanks, Gus." I'd tried not to worry and hadn't been doing a very good job. Knowing there was an officer on duty would ease my sleep — only a little, but even a smidgen would be nice. "So you're not investigating the murder at all?"

"Nope."

"But if you get information, you tell the sheriff, right?" I persisted. "Or that Deputy Wheeler?"

Gus put his elbows on the desk. "Why don't you tell me what's on your mind, Beth? If I think it's important, I'll pass it up the line."

I blew out a breath. That was the answer I wanted. I didn't have to talk to Sharon Wheeler again; I could chat amicably with my friend Gus. So I told him about the call to Gloria, my subsequent task of refrigerator cleaning, Agnes's hockey fandom, and her connection with the Republican Party.

Gus sat back in his chair. "You think some Democratic Chicago Blackhawks fan killed Agnes?" A smile came and went.

"I knew you'd laugh at me. But we thought someone should know."

He leaned back a little farther and put his hands behind his head. "Did you read that blog this morning?"

"WisconSINs? No."

"It spent a lot of time raising questions about the whereabouts of a certain white-haired and overweight gentleman the night Agnes was killed."

I thought a moment. "Randy Jarvis?"

"Don't know who else it could be. Tell you what. I'll call the sheriff and tell him about Randy and slide in a mention of Agnes's right-wing persuasion. What's important isn't the fact itself, but that she kept it a secret."

"Thanks, Gus."

I was opening the door when he said, "Are

you going to the memorial service?"

"The what?"

"Didn't you know? There's a memorial service for Agnes tomorrow afternoon. I thought it was the PTA's deal."

"No." I opened the door roughly. But I could guess whose idea it was.

I took care of the worst of Paoze's clothing issues with safety pins and whip stitches. Once again, the Mom Sewing Kit saved the day. He was set to walk the five miles to Madison when I stopped him. "If you work until the end of the day, I'll drive you home."

"Mrs. Kennedy, you do not need to do this."

"If you hadn't been working here, your bike wouldn't have been stolen. That makes it my responsibility." He looked dubious, so I started making things up. "And I have to go to Madison tonight. I'm meeting a friend for dinner." A little more arm-twisting, and I had him convinced. Come closing time, we companionably tallied the day's receipts and locked the doors.

"But this is not the way to Madison." Paoze frowned as I turned left instead of right.

"There's a stop I need to make."

168

A few minutes later, I pulled into the driveway and pushed the button to open the garage door.

"This is your house?" Paoze asked.

"For now." As long as Richard kept up with the hefty child-support payments, the kids and I could stay. If, for whatever reason, the payments stopped coming, the house would be up for sale faster than water froze in January.

We walked into the garage, Paoze trailing behind. "Could you help me get this down?" I indicated the mountain bike on the wall, looming above a trio of bikes standing on the garage floor. Together, we wrestled it off the yellow hooks and bounced it onto the concrete.

I left Paoze holding the bike upright while I rummaged through a plastic bin of sports equipment. Down at the bottom, beneath the soccer balls and jump ropes and baseball gloves, I found a keyed bicycle lock with a key still in the slot. "Ha!" I pulled it out and handed it to Paoze. "That should do you."

He held the lock with his arm straight out. "Mrs. Kennedy, I do not understand."

"For you." I waved at the lock and the bike. They were Richard's castoffs. He'd bought new equipment last summer.

169

"I cannot take this."

Paoze tried to hand me the lock, but I put my hands behind my back. "Your bike was stolen from my store, and it's up to me to replace it."

"That is not right." Paoze put the lock back into the bin. "I cannot take this gift."

"You can't walk back and forth from Madison, and the bus schedule doesn't fit store hours. If you don't have a bike, you'll have to quit, and I don't want to lose you."

"Mrs. Kennedy, I cannot."

Stubborn kid. "Then think of it as a loan. If you get your bike back, you can return this."

"A loan?" He looked at the bike. It was tricked out with more gears than anyone living five hundred miles from a mountain range needed. It also had a fancy computer that gave mileage, speed, elapsed time, and the time of day in Guam, for all I knew.

I saw him weakening, and I pressed the advantage. "A loan. If you decide you want to buy it, I can deduct something from your paychecks."

"Deduct." He stroked the handlebars with his index finger.

"Sure. We can agree on a price and I'll divide it by, say, twenty-six, and subtract that amount out of every paycheck." I watched him eye the gears. "But it's an old bike" — all of four years old — "and it hasn't been maintained at all the last year, so I can cut you a pretty good deal."

A bolt of lightning cracked, and we both jumped. Automatically, I counted seconds. At four seconds a crash of thunder came, loud enough to rattle the glass in the garage window. The storm was close.

"Let's get that bike in the car." I made a come-along gesture and walked out into a strong wind. "The front wheel is quick release. Let me show you."

Paoze clutched the handlebars tight. "Thank you, Mrs. Kennedy, but I can ride now. Thank you for the bicycle. I will —"

"You'll put that bike in the car right now, is what you'll do. Look at that sky. I wouldn't put a dog out on a night like this." Paoze looked at the dark clouds, masses of fast-moving black and gray. A fat drop of rain splattered on the driveway. "Hurry." I opened the car door and popped the trunk. "You don't want your new bike getting wet, do you?"

Rain pelted the windshield as we drove through the streets of Madison. The windshield wipers, even on high speed, weren't keeping up with Mother Nature. I stayed off the busiest streets and tried to keep away from puddles and overflowing catch basins.

Paoze gave directions, almost shouting in order to be heard over the rain. "Please turn left. My street is there."

I flipped on the turn signal and started down a street I'd never noticed before. The houses grew smaller and dingier. Peeling paint was ubiquitous, plywood covered random windows, and the tiny front yards were nothing but beaten earth.

"Here." Paoze indicated a miserable-looking house. The roof was a shingle patchwork, not a single window was intact, and the spalling concrete front porch looked downright dangerous.

I didn't want to look, yet I couldn't look away. Paoze, the ever-helpful, always clean-cut young man, lived *here?* Appalled didn't come close to what I was feeling. But what could I say? The kid was on tuition scholarship, but he had to come up with room and board. From what little he'd said about his parents, they were having a hard enough time paying their own bills, forget having anything left over for their son. If Paoze was paying rent and buying groceries solely on the paychecks I was signing, he must be eating a lot of macaroni and cheese.

He opened his door. "Thank you very

much for the ride, Mrs. Kennedy. I will borrow the bicycle this time and consider purchasing." And he was gone into the rain.

I popped open the trunk and felt the car move as he lifted out the bike. He shut the trunk lid and moved through the rain, carrying the bike's loose front tire with one hand and hanging on to the handlebars with the other. Through the curtains of sweeping rain, I watched him reinstall the front tire, unlock the front door, and wheel the bike inside. The glimpse I got of the interior stairway was of stained carpet, warped paneling, and a bare bulb sticking out of the ceiling. Without even knowing, I could smell the mold, the cigarettes, and the greasy odor of old cooking.

The door shut. He hadn't even waved good-bye.

I was halfway home when my cell phone rang. "Oh, hi, Beth. I didn't expect you to answer." The woman giggled. "I don't know why, but I didn't. Sometimes I have no idea why I do things."

Pointless conversations give me headaches. I'd pulled over to the curb when the phone rang, and now I tapped the steering wheel as red taillights went wetly past. Conversations like this also brought out the worst in me.

"This is Beth Kennedy," I said. "To whom am I speaking, please?"

"To whom?" she mimicked. "Never knew anyone to say 'whom' other than *youm*." She giggled again. "This is Claudia. Claudia Wolff in case you know more than one Claudia."

"Hi, Claudia. What can I do for you?"

"You can tell me you haven't heard about the break-in at Tarver. Did you know? Someone smashed half the windows in the school. Sprayed graffiti all over and stole a bunch of computers."

This was why I didn't care for gossip. Almost everything she'd said was wrong. "I talked to Gus about it earlier today."

"Oh." Her voice drooped, but it took her only a moment to perk back up again. "Well, anyway, that's not why I called. Erica, our PTA president? She asked me to set up a memorial service for Agnes."

Ten bucks said a service was Claudia's idea from the get-go, and Erica had washed her hands of it by saying the project was all hers.

"So I'm putting together a program," she said, "and that takes hours and *hours* to do a nice job. But it's for Agnes, so I want to

174

do it right."

"Mmm." I made a noncommittal noise. Claudia was one of those perennially underappreciated volunteers, according to Claudia. And, to be fair, she was probably right. She did a tremendous amount of PTA work, but it was hard to feel sorry for someone who spent a lot of time asking for people to feel sorry for her.

"Listen to this," she said. "None of Agnes's family can make it tomorrow. Can you believe it? Six brothers and sisters and none of them is driving down!"

"Mmm," I said. Engaging her in conversation was like making eye contact with a large slobbery dog. You didn't want to do it unless it was absolutely unavoidable. Either one could be a long, messy process.

"So," she said, "it only makes sense that everyone on the PTA committee says a few words. Service starts at two in the auditorium. Be there fifteen minutes early, okay? See you!"

"No, wait. Claudia —" But she was gone. I pushed the buttons to call her back and got a busy signal. I tried again; still busy.

I stared at the phone cross-eyed, making my headache worse. I didn't want to speak at the memorial service. I didn't even want to go, though I would because I was a Good

Girl. But speaking? What on earth could I say that wouldn't make me worry about lightning striking me dead? Maybe I'd get Marina to help. I considered the possibility for half a second, then rejected it completely. The cat would be better help than Marina.

My phone rang again. "Beth? This is Gloria Kuri, Agnes's sister."

"Hi, Gloria. Sorry you can't make it down to the memorial service tomorrow. I'm sure there will be a good turnout." I wasn't sure at all, and for my own sake I was hoping for a small showing. Public speaking wasn't my forte, and the smaller the crowd, the less my knees would be knocking.

"Yeah, well."

I massaged the skin at the middle of my forehead. My siblings and I weren't the closest, but if one of them died, I'd move heaven and earth to attend a service given in their honor. Clearly, Agnes's family was even more messed up than mine.

Gloria went on. "You know, I was wondering if you already went to Agnes's house and cleaned out the fridge and stuff."

"Did it this morning."

"Oh." There was a pause in which no profusion of thanks was forthcoming. "Then I wonder if I could ask you one more favor."

I could tell how this was going to go.

Every week one sibling or other would remember that Agnes had something he or she wanted. Gloria would call me and I'd be asked to trot over to the house and hunt for an object I may or may not find, then box it up, and ship it north. The object would undoubtedly be ungodly heavy and cost me a fortune in postage, a fortune for which I'd get promises of repayment, but repayment would mysteriously never appear. "Well . . ."

"I'm looking for a photo album," Gloria said. "Agnes was the oldest daughter, so she got all the family photos when Momma died. Now I'm oldest, and I don't want that album sitting in an empty house all winter. I'm sending you money ahead for the postage, so you don't have to worry about that."

Shame heated my face. Misjudgment was my new middle name.

"Sure," I told Gloria. "I'll stop by tomorrow before the service and get it in Monday's mail."

We disconnected, and I wondered if I'd misjudged Claudia, too. Maybe I should stop judging altogether. Maybe I should assume that people's intentions were honest and kind, and if their actions didn't show that, well, then, there was some miscommunication — that was all.

177

I'd almost convinced myself when I remembered the stricken expression on Paoze's face after his bike had been stolen — and the scattered papers in Agnes's office at Tarver and the stain on Agnes's living room floor.

My headache throbbed in time to the beat of the windshield wipers. Swish, swish, swish.

To my right, dark figures hurried down the sidewalk, bending their heads against the rain. I watched them for a while — watched one particular large and lumbering figure for quite some time — then I put the transmission in drive, signaled, and when the road was clear, merged into the eastbound traffic.

Without Marina at my side, Agnes's house seemed darker than before. I turned on all the lights in the living room, but none of them penetrated the gloom. The scent of the stain remover Marina used had faded away, and the house already had the stale smell of abandonment.

I strained to hear something — the ticking of a clock, the hum of a furnace, any noise at all — but the only sound was that of my own breathing. On this quiet postchurch Sunday noon, no noises penetrated from outside. There were no car doors shutting, no children's voices calling. The owner of this house was dead, and the house was, too.

"Stop that," I said out loud. If I creeped myself out, I wouldn't be in any shape to read what I'd prepared for the memorial service.

I checked the living room end tables and looked through the entertainment center. No photo albums. Not even any photos.

I bypassed the kitchen and headed down the carpeted hallway. In the soulless guest bedroom there were books on the shelves of one of the nightstands. Automatically, I glanced at the titles. Maybe nine out of ten women peeked into medicine cabinets; I did my peeking at bookshelves. Books said a lot about a person. Plus they were in plain sight, so there was no need to feel guilty about snooping.

The collection included *Little Women,* hardcover, bound in a deep rich blue and inscribed "Agnes Heikkinen" on the inside cover in a young hand; seven Nancy Drews, paper dustcovers intact; *The Little Colonel;* a couple of dingy Bobbsey Twins books. I took down a copy of *The Princess and the Goblin.* Inscribed on the front flyleaf was

"To Agnes, from her aunt Agnes, Christmas 1910."

From Agnes to Agnes, and then passed to our Agnes. A triple play. I slid the book back onto the shelf and was grateful that my family didn't curse succeeding generations with increasingly inappropriate names. I'd have to thank my mother next time I talked to her — which might be before Christmas, or might not.

Since the most likely place for the photo album was also the place it would take longest to search — the book-lined study — I took on Agnes's bedroom next.

I looked at the nightstand. The specifications for the school that had been Agnes's last nighttime reading was thicker than the Chicagoland phone book. I flipped to the end and whistled — 829 pages. Why on earth was Agnes reading this? It was something for builders to read: contractors, plumbers, electricians, but not school principals, for heaven's sake.

"This isn't frying the eggs," I told myself, quoting Marina. If I didn't get a move on, I'd have to come back after the memorial service, when darkness was closing in.

With sturdy resolve, I opened the dresser drawers. I pushed my hands through the stacks of clothing and felt around for any booklike shape. Nothing.

I shut the last drawer with a bang and opened the bifold closet doors. A long line of gray, navy, and maroon suits marched down the clothes rod: an army of lifeless, flat Agneses. I shivered, hoping the image wouldn't slide into tonight's dreams.

The shelf above the suits was crowded with hat boxes. Which was odd, because I couldn't once remember seeing Agnes under a hat. I reached up and jiggled a box. The first box I tried with a pink faded chintz pattern was light. So was the next box, a red-and-white stripe. The next box was also light, and the next, and the next. None contained any photo albums, then.

My body acted on its own volition, fast and with no thought. I grabbed the last box on the shelf and fumbled off the lid.

It was a hat.

So much for that mystery. I started to replace it, but stopped and took a closer look.

The hat was a cloche, made in a rich maroon so dark it was almost black. A light netting was sewn onto the front brim, something else I hadn't seen on a hat in years. I turned the hat upside down. FAYE'S MILLINERY, read the label. CHICAGO, ILLINOIS. The name wasn't familiar, but as I'd never bought a formal hat in my life, that wasn't a huge surprise.

What was a surprise was that Agnes owned expensive hats she never wore. She'd always struck me as one of those people who went through her closet once a year and got rid of anything not worn in the last twelve months. Yet if that was Agnes, why all these hats?

I replaced the box and pushed aside the suits to check the closet floor.

"Oh . . ."

I backed up until I ran into the bed. I sat down fast. My vision clouded with a moisture that could only be tears.

It was always the shoes.

Shoes are worn year after year, collecting memories and miles and dirt from vacations and drops of paint from home-improvement projects. Shoes show how a life is lived. I'd packed away my grandmother's dresses without a quiver, but when I'd picked up her shoes, I'd fallen apart. I looked at a pair of Agnes's slippers, worn through at one toe, and wept.

When the tears stopped, I wiped my eyes. "I'm so sorry, Agnes," I whispered. "So very, very sorry."

I shut the closet door and went to the bathroom to rinse my face. The mirror showed red-rimmed eyes, but the color would fade by the time I had to stand in front of an auditorium full of people. My hair, however, had to be fixed. I dragged my fingers through the strands, which didn't help matters at all. My purse with its resident comb and brush was in the car, so I whispered an apology to Agnes and opened the door of her medicine cabinet.

I blinked. "Wow."

A veritable pharmacy had taken up residence inside — big brown bottles, little clear bottles, medium white bottles, and all sorts of sizes in between. I recognized some as herbal medications; some were vitamins; others were prescription. The prescription labels were from the Hunter Center, an office with which I wasn't familiar. I didn't recognize the medications, either. Agnes always prided herself on being healthy, and she had made a big ceremony out of awarding Tarver's perfect attendance certificates. If she was so healthy, why was —

Oh. My. I was peeking in Agnes's medicine cabinet.

I shut the door fast. There'd be time to fix my hair at the school. Using someone else's comb was icky, anyway, and even worse if that someone was dead.

I turned off the lights and scooted down

the hall. The study, when I turned on all the lights, wasn't as dismal as I'd remembered. In a dark and slightly claustrophobic way, it was almost cozy. I crouched down to look at the low-lying books — educational texts, books on economics and financial management. Next up was a shelf of architecture and construction books.

I stood and looked through the next bookcase. History, biography, American history. The last two bookcases had shelves above and closed cabinets below. Inside, one shelf was empty, but the other held a few photo albums. I took down the leftmost one. Its thick burlap cover was promising, but the pages were the sticky cardboard layered with thin clear plastic. It was not the album Gloria wanted. The photos, judging from the clothing and hairstyles, were from the midseventies.

Curiosity made me look closer. Instead of dour faces in formal portraits, I saw photos of a smiling Agnes. Her hair, past her shoulders with feathered bangs, was the same hairstyle she'd been wearing the last time I saw her.

Except for the hair, Happy Agnes didn't look anything like the Agnes I'd known. She was young and thin and, well, happy. Who, I wondered, had taken the photo? Who had

inspired that shining joy? When I turned the
page, I knew.

CHAPTER 10

I slipped into my reserved front-row seat. "Thought you were going to be late," Erica said. Claudia stepped up to the podium and tapped the microphone with dark red fingernails.

"Good afternoon," she said somberly. "I'd like to start this memorial service for Agnes Mephisto by asking Pastor Calvin to lead us in prayer." A black-robed pastor took the microphone. "Let us pray," he said, and an auditorium full of people bowed their heads.

I tried to pay attention, but Pastor Calvin was famous for his long-windedness, and it became clear that he hadn't known Agnes at all. The third time he called her "our deeply beloved sister," I tuned him out completely and took myself back to Agnes's study. Once I'd recovered from my startling discovery, I'd found the family album quickly enough.

Bound in cracking leather, the black pages

were filled with sepia-toned photos stuck on with black adhesive corners. I saw horses and hayfields and ponies and women in long dresses. Most of the photos were labeled with names; some had names and dates. The album was a treasure, and I didn't blame Gloria for wanting it closer at hand.

I'd laid the old album aside and looked at Happy Agnes one more time. There were also a tanned Agnes and a relaxed Agnes. And, according to the photos on the next page, a married Agnes.

"Dear Father, please take to your heart our sister . . ."

On the second page, Agnes and her husband, John Mephisto, were dressed in their wedding clothes. He was in jeans, a dress shirt and tie, with long hair loose to his shoulders. She was in a white dress that looked like a long T-shirt, her long hair loose. Agnes carried daisies, and she and John were both barefoot.

The next few album pages had snapshots of Agnes and John posing at beaches, at the edge of the Grand Canyon, in front of Mount Rushmore. John was good-looking, if you liked tall, dark, and handsome, and the top of Agnes's head almost reached his shoulder. Each picture showed Happy Agnes with her expansive smile and one hand holding on tight to her husband. The husband's smile wasn't nearly so wide, and his gaze often wandered from the camera.

"And let us remember our own souls. . . ."

Then came two pages of Christmas pictures, then nothing. Most of the album was blank.

"Amen."

The minister stepped away from the microphone. Claudia took charge. "Thank you, Pastor. I'd like to ask Erica Hale, president of the Tarver Elementary Parent Teacher Association, to say a few words. Erica?"

In a navy blue skirt and jacket over a staid white blouse, Erica looked the part of the grieving colleague. But Agnes and Erica had shouted at each other more times than first graders could count, and our esteemed president had been checking off the days until her term as PTA president was over.

At her house the other night, I'd stayed after Randy and Julie left to beg for gardening tips and had learned a little too much about how Erica felt about the recently deceased principal. "It's a relief," she'd said, "to have that woman gone."

I watched Erica adjust the microphone to suit her short stature and wondered if she would manage to avoid hypocrisy.

"Agnes Mephisto," she began, "was principal of this school for ten years. Under her guidance, test scores rose, money was saved, and a new era in administration-teacher relations was achieved. . . ."

The level of relations was a new low, but it was new.

"Agnes was an original, and she will be deeply missed."

I thought about that as Erica came down the stage steps and sat back down. "No lies," I whispered.

"I didn't get straight As in law school for nothing."

"Randy Jarvis is the treasurer of the Tarver PTA," Claudia was saying. "Randy?"

Mr. Jarvis laboriously stumped up the stairs, one foot up, next foot beside it. One foot up. Next foot beside it. He swayed and flailed his arms at the top, but he regained his balance and plodded to center stage. A large, soft exhalation ran around the room; I hadn't been alone in holding my breath.

Randy moved the microphone up and stood a moment with his hands on both sides of the lectern. "I met Agnes ten years ago this August." He looked out across the audience. "Remember that August? Hot as Hades and not a drop of rain. Humid as all get out past Labor Day."

That sounded like every August, but ten years ago I'd been enamored of an infant Jenna, so I wasn't the best judge.

"Agnes came into the store and told me she was the new Tarver principal. Asked if I had any kids in the school."

Randy was starting to ramble. I wondered if there would be a plot, or if it was going to be your average Randy story: long, tedious, and point-free. I deeply wanted to twist around and find Marina. This didn't sound like the crazy-with-love-for-Agnes Randy she'd theorized.

"That day," he went on, "Agnes bought a Diet Coke and a bag of Doritos." He paused. "And an ice-cream sandwich. I nearly forgot about the ice cream."

Randy held a roomful of people captive while he recited the junk food that Agnes regularly purchased — Doritos and ice cream in summer; potato chips and beef jerky in winter. "I always knew when winter was coming, just by what Agnes bought." Randy chuckled. No one else did. "Just two weeks ago, Agnes bought potato chips but no jerky. I asked her if that meant we were only going to get half a winter. But she said she just wasn't hungry."

Mercifully, he stopped there. He nodded and made his ungainly way down the stairs.

"Our next speaker," Claudia said, "is Beth Kennedy. Beth became secretary of our PTA only a few weeks ago, but she's been a part of Tarver for many years. She's also the owner of the Children's Bookshelf. Beth?"

I climbed the stage stairs, which suddenly seemed taller and steeper than Mount Everest. At the top, I stopped, catching my breath. What was I doing up here?

The night before, I'd sat in front of the computer and written draft after draft of words appropriate for the occasion — bland words that edged toward hypocrisy without quite tumbling into the pit. I glanced down at them now. "Agnes Mephisto's love of books was our common bond. . . . Agnes had a strong and admirable drive to push Tarver Elementary to great heights."

Gag me.

I looked out across the upturned faces — Erica, Randy, overly pregnant Julie, and on the other side of Erica, the school superintendent and administrative staff. Scattered around were teachers and local business owners, a few parents — Debra O'Conner and her husband, CeeCee Daniels and husband, Claudia Wolff, Tina Heller. All of them were here because they were supposed to be; none of them were here because they cared about Agnes.

A sudden surge of anger roared through me. I grabbed the paper and held it high. "Claudia asked me to say a few words, and I spent last night working on this speech. Until ten seconds ago my intentions were to read it." I crumpled the sheet into a lump and hurled it to the floor. "But it's crap."

There were lots of sidelong glances and a soft rustling. Behind me I heard scuffing feet, and I figured Claudia was perching on the edge of her chair, looking around for a hook she could use to yank me away from the microphone.

"Crap," I repeated. "We can stand up here and say pleasant things about Agnes, but did any of us truly know her? How many of us invited her into our homes? Stopped in her office just to chat?"

More feet were shuffling. I plunged on. "If we're here to memorialize Agnes, let's talk about what she was really like."

Air left the room as two hundred people sucked in a breath at the same time. "Beth!" whispered Claudia. "You can't —"

I ran over her strangled cry of distress. "Did anyone know Agnes was named for her aunt Agnes? At least three generations of her family had the name. Did anyone know Agnes was from Superior?"

There wasn't a single nod of confirmation. A movement in the back of the room caught my eye, but I couldn't make out who it was. "Agnes," I said, "was a Perry Como fan, and she was a big believer in vitamins."

I spotted Marina's red hair. She was grinning, and I realized that I'd given away that I'd gone back into Agnes's house and . . . well . . . snooped. The fact that I hadn't *intended* to snoop wouldn't shield me from the grief I was sure to get. Ah, well.

"Agnes had a marvelous collection of 1930s hats. Her guest room —" My voice cracked as I once again saw that lonely, unloved room. "In her guest room was a shelf of children's books. Nancy Drew, the Narnia books, *Wind in the Willows*."

In the second row, Debra put her fingers to her lips. A couple of rows behind her, CeeCee tucked her hair behind her ears as she surreptitiously wiped the outsides of her eyes.

I put my elbows on the lectern. "And Agnes was a hockey fan. Did anyone know that? No one here cared enough about Agnes to learn about her passions. If I had to do it over again, would I? Who knows? But now I'll never get the chance. Agnes is dead." I bit my lower lip. "Murdered."

Ignoring the rustling, I went on. "There's no sugarcoating this. Agnes was murdered.

Years taken away from her." My voice hardened. "Whoever stole those years did a great wrong. He stole Agnes's life. And it's our own fault that we hardly knew her."

There wasn't anything left for me to say, so I stopped. "Thank you," I said, and started back to my seat. Claudia gave me the stink eye, but I pretended not to see.

Erica leaned over as I sat down. "Where's your hair shirt?" she asked softly. "No public penance can be complete without one."

"Too itchy," I whispered. Erica turned a laugh into a cough as Claudia introduced the next speaker: the superintendent of the Rynwood School District.

Mack Vogel took the microphone and gave me a wary glance. "Good afternoon, ladies and gentlemen. On this sad occasion, I'd like to say a few words on the contributions Agnes Mephisto made in the ten years she served as principal of Tarver Elementary."

One sentence later, we were listening to the sanitized version of Agnes.

I sighed. Erica patted my arm and whispered, "Not everyone is as brave as you."

But I knew it wasn't bravery that had made me toss my speech to the floor. It was sheer unadulterated fury. Agnes should not be dead, and she deserved to be remembered as she truly was, not as some mythical, perfect principal.

Mack was steaming on strong. "Of the many fine attributes we'll miss in Agnes, at the top of the list must be the dedication she always exhibited."

I sighed again and tried to think of something else.

At long last, the pastor closed the service with another prayer. "Amen," he finally said. Immediately, people stood and started making their way to the exits. Claudia fixed me with a beady stare as she came down the steps. I said good-bye to my fellow PTA committee members amidst a flutter of questions about the school break-in and the absence of a murder suspect, and I snaked into the departing crowd.

I'd almost made it to the back door when someone spoke into my ear. "I knew," he said in a low voice. I stopped and the crowd flowed around us. The man was dressed in a black polyester suit with sleeves two inches too short. He looked like someone I should know, but I couldn't quite place him.

He nodded. "I knew all about Agnes and her hockey."

It was Harry, the school's security guard and janitor. No wonder I didn't recognize him; I'd never seen him out of the navy blue slacks and light blue dress shirt that passed for his uniform.

"Are you a hockey fan, too?" I asked.

"Blackhawks," he said, referring to the NHL team in Chicago. "But Agnes and me got along anyway."

I remembered the night Agnes presented the school renovation design. She and Harry had stood together in back, beforehand. So much for my assumption that they were talking about what time to turn down the lights.

"Agnes knew hockey," Harry said. "She played goalie. Best kid goalie in Superior until they wouldn't let her play anymore 'cause she was a girl." He looked at the floor.

I laid my hand on Harry's thin arm. "I'm sorry. She shouldn't be dead."

"No, she shouldn't. She really shouldn't." His voice shook. "I'll miss her," he said. "A lot."

I squeezed his arm. "She was a fine principal. We'll all miss her. We'll —"

Harry jerked his arm away. "Bull," he said loudly.

I shrank away. I knew what was coming next. Harry was going to blast me, the PTA, the administration, the teachers, and the parents with being sanctimonious, self-righteous snobs who couldn't stand Agnes in life and didn't have the courage to say so at her death. He was going to say none of us should be here. And he'd be right.

Harry's shoulders went back and his chin lifted. I dove deep into my imagination, and the unironed collar of his shirt disappeared. The black suit expanded into a voluminous cape. He surveyed the people streaming by with a fierce and challenging glare. "She deserved better." He turned on his heel, swirling the cape gracefully, and strode off.

I watched him go, hearing the jangling of spurs on leather riding boots. Poor Harry, born four hundred years too late. He would have made a wonderful defender of feminine virtue.

"Was that Harry?" Marina came up beside me. "He looks different. The suit, I guess." But there was doubt in her voice.

"Mmm." She kept talking, but my thoughts were back in the Elizabethan era with Sir Walter Raleigh and mud puddles, so it took me a moment to come back to the present. "Sorry. What did you say?"

"Oh, for crying out loud." She waited until a passing group was out of earshot. Then she leaned close. "I know who killed Agnes."

197

CHAPTER 11

I sat at Marina's kitchen table, drinking decaf and shooting holes in her latest who-killed-Agnes theory. "Agnes and her ex-husband have been divorced for more than twenty years," I said. "Why on earth would he wait until now to kill her?"

Marina twiddled her fingers in the air in a don't-bother-me-with-mere-details gesture. "It's always the ex-husband. There are lots of reasons why he waited this long."

"Name three."

Though Marina's lower lip had momentarily drooped when I'd said I already knew Agnes had been married once upon a time, she'd recovered as she retold her tale of grilling Randy Jarvis for Agnes information while buying a candy bar. The empty wrapper now lay on the table in front of us, and I spun it in circles while I waited for Marina.

"Maybe," she said, "Agnes changed her

last name and it took this long for him to find her. Sure." She warmed to the idea. "Other than those expensive shoes, who ever heard of a name like Mephisto? Mephistopheles, Mephisto, the devil, same thing. No one would marry a guy with a name like that."

"Agnes did," I said. "John Mephisto, in 1975. There was a wedding invitation in the photo album."

"Well, fooey." Marina licked her finger and touched it to the candy wrapper, sticking on the tiniest of chocolate scraps. "How about Agnes was stalking him for years, making his life miserable, and he finally snapped?"

"Hard for someone in Rynwood to stalk someone who lives in California."

"Aren't you the party pooper? She could have been cyberstalking. Maybe she stole his identity. Maybe she —"

The alarm on my watch started beeping. I pushed the stem to shut it off and got up. "Much as I'd love to stay and listen to you flounder for theories, I need to get home before Richard drops off the kids."

"I'm not floundering."

"Okay, you're not." I slid on my coat. "But you're taking on a lot of water."

"Oh, hah very hah."

199

I was turning the doorknob when she said, "Hey, Beth?" She was sticking her finger into the chocolate wrapper again. "Nice speech." She didn't look up at me. "At the memorial service. That was really nice."

"Oh." I was used to Marina's carefree dispensation of compliments, but this sounded deep and real. "Well, thanks."

"You were right. None of us really knew her."

I thought of Harry. There was one person. But just one.

"Anyway, I just wanted to say you did good." Marina looked up and grinned. "Who would have guessed?"

I stuck my tongue out at her and went into the black night.

Three hours later, Jenna and Oliver were hugged, unpacked, and sound asleep. I took their dirty clothes to the laundry room, wondering if I'd done the right thing in divorcing Richard. Did every divorced mother wonder the same thing? How much damage had I done to my children by removing their father from their daily life?

Not that he'd been home every day. His job put him on the road three weeks out of four, and I'd thought divorce wouldn't be all that different for the kids. "Wrong again," I told the jug of laundry detergent.

Bam! Bam! Bam!

I jumped. Who would be pounding on the back door at this time of night? I started the washing machine and went through the kitchen. Marina's face was on the glass, pressing her nose flat and making a mark I'd have to clean off later. I waved her in. She rattled the door, and I remembered I'd already turned the dead bolt.

The second the door was unlocked, Marina shot inside. "It's me. It's me," she wailed. Her hair flew around her head in a red nimbus.

"I know it's you." I shut the door behind her. "Who else would I let into my house late on a Sunday night?"

"No, no. It's me. I'm doing it. And now he's after me. What am I going to say to the Devoted Husband? I can't tell the DH — I just can't." She paced the room in a very un-Marina-like way. Nervous energy and Marina weren't on regular speaking terms, but she was tapping her knuckles together and whirling around as if to the manor born.

"What am I going to do?" Marina said over and over, each repetition growing louder and louder. "What am I going to do?"

"I'd suggest taking a deep breath and

calming down."

"You don't understand!" Her eyes darted around. "I'm in danger. I'll put you in danger." A horrified look crossed her face. "I've put your kids in danger just by being here! I can't —"

"Yes, you can." There was a chair nearby, and I shoved her toward it. "Sit down and calm down."

"But I can't." She tried to rise.

I pressed on her shoulder and didn't let her up. "Sit." When she remained motionless for a full second, I said, "Deep breaths. No arguing. We'll do them together. Ready? One." After we'd done three, I sat in the chair next to her. "Now, start at the beginning and go to the end. Don't leave anything out."

She gave a shaky laugh. "I knew this was the right place to come. You're the best person in a crisis I've ever known."

"Hah. I'm a mom, that's all. Moms know crises."

"That's not true. Some moms freak out at the sight of blood."

I shut one eye and scanned her from head to toe. "Are you bleeding somewhere that doesn't show? Because if you are —"

"See? You're doing it already. I'd worked myself into a panic attack, and now I'm almost laughing."

Almost, but not quite. "I could tell the bloop joke."

"No, no!" She put her index fingers into the shape of a cross and thrust them at me. "Not the bloop joke. Anything but that." She giggled, and I knew her worst fear had faded.

"In the beginning," I started, "Marina Annesley, now Marina Neff, was born in Sheboygan, Wisconsin. Fast-forward forty-some years." I rolled my index fingers, indicating time passing. "Your turn."

"I'm the —" She spoke so quietly that I couldn't hear.

"Sorry? The what?"

"The WisconSINista."

I knew the term "barista," though I'd never plucked up the courage to order a cup of coffee from one. Fancy coffee shops with mile-long menus written on chalkboards intimidated me. But what was a Wisconsinista? A new name for Wisconsin natives? A University of Wisconsin football fan?

"The what?" I asked.

She pushed her thumbs up against each other hard enough to whiten the skin around her nails. "The Wiscon—"

"I heard you the first time. What's a Wisconsinista?"

"Why did I know I'd have to explain this to you? I write that blog. You know, Wiscon-SINs? The one everybody is talking about?" In spite of the angst hanging off her, she sounded proud of herself.

"Oh." The anonymous blog my staff kept crowding around and reading. The one Gus mentioned. The one that was offering up Randy Jarvis as Agnes's killer. The anonymous blog I'd thought Lois might be authoring. So. Not written by my staff, but written by my best friend. My mouth twisted a fraction.

"Yeah, yeah," Marina said. "Nothing but a bunch of gossip, right? But it's been fun. You wouldn't believe some of the e-mail I've gotten. And who it's been about." She grinned. "Did you know —"

I held up my hand. "Please. Don't know. Don't want to know."

"Spoilsport."

"My kids tell me that on a daily basis."

"No surprise there." She rolled her eyes. "I started this blog in September, when Zach went back to school. Had to do something to keep from going wacko. Anyway, I got maybe thirty, forty hits a day until Agnes was murdered. Then ka-blooey!" She threw out her arms. "The day after? Thousands! And I'm still getting hundreds."

"How nice for you," I said. "But if it's that much fun, why are you here?"

The glow on her face faded to a white that made her freckles stand out sharply. "Because tonight one of those e-mails was different. It came just after I posted about there having to be a connection between the school B and E and the murder. This e-mail was a threat."

"Like a cease-and-desist threat?"

"No." She covered her mouth with her fingers and spoke through them. "It was 'Keep trying to find the guy who offed Agnes and you could be next.' "

" 'You could be . . .' " The sentence was impossible to finish.

Time at the kitchen table stopped. The refrigerator hummed, the wall clock ticked, and the washing machine sloshed. But Marina and I, despite being seated comfortably, hung in midair, our feet dangling and our toes frantically trying to touch the ground.

"That's a death threat," I whispered.

She nodded, and the ground fell farther away. Multiple emotions competed for the top slot. Fear, panic, and a deep and desperate love for this woman who had given me so much. Marina? Dead? Reality had changed in an instant and I didn't care for it.

I took one of her hands and flinched at the chill in her skin. "Do you want me to call Gus for you?"

"No."

"Right. It's probably better if you call." I gave her hand a pat. "I'll get the phone and —"

"No!" She grabbed out and jerked me back down. "No police."

This was starting to sound like a B movie. The kidnappers said no police, but one of the parents always ended up calling them. Something would go wrong and a rogue cop would save the kid, retrieve the money, and get a promotion. "What do you mean, no police?"

"Just what I said." Color was coming back into her face. "No police."

"Marina, you just had a death threat! We're calling Gus right now."

"Call the police and I swear I'll deny everything."

"Are you nuts?"

"Yes! I mean, no. If I go to the police, I'll have to tell them I write WisconSINs! I'll lose my anonymity, I'll get more threats from people who didn't like what I wrote about whoever, and I'll have to shut down

206

the blog. The whole town will hate me."

"Gee," I said dryly. "Shut down the blog or get killed. How on earth will you decide?"

"I'm not going to get killed." She put up her chin. "It's common knowledge that people who send anonymous threats never carry them out."

"Is this the same common knowledge that says you can see the Great Wall of China from the moon? The same common knowledge that says chameleons change color to match their surroundings?"

"They don't?"

"No."

"Well, I don't think this guy is dangerous."

"So why are you sitting in my kitchen late on a Sunday night?"

"He just wanted to scare me, that's all."

"Uh-huh." I put my elbow on the table and propped up my chin with my hand. "And you know this how, exactly?"

"If he wanted me dead, I'd be dead." She ran an index finger across her throat and made a gurgling noise that sounded more like something you'd hear in a dentist's office than in a dark alley. "He wants two things. That I stop trying to figure out who broke into the school, and that I stop trying to figure out who killed Agnes."

"Is that what you've been doing?"

"Sure. Me and half the people in Ryn-wood." She flipped her hair back over her shoulders. "I'm just the one with an audience."

"And you like that."

"Daahling. Everyone loves an audience." The imaginary cigarette holder she suddenly held was two feet long, and the imaginary smoke ring she blew wafted up toward the ceiling. "I'm just honest enough to admit it."

That comment wasn't worth responding to. "So if you agree to stop trying to figure it out, he'll stop threatening you."

"So he says."

"Then it's easy," I said. "Stop."

"Why did I know you'd say that?"

"Gee, can't imagine." I drummed my fingers on my cheek. "Maybe because I'm right?"

"Daahling." She tipped ashes off the ghostly cigarette and onto the linoleum. "You could be right of Rush and I'd still love you, but there is another alternative." Her glance slewed sideways, and the Greta Garbo facade faded.

Ahh. "You have an ulterior motive, don't you?"

Her mouth opened slightly. *"Moi?"* She laid

her hands flat on her collarbone.

"Yes." I folded my arms. "You're about to ask me to do something I don't want to do. Last time you did that, I ended up as the PTA's secretary."

"And you enjoy it." Marina smirked. "Don't give me that look. You're having a good time. You and Erica are getting along like a house afire. Has she stopped by yet to give you landscaping advice?"

Erica had said she'd drop by next weekend, but I wasn't going to tell Marina that. "Whatever you want, I don't have the time, I don't have the money, I don't know how, and . . . and . . ."

"And you don't want to help me." Marina slumped.

"Cut it out. You're not guilting me into participating in whatever nefarious plan is cooking in that red-haired brain."

"Nefarious? I'm as law abiding as they come."

"Sneaky, then."

She gave me an injured-kitten look. "All I want is a little help."

"Let the police handle it," I said.

"I'll lose the blog."

I shrugged. "Start another."

"You don't understand."

"You're right. I don't. Why on earth would

you risk your life over something as trivial as a blog?"

Marina's forehead started to turn pink, and I knew I'd said the wrong thing.

"Trivial?" she said loudly. "Providing information is trivial? People are starved for this kind of knowledge. I get e-mails almost every day, thanking me for doing the blog."

That was easy to believe. "Dear Blogger, thanks so much for telling all about Jane Doe. I always knew there was something funny about her, and now I have proof. Can't wait to tell my neighbor about Jane's five ex-husbands."

"It may be gossip to you," Marina was saying, "but to some people, lots of people, it's the foundation communities are based on. Everyone has secrets, but the more we share, the more we can understand each other."

I didn't quite buy it. "How does knowing that Don Hatcher is getting a hair transplant help me understand him?"

"Because," Marina said patiently, "now we know to what extremes he'll go to preserve his vanity."

I tilted my head to one side and squinted one eye. "What about Carla going to that spa?"

"She's finally serious about losing weight,

and everyone should help her and not sabotage her new diet."

"Well," I said slowly, "that's one way to look at it."

"Beth finally comes around!" Marina pumped her fist. "Break out the chocolate."

"Just don't tell my mother." I looked left and right. "She doesn't believe in gossip."

"And I bet she doesn't have a single friend to have over for coffee on Monday mornings, let alone someone to go to late on a Sunday night."

It was true. Mom had a boatload of acquaintances, but she didn't have anyone to call her best friend. Maybe there was a tie between gossiping and friendship. Maybe talking about other people tightened connections and secured bonds and —

"So you'll help me, right?"

This was the woman who'd cured my morning sickness; the woman who had shown me how to get gum out of carpet; the woman who had comforted me the night Richard left for good. And all without my asking. If I didn't help her when she did ask, what kind of friend was I?

"The blog may be silly to you," she said, "but it's all I have. You have the store and the kids and the PTA. I have a husband who's hardly ever home and a son who hasn't wanted me around since he was five. I need this, Beth."

I couldn't stand the entreaty sculpted on her face. "Of course I'll help you."

"Really?"

"Sure. Anything you want. Just ask."

"What?" She put her hands to her face in mock horror. "No caveats? No amendments?"

Though spoken in jest, her words wounded me. I'd always thought of myself as a good friend, but maybe I'd slid into selfishness.

"No limits," I said. "What do you want me to do?"

The next morning, ignoring the protestations of my manager, I shut myself in my office and fired up the computer. Lois stood outside the door and scolded me. "What are you doing in there? We need to finish planning the Halloween party. We need to figure out the November work schedule. We need to figure out how to shoehorn two author events into December."

"Later."

With a pencil and a pad of paper at the ready, I read Marina's WisconSINs blog archives.

Each posting began the same way: "Good

morning, Rynwood!" The only variation was the number of exclamation points. The juicier the gossip, the more punctuation it was awarded.

I waded through the September news about summer vacations ("Thanks to the magic of cell phones with cameras, does anyone think what happened to C.P. in Vegas is going to stay in Vegas?"), college back-to-school parties ("Yet another freshman discovered the joys of Everclear. How's that hangover doing, J.M.?"), and tan lines ("There's a thin, pale band around the ring finger of D's left hand. Could this year's split be the final one for D and J?"), but there wasn't anything related to Agnes or Tarver Elementary.

With my pad of paper stubbornly blank, I closed out of the September archives and opened October's.

"WisconSINs applauds anyone who tries new things. While many people resist change, there are those who accept new ventures with a song in their hearts and a smile on their lips. Attitude, my daahlings, it's all about attitude! Get out of your rut and try something new today. There's a whole world out there just waiting for you!"

The post's date was the same day I'd agreed to become the PTA's secretary. The truly annoying part was she'd been right; I had needed to get out. My rut had been getting deeper and more comfortable on a daily basis. The sharp edge I'd honed in college had dulled to a butter knife. What had happened to me?

I stood up and paced. When had my thirst for learning and knowledge been replaced by complacency and contentment? When had I stopped subscribing to *The Atlantic Monthly*? When had I quit watching *NewsHour* with Jim Lehrer?

Silly questions. All that had come to an abrupt halt with the arrival of my daughter. And I didn't regret it a bit.

I sat back down and picked up the pencil. I wrote a title, "Murder Suspects." Now the page wasn't blank. Back at Marina's blog, the date of Agnes's murder was fast approaching. The week before, K.O. was mentioned in passing as a contender for a big competition. K.O. Kirk Olsen. I felt a rush of detection and wrote the name: Kirk Olsen, of the school bus incident.

When Agnes had ordered the long-established school bus routes reconfigured, Kirk's children had ended up with a twenty-five-minute bus ride instead of a ten-minute one. He hadn't been pleased, and he'd been extremely vocal with his opinions. The rerouting had resulted in fewer stops for the buses, lower gas mileage, and the elimination of one bus altogether, but for a week or two, teachers and staff had kept a sharp watch on the school entrances. Kirk went to deer camp every fall and regularly showed up in the paper as the winner of shooting competitions.

Where there was one name, there must be more.

The day before the murder, the blog suggested a new law that prevented parents from naming their children with rhyming first names, especially rhyming boy names with alliteration.

That could only be a reference to Claudia Wolff with her wild brood of Tyler, Taylor, and Taynor. And hadn't there been . . . I clicked through more posts, all the way to the day after the murder. Yes. There had been mention of the Fish Fry Friday disaster *and* mention of the school bus incident.

Claudia had gone ballistic when Agnes tried to cancel Fish Fry Friday — held in perpetuity on Friday evenings in the school cafeteria — and she'd almost taken her boys out of Tarver. I wrote down her name as Suspect Number Two.

This was getting kind of fun. Whom else had Marina written about?

I wrote down another name without even looking. Randy Jarvis. But the pencil's tip hovered over his name. The night I'd dropped Paoze off at his house, I had seen the silhouette of someone who might have been Randy. But what would Randy have been doing in Madison on a Tuesday night?

Back to the blog.

Two days after the murder, WisconSINs rehashed the Bike Trail Incident. A few years back, a group of residents had mounted a campaign to put a bike trail in Rynwood. The proposed path had traversed school grounds, and Agnes had stamped the idea flat. Nick Casassa (father of Patrick and Tricia) was a member of the Rynwood City Council and had been a big proponent of the trail. He hadn't taken the defeat well.

I tapped the list. Four names didn't seem nearly enough. I drew a squiggly line to illustrate the end of the blog suspects and started writing the names of everyone who hated Agnes. Mere dislike wasn't enough. If it was, I might as well use the phone book for a list.

Who had hated Agnes? Hated her enough to kill her?

Dan Daniels. CeeCee's husband. Flossie had mentioned him at lunch. His goatee alone made me nervous. No completely innocent man would grow one of those.

Cindy Irving. Currently she was doing landscaping for the city, but not that long ago she'd been a teacher at Tarver. Agnes had asked her to apply for early retirement. Cindy's reaction hadn't been pretty.

Who else?

Joe Sabatini. I didn't know him, but I'd heard about a scene starring him and Agnes circa last year. After a fifth-grade class had a pizza party in his restaurant, half the kids had become sick. Agnes blamed his food. Though the culprit turned out to be the cream cheese frosting on someone's mother's cupcakes, thus ending all homemade treats, no classes were ever again welcome at Sabatini's. And if Marina's theory about his being a member of the mob was true . . . well, anything was possible.

Reluctantly I wrote down Erica's name. Our PTA president had a violent temper. Though she almost always kept it in check, I'd once watched her browbeat a man twice her size into complete submission. He'd been beating a dog, and I was on Erica's side from beginning to end, but the red-hot intensity of her rage had made me back up a step or three.

Of course, hate wasn't the only thing that inspired rage. Love could do it, too. I thought for a while, then wrote one last name.

Harry, the Tarver janitor/security guard.

"Lois, could you give me a hand?" I strained to push an unused display unit from my office to the front of the store. Somewhere in the middle of making the suspect list, I'd had the bright idea to rearrange the movable shelving up front. If it was good for grocery store sales to move products around every so often, why wouldn't it be good for a bookstore?

Between oomphs, I said as much to Lois.

"It'll never work." Lois shook her head, putting the amethyst crystals that dangled from her ears to flight. Today's outfit consisted of a tie-dyed headband, an embroidered smock top, and a denim skirt over scuffed cowboy boots. "People like stores to stay the same. It annoys them when they can't find things."

With a solid hip check, I shoved the display unit farther north. "Maybe." The unit went forward another foot. I heard a thud from low down and leaned around to see what I'd done. The last shove had pushed an oversized book to the floor.

"And look at what you're doing!" Lois walked around the end of the shelving and picked up the book. "Just look." She held it out, and I saw that the lower corner wasn't a nice sharp point any longer. "That has to go in the clearance bin."

Knowing I'd been careless sent me over the top. "Thanks for your assistance, Lois," I said tightly. "Next time I want advice on how to run my business, I'll be sure to ask you."

"There's no need to be snippy," Lois said. "I'm only trying to help."

The front bells jangled, and we both put on smiles to greet the first customer of the day.

"Good morning, ladies." Evan smiled. "I was walking past and saw you were doing some furniture rearranging. Need some help?"

Lois turned and walked away. I said loudly, "Why, yes, thank you."

Evan looked at Lois's retreating back, then at me. "Was it something I said?"

I wiped my forehead with the back of my wrist. Sweaty before eleven a.m. Yee-hah. "No," I said. "Just a little miscommunication." Or something.

"Happens." Evan looked at the unit. "Where does this want to go?"

He pushed it up front, centering it between the front window and a paper skeleton hanging from the ceiling. I came behind with a smaller set of shelves, and we positioned and repositioned until I was happy. We'd never had middle-grade books up front. Maybe the prominent positioning would help sales. Anyway, it didn't hurt to try.

"Thanks for helping," I told Evan. A muted sniff came from the back of the store.

"There's a small fee," he said. "How about dinner?"

"Dinner?" The store suddenly seemed tiny, its walls closing in on me, pressing tight. Breathing, normally something I did without thinking, became a conscious effort. "Um . . ." A couple of lunches with this outstandingly gorgeous man I could pass off as business, but dinner? That was a solid move into the personal relationship category.

"How about tonight?"

"Sorry. My kids and I already have plans."

"Oh." His mouth turned down. "I understand. Some other time, then?"

"Sure." Maybe in another year, or when Oliver went off to college, whichever came first.

"There is one other thing," he said. "I need a favor."

■ ■ ■ ■

"But I've been in the hardware only twice in ten years." My legs, half as long as Evan's, were whiffing along at time and a half to keep up. I was happy the store was only a block away. Any farther and I'd have had to beg for mercy.

"Perfect."

When we'd huffed past the barbershop, the shoe store, and the art gallery, I glanced up at him. "Are you . . . ? Uh-oh."

"What's the matter?"

"Prepare yourself," I said.

"For what?"

But it was too late to warn him properly. Don Hatcher, dry cleaner and alleged participant in the affairs of Marina's next-door neighbor, was fast approaching. I sneaked a look at his hair. Maybe Wisconsins was right. His hair did look different.

"Hello, Beth." Don stopped in the middle of the sidewalk.

I slowed and stopped a little too far away for comfortable conversation. "Hello, Don. How are you?"

"Got a new one. Ready?"

No.

"Knock knock," Don said.

"Um, who's there?" I asked.

"Sabina."

Oh, dear. "Sabina who?"

"Sabina long time since I've seen you." He threw his head back and laughed. "Get it? Sabina? It's been a?"

I smiled. Sort of. "Haven't heard that before."

"Got it off the Internet." He winked. "Don't tell, okay? You know, I haven't seen you much lately. You're not taking your cleaning to Madison, are you?" He stepped close as a cloudy frown took up too much of his face.

With Richard and his suits out of the house, my dry-cleaning bill had dropped to almost nothing. "And miss your jokes?" I edged over to Evan's side. "How could I? And I sent those drapes from Agnes's house to you. Don't those count?" Well, Marina had sent them, actually, but I was part of the cleaning team.

"Working on them," he said. "There's a spot that's resisting me — can you believe it?" He winked. "Knock knock."

"Who's there," I said weakly.

"Ally."

"Ally who?"

"Ally gator. See you!" Laughing, he nodded at the two of us and sauntered off to find another victim.

Evan watched him go. "Is it always knock-knock jokes?"

"This year." We started walking again. "Last year it was lightbulb jokes."

"As in how many whatevers does it take to screw in a lightbulb?"

"Yup." I wondered what kind of joke Don would be telling next year. Lois guessed limericks, but even cannibal jokes would be better than that.

We'd come to the front door of the hardware. Evan pulled open the wooden door with its large glass panel and bowed. "Milady."

If I'd been Dorrie with no Jim, I would have tittered and batted my eyelashes. If I'd been Marina, I would have curtsied and said, "Thank you, milord," and swished billowing skirts through the doorway. But since I was just me, I flushed a fast bright red, stammered out, "Um, thanks," and stumbled over the threshold.

Gone were the scary-looking power tools. In their place was a friendly display of doorknobs and door knockers. And where plumbing parts had once awed me to speechlessness, a small lighted Christmas village was spread out across a large table coated with artificial snow. Tiny skaters raced on a mirror pond. A miniature horse and sleigh traveled through a downtown out of Currier and Ives.

"I know it's not even Halloween," Evan said, "but —"

"It's wonderful." I was entranced by a two-inch-tall chimney sweep. "No one else in town sells these. Look!" I pointed at a miniature cat being chased by a dog. "They even left footprints in the snow."

"Toothpick." He stood next to me, hands in his pockets. "Took me forever to get it right."

"You did this?" I looked at the complicated display, at him, then back to the display. "All by yourself?"

"I detect surprise." He grinned. "I think my feelings are hurt."

"Well." I fumbled to say something that didn't sound patronizing. "Of course I'm surprised. I'm surprised you had time." Good answer, Beth. He'd buy that.

Evan looked at me. "Did you know your earlobes turn red when you lie?"

I covered my ears. "They do not." But they did. Always had.

"First time I noticed it was the second week of kindergarten. It was your turn for show-and-tell, you and Dave Kravis. But he forgot and started crying, and you told him

224

you'd forgotten, too."

"I don't remember."

"You'd brought a bag to school that morning and hung it on your hook."

Good heavens, the man remembered more about me than I did.

"You didn't normally carry a bag," Evan was saying. "So I looked inside and saw a ring of skeleton keys. No five-year-old carries skeleton keys. You'd brought them for show-and-tell, but you didn't want to make Dave feel bad, so you lied, and your ears turned red."

I stuck to the faulty-memory story. "Don't remember." The whole red-ear thing had been an embarrassment my entire life. Ninety-nine point nine percent of the time I simply told the truth — lying was almost always wrong, and keeping track of lies was hard work — but every so often I wished for the ability to, if not lie, at least dissemble.

"So," Evan said, "I hear you're the new secretary for the local PTA. How did you get talked into that job?"

"It was . . ." Spinelessness. Irresolution. Weak-willed timidity. "It's something I wanted to try."

"Why?"

I looked at him. Finally, he was shedding

his mask and turning into the jerk he was destined to be. "What do you mean, why?"

"This probaby isn't the right time for this conversation."

"When better? Go on, you can tell me the truth."

He half turned away from me, his gaze falling on a girl and her father hauling a fresh-cut Christmas tree through the snow. "The truth is, I'm interested in everything you do."

"Umm. . . ." This wasn't the kind of truth I wanted. Why couldn't he have said something about having an insatiable interest in PTA committees? Or that he was a feng shui master and had recommendations for the school addition?

His arm brushed up against mine. Had I stepped closer to him, or had he moved closer to me? His hands touched my hair. "Beth," he whispered, his eyes going a deeper blue with each breath. "Kind, sweet Beth."

The front door opened, and I sprang back.

"The display looks great," I said loudly. "Really great. I'll see if my mother still collects these. Last Christmas she had them on so many tables, she ended up eating at the kitchen counter until January." I smiled at the stooped man walking through the door. "Hello, Mr. Brinkley. Evan was just showing me his line of collectibles. They're nice, aren't they?" I was in hapless babble mode. Escape was the only solution. "Well, I have to be going now. Bye!"

My escape was slowed by Mr. Brinkley's quavery chuckle. "My eyesight isn't what it used to be, but it sure looked like he was showing you something else."

I fled.

I did my best to smooth things over with Lois. I hadn't done a very good job, though, because at two o'clock she appeared in front of me, arms folded.

"What are you doing?" she asked.

I sat up straight enough to make my grandmother proud, but my earlobes were already feeling hot in preparation of the lie I was going to tell. "Thinking about how many copies of *The Polar Express* to order for Christmas." Which was a dumb thing to say because the only thing on the legal pad I was clutching to my chest was a list of names.

"Mmm-hmm. Looks to me like you were doing nothing but staring at that list. What's it a list of, anyway?"

"Oh . . . nothing."

"Really," she said flatly. "I thought when

227

we moved the displays around —"

What "we" was she talking about, exactly? As far as I could recall, all Lois had done was head up the Overly Critical section of the cheerleading squad.

"That maybe you wanted to track customer movement patterns," Lois continued. "Looks more like you're daydreaming about that Evan."

A Marcia giggle came from the back of the room. She'd come in at noon, stared at the changes, and said nothing. Marcia wasn't into confrontation; she was more the type to offer her opinion in whispery teapot confidences.

"Don't be ridiculous," I said. "The only daydreams I have are about banana splits with hot fudge topping."

Marcia giggled again. Both Lois and I looked at her. Whose side was she on, anyway?

By the end of the day, Lois had thawed to polite conversation. I'd caved by three thirty and gone out for chocolate and tossed in the promise of a new tea variety for the next morning. As the superintendent of schools had said, I was the conciliatory sort. Lois looked up from the cash register drawer she was closing out. "Big plans for the evening?"

"Plans, yes. Big? No."

Lois raised one eyebrow but turned her attention back to the drawer. "Five, ten, fifteen, twenty. Have fun with your little plans."

Between the nonconsultation with her on the rearrangements and the fact that I hadn't shown her the contents of my list, she was still a little annoyed. But how could I tell her the truth about the list? If I told her that Marina, who was the name behind the anonymous WisconSINs blogger, had received a death threat and I was making a list of suspects, the news would be all over Rynwood within hours and I wouldn't be any help to Marina at all.

"Fun?" I zipped up my coat. "This will be almost as much fun as going to the dentist. And not nearly as much fun as getting a mammogram."

CHAPTER 12

"All in all, Beth, she's done well this marking period, with respect to grades." Jenna's teacher, Paul Richey, closed the manila folder. "Did she and Bailey Scharff know each other before this year? Those two have formed a tight friendship."

"Not very well."

"Mmm." Paul drummed his fingers on the folder.

The memory of Evan telling me he had two daughters popped into my head. This was followed by the memory of his elbow brushing my arm and the smell of his skin and —

"Beth?"

I blinked. "Sorry. You were saying?"

Paul was frowning. "Are you all right?"

"What? I'm fine. Just a little distracted. Sorry." A good mother would be fully present at her daughter's parent-teacher conference, not daydreaming about a man.

Once again, I wouldn't be a candidate for the Mother of the Year Award. Since Jenna was ten, this would be the tenth year in a row.

"Understandable," Paul said. "Concentration has been hard for everyone since Agnes was killed."

"Yes."

We sat quietly. At the bookstore, Paul had more than once railed against Agnes and her heavy-handed management techniques, her habit of dictating rather than building consensus, and her unwavering belief that her opinions were correct ones. But every Tarver Elementary teacher had the same complaints, and if complaining about the boss made a person a murder suspect, then if I died the police would have to put Lois and Marcia on the list.

Paul sighed. "I can't say I'm sad she's gone. But she didn't deserve to be murdered."

"No."

We sat a few moments longer, thinking our own thoughts. Then Paul stirred and advised me that it might be best for Jenna to have more than one friend.

I thanked him, gathered my purse and coat, and walked out of the room. Onward and upward — or at least onward.

"Beth!"

I flinched at the reverberations echoing off the hallway's hard surfaces. "Oh, Debra. Hi." If Harry the janitor could see the marks her high heels were leaving on the floor, he'd have a coronary.

"Can I talk to you?"

As always, Debra's hair looked perfect. With an iron will, I kept my hands still and didn't check for stray strands. "Sure. But I'm meeting with Oliver's teacher in a few minutes."

"It's about the memorial service," she said. "You were right. None of us knew Agnes. We were a bunch of hypocrites, pretending we cared, pretending she mattered to us."

"Oh," I said faintly. Someone had paid attention? I'd have to be more careful next time I spoke in public. Or here was an even better idea — never again open my mouth in any group of more than four people.

"I sat up most of the night, thinking." Debra chewed on her lower lip, mussing the perfectly applied lipstick. "There are a lot of hypocritical things in my life. Agnes was just the tip of the iceberg. My career, my house, my car, even my hair." She tousled the artful coiffure. "Everything I've ever done was to impress or please someone. I wouldn't know a real emotion if it bit me on the hind end."

I stared at her and couldn't think of a thing to say.

"So I'm going to change."

"You are?"

"Yes. Starting tomorrow." She nodded decisively. "Why wait?"

Good heavens. "Um, big changes are worth a few days of thinking, don't you think?"

Behind us, a door opened. "Good-bye, Mr. Egoscue, Mrs. Egoscue," chirped an unbelievably young voice. "Thanks for coming! Oh, good, Mrs. Kennedy. Right on time. Come on in. I'm ready for you."

I didn't move. "Debra, let's go to the Green Tractor. I can meet you there in twenty minutes. We'll get Ruthie to make us ice-cream sundaes and brew up a pot of decaf."

"I appreciate the offer," Debra said, "but I have errands to run. I just wanted to thank you." She hurried off.

"Mrs. Kennedy?" Lauren Atchinson stood in the classroom door.

What was the right thing to do? Since it was my speechifying that had affected Debra, wasn't it my responsibility to go after her and offer my help, as little as that might be? On the other hand, I needed to talk to Ms. Atchinson about my son.

"Mrs. Kennedy?"

On the other hand, because of me, Debra might be hurtling onto a path of self-destruction. How could I turn away from her now?

"Mrs. Kennedy, if you need to reschedule, I might have time the week after next."

But it was no contest. Motherhood trumped everything, every time.

In Oliver's classroom construction paper pumpkins spattered the concrete block walls, each one decorated with leering grins and a child's scrawled name. I looked for Oliver's and finally found it, a lopsided one-toothed visage.

"First off," Lauren said, "Oliver is a very nice little boy."

"Thank you."

"For an older parent, you're doing a great job of socializing him with peers."

"A what?" Had she really said what I thought she'd said?

She opened a manila folder. "You can't have a lot in common with people my age, and I just wanted to say I think you're doing a great job."

Responses rushed into my head. They all jammed up together, making an outraged bottleneck, and not a single word made its way out of my open mouth.

"So." Lauren handed me a sheet of paper. "Here's a chart of Oliver's progress."

Young, I thought. She's not even twenty-five. She knows not what she does.

I studied the graph. On the left were the titles of Language Arts, Mathematics, Science, Social Studies, Physical Education, and Other. All the titles had a series of horizontal lines extending across the sheet, and on the right was a scale of one to ten for each. Across the sheet's bottom was a label for each week in the six-week marking period.

"As I'm sure you can see," Lauren said, "there's been a falling off."

She had a gift for understatement. At the beginning of the year, Oliver was scoring between seven and nine for each subject. The lines jiggled a bit until the last two weeks. After that, each line looked like the Dow Jones in 2009. *Crash!*

"Have there been problems at home?" Lauren frowned, tilting her head to one side. "Is there anything I can do? I'd honestly like to help."

She looked earnest and caring, but what was I going to say? That he and his sister wanted a puppy and I didn't? That he was suddenly afraid of eating spaghetti? That the idea of a man in my life frightened him? That he'd gone back to wetting his bed?

"Mrs. Mephisto's death has been hard on him," I said. "He's known only one other person who died. That she was murdered makes it even more difficult."

"It's so hard to think someone in Rynwood was murdered." She fidgeted with her necklace. "The police came around and talked to all the teachers, did you know? They said they were just gathering information, but funny thing is they were asking us all what we were doing that night."

I smiled. "Where's an alibi when you need one?" I suddenly remembered Lauren's vehement recommendation of appointing Gary Kemmerer as principal. Maybe I should add the two of them to the list. Who knew what ten years of working under Agnes could do to a man? And Lauren might have the kind of malleable personality that could be manipulated to do the direst of deeds.

"Oh, I had an alibi," she said. "Tuesdays are my ballet nights. I was in Madison helping to block out a scene from *The Nutcracker.* The choreographer and the director and I were there past midnight."

Mentally, I added Lauren and Gary to the

list, then crossed off Lauren's name. I wasn't obsessive about my lists; I was just accurate.

"The police will catch the killer," I said. "I'm sure that will help Oliver."

Lauren nodded. "So you can directly correlate his downturn with the death of Mrs. Mephisto?"

"Yes."

"Is he showing other signs of grief or stress?"

Though I knew she was only trying to help, my irritation level was rising. Clearly, obfuscation was in order. "He has a history of enuresis," I said. "I've been following the recommendations of his pediatrician and expect to eliminate the problem in a short time frame."

"I didn't realize Oliver had bed-wetting issues."

So much for that idea. "It's not uncommon," I said calmly.

"No." Her gaze lost its intensity and wandered off. "Kids can't help themselves. They don't do it on purpose."

"Of course not."

"There are all sorts of reasons for enuresis." Her cheeks were developing round red spots. "A child could simply have a genetic predisposition. A urinary tract infection.

Sleep apnea. Diabetes, even."

"Yes, I know."

"And some people are born with small bladders. It's not a character flaw. It's just the way you were made."

I'd struck a nerve, and I didn't quite know how to unstrike it. "Exactly," I said.

After a pause, the conference went on. At long last she closed the folder. "Mrs. Kennedy, would you consider making an appointment for Oliver with the school psychologist? I'm sure we both agree it's in his best interest to work through his problems."

I bit my cheeks. "I'm sure my son will be fine."

"You could be right," she said doubtfully, leaving hanging the insinuation that though I *could* be right, I was probably wrong. "But I think it's better to act sooner rather than later."

"Good advice." I gathered up my purse and the materials she'd handed over. On my way out, I counted the months until the end of school and came up with a number much bigger than the optimal zero — eight and a half more months of Lauren Atchinson.

This could be a very long year.

I picked up the kids at Marina's house. "So

how did it go?" she asked. Her gaze was bright and shifty, darting toward me, toward the laptop computer on the kitchen table, toward the family room where her son Zach was playing with Oliver and Jenna. She was making me dizzy.

"Jenna's teacher said she's doing fine, but Lauren Atchinson wants Oliver to start therapy."

"For what, having to be in her classroom all year? Piffle." She waved off the idea with bright orange fingernails. "And that wasn't what I was asking about." The glancing eyes made another circuit. "Did you find out anything? You know, about you-know-what?" She made a big sideways nod toward the laptop.

"You mean finding out the you-know-what of the you-know-who who did you-know-what you-know-when?"

"Stop that." She shook her finger at me. "You know what I mean."

And, of course, I did. "Not yet."

"Oh." She deflated half a size.

"You didn't really expect me to figure it out this fast, did you?"

She pointed at her head. "Here? No. Down here is another story." She put her hands on her heart. Though she didn't look as rough as she had last night, there were telltale signs of Marina-stress. Hair loose on her shoulders, boxes from frozen dinners on the counter, no coffee brewing. "This morning," she said, "the Dear Husband actually asked if anything was wrong. I said the sad plight of the African swallows was keeping me awake at night."

I laughed. "Could you possibly have come up with a worse lie?"

"Well, I had to tell him something." The fun left her face, and worry appeared in its place. "I'm sure the you-know-what threat isn't real." She twisted a strand of hair around her fingers. "This will all turn out okay, won't it?"

"It'll be fine," I said. "Promise."

But I should have known better. Making a promise like that is just asking for trouble.

I drove us home through a rain that couldn't make up its mind what it wanted to be. For two blocks the drops came down hard enough for me to turn the windshield wipers on high. In another block the rubber scraped dry on the glass. Half a block later, it was a steady drizzle.

In the backseat, Jenna wiped her fogged-up window with her hand. "What did Mr. Richey say about me?"

I smiled into the rearview mirror. "That

you're the smartest, nicest, most talented little girl he's ever taught."

"No, really. What did he say?"

This was the first time Jenna had paid any attention to a parent-teacher conference. "What do you think he said?"

Her palm scrubbed harder at the window. Soon it was clear from top to bottom, and from left to right. "It was only the one time."

Uh-oh. "Are you sure?" It didn't take a great leap of reasoning to figure this was something to do with Bailey Scharff. Pete had given me a general warning; the rest was up to me. For the first time in months I felt a wave of longing for Richard. I couldn't do this by myself. I wasn't smart enough to raise two children all alone. I was too old, too out of touch, too —

Jenna whipped around and thumped her back against the back of the seat. She folded her arms. "Yes, I'm sure," she said sullenly.

I glanced over at Oliver. He was tipping his head back and forth with the windshield wipers, counting the beats. "Fifty-five, fifty-six . . ."

"Why did you do it even once?"

"Don't know."

I flicked on the turn signal and turned left. Half a dozen blocks and we'd be home. The kids would jump out, rush inside, and the opportunity for car-inspired confidences would be gone. Richard had always wanted the kids to take the school bus in the morning, saying they needed to learn to interact with children of all ages. Maybe he was right, but I'd discovered more about my children's lives on these rides than in any other situation. "Who started it?" I asked, intentionally not mentioning Bailey's name.

"Not sure."

I slowed down a little more. This felt like a ten-block conversation. "Are you going to do it again?"

"No," she muttered.

All I could see was the top of her head. The part in her hair was straight as a ruler, the two ponytails drooping down. For no known reason, tears smarted in my eyes. I loved her so much. . . . I winked the wetness away. "Are you sorry you did it?"

She didn't move. She didn't say anything.

"Jenna? Are you sorry?"

"Do you think he hates me?" Jenna whispered.

This conversation was like the quote about writing a novel; it was like driving from coast to coast in a dark fog, seeing only a hundred feet of pavement in front of the headlights. "Do you think he does?" If we were talking about Paul Richey, the answer was no. If we were talking about a boy in her school, the answer might be different.

"I would if I were him," she said.

To my right, Oliver was still busy counting. "Ninety-one, ninety-two . . ."

Three blocks to go. Time for Mom to come up with some miraculous way of making everything better. Unfortunately, my bag of magic was flat empty. Well, except for the one surefire trick. "Have you told him you're sorry?"

Half a block later, the answer came like a soft breeze. "No."

"Do you think apologizing would help?"

"Maybe."

"If you were him and he was you" — I grimaced at the atrocious grammar, but communication was the important thing — "would you want him to apologize?"

We drove the last block; then I clicked on the turn signal for the approach up our driveway. From the backseat came a very, very quiet "Yeah."

"Maybe you should do it tomorrow." I pulled the garage door opener off the visor and handed it to Oliver. He pushed the button with his thumb, and the door rolled up. "Get it done, and then you don't have to think about it anymore," I said.

We rolled onto the garage's dry concrete,

and I turned off the windshield wipers. "A hundred and thirty-seven," Oliver said firmly. "I counted all the way from Mrs. Neff's house."

"Good job, Ollster," I said. "You're the King of Counting."

Jenna unbuckled her seat belt, grabbed her backpack, and rushed inside. I helped Oliver with his buckle and held the booster seat while he jumped out. "What did Jenna do?" he asked. "Is she in trouble?"

So much for his not paying attention. "If Jenna wants to tell you, she will." That meant he'd never know; Jenna wasn't prone to sharing confidences with her little brother. I had high hopes that someday they'd be friends, but that day was probably decades distant.

"Oh."

His voice sounded even smaller than usual. As we shut the car doors and headed into the warmth of the house, I studied him with the eagle eyes of a concerned mother. Oliver had a naturally cheerful personality, but now all I could see were sagging shoulders and dragging feet, and the voice in my head was Lauren Atchinson's. *Is he showing other signs of grief or stress? Would you consider making an appointment with the school psychologist?*

I hadn't seen eye to eye with the school psychologist since she'd suggested Jenna's basic nonreaction to the divorce could be linked to a deep fear of men's genitals. But I knew a way to bring Oliver back to life. And with any luck it would bring Jenna and Oliver closer together, too.

Not so very long ago I would have called Richard before making a decision like this. He was their father, after all, and had a right to be involved in anything that affected their lives. But he was out of town, and Oliver needed this right away. Besides, I knew what Richard would say.

I dropped my purse in the study and headed to the kitchen. Jenna had already run upstairs, but Oliver had put his backpack on the kitchen table and, kneeling on the seat of a chair, was sorting through the contents.

"Mommy?" He turned, holding out a scribbly drawing. "Robert says this looks like a whale, but I want it to be a dolphin."

Jenna plopped into the chair next to Oliver. "What's that? Looks like a shark."

"It's a dolphin!"

Time to head off the impending argument. "Who wants some popcorn before dinner?"

Five minutes later the popping slowed to

a stop. I poured the popcorn into a bowl, then drizzled melted butter and salt over the top. "Ready?" We ate the first ritual piece solemnly, then dug in for great greasy handfuls. "Normally," I said, "we have popcorn on Sunday, right?"

"Um-hmm." Grunts of agreement came through stuffed mouths.

"And sometimes we have it when someone is sick. Why else do we have popcorn during the week? No talking with your mouth full, please."

Oliver reached for another handful. "We had popcorn when Mr. Stolz died."

Oh, geez. I'd forgotten about that. The kids had been all excited about its being their turn to run the garden train and had run down the street, only to find an empty house and drawn shades. I'd given them hugs, talked about heaven, then done my best to distract them with food.

Jenna looked at me, her hand midway to the bowl. "Are we having popcorn because Mrs. Mephisto died?"

"Partly."

"Whaf's fe ofer pah?" Oliver asked.

"No talking with your mouth full."

He swallowed hugely. "What's the other part?"

I wiped my buttery fingers on a napkin.

"Remember the time we had popcorn when I told you about our trip to Florida?"

The spring break trip had been a gift from Richard. "Take the tickets," he'd said gruffly, and I'd cried myself to sleep that night, certain the divorce had been a horrible mistake. The next day he'd e-mailed the itinerary he'd worked up for the trip — new activities every thirty minutes, kids! — and I hadn't cried over him since.

"Are we going to Disney World again?" Jenna's eyes went round.

"No."

She heaved a tremendous sigh, then shoved a massive handful of popcorn into her mouth. Her cheeks pouched out like a chipmunk's. I closed my eyes briefly and decided to let this skirmish go. "You have to pick your battles," my sister Darlene once told me. She had four children, and all four had evolved into functional young adults, so she must have done a few things right.

"We're not going to Disney World," I said, "but we are getting something."

"Are we getting . . ." Oliver didn't finish the sentence. His gaze was locked on me. "Are we. . . ." Hope was in his eyes, his face, his hands, his entire body.

"Wha— ?" Jenna said, spitting out a wet and half-chewed kernel. "Are we what?"

I looked at Oliver. He knew.

His grin started small, then grew and went from ear to ear and practically all the way around his head. He jumped out of his chair and hurtled around the table in leaps and bounds. "We're getting a dog, Jen! We're getting a *dog!*"

The store was quiet. The lone customer was having a grand time chuckling over picture books by Kevin Henkes. Lois was at the front computer, working on a flyer for the Halloween party and humming an ABBA tune.

I found Paoze in the back corner, dusting the wooden puzzles with the raggedy feather duster that had been in the store as long as the store had existed. One of these days I'd have to get a new one.

"Paoze, I need to talk to you."

He sprang to attention. "Yes, Mrs. Kennedy."

I led the way to my office. "Don't worry. You're not in trouble." I closed the door behind us. "And this is more of a personal matter, anyway."

"Yes, Mrs. Kennedy."

Time and time again, I'd asked him to call me Beth. "I cannot, Mrs. Kennedy," he always said. "It would be disrespectful."

Maybe to him it was disrespectful, but it made me feel as if my mother-in-law were standing behind me.

I sat in my desk chair and Paoze perched on the edge of the chair facing me. "Remember the night I dropped you off at your house?" I asked. "Well, a couple of blocks away I thought I saw a . . . a friend of mine. This friend went into a two-story house, a white house with black shutters and what looked like a metal door." It also had bars on the windows, but so did most houses in that neighborhood.

Paoze didn't say anything.

"Do you know the house?" I asked.

He looked at his knees, at his hands, at his knees. "Yes."

The drawn-out hesitation kicked my anxiety into alert mode. He knew something about the house. Something bad. It was a drug house. It was a brothel. It was —

Paoze looked up and met my gaze. "This friend. Do you know her well?"

I frowned. "Her? It's not a she at all. It's a he."

The boy's brown eyes opened wide. "A man? At that house?" His fingers began tap-tap-tapping his kneecaps. "No man should be going to that house. No man should be let in the door. It is not safe."

"Not safe? What are you talking about? Randy went up to the door and knocked. The door opened, and he went inside. What's unsafe about that?"

"Randy? Big Mr. Jarvis?" Paoze spread his arms wide.

"Well, yes."

The kid smiled, and the tension left his body. "Then this is right. Mr. Jarvis belongs there."

This conversation might have made sense to Paoze, but I was missing something — like the whole thing. "Belongs where?"

"I . . ." He went back to studying his knees. "I should not tell."

Shouldn't or couldn't? Or wouldn't? Though his grasp of the English language was firm in a general way, sometimes mistakes slipped into his speech. "Why not?" I asked. "Mr. Jarvis isn't doing something wrong, is he?"

"Oh, no." Paoze shook his head vigorously. "Mr. Jarvis is a very good man. I wish to be like him when I grow older."

Randy as a role model? The mind boggled.

"Kayla says —" He came to an abrupt halt.

"Sara's roommate?"

"Yes," he said quietly. "And I should not say more."

Curiouser and curiouser. What could involve an attractive college junior and a sixtysomething man from Rynwood who ran a gas station and ate large bags of nacho chips for breakfast? I knew Sara, Kayla, and Paoze had a comfortable friendship, but how did Randy figure into the mix? "I don't want you to break a confidence," I said. "I just . . ." Just what? What exactly was I trying to do here?

"Kayla only goes during the week." Paoze's hands were gripping each other. "I am glad she does not volunteer on weekends. That is when it can get very bad."

What could Kayla be doing as a volunteer at a place with a metal door and bars on the windows? "Mr. Jarvis is also a volunteer."

"Yes."

I thought about this. Randy, a volunteer. Kayla, a volunteer. Kayla's major was social work. Randy was the treasurer for the Tarver PTA, a child advocacy organization. There were dots here to connect, but the dots were a little too far apart for me to make the leaps.

"Kayla said Mr. Jarvis is very brave," Paoze said. "I do not worry about her when Mr. Jarvis is there."

Dot to dot to dot. I'd figured it out. "That

house is a women's shelter," I said. "Where women and children can go if they feel they're in danger."

Paoze's brown face went very still. "I should not have said. It is much of a secret."

"Don't worry." I smiled at him. "The secret is safe with me."

"You will not tell?"

"I will not tell, Paoze. And neither did you," I said softly. "I reached my own conclusions, that's all."

After he left, I took the list out of my desk drawer and picked up a pen. I drew a line through the name of Randy Jarvis.

Two down, nine to go.

"Thank you for meeting with me." Gary Kemmerer, Tarver's acting principal, folded his hands on top of the desk. Erica, Randy, Julie, and I were representing the PTA, and all four of us were uncomfortable. Five, I amended, as I heard Gary's toes tapping under the desk.

"As acting principal," Gary said, "I might not remain in this office for long. The school board is starting a search, and they're anxious to appoint a new principal as soon as possible."

"You apply for the job?" Randy asked.

Erica and I blinked at his tactlessness. Julie moved her hands over her oversized belly and looked radiant.

"Yes, in fact, I did." Gary frowned at Randy. "But that's not the purpose of this meeting. I invited you here to establish common ground with the PTA. The past ten years have seen a fair share of adversarial instances, and I want to say I'll do my best to . . ."

He was lapsing into corporate-speak. I put a noncommittal expression on my face and drifted away. Jenna and her apology for whatever. Oliver and enuresis. Paoze. Marina. WisconSINs. Halloween. The threatening e-mails.

"Beth? You don't approve of this idea?" Gary asked.

I jerked back from the memory of a Marina too frightened to talk. "Um . . ."

"The PTA," Erica said, "is more than pleased to work hand in hand with Tarver's leadership —"

"What if the police don't find the killer?" I blurted out. "I'm worried about these kids if the murderer goes free."

Erica, Randy, Julie, and Gary all stared at me.

"I know this isn't what we came here to discuss," I said, "but it's a huge concern of mine." For lots of reasons. "I hear the police have been talking to the teachers. Have they been talking to the staff and administration, too?"

"Good point," Erica said. "Staff dealt with Agnes from eight thirty in the morning to four in the afternoon. I'm sure most of them had occasional run-ins with her. How about you, Gary?"

"What about me?" His chin went up.

"Do you have an alibi?" Erica smiled, but the steel wasn't far below the surface.

"As a matter of fact, yes. Now about this —"

"What is it?" Julie asked.

"What is what?"

"Your alibi." She folded her hands over her tummy. "I think the parents of Tarver children deserve to know that the acting principal has a solid alibi."

"The police were satisfied."

"But I'm not."

They stared at each other, grim-faced, until Erica spoke up. "She has a point, Gary. If you tell us, we can reassure everyone that Tarver is in good hands."

"The police —"

Erica shook her head. "What the police think doesn't matter. It's what the Tarver parents think that counts. And," she added, "what the school board thinks. How satisfied is Mack Vogel that you had nothing to do with Agnes's murder?"

"I . . ." His chin sank down. "It's personal."

Randy chuckled. "You're not taking figure skating lessons, are you? Those toe picks mess up the ice something fierce."

Gary mumbled something.

The four of us leaned forward. "What did you say?" I asked.

He sighed and spoke louder. "I take lessons on Tuesday nights. I've driven to Chicago on Tuesday nights for five years. But it's not figure skating. Or hockey or curling, for that matter."

"Then what?" Erica asked impatiently.

"I take opera lessons."

"You . . . what?"

"Don't spread it around," he pleaded. "I don't want people to ask me to sing in church or at weddings. Or here at school. Can you just see the kids' reaction to *Tosca*'s 'Recondita armonia'? I mean, please." He spread his hands wide, palms up, in entreaty. "Opera is the only music I sing. It's the only music that really matters, you know."

I didn't dare look at Erica. I knew she hated opera with a passion.

"Thank you for sharing, Gary," she said. "If the news of your Tuesday lessons

255

spreads, it won't be because of anyone in this room."

We went on with the rest of our meeting. Somewhere between discussion of how the PTA's mission statement meshed with Tarver's core values, I pulled out the list and a pencil.

Three down, eight to go.

"You're getting a what?" Richard asked.

"A dog." My chin pressed the phone harder into my shoulder as I whacked a few keys on the store's computer keyboard.

"They're too young," he said. "They're not old enough to take care of a dog. You'll end up doing all the work yourself."

It was the exact Richard response I'd predicted. I didn't say anything, just kept looking at the photos on the local animal shelter Web site. A parrot? Who would leave a parrot at an animal shelter?

"You don't even like dogs."

"I love dogs."

"When they're someone else's," he said.

Why did I keep forgetting that Richard knew everything about me? "The kids could use a little responsibility. It'll be good for them. Besides" — I enlarged a picture of a tabby cat — "Oliver says if Agnes Mephisto had a dog, she'd still be alive."

Richard was quiet for a moment. "I can't have it on my weekends," he finally said. "My condo doesn't allow dogs."

Rats. "Fine," I said.

"What breeds are you considering?" He launched into a speech on the characteristics of the dogs best suited for young children.

I let him talk while I poked around the animal shelter Web site a little more. When he said he'd e-mail me a list of respected Lagotto Romagnolo breeders, I said, "Thank you, Richard. The store's getting busy now, so I have to go. Bye."

Lois looked at me, then looked at the empty store. "Busy must mean something different from what I thought it meant."

"Words evolve."

"Mmm." She flicked her feather duster over the shelves of board books. "Did you see the WisconSINs blog this morning?"

Uh-oh. "What does it say?"

Lois cast me a glance laden with overtones. Surprise, suspicion, pleasure, and anticipation were all wrapped up together in her small smile and lifted eyebrows.

"Thought you didn't hold with gossip," she said.

"Everyone is talking about that blog." I tossed off what I hoped was an eloquent shrug.

The small smile turned large. "And you don't want to be the last one to know?"

"Well, no one does."

She cackled with delight. "Where's the calendar? It's a red-letter day." Next to the cash register was a canister of pens, and she reached for a red one. "I can't wait to tell Marcia." She turned to the calendar on the wall behind the counter and wrote. "There!" She spun back around and clunked the pen back into the canister.

The calendar I'd mounted on the wall was filled with notations for party dates, author signings, and staff scheduling. Today's square, however, had the added touch of a small stick drawing. The triangle skirt and hair ending at the shoulders denoted it as female. The outstretched fingers and O-shaped mouth showed the figure's surprise. Above her head was a lightbulb, and inside the bulb was the word "people."

I stared at the drawing. People.

"It's supposed to be funny," Lois said uncertainly. "You know, silly? Beth finally admits that knowing things about people is important. Hah hah?"

People. I wanted to smack my palm against my forehead. "Thanks, Lois. You've been a big help."

"I have? I mean, good."

A customer came in and asked for middle-grade books for boys not very interested in reading. Lois took her in hand. I went to my desk and fired up the WisconSINs blog. I glanced at the bottom of today's entry. Barely ten o'clock in the morning and more than a dozen people had already left comments. Oh, dear.

"Fresh Help for Finding Murderer," it started. "This blogger is giving you the good news that a new recruit will breathe life into the campaign to ferret out Agnes Mephisto's killer.

"No longer will the citizens of Rynwood need to wait for the slow wheels of justice to grind out the answer we so desperately crave. Why should we be afraid to walk the streets at night? Why should we quake under our blankets, shivering with the numbing thought that We Could Be Next?

"My friends, it's time to fight back, and this blogger has enlisted a new vigilante to fight for the cause. Come back tomorrow, dear Readers, for the next installment in the efforts to Take Back the Rynwood Night."

I closed my eyes. "Oh, Marina," I whispered. "What have you done?"

CHAPTER 13

I crossed my arms. "Vigilante?"

Marina chuckled. "Isn't that a great word? The exact definition is 'a self-appointed —.'"

"I know what 'vigilante' means."

"Bookish Beth." She rolled a pencil toward me. It bounced across her kitchen table and came to rest against my yellow pad of paper. "Can't you just see it?" she asked. "You and me and all the other people who want to see justice done, banding together for the maintenance of order. Maybe we should get uniforms. A dark green would be just the ticket."

People, whispered a voice in my brain. What people do is important; what people think is important; what people feel is important. Our job was figuring out which particular people were significant to Agnes, and then we could work on motivations. And motivations are the origins of actions.

Find the motivation, find the killer.

"Or a mustache." Marina's cheeks were flushing a pale shade of pink. "Don't you just love those handlebar types?" She twisted the ends of her imaginary mustache.

"No mustaches until we figure out who's threatening you."

"Aren't you the party pooper."

"Richard is dropping off the kids at eight. I don't have all night."

"Sad, but true. Ah, for the days of unencumbered youth." She heaved a bosom-raising sigh.

"Take off your rose-colored glasses. We need to get to work." I thumped my pad of paper. "We need a plan."

"Oh, goodie." She clapped her hands. "I love plans."

"When was the last time you went along with a plan? 1983?"

She pulled her mustache tips out straight. "I'll have you know I'm completely capable of following a plan."

"You can, but will you?"

"Wasting time, my sweet, we're wasting time."

"Fine." I picked up the pencil. "Tonight is brainstorming night. I ran into Gus at the grocery store, and he says the sheriff's department says the investigation is proceeding, but that could mean anything."

"Means they're getting nowhere," Marina said darkly.

"We don't know that."

She looked at the ceiling. "Is she truly this innocent?" she asked the white paint. "I know she doesn't get out much, and she has a history of serious shyness, so she's the worst person on the planet to hunt down a killer —"

"Hey!"

"But she's the best thing I've got."

"Gee, thanks."

She stopped fiddling with the mustache. "You don't have to do this." Her voice was quiet. "Help me, I mean. This kind of stuff isn't your style."

A sense of relief filled me. I was off the hook! I could go home, back to my journal and dirty laundry. No threats, no murders, no pushing myself into a shape that didn't suit me. "Well . . ."

"No, really. This is going to mean tracking down clues and figuring things out about suspects and eliminating possibilities. You'd have to get out and do stuff you don't like to do. I pushed you to be PTA secretary, and that's as much pushing as I should do. You're quiet and retiring, and you don't like all that . . . that *doing*."

The relief was replaced by irritation. "I'm not exactly a hermit. You make it sound as if I live in an ivory tower. Did you forget I was a journalism major? I know all sorts of techniques that would be useful for this."

She gave me one of those you're-being-argumentative-for-no-good-reason looks. "Only on paper. You don't know anything about real investigating."

"And you do?"

"I'm the one being threatened. Dragging you into this is pure selfishness on my part. This kind of stuff isn't for you, Beth. You'd have to make people talk to you. Make people *want* to talk to you."

That people thing again.

"It's so not you." She leaned forward and placed her warm hands on my chill ones. "You'd have to change, and I don't want that. I love you the way you are, dear heart."

There was no good choice. If I helped Marina, I'd be stressed out and uncomfortable and cranky and impatient with my children. If I didn't help, I'd feel guilty the rest of my life that I didn't help my best friend in her hour of need.

The scrunchie in Marina's hair dropped to the floor with a small *plop*. "I should never have asked you to help." She patted my hands. "Forget I ever brought it up.

263

Let's talk about something else. What are you doing for Jenna's and Oliver's Halloween costumes?"

She chattered on about costumes she'd once made for her older children, and I listened with half an ear as my conscience fought with my stick-in-the-mud-ness.

I didn't want to do things that made me uncomfortable. I didn't want to change. But there were dark circles under Marina's eyes, something I'd never seen before. And there were the hat boxes in Agnes's closet.

No, there wasn't a good choice here, but there was only one I could make.

I waited for a pause in Marina's description of a gladiator outfit she'd made for her daughter. "Like it or not," I said, "I'm going to help you."

"You will?" Marina looked at me. "For really real?"

"Yup."

"Hooray!" She leaped up out of her chair and ran around the table. "You're the best friend ever, ever, ever." The hug she gave me squeezed my breath away. "Ever!"

And after all, maybe I'd have to change only a little.

Denise twirled my chair to face the mirror and flung a plastic cutting cape over my top half. "What are we doing today?" she asked.

I glanced briefly at my image in the mirror, then looked away. "How about auburn hair just past my shoulders that has enough body to hold a curl, but not enough curl to be unmanageable?"

"Honey, I'm a hairdresser, not a magician."

She twirled me around again and released the chair's back. The base of my skull snugged into the guillotine-like gap in the sink. I relaxed as Denise ran warm water over my head.

"Normal cut?" she asked. "Two inches off the bottom?"

"I wish you could take two inches off my bottom."

She laughed. "Not with scissors, you don't." The shampoo bottle squeaked as she pumped out a dollop of goo. "I hear you're cozy with Erica Hale these days."

"I'm on the PTA committee, that's all. Erica's okay."

"Don't get on her bad side." Denise rubbed shampoo into my temples. "She can be vicious as a cat with kittens. Uh-oh. Did I scrub too hard? Sorry. I get carried away when I talk about the lawyer my so very ex-husband hired."

I winced away from her overeager shampooing. "Divorce is never easy."

"You got that right." She rinsed my hair, put a towel around my head, and sat me up straight. "Speaking of divorce, do you know about Dorrie and Jim? According to Dorrie, it's really over this time."

"That's what she said the last time."

Denise started combing out my hair. "And probably the time before that. Two inches?"

As she snipped away, I wondered what the difference was between an expensive haircut and a normal one. I'd always figured it was about sixty dollars, but maybe Debra was onto something. Maybe one of these days I'd spring for a fancy salon cut. Like after the kids were married and before I became a grandmother.

But why was I wasting my time with idle thoughts? I had questions to pose, things to do.

"So how's your brother these days?" I asked. "Haven't seen Nick or Carol at any PTA meetings lately."

"Oh, they're fine."

I watched her in the mirror. Such a short answer wasn't typical for Denise. "Really? I kept looking for Nick at the meetings about the school addition, you know, before Agnes was killed." Small lie, but not a big one. My ears couldn't be more than a faint pink.

"They're stuck in Florida," she whispered. Snip snip snip went the scissors.

"Stuck? In Florida?"

"Shhhh." Denise looked around. "Carol's really embarrassed about it. She doesn't want anyone to know, okay? She's afraid of it coming out on . . . on that blog."

My gaze met her mirrored one. "Carol's okay, isn't she?"

"She will be."

"What happened?"

"A week or two ago they went on a Caribbean cruise. For their twenty-fifth wedding anniversary, you know?"

"Sounds nice," I said.

"It was all fine and dandy until Carol came down with some weird tropical disease."

"How weird is it?"

"Weird enough that she won't tell me any details." Denise sounded miffed. "All that sister-in-law of mine will say is that she's not coming back for a while, not until small children won't run away from her, screaming for their mothers."

"Some skin disease?"

"That's my guess."

Ick.

"But," Denise said, "she's also losing some serious weight, so she's not exactly down in the dumps about the whole thing."

I laughed. "How long have they been gone? Do they even know that Agnes Mephisto is dead?"

"They left the Friday before, so they weren't here, but I told them when they called in to say Carol was sick. Nick didn't sound one bit sorry. I know he didn't like her and all, but he could at least have faked a little sympathy!" She went on to list her brother's faults, one of which was apparently the ability to telecommute from Florida while his wife was in the hospital.

My head nodded at appropriate times, but my mind was miles away.

As Bike Trail Nick clearly wasn't the killer, one more name could be struck from the list. I smiled into the mirror. At this rate I'd have the case solved by the end of next week.

Friday night the kids and I went to Marina's house and ate more pizza than was good for us. When I mentioned this, she drew herself up and put her nose in the air. "My pizza," she said with a horrible Italian accent, "iz made of ze freshest ingredients, no?" The three youngsters giggled, egging her on. "Flour from ze new bag. Yeast from ze unopened packet. Tomato sauce from ze can bought only this morning."

I forked off a piece of thick-crusted pep-peroni and sausage. Guy pizza, but every once in a while it hit the spot. "Your Italian accent sounds like it has spent too much time watching old French movies."

"The Swedish chef," Jenna said, and for some reason this sent Oliver and Zach into paroxysms of laughter.

Oliver recovered first. "Know what?" He thrust his pizza-laden fork into the air. "We're getting a dog!"

"You are?" Marina looked at him, then looked at me. "You are?"

"Um, yes."

"When did this come about?" And why? her tone implied.

"Oh, we've been talking about it for a while." On and off. Mainly off.

"Really?" Marina arched her eyebrows. "You never mentioned it."

"Not a dog," Jenna said. "A puppy."

"Future dog." Zach's face lit up. "Cool. I've never had a dog. What kind are you get-ting?"

"Snoopy dog!" Oliver shouted.

"I want a golden retriever," Jenna said.

Zach looked thoughtful. "Nathan O'Conner has a chocolate Lab. He jumps into the water and catches tennis balls."

"Don't want a Lab dog," Oliver said. The three children started talking at once, each arguing at the top of his or her lungs for the breed of his or her choice.

I put my fingers in my mouth and whistled loud enough to make us all wince. The kids fell silent. Whistling was my best trick, but it didn't do to use it too often.

Marina fixed her gaze on her son. "You'll take the plates." She pointed at Jenna. "You'll be in charge of the silverware."

Oliver bounced in his chair. "What do I do?"

"Hmm." Marina tapped her nose. "Reroof the garage?"

He giggled and, once again, my heart melted into a puddle of love.

"Maybe eliminate national debt?" Marina frowned; then her face cleared. "I know. How about you find a cure for avaricious greed?"

Oliver tried to repeat the word, looking like a little bird hoping for worms to be dropped into his mouth.

"No." Marina drummed her fingers on the table. "Eliminating avaricious greed might take longer than one night. What do you think about putting the napkins in the trash instead?" Oliver nodded happily. "Ready?" The three kids half rose. "Back, back, back,"

Marina ordered. "Down, down, down." They dropped their hind ends in their chairs and she held up her closed fist. "On three." She put up her index finger. "One. Two." A second finger went up next to the first. "Three!"

Before her third finger went up, the kids were hurrying around the table, collecting and clearing like professionals. Table clear, dirties in the dishwasher, they scampered off to the family room with only empty place mats to show they'd ever sat down with us.

I looked at Marina with admiration. "How did you do that?"

"Bribery."

"Why doesn't it work that well for me?"

"Got to bribe them with the right stuff. Next time," she said, nodding sagely, "try cold, hard cash."

"Marina, you didn't!"

She crossed her eyes at me. "Sucker. We've been playing restaurant after school all week. I told them if they kept quiet about it and did well tonight, they could watch two movies."

"You are a devious woman."

"Why, thank you."

"Speaking of devious." I got up and fetched my purse. "So, the other day I went through the WisconSINs blog posts and made a list of —"

"Great God in heaven." Marina flopped forward and thunked her forehead against the table. "Not a list. Please, anything but a list."

"Do you want my help or not?" I asked. Marina made a small mewing sound that was probably a yes. She'd once dared me to go a full week without a list. I'd lasted two days, but I had broken down upon realizing we'd needed milk, eggs, bread, *and* bananas. Three things I could keep in my head. Four things were one too many.

"So what's the title of this list?" Marina lifted her head and propped it up with her two fists, one atop the other.

All my lists had titles. Why anyone found this amusing, I had no idea. I unfolded the piece of lined yellow paper. "Murder Suspects."

"So descriptive," Marina murmured.

Brushing the paper flat, I said, "Some of these people are identified on your blog as potential suspects."

Marina jumped her chair around the table to sit side by side with me. "Lemme see, lemme see." It sounded as if she were repeating a take-out order for a Chinese restaurant.

"Not so fast, twinkle toes." I held the paper out of her reach. "First, the introduction."

She slumped back and folded her arms across her chest.

"Cut that out." I opened the paper a few inches, then closed it up again. "There is no order to this list. Not most likely suspect to least likely, and not least likely to most. I just wrote names down as they came to me."

Marina looked heavenward. "On with it, O Queen of the Lists."

I held the paper a little farther out of her grasp. "Suspect number one: Kirk Olsen."

She nodded. "The affair of the school buses."

"Suspect number two is Claudia Wolff."

"Ooo, the Dysfunction from Fish Fry Friday." Marina perked up. "I could stand it if Claudia was the killer. Sad for those horrible children, though." She looked downcast for a moment, then brightened. "Growing up without a mom would be bad, but could it be any worse than having Claudia Wolff as your primary caregiver?"

"Well . . ."

"Can't be Claudia, though," she said, sighing.

"Why not?"

"She was up with a sick kid that night.

Taylor? Tyner? One of those. Claudia was calling around to borrow a vaporizer. She called me around eleven." Marina shook her head sadly. "Another good suspect toasted. Who's next?"

The lyrics of a Tom Lehrer song went through my head. I tried to turn them off, but I knew they'd keep coming back until I replaced them with something else. I crossed off Claudia. "Next is Randy Jarvis."

"Ah." She looked left and right. "He's my favorite," she whispered.

Their relationship had been strained at best since the time she and Randy had gone at each other hammer and tongs over the end-of-school gift the PTA gave out. Randy had pushed for root beer floats; Marina had wanted to hand out paperback books. After too many hours of discussion, Erica banged her gavel and said they'd hand out gift certificates to the Children's Bookshelf.

"Randy and Agnes were having it on," Marina said. "I'm sure of it. I know he didn't look grief-stricken at the memorial service, but he's a man, and he's from Wisconsin. He wouldn't show public grief if his mother was run over by a truck right in front of him."

I didn't see how Randy's not crying at the memorial service proved he'd been involved with Agnes, but I didn't pursue the issue. "Randy didn't kill Agnes," I said.

"Yes, he did." She spread her arms wide. "Here's how it worked. The meeting at the school ended. Everybody left. Randy hung around, left his car at the school, and walked to Agnes's house for an assignation. They had an argument. In the heat of anger he picked up something heavy" — she picked up an invisible object — "and hit her on the head." Her arm swung down. I winced as her hand thudded against the table. "After that, he sneaked out the back door."

"You really think Randy would have walked three blocks?"

She wavered, in love with her theory, but seeing the flaw. Randy hadn't walked that far in years. "Well . . ."

"Marina, Randy wasn't even in town that night."

"Don't be silly. Where else would he be? No, wait. Let me guess." She started playing an air guitar. "He plays guitar for a classic-rock band. They play in nasty little bars all over the county. But, wait! A discerning crowd hears the emotion Randy pours into the solo for 'Free Bird,' and the applause doesn't stop for half an hour." Her hair bounced all around as she bobbed her head in time to music only she could hear.

Suddenly I was tired of the game. A murderer was roaming free while my children were watching *Free Willy.* Not that, deep down, I thought they were in any danger, but still . . . "On Tuesday nights," I said, "Randy is a volunteer."

Marina's mouth slacked open. "He's a what?"

"Every Tuesday and one Saturday a month. And don't ask where he's volunteering, because I'm not going to tell you. Confidential sources."

She stuck her tongue out at me. "Don't you hate it when someone you can't stand turns out to be a good person? What a waste of a perfectly good suspect. Who's next on the list?"

I rattled off the rest of the names. "Nick Casassa, Dan Daniels, Cindy Irving, Joe Sabatini, Erica Hale, Harry the janitor, Lauren Atchinson, and Gary Kemmerer."

"Lauren Atchinson?"

I shrugged and told her that Nick, Lauren, and Gary all had solid alibis.

"What are they?" Her eyes were bright.

"Not saying."

"Come on, pretty please?"

"Nope. Not a chance. Move on to the next question, please."

She pouted and flounced her hair a few times, but I didn't budge. She sighed dramatically. "How about Agnes's ex-husband?"

"Do you want the long or the short version?"

She cocked her head, listening to the sounds emanating from the family room. "Isn't that the start of *The Willy Show*? We have time for all the details." She rubbed her palms together.

I dug into my purse for another set of notes. If I was going to keep on with this investigating stuff, I was going to need a bigger purse. "John Mephisto remarried a week and a half after his divorce from Agnes."

Marina blew a soft, sympathetic whistle. "Ouch."

"Yup."

"What was that all about?"

"Agnes and John got married the summer after they graduated from college. University of Wisconsin, Eau Claire. After driving around the country for a summer in a VW bus —"

"How very seventies," Marina said.

"Agnes went on to graduate school here in Madison. John Mephisto started working as a junior loan officer for the State Bank of

Madison. Agnes, one of a handful of females in the doctoral program —"

"Agnes had a PhD?"

"She was taking her studies very seriously. Mephisto was left to his own devices in a town where he knew very few people."

Marina made a slicing motion across her neck. "Never mind the rest. So what wife is Mephisto on now? Three? Four?"

"Still on two, actually. They live near San Diego."

"Hmm." Marina frowned. "Doesn't sound like he holds a grudge against Agnes."

"Plus he was in Las Vegas the week Agnes died, attending a regional business leaders' conference."

Marina's face lit up. "So he could have sneaked out and flown here. Done the deed and zipped back to Vegas."

"Nope." I shook my head. "At the approximate time Agnes was killed, he was accepting an award for 'most environmentally friendly office management.' "

"Well, shoot." Marina stuck her lower lip out. "It would have been okay if he'd done it."

"Sorry."

She flicked at my notes. "Where'd you get this, anyway?"

"A few phone calls, a few Web site

searches." Actually, most of the information had come from Agnes's sister, Gloria. I'd called, ostensibly to confirm that the photo album had arrived. With only a small push, she'd been more than pleased to dish up the dirty on her sister's failed marriage. Turned out Mephisto had also been from Superior. "He was slime," Gloria said. "He went after Agnes for one reason and one reason only."

Marina leaned down and picked a fallen scrunchie off the floor. She set it on the table and spun it around her index finger. "So many people with alibis." Twirl, twirl. "This never happened on *Dragnet*." She held on to the table and tipped her chair back. If any of our children had done that, we'd have scolded, "Four on the floor." But since it was just us, we didn't have to be adults. "So now what? Do you want to split up the rest of the names, or are you still gung ho on doing this yourself?"

"Mom?" Zach ran into the room. "We get to watch another movie, right?"

The chair thudded down, and Marina spread her arms wide. "Come here, my son, and let me bestow upon you the kiss of motherhood."

He wrinkled his nose and looked like a young male version of his mother. "Aw, quit. I'm too old for that." Marina's arms drooped and her lower lip trembled, but Zach only rolled his eyes. "Stop that, too," he said. "Hey, can we have popcorn during the second movie?"

Marina heaved a loud sigh. "Despite the scorn heaped on my head, I will indeed labor and sweat to bring you corn that is popped."

"None of that air crap."

"Young princeling, your wish is my command."

"Cool." He ran off, then turned and trotted backward. "Thanks, Mom! You're okay, even if you do talk funny sometimes."

"He's getting so big," Marina said softly. "A few more years and he'll be gone, too."

I was quiet, remembering that sunny September day when I'd taken Oliver to his first-grade classroom. Preschool and kindergarten hadn't seemed real, somehow, filled with naptime and tambourines and construction paper. First grade was the beginning of Oliver's true education, and the real start of his growing away from me.

"Well." Marina pushed herself to her feet. "That's what motherhood is all about. Love 'em and leave 'em go. Want some popcorn?"

"Sure." The reason I even owned a stovetop cooker was because I'd tasted Marina's

280

popcorn. That microwaved gunk hadn't come into our house for years.

With metallic screeches, she slid aside the cast-iron pan that lived permanently on the range and took the popcorn cooker out of a cabinet. "I'll make a second batch for us. Garlic, cheese, and just a touch of chili powder." With her head in the refrigerator, she asked, "You're not planning on kissing anyone later on tonight, are you?"

My thoughts immediately went to Evan, and my cheeks flamed. "No-o," I stammered. Rats. There were one or two things I wanted to keep to myself, and Marina would be all over that stutter faster than a first-time mother on a dropped pacifier.

Wildly, I looked around for a subject changer. Marina's laptop computer sat at the end of the counter, booted up and ready for service. I sidled toward it as Marina came out of the fridge, butter in hand and eyebrows raised. "Hey." I angled the screen toward her. "You have mail."

She squinted at the screen. "My reading glasses are AWOL. What's the subject line say?"

"There are three of them."

"Read on, my dear." She sliced off a chunk of butter and put it in a glass measuring cup. "Now that you're party to my blog-

281

gership, there is nothing about me you do not know."

Without even meaning to, she was making me feel guilty. "Um, the first one is from Lands' End. A shipment is on its way."

"New jeans for Zach, winter coat for the DH."

"Where is he, anyway?"

"The DH," she said, "is at this moment traversing the state with three other like-minded men. Tomorrow's plans include setting up a grill in a parking lot at eight in the morning, cooking, and eating vast amounts of fatty foods, then sitting on cold concrete for a minimum of three hours watching young men run, throw an inflated leather object, and collide against one another with sickening thuds."

"Ah." I looked back at the screen. "E-mail number two is an advertisement from the Hawaii Visitors and Convention Bureau. How many years have you been trying to get your DH to take you there?"

She counted on her fingers, ran through all the digits, and started over on the right hand. "Too many. Something always seems to come up. New car, college tuition, new roof, college room and board, new carpet, college textbooks, new furnace, college fees, et cetera, et cetera."

College. I hadn't put a dime into the kids' college funds since the divorce. One of these days I'd have to talk to Richard about it — after school let out for the summer, maybe.

"E-mail number three," I said, "is from a gobbledygook e-mail address of letters and numbers. Why do people do that?"

"What's the address?" Marina asked hoarsely.

"Are you getting a cold?" I put my finger on the screen — bad Beth! — to help me read along. "It's 1t94z4a at rynwood dot com. Is that anyone you know? Marina?"

I turned around. Marina was standing statue still, staring out the window. But since it was dark outside, there wasn't anything to see except her reflection. Her mouth opened, then closed without a sound coming out.

"It's him, isn't it?" I asked.

"Read it," she said dully. "Then delete it."

"But —"

"Just do it!"

A loud *pop* echoed across the kitchen; we both jumped. There was another *pop* and another, and then a flurry of popcorn burst into full flower. Marina started cranking the wooden knob. "Are you going to read it or what?"

I read it, then desperately wished I hadn't.

Once, twice, three times, I tried to speak, but nothing came out. Repeating the words on that screen wasn't possible. If I spoke them, they might come true.

"Oh, for Pete's sake," Marina said. "It can't be that bad." With a heaping popcorn bowl in hand, she gave me a friendly hip check and pushed me aside. She leaned close to the screen, squinting, and started to read aloud, but fell silent. Her hands began to tremble.

I watched the tremors grow from a one on the Richter scale to a seven. The popcorn bowl plunged to the vinyl floor with a loud whack, and hot buttered popcorn went everywhere.

"He says —"

"Yes." I put my hands on her shoulders.

"He says he's going to —"

"Don't," I whispered, and put my arms around her waist. Whoever had sent that e-mail had a vivid and bloody imagination. "Just don't."

She gripped my hands hard enough to hurt. "Beth, what are we going to do?" Panic pushed her voice high. "What am I going to do?"

"Shhh." I put my forehead against the back of her neck. Her whole body was shivering, but after reading the new threat, I didn't blame her a bit. "Shhh," I whispered. "It'll be all right."

"How can you say that?" The panic was rising, threatening to take her off in its dark, dirty claws. "How can you know?"

I gave her the firmest, sturdiest, most reassuring hug possible. "Because I have a plan."

A thundering herd pounded up the hallway. When it reached the kitchen, it resolved down to three preadolescents. "Something fell!" "Did you drop the popcorn?"

Marina and I were already back in Mom Mode. Pleasant faces, no sign of fear or anxiety. Happy, happy, happy. "Just a mere slip of the elbow, dear young ones," Marina said. "Demonstrating once again that anyone can make mistakes, *tu comprends?*"

"She's talking French again," Zach said to my children. "I hate it when she does that."

Oliver looked at the scattered mess. "Does this mean we're not getting popcorn?"

"Fear not, young friend." Marina handed me a broom and dustpan. "If yon minion will complete the tidying, the master chef will commence replacement."

Oliver turned to Zach and whispered, "What did she say?"

"That she'll make some more," Zach said.

Jenna headed back to the family room.

"C'mon, we're missing the movie."

I got the wastebasket out from under the sink and started dumping popcorn into it. "This part of the floor needs a wash."

Her head was in the fridge. "Don't bother. I'll get it later."

I turned the laptop my way and hit a few keystrokes. "Later the kids will have tracked butter all over the house. It'll only take a minute to mop up."

"You're the best friend in the whole wide world." Marina shut the refrigerator door and looked at what was in her hand. "Why am I holding this?"

I was willing to bet it wasn't because she wanted to add oyster sauce to the popcorn. "It was in front of the butter." Which wouldn't have made any sense whatsoever in most households, but Marina ran hers with a special brand of logic. "You wanted butter," I reminded her gently. "For more popcorn."

"Did you delete that e-mail?" she asked the oyster sauce.

"From the in-box and from the deleted folder."

She tightened the lid on the jar. "Do you really have a plan?"

What she wanted to know was if I had a way to end the e-mails. If I could help her find a way out of the fear. If I could make it all go away and never come back. For the very first time in our friendship, I needed to be the mother figure.

"Fear not, young maiden." I headed for the laundry room and a mop and bucket. "Salvation is at hand."

As I'd hoped, she snorted out a laugh. I went into the laundry room and made rattling noises until I heard the fridge door open again. Softly, slowly, I went one room farther, into the study. Marina's DH used a wireless server to give all the computers in the house printer access. I tiptoed in and collected the e-mail I'd printed. It was just as frightening when read the second time. I folded the sheet of paper and slid it into my pants pocket.

"Did you find it?" Marina called.

I slipped out of the study and went to find a mop.

CHAPTER 14

The next morning I woke to a whispered darkness. "Mom?" came a hushed voice. "Are you awake yet?"

I rolled over, eliciting a protest from the cat. "I am now."

"Good." Oliver turned on the overhead light, blasting the room with too many lumens. Before my eyes unsquinched, he'd jumped onto the bed and settled down as he had so many other mornings; his back against the footboard, feet out straight, a stuffed animal on his lap. Today's animal choice was a large dog of an unlikely shade of navy blue.

"When are we going?" Oliver wiggled his feet. "I'm not hungry. Can we skip breakfast?"

"No," I said automatically. "Breakfast is the most important meal of the day." My brain, fuzzy with too little sleep, tried to remember what today's big event might be.

It was the store's Halloween party, but that wasn't until afternoon. I rubbed my eyes. Focusing was difficult because I'd stayed up late trying to figure out who'd sent that e-mail to Marina.

When we'd come home last night, I'd called Sara, my part-time helper, on her cell phone. "What's up, Mrs. Kennedy?"

"Sorry to call so late, Sara." Since it was past ten, I'd debated about calling at all.

"Late?" She laughed. "We're getting ready to go to a party. Want to come?"

Ah, youth. I didn't miss it. "Then I won't keep you long. A while back, you said there are ways you can find out who sent an e-mail."

"Sure. It's really easy sometimes." Sara's minor had something to do with computers. More than once she'd tried to explain, but my eyes always got glassy somewhere in her second sentence.

"Great. Can you tell me how to do it?"

"Oh. Wow. Well . . ."

Clearly it wasn't *that* easy. "Never mind. I'll just —"

"No, hang on a sec." Her voice went far away. "Kayla, where'd my laptop go? No, it's not on the couch. . . . There it is." She came back. "Mrs. Kennedy? Hang on." She tapped at the keyboard. "Got a pencil?

Here's a Web site that'll walk you through the basic steps." She told me the URL. "If you have troubles, bring the e-mail to the store and I'll help you out, okay?"

I'd thanked her and hung up. I wanted to take the e-mail to Gus, but Marina had threatened her own unique brand of terror if I did any such thing. The best remaining choice was to try and figure out on my own who sent it. In the wee hours of the morning, I determined that the sender's IP address was a string of meaningless numbers and that the sender had a computer name of dh4cln.

Well, yee-hah.

The victory was hollow at best, and I'd trudged up the stairs, trying to beat down the feeling that I'd failed Marina.

Now, Oliver was banging his feet against the mattress, jouncing my bladder a little past comfort. "All I want is cereal." He held the stuffed animal at arm's length and flew him left and right. "You're going to get a brother, Big Nose!" He pulled the dog to his chest, hugging it tight.

Right. Today was Dog Day.

Jenna came into the room. Dressed in her favorite weekend jeans and a Door County sweatshirt, she was ready for action. "I can't believe you're not out of bed yet. We've been up for *hours*. All the good dogs will be gone if you don't hurry."

I pulled the covers over my head and gave them the cue. "Can't. I'm stuck."

Jenna giggled. "I'll help unstuck you."

"Me, too!" Oliver shouted. The kids launched themselves at me. The next few minutes were a glorious riot of tussling and tugging and hugging and laughter and, even if they didn't know it, an outpouring of love. For, oh, how I loved my children.

Three hours later, the love was wearing thin.

Hands on hips, I stood in the animal shelter's dog wing, looking around at dozens of caged canines. "I can't believe you two have rejected all of these dogs."

"It's not me." Jenna stood with her hands on her own hips. "It's him." She pointed at the only full sibling she'd ever have. "Every dog I like, he hates."

Oliver's lower lip was pushed out as far as it could go. "Every dog I like, *she* hates."

"That's because you only like dumb ones."

"I do not."

"Do, too!"

"Kids," I warned. After one final round of do-not-do-too, they subsided. I looked at the ceiling, hoping to find divine guidance, but saw only white acoustical tile. In after-

291

school specials this would have been a happy family outing.

"Since you two can't agree," I said, "I'll pick the dog."

The attendant smiled weakly. "That's a wonderful idea." She gestured at the plethora of doggy life. "We were fortunate enough to get a very generous donation from an anonymous donor a few years ago, and not only did we have the money to build this new facility, but now we have the staff for training."

Anonymous donors were thick around here these days. Too bad one that supported children's bookstores didn't fall into my lap.

"All our dogs are housebroken and trained to a leash," the attendant went on. "Every single one would make a wonderful pet."

I tried not to look cynical. She was trying to sell something; of course all the dogs were wonderful. Every one would probably fetch my slippers, bring in a slobbery paper, and text me at the store about Timmy falling down a well.

The puppy Jenna and Oliver originally fell in love with had been a neighbor's expensive purebred destined for special diets and expensive shampoos and show rings. When I'd broken the news that a dog like that wouldn't be happy at our house, they'd stormed and raged but had eventually come around to the idea of bringing home a dog from the animal shelter.

"We'll be saving it, right?" Jenna had said.

The shelter was no-kill, but in lots of ways she was correct.

"I want a puppy." Oliver had been adamant. "I want a puppy, I want a puppy, I want —"

"Enough." My voice was calm but firm, and my son's chant had died away. "We'll go to the animal shelter and see what's available."

"But I want a puppy!" Oliver's lower lip had started to tremble.

"We'll see what's available," I'd said. "Cheer up, kiddos. On Saturday we'll go to the shelter. They're bound to have a dog we'll all love."

And now it was Saturday. There wasn't a single dog my kids could agree on, and I was not — repeat *not* — going to take two dogs home. Jenna stalked over to stand in front of the dog of her choice: an Airedale. Oliver grabbed a boxer's cage door and held on tight. "I'd feel really, really safe if we had him."

"It's not a puppy," Jenna said.

"I don't care." Oliver took on the mulish

look Jenna had sported of late. "He loves me."

The tag on the door said BONNIE. I smiled at him. "You mean *she* loves you."

Oliver jumped away. "He's a girl?" His look of horror almost made me laugh out loud.

"What's wrong with a girl?" Jenna asked, her eyes narrowing.

"Any more bickering," I said, "and we're going straight home. All these dogs would love to come with us. They all want kids to play with and a food bowl with their name on it. We just have to look for the one who fits into our family."

"This one," Jenna said.

I squatted down and looked the Airedale in the face. Even standing still, he looked as if he were bouncing. "Hey, there," I said softly. Instantly he erupted into leaps so high he bashed his head against the top of the cage and started a frenzied barking that set off the other dogs.

We held our hands over our ears and waited for the din to die down. Either the attendant was hard of hearing or she was used to it.

"I'm not so sure," I told Jenna, "that he's the best choice."

In spite of her square stance in front of

the cage, she'd taken on a doubtful look. "He is pretty noisy."

I walked down the aisle. There were so many dogs in so many shapes, sizes, and colors. Big dogs, little dogs, medium-sized dogs. Old dogs, young dogs. Short-haired, long-haired. Black, brown, yellow, white. So many dogs without a home, so many dogs without anyone to love them. If the shelter hadn't been no-kill, I might have started crying then and there.

The last cage at the end of the row looked empty. "I thought you were full up," I said. "Did someone adopt a dog today?"

"That's Spot," the attendant said. "He's a little shy."

I hunkered down and peered in. Way in the back corner, a medium-sized lump of fur was curled into a ball. "Spot?" My whisper had no effect. "Hey, guy. Are you in there?" His eyes opened to small slits. We stared at each other for a moment, long enough for him to communicate his entire life history — born to an unwed mother; grown up in a foster home that didn't have time for him; tossed into this shelter without a wave good-bye.

"You poor thing." The tip of his brown tail beat a quiet tattoo against the blanket. I looked up at the attendant. "Spot?" From muzzle to tail, everything about him was brown.

"Someone's idea of a joke, I guess." She shrugged. "We have some golden retriever mixes that are good with kids. I could get one out."

"No, thanks." My knees creaked as I stood. "We're taking Spot."

Within seconds of our return home, the phone rang. It was Jenna's friend Bailey. "Oh, sure," Jenna told her, "we got a dog. You wouldn't believe the lame thing my mom picked out. He's scared of everything."

I put down the expensive bag filled with dog treats, dog toys, dog leash, and collar, and I headed back to the garage. Oliver and Spot were sitting together in the backseat, waiting for doggy arrangements to be made in the laundry room. When I came back to the kitchen with two bags of expensive dog food, Jenna was saying, "Yeah, some guard dog he's going to be. If a burglar comes, I bet he hides in the closet faster than Oliver does."

Her laughter was loud and raucous and mean. The sound was so unlike my happy Jenna's laughs that I couldn't believe it came out of the same person. Where had my daughter gone? Even more important, how was I going to get her back?

"Five minutes," I said, holding up one hand, fingers spread wide.

She turned her back to me.

For a moment I stood there. Jenna was only ten, far away from the dreaded teenage years. If she was snubbing me now, how would she treat me at fifteen? Images flashed. Jenna with blue spiked hair and rings in her nose. Jenna skipping school . . .

"No," I said. "This is not going to happen."

Jenna gave me a startled look. "Uh, Bailey? I guess I gotta go. Yeah. See ya later." She hung up the phone. Wariness dominated the mix of emotions on her face. "Um . . ." She stopped, not knowing where to go next.

I didn't know, either, but since I was the adult in the house, I had to take a stab at it. Pretending this was about the dog would be the easiest way to go, and it was a tempting route, but my mom instincts were telling me to take the road less traveled.

"Why don't you play with your old friends anymore?" I asked.

"You mean Alexis?"

"Alexis and Sydney. The three of you were such good friends last year."

Her shoes were, apparently, worthy of sudden and intense examination. "Bailey says

Sydney is dumb. That she doesn't know anything about clothes and is stupid about music. She says the only thing Sydney knows how to do is play the piano, and who cares about that?"

"Okay." I resisted the impulse to do some Bailey bashing. "Is that what you think, too?"

"I dunno."

"How about Alexis?"

She shrugged, but it was a halfhearted movement. The seed, however, had been planted. She needed to find her own way, but please God, I wanted it to be a fine and upright way.

"Anyway," I said, "if a burglar breaks in, a closet is the safest place to be."

She frowned, not making the leap back to her phone conversation. Then her face cleared of confusion and went straight on to another expression altogether — shame. "I didn't mean that about Oliver," she said in a low voice. "He's pretty brave for a little kid. When I was seven, there's no way I would've gone up in the big tree at Mrs. Neff's."

I felt a rush of relief that, for today at least, my Jenna was back. "And you're pretty brave for a big kid."

"Can we come in?" Oliver called. "I think

Spot really wants to see his new house."

"What do you say, favorite daughter?" I kissed the top of her head, then rubbed the kiss into her hair, just as I'd done for years. "Want to help me with the food and water bowls?"

She squeezed me tight. "Sure. But, Mom? Can we call him something else? Spot is sooo dumb."

I laughed. "The name doesn't seem to fit, does it?"

"Mom!" Oliver yelled. "I think Spot just leaked!"

On the other hand, there could have been a very good reason for calling him Spot.

Sara looked at me critically. "Your pinafore is crooked."

For the fortieth time since I'd arrived at the store, I straightened the straps on the apron of my Mother Goose costume. If I'd been better endowed in the chest area, it might have stayed in place. "Next year," I said, "I'm getting a new costume."

Sara herself looked fetching in a Red Riding Hood costume. Lois was the Cat in the Hat, Paoze made a wonderful Robin Hood, and Marcia was the Princess and the Pea.

"Every year you say you're going to get a

new costume." Lois plugged in the fog machine. "And every year you wear that Mother Goose outfit that has never fit you properly."

"It was my sister's." And it had been free, always my favorite price.

The fog machine hummed, burped out a few clouds of fog, then started spitting out a stream of water.

"Huh." Lois frowned at the machine. "That doesn't seem right." She gave it a good, swift kick, and the fog came out in a steady flow. "Like my dad always told me," she said, "if it doesn't work, get a bigger hammer."

"But you did not use a hammer," Paoze said. "You used your foot."

"Paw," Lois corrected, pointing at her costume's furry feet. "That's why it worked. Shoes wouldn't have done the job at all. If you're going to kick a machine, you need to use a paw."

Paoze plucked the string of the bow slung over his shoulder. "I do not believe you. This is a joke."

I laughed and patted him on the shoulder. "You're catching on, kid."

Lois sniffed. "Okay, so that wasn't my best effort. Next time he won't see it coming."

Sara and Paoze slid a long table over the

fog machine. Lois and I unfolded a large black and orange plaid tablecloth, and Marcia started ferrying snacks from the kitchenette. In no time at all the table was covered with goodies and punch. Fog trickled out from the edges of the tablecloth, creating a satisfyingly eerie effect.

"Let 'em come," Lois said. "We're ready!"

I unlocked the front door and braced myself for the rush. At one, the store had closed for a bare hour. While I was telling the babysitter about the new dog and rushing around putting on my costume, my faithful staff had done the work of setting up games and prizes. I didn't like shutting the store even for an hour, but logistically it worked out better this way. Lois was convinced it added more attraction to the event, and she might have been right.

Half an hour later, Sara was organizing a Pin the Tail on the Black Cat game, Paoze was helping kids create their own construction paper masks, Lois was drying the face of a child who'd just bobbed for an apple, and Marcia was reading Erica Silverman's *Big Pumpkin* to an enthralled collection of children and parents.

I was running myself frazzled trying to help customers find books, running the register, and answer questions for anyone who asked.

"Hey."

There was a tug on the lower corner of my apron. I looked down. A kindergarten-sized child was looking up at me. "Hi, there," I said. "What's your name?"

"Avery Olsen."

"Hi, Avery." My brain went *click!* Avery was Kirk and Isabel Olsen's daughter — Kirk of the school bus incident. "Are your mommy and daddy here?"

"My mommy is over there." She pointed to Marcia's reading circle. "My daddy's gone. But he's almost home."

"I see." Or not. "What can I do for you, Avery?"

"Potty."

Clearly, Avery was a girl of few words. "I'll take you there, okay?"

She nodded solemnly. I put my hand on the back of her head and guided her toward the back of the store. On the way past Isabel and her son, Neal, I tapped Isabel's shoulder and nodded at Avery, whispering, "Bathroom. Do you want to . . . ?"

"Go ahead," she said. "She'll be fine."

That hadn't been what I meant. I'd meant for her to take responsibility for her daughter; I'd meant to imply that I wasn't a babysitter and that I had a store to run.

"Oh," I said. "Okay."

I shut the bathroom door behind Avery. "Do you need any help?"

"No." She stood tall. "I'm a big girl now. I'm *five*."

"That is a big-girl age, isn't it?"

"Yup." She began bathroom preparations and climbed aboard. "My daddy says when I'm big enough, I can go and shoot things with him."

"Really?"

"At first it won't be real things. Just paper." She sounded disgusted with the idea. "But when I get biggerer, I can shoot real things."

"Oh. How nice."

She nodded emphatically. "Neal doesn't like guns, but I do. I want to go with Daddy next time he goes away. He's far away now."

"He is?"

"Yup." She hopped down and finished the job. "But he'll be back soon. I bet he got lots of real things. He shoots good." She pushed the toilet's lever with both hands. "I want to be just like him when I grow up."

Job done and hands washed, we went back to the party. Marcia had finished the story and was glowing at the enthusiastic applause. I handed Avery over to Isabel. "Your daughter says Kirk's out of town. Is he on a hunting trip?"

Isabel nodded. "A two-week guided hunt in the Canadian Rockies. It's his thirtieth-birthday present. Everyone chipped in: his parents, his brothers, a bunch of his friends, everybody. You should have seen his face when we told him."

I tried to figure out the dates in my head. "So he's been gone two weeks." That would put him in Rynwood the day Agnes was murdered.

"Almost three. He decided to get there early and spend some time getting used to the altitude." She dug into her purse. "The guide e-mailed me some pictures, and I made lots of copies. Want to see?"

I called Marina that night and gave her the news. "Kirk Olsen was in Canada on a hunting trip the night Agnes was killed." I turned on my computer and scanner.

"Maybe he sneaked home early," Marina said, "killed Agnes, then sneaked back."

"Nope." I put Isabel's photo on the scanner and clicked the appropriate buttons. "His wife gave me a date-stamped picture. I'm e-mailing it to you right now."

"Hang on . . . Oh, eww," Marina said. "He's got a dead thing. A big dead thing."

"Male moose weigh more than a thousand

pounds."

"Hokey Pete." Marina whistled. "But, say, maybe it's not a real picture. You said there's a computer up at that hunting camp. Maybe Kirk Photoshopped it for a perfect alibi."

"Are you serious?" Kirk was prodigious in his computer illiteracy. I'd once seen him puzzling over an ATM machine.

Marina sighed. "Okay. It's not Kirk Olsen. And I have more bad news. It's not Dan Daniels, either."

"No?"

"Nope. I was talking to CeeCee, and she said her sainted husband — she didn't say that, but that's how she feels about him, you know — has hockey league on Tuesday nights, and he had a late game. Didn't even get on the ice until eleven."

"Lucky," I muttered.

"Your time will come, my sweet. Another five years and the kids will be old enough for you to risk life and limb by playing something as silly as hockey."

"Hockey isn't silly."

"And neither is my writing the blog."

I started to protest, but my computer dinged as an e-mail came in. It was from Marina, and there was a single word in the body of the text: "Hypocrite!"

Okay, so she had a point.

305

"Silly is in the eye of the beholder," she said. "Put that in my obituary, will you?"

Thinking about Marina's obituary was pretty much the last thing I wanted to think about. I'd rather think about writing my own. I was halfway through the second paragraph when Marina interrupted.

"Who's left? You know, on The List?" She capitalized the words.

I pulled the by-now-tattered piece of paper out of the inside pocket of my purse. "Cindy Irving, Joe Sabatini, Erica, and Harry."

"That's not very many," she said.

I didn't say anything.

"You don't want it to be Erica, do you?" she asked softly.

Not in the least. I got out my pen and crossed off Kirk and Dan. "What matters is keeping you safe and getting the killer into prison. What I want really doesn't matter."

Seven down, four to go.

"Did you see WisconSINs this morning?" Lois asked.

I almost dropped the load of books piled high in my arms. What had Marina done now?

"You know," Lois said, rescuing a stack of Magic Tree Houses before they cascaded to the floor, "if you used the book cart, these things wouldn't happen."

"Too far away," I said vaguely. "What's on the blog?" I asked. Friday night I'd told Marina that it might be good to take a few days off from blogging. So much for my powers of persuasion. Her identity had become intertwined with that of WisconSINs, and it would take an act of Congress to separate her from the blog.

"Brand-new suspect for Agnes Mephisto's murder." Lois grinned. Today she was wearing a flowing white poet shirt over pale pink wide-legged slacks and black ballet slippers. I didn't have the figure for the pants, but I coveted the shirt. "If I still had kids at Tarver, I'd probably be hauled down to the police station myself."

"What?" Aghast, I stared at her.

"Not that I'd kill anyone," Lois said, "unless she was after me or mine, but if she got me all riled up, who knows what might happen?"

"No, no." I shook my head impatiently, and another book started sliding. "The blog. What does it say?"

"You know how it doesn't name names, but it says the police should look at the mob connections in town."

"The mob?"

"They're everywhere," Lois said seriously. "WisconSINs says there's a restaurant in town that the police should look at. And that's got to be Sabatini's. It's the only place in town even close to Italian."

There was a loud banging on the back door. "Could you unlock that?"

"Sure." Lois dumped the books she was holding back into my arms and went to flirt with the UPS guy.

I hurried to my desk, found a semiclear space for the books, and called Marina. "What are you thinking?" I whispered fiercely. "You're getting death threats, and you're *still* putting up posts about the murder? That's what he said *not* to do!"

"Quit worrying," she said over a background noise of toddler-sized shrieks. "I can only be safe when Agnes's murderer is locked up and the key thrown away. What better way to speed the process than to help the police? I'm sure they're reading Wisconsins. Everyone is."

I rubbed my forehead. "You read that e-mail Friday night. You were scared. Scared silly. Did you forget about that?"

"The only thing we have to fear is fear itself," she said airily. "If General Mac-Arthur wasn't afraid, I'm not going to be."

"That was Franklin Roosevelt's quote,

and both he and Douglas MacArthur are dead."

I banged down the receiver. "This is so stupid," I muttered. "How can I help her if she's going to ignore everything I say? Let her stew."

"In her own juice?"

I jumped and looked up — way up — at Evan Garrett. When had he come in? It was just now ten o'clock; I hadn't even realized we'd unlocked the front door. "Yes," I said. "In a big pot, in lots of her own juice. A big fire might tenderize her. Make her easier to deal with."

"Possible." He looked thoughtful. "Or she might just get hot. And cranky."

Suddenly, though the sky outside was October gray, the day felt bright.

"What do you say to a coffee break?" Evan asked. "Doughnut included."

Lois was nearby, alphabetizing an end cap display of Harry Potter books, something I knew she'd already done.

"Lois?"

"Oh!" She gave a very fake jump. "Yes?"

"I'm going to show Mr. Garrett here the cookies at you-know-where. Would you like anything?"

In a few short minutes we were seated at a small round wooden table that had lived the best years of its life in the Rynwood Pharmacy. A few years ago new owners had taken out the pharmacy soda fountain, and Alice and Alan, owners of the cleverly named Rynwood Antique Mall, bought the furniture so Alice could sell the cookies she made instead of eating them all. "Getting big as a house," she'd told me, thumping her hips with her fists. "Time to do something about it."

I perched on the front edge of the chair, not wanting to lean against the stunningly uncomfortable wire-backed soda fountain chair.

Evan was on his second chocolate-chip cookie. I was almost done with my oatmeal and was debating whether to eat raisin next or go for the peanut butter. But I was finding it hard to make a decision because concern for Marina was taking up most of the space in my brain.

"What's going on up there?" Evan asked. He tapped my head, just above my ear.

I twitched away, then smiled, but it was a weak attempt. "Sorry. I'm a little pre-occupied these days."

"Work? Kids? Parents?" He didn't seem offended that I'd backed off from his touch.

"Um, not exactly." The cookies sat there, getting stale.

"You're my oldest friend, Beth." Evan's voice was soft. "Let me help."

The blue eyes were close enough for me to drown in them. My breaths grew short, and before I fell onto the floor in a hyperventilation faint, I tore my gaze away and grabbed a cookie. "What would you do," I said around small bits of peanut, "if your really stubborn, um, sister was doing something you considered dangerous?"

He considered the question. At least he wasn't laughing out loud. "Can I assume she isn't listening to the wise counsel of siblings?"

I waved the last half of the cookie at him. "Assume away."

"Is what she doing illegal?"

"Not to my knowledge."

"But dangerous, you said. Dangerous only to her, or will her actions endanger others?"

The phrase rang oddly in my ear, and I suddenly remembered that, until recently, Evan had been a lawyer — a big-shot lawyer who'd probably charged more per hour than I made in a week. "Right now it's just Ma . . . my theoretical sister."

"But there is a possibility of future endangerment to others." He made it a statement.

If the bad guy decided to kidnap Zach, yes. If the bad guy decided to burn down

311

Marina's house and all who were in it. If, if, if. "I suppose."

"How will you feel if you do nothing?" Evan asked.

"Depends. If nothing happens to her, none of this matters." I shrugged. "But if something does happen . . ." Friday's e-mail came back in a rush, with its promise of pain and blood. I looked straight at Evan. "If something does happen, I'll never forgive myself."

"Then you have to do what you can," he said.

"Why did I have a feeling you were going to say that?"

"Because in addition to your being my oldest friend, I'm yours." He leaned forward. My eyes closed and his lips, feeling soft and warm as an August evening, touched mine.

The feel of Evan's kiss lingered long after we went back to our respective stores. I found myself touching my mouth from time to time, reliving the moment, until Lois asked, "Getting chapped lips, huh? Have you tried that Burt's stuff?"

I locked the door promptly at closing time and left the banking chores for the next morning. This evening, I had a Thing to Do.

Hot tomato sauce and garlic scented the parking lot and was positively overwhelming when I opened the door to Sabatini's. "Hi!" chirped the teenager at the counter. Her plastic name tag gave her the unlikely name of Valley. "I'll be with you in a sec, okay?" She handed change to a man standing in front of me. "Here you go, sir. Have a good night."

The man picked up his pizza and turned. It took me a long second to come up with his name. Recognizing people out of their normal environment didn't come easy to me. "Hi, Harry," I said. "How are you?"

Tarver's security guard and janitor looked at me over the top of the cardboard box. "Hello, Mrs. Kennedy."

Harry's eyes looked even darker and more sunken than normal. His hair was longer than I'd ever seen it, and grime was crusted underneath his fingernails. He was the embodiment of grief, sliding ever so slowly into depression. But at least he was eating. That had to be a good sign.

"The police were asking me if I did it," he said. "They kept asking and asking, and nothing I told them mattered."

Poor Harry. "Didn't they believe you?"

"They wanted an alibi, and I was waxing the floors at the school. I usually do it

Saturdays, but that Saturday the machine was broken, and I couldn't do it on Monday because of the meeting, so I did it Tuesday."

It was an ironclad alibi. Everyone knew how Harry was about the floors — everybody, that is, except the sheriff's department.

"It'll be okay." I put a light hand on his arm. "Take care of yourself, Harry."

"Yes." He nodded slowly and left.

I sighed and turned my attention back to the business at hand.

"Can I help you?" The clerk looked positively perky.

I gestured at her name tag. "You're probably tired of answering this, but . . . Valley?"

She crossed her eyes. "If I had a dollar for every time someone asked me about my name, I could buy my car instead of making all these stupid payments." She heaved a world-class sigh. "My mom and dad are big skiers. I was born nine months after a trip to Sun Valley."

So original, yet so banal. "At least they didn't name you Sunny."

Her grimace eased. "I never thought of that. At least Valley isn't, like, gag-me cutesy."

"And they didn't end it with an *i*."

We smiled at each other, rapport established. "I'd like to order a large pizza to go," I said. "Pepperoni and sausage on half, cheese only on the other half."

She had a pen and order pad at the ready and scribbled away. "Cheese only?" She looked up, grinning. "Kids?"

"A daughter who turns up her nose at any dinner without meat, and a son who is sliding toward vegetarianism."

"Usually the other way around, isn't it?" She spun around, tucked the order onto a circular rack, then turned back to me. "I mean, aren't girls usually the ones who do the veggie thing?" She plopped her arms on the counter. "I tried to be a vegan once, back when I was little." This from a girl who looked as if she might be seventeen. "But then it was Thanksgiving, and how can you have Thanksgiving without turkey?"

"Plus it'd be hard to be vegan in a place like this." Clever Beth, manipulating the conversation. "How long have you been working here?"

"Joe hired me two summers ago, right when he opened."

"That's Joe Sabatini?"

She giggled. "Want to know a secret?" She looked left and right and motioned me close. "Joe's last name isn't Sabatini," she whispered. "It's Pigg."

"Pig?"

"With two *g*s. P-i-g-g." Her giggle went loud, and she clapped her hands over her mouth. "Isn't that too funny?" she said through her fingers. "I could be working at Pigg Pizza." Her shoulders heaved with the effort of not laughing out loud. "At Pizza for Piggs!"

"So where did the Sabatini come from?"

"The Pigg's Pizza Parlor." Tears of laughter squeaked out of her eyes. "Oh, geez. Sabatini is some sports person. Like baseball?"

Even I'd heard of that Sabatini. "Gabriela. She plays tennis."

"Yeah, that's it. Joe's a big fan, I guess. He's from South Dakota, came here to go to Wisconsin." She shrugged. "All that school and money, and he ended up in dumpy Rynwood running a pizza place. Makes you wonder if college is worth it."

I walked out with dinner. Joe wasn't Italian, and he was from South Dakota. Okay, he could still have mob ties, but the likelihood had plummeted from "maybe" to "oh, please."

And now I'd eliminated everyone Marina had mentioned as a suspect, which didn't make sense. The bad guy wanted her to quit blogging, but if he wasn't called out in WisconSINs, why would he care? Because Marina was poking around? What kind of sense did that make? None.

I drove to pick up Jenna and Oliver, pushing other ideas around in my head. Nothing jelled, nothing came together, nothing clicked. As a detective, I made a pretty good children's bookstore owner.

The change in the evening's meal plan from stew to pizza was a success with the kids — so successful, in fact, that I didn't hear a single complaint when I said we needed to take Spot for a family walk. There was, however, a bit of jockeying over who carried the plastic bag. "We'll put a schedule on the calendar," I said. "Since I'm doing dog duty while you two are at your father's, I'll take one turn a week, no more. Yesterday was my turn. Tonight is Jenna's."

The "But, Mom" whines instantly quelled when I said, "You two wanted this dog, not me. If you can't handle the responsibility of a dog, he's going back to the shelter."

It would have taken a court order to force me to return Spot, but they didn't know that. He'd spent Saturday cowering in the laundry room, but by Sunday morning he'd turned into a real dog. He played catch with Jenna. He lay quietly on Oliver's bed while stuffed animals were piled on top of him.

317

He warmed my feet while I worked on the computer late at night. He'd even forged an early truce with the cat, who had taken one look at the interloper, hissed, and inflated to twice his normal size. A tail-wagging Spot just gazed at George, happy, tolerant, and unthreatening. George won the stare-down. Cats always did, but Spot didn't care. Now that he had a family, he was a Happy Dog.

The sidewalk was unevenly lit by street-lights, but there was enough ambient light to let us walk without squinting at our feet. Oliver held the leash and ran to the corner. "C'mon, Spot!"

"He's not such a bad dog," Jenna said.

"Maybe even a good dog?"

"Maybe." But she was cheerful, not cautious, or — much worse — sarcastic.

If I'd been the optimistic sort, I would have cheered the occasion as evidence of a lessening of Bailey's influence. But I was more the wait-and-see type.

"What would you think," I said, "if I asked someone over to have dinner with us?"

"Like Mrs. Neff? Sure. She's fun."

"No, more like Mr. Garrett."

"Who's that?" Jenna, who had been skipping, stopped dead.

"He's a friend of mine."

We stood in the dappled shadows cast by

streetlights and barren maple trees. "A boyfriend?" she asked.

"I knew him when I was a little girl."

She studied me with eyes that knew too much. "Does Gramma Emmerling like him?"

"We can call your grandmother and ask. But I'm not sure if she'll remember him. He moved away after kindergarten."

"So you haven't seen him since you were, like, five?"

"He's the new owner of the hardware. He just moved here a few weeks ago."

"Doesn't he have a family of his own?"

I gave her Evan's vital statistics, and somewhere in the details about his younger daughter, Jenna relaxed. "I guess it'd be okay if he came over." She started walking again. "Can you make meat loaf and baked potatoes?"

I took her hand. "Steak sauce on the meat loaf?"

Her hand, which didn't feel much smaller than my own, squeezed back. "And ketchup on the baked potatoes!"

"Oh, eww."

She giggled and dropped my hand as she raced to catch up to her brother. "I know something you don't know," she called ahead.

"Tell me," he said, beginning the inane rhyme they'd developed last summer. "Tell me in a tree, show me a bee, tell me for free, show me and I'll go hee hee hee!" He gave a loud and artificial laugh.

But for once I didn't shush him. Part of the rhyme had finally shaken something loose in my head.

Show me.

Show me the money.

I smiled. Finally, I knew how to start looking for Agnes's killer.

CHAPTER 15

Hal Hopkins of Hopkins Surveying stared at me from the other side of his desk, then repeated the question I'd just asked. "Where did the money for the school addition come from?" His desk was so coated with folders, large papers folded awkwardly small, and large rolls of paper that there wasn't even space for coffee. Hopkins held a mug in his left hand and fidgeted with his cell phone with the right. "Why do you want to know?"

Good question. I'd have to stop by the library's video section and study Jessica Fletcher's techniques. Meanwhile, I summoned my inner bureaucrat. "As a member of the PTA," I said, "I consider it my duty to tie up loose ends. Agnes didn't tell us anything about the donor, and before we can make any recommendations on whether or not to proceed with the renovation, we should make every attempt to discover the money's origins."

"Oh." Hal blew the steam off his mug and his wire-rimmed glasses steamed up. From behind the fog, he said, "I guess that makes sense."

Good. I didn't have time to watch all those DVDs, anyway.

Hal noisily slurped some coffee. Clearly, his mother hadn't raised him very well. I made a mental note to work on table manners tonight.

"Wish I could help," he said, "but I don't know anything about the money."

Though I hadn't expected to have the answer spill from the lips of the first person I questioned, I had harbored a tiny spark of hope. Which had just been extinguished by a great wave of reality. It had been luck enough that the only surveyor in town had done the addition's construction staking. Why had I expected more?

I held out one of my seldom-used business cards. He looked for a place to put his cell phone, but he couldn't find one. When he put down his mug instead, it started sliding down the slippery slope of folders. He grabbed the coffee, and I placed the card on a folder. "If you think of anything else," I said.

"Sure. You bet."

I was sure the card would disappear within

a day into the desk's maw, never again to see the light of day. I thanked him for his time and turned to go.

"Hey." He gestured at me with his cell phone. "Have you talked to the architect? Browne and Browne?"

"Not yet."

"Bick Lewis is the project manager," Hal said. "He's sharp. He might know."

I didn't want to drive to Chicago, and I certainly didn't want to talk to anyone named Bick.

"Thanks," I said. "I'll do that."

"Mrs. Kennedy?"

I looked up from a stack of invoices with which I was playing eeny, meeny, miny, moe, catch a past-due statement by its toe. "What's up, Paoze?"

"Have the police found my bicycle?"

Between Marina's death threats and Evan and Spot and the store's upcoming Halloween party, I'd completely forgotten about the bike. "I haven't heard." Prevarication, thy name is Beth. I shuffled the bills, picked one at random, and put it on top. Done. "But there's no reason why we can't ask. Get your coat."

Once again, Paoze hung back as we walked up the police station's front steps. And, once again, Cindy was working on the flower beds. She was cleaning leaves from behind the shrubbery, and a basket of deadheaded mums spoke of earlier work.

I stopped. "Hi, Cindy."

She sat up and brushed at her face with the back of her wrist. "Hey, Beth. Paoze. You're not here to ask about Agnes's killer, are you? Because they haven't found him yet."

"That's too bad," I said. "Have you heard anything else? Suspects? Bad alibis? Anything?"

Dust flew as she slapped her hands on her knees. "No, and you know what's driving me nuts? I wasn't even here that night. I missed the whole thing, thanks to my niece."

"Chrissie?"

Cindy nodded. "Her husband was out of town on business a couple days, so I volunteered to babysit her kids while she was working, and she got mandated to stay an extra shift. I didn't get home until the next morning."

She talked on, but I wasn't paying attention. Ten down, one to go. I *had* to find more suspects. There was no way Erica had killed Agnes — no way whatsoever.

Five minutes later, we were in Gus's office, sitting in our appointed seats. "Sorry, son," Gus said. "We're doing what we can, but it's pretty easy to hide a bike."

Paoze nodded. "Thank you, sir." His voice was as expressionless as his face.

Gus's response was what both Paoze and I had expected, but that didn't make it any easier to hear. "Paoze, I need to talk to Gus a minute. Why don't you head back to the store?"

Once the door closed softly behind him, I fixed Gus with a stern eye. "You know who took his bike, don't you? You said as much last time we were here."

"Knowing is different than proving."

"What does proving have to do with anything? It's just a cheap bike. Talk to the kid's parents and get it back." I waited a beat, but Gus stayed silent. "All Paoze wants is his bike. He doesn't want anyone to get in trouble." Silence. "This isn't the big city; this is Rynwood," I said in exasperation. "Why is this a problem?"

"It isn't just the theft of a bike."

"What?" Maybe it was time for Gus to get out of police work. Maybe he and Winnie could sell her garage sale finds on eBay, or maybe he could tutor kids in Latin. "What else could it be? Bike's here, bike's gone. Bike's stolen. What else could . . ." A teeny-weeny lightbulb went off in my slow brain.

"Oh," I said.

"Exactly."

We sat in silence, contemplating the ugliness of racism. The Hmong immigrants hadn't been welcomed with open arms by all of Wisconsin. I didn't bother asking how Gus had determined who stole the bike. Any small-town cop worthy of the name knew the usual suspects and would have traced down the miscreants long ago.

The fact that Paoze's bike hadn't been returned meant the parents weren't cooperating. "Not my kid," the mother would have said. "He was in his room that afternoon doing his homework."

Or the father would have done the talking. "Son, did you steal that bike? You wouldn't take anything from one of those kids, would you?" He'd have ruffled his boy's blond hair.

In Gus's office, dust motes spun in lazy circles. "I don't suppose," I said, "that you'll tell me who took the bike."

"You suppose correctly."

My involuntary sigh made him smile. "But," he said, "I'll give you a little unsolicited advice. There's a Robert Laird over on Crowley Drive, that short road behind the elementary school, who's the same age as your Oliver."

Robert of the spaghetti worms?

"He has a couple of older brothers," Gus went on, "and let's just say I doubt either one cares about making the honor roll."

Jenna and Bailey; now Oliver and Robert. I suddenly saw it all — Robert and Oliver stealing lawn ornaments and putting them in front of the school; Robert and Oliver bashing mailboxes with baseball bats; Robert and Oliver driving down the road with a backseat full of empty beer cans, the radio turned to volume eleven, seat belts flopping loose, a gravel truck pulling in front of them . . .

I shook the images away. "What about the parents?"

Gus looked grim. "The ex-husband? He lives on the other side of town and picks up the boys maybe once in three visitations, hangs around long enough to mess up their heads. The mother has had a series of live-in boyfriends who get younger and younger. No one disciplines those kids. Maybe a slap every once in a while."

Inviting Evan over for dinner suddenly seemed like a very bad idea. Not that he was my boyfriend, of course, but still . . .

"If I were going to pick a friend for my son," Gus said, "it wouldn't be one of the Laird boys."

I wanted to say that maybe Robert was different. That maybe Oliver would be a good influence on a troubled child, that maybe Oliver's kindness and compassion would bring out the best in young Robert, that Robert would graduate from high school, be the first in his family to go to college, marry happily and raise a large, loving family whose only thoughts were to do good in the world.

But this wasn't a fairy tale, and none of that was likely.

The next day I left Lois in charge. It had taken a promise of time off between Thanksgiving and New Year's to get Marcia to come in and help. I'd tried Paoze and Sara first, but Paoze had an exam in Shakespearean drama and Sara's organic chemistry lab was something she couldn't skip. "Sorry, Mrs. K," she said, "but I'm not getting this section on ring systems, and if I miss this lab, I'm toast."

The expressway extended ahead in a long curve. It was a sight that, for me, inspired meditative thoughts. When driving long distances, I rarely played the radio or listened to CDs. Today's meditation was "Come Up with a Brilliant Observation

That Will Lead to the Conviction of Agnes's Killer."

I spent fifty miles coming up dry. Clearly, it was time to lower my expectations. Maybe by the time I got to Chicago, I'd have figured how to manage Marcia better.

Fifteen miles later, I switched to calculating the odds of both of my children choosing unfortunate friendships in the same year.

Ten miles after that, I turned on the radio.

"Good morning." The receptionist at Browne and Browne smiled at me. The office was high rent, with colors and decor and lighting courtesy of expensive interior decorators. The complex shadows cast by the skylight and black stainless steel light fixtures didn't come cheap.

"How may I help you?" she asked. I approached the counter. Made of glass block and lit from within by deep green lights, it spoke softly of cleverness and luxury and a dose of magic. The woman, roughly my own age but model skinny and with dangerously long fingernails, tilted her head slightly to one side.

"I have an eleven o'clock appointment with Bick Lewis." I gave her my name.

She lifted the phone receiver from a base

that had as many buttons and flashing lights as an aircraft cockpit. "You're welcome to have a seat."

I thanked her and ambled over to the waiting area, my shoes making a slight squishing noise on the hard floor. I eyed the copies of *Structural Engineer* and *Architectural Digest,* glanced at the leather and metal chairs, a sure trap for the unwary, and elected to stand.

"Hello, hello."

Yesterday I'd heard the same voice through a hundred and fifty miles of phone wire and had envisioned a well-rounded sixtyish man with oxford shoes, white shirt, and a red paisley tie to match the suspenders that hid beneath a black suit coat. The reality was a little different.

"Beth Kennedy, right?" A thin man, maybe thirty years old, pumped my hand. "Good to meet you, good to meet you."

The top of his head was in my direct line of vision. I looked down to see into his face.

"Thanks for meeting with me on such short notice."

"No problem." He whisked me through a low-ceilinged hallway lined with photos of what I assumed were buildings designed by Browne and Co. A few I recognized — a Chicago skyscraper, a Madison library —

but the palatial residences were just blurs on my vision.

"Here we are, here we are." Bick ushered me inside an office. As I gingerly sat in a twin of the lobby chairs, Bick spun around a leather monstrosity and plopped down. Inside the huge chair he looked like a small child in his father's office.

"D'you mind?" He held up a pipe and a pouch of tobacco.

"You're allowed to smoke in here?"

He grinned. "Partners get privileges. Yes, yes, I know. How does an undersized, pipe-smoking punk make partner of one of the largest architectural firms east of the Mississippi? Well, it ain't my innovative designs." He started stuffing his pipe with tobacco. "And it ain't my engineering expertise."

"Then what is it?" What could matter more than architecture at an architecture firm? It'd be like a doctor not knowing how to diagnose shingles. Or a children's bookstore owner not knowing the plot of *The Indian in the Cupboard*.

"I'm the best rainmaker they've ever had." He ripped a paper match out of a matchbook, and a small flame flared. The stink of sulfur wafted by as Bick held the match close to the pipe's bowl and puffed furiously. A small cloud of smoke billowed

331

around his head. He opened another desk drawer and set out a plastic rectangular box the size of a four-slice toaster. It whirred into motion, and the smoke was sucked into a vent.

Bick caught my lifted eyebrows. "Compromise, compromise," he said. "I can smoke if I use this little guy. It's not the same, though." He looked around the room. It was the size of a small master bedroom. "There's nothing like a room filled with pipe smoke."

"No doubt."

His laugh was as deep and rich as his speaking voice. If he sang, it'd be a low bass. "Are you married?" he asked.

I looked at my empty left ring finger. Taking off those rings had been one of the hardest things I'd ever done. The sudden and overwhelming sense of failure had taken me by surprise. I'd been prepared for sorrow, but not for such a stunning sense of disappointment in myself. So much for those vows I'd taken for life. I'd meant every word, every syllable, and now I was raising two children by myself. Where had I gone wrong? What was wrong with me?

My voice didn't want to work, but I coughed it loose. "Why would you guess I'm not married?"

"Not a guess, not a guess." He aimed the

pipe's stem at me and, for the first time, I took note of the intelligence in his face. "Facts. You and your husband divorced last year. You own a bookstore. You became the Tarver PTA's secretary a month ago."

I stared at him. Half of me was annoyed at what felt like a personal invasion; the other half was impressed. A tiny portion was flattered, but I stomped hard on that part. "I called yesterday afternoon at three thirty. How do you know all that?"

"Did my homework." He blew a lazy smoke ring.

Hal the surveyor had been right; Bick was sharp. "Did you do your homework on the Tarver Elementary School addition?"

Another smoke ring. "Ask me a question about Tarver Elementary, any question."

"What year was it built?"

He gave me a slitted glance. "The original school or the one built after the explosion?"

"What explosion?"

"One score for me." He held up his index finger. "The original building was completed in 1930. A disgruntled janitor dynamited the place in 1947. The guy wired dynamite all through the crawl space and set it off by touching together two exposed wires."

Horror fluttered in my heart. "Tell me he

333

didn't do that during school hours."

"No, no. July. They rebuilt the new school on the same spot. No crawl space, though." His cheeks sank deep as he drew on the pipe. "That particular barn door is locked tight."

I tried to shake away a sight I'd never seen. "An explosion. I can't believe I've never heard about it."

Bick shrugged. "Long time ago."

Next time I saw Auntie May in her wheelchair, I'd ask her about it — if she didn't run me over first. "Why is there a step between the early-elementary wing and the main hall?" A ramp had been added to allow the building to be handicapped accessible, but I'd always wondered why the step existed.

"Builder error," he said promptly. "They were in a hurry to get the school built, so they started laying block at both ends. When they met in the middle, things weren't quite right."

"You're making that up."

"Construction isn't about getting everything right. It's about how to best cover up your mistakes."

"I didn't need to know that."

He smiled. "Then go back to thinking I made that part up."

"I will. Last question," I said. "Who put up the money for the Tarver addition?" My heart thudded against my ribs. Please, let him tell me. Please, don't let Marina get hurt. Please . . .

His sharp gaze focused tight and drilled into me. "Hmm." He puffed on his pipe, blowing tiny smoke signals into the air. I tried not to squirm under the intensity and failed miserably. He blew a big puff, took the pipe out of his mouth, and asked, "How about dinner tonight?"

"I . . . I'm sorry. What did you say?"

"Never mind, never mind." He studied his pipe. "The money for Tarver. Interesting question." We both watched the smoke for a minute. I wondered if Native Americans truly had sent up smoke signals, or if the whole thing was a Hollywood invention.

"Why," Bick asked, "do you want to know?"

I spouted out what I'd told Hal the previous day — member of the PTA, wanted to be responsible, blah, blah, blah. My explanation tailed off. "And that's about it."

Bick's focus tightened even closer. I kept up the stare-down for almost a full second before looking away. He didn't believe a word of it. And here I'd thought the ability to detect lies was a Mom Skill.

"Actually, I have no idea where the money came from," Bick said. "Agnes never gave out more information than necessary."

Was there such a thing as architect/client confidentiality? As with attorneys and priests? I'd never heard of it, but there were many things I didn't know and even more things I didn't understand — golf handicapping, for one.

Bick pulled out a lower desk drawer and propped his foot up. The look projected comfort and ease, but I detected small vertical lines between his eyebrows, lines that hadn't been there earlier. "So," he said, "have you heard anything? I talked to Mack Vogel last Thursday, and he said the board was going to bring it to a vote this week."

"Bring what to vote?"

"The project." He spoke slowly, as if to a child. "The Tarver Elementary addition, remember it?"

Ah. So this was why I'd been invited into the inner sanctum on such short notice. Old Bick wanted to continue to be the company rainmaker, and he was feeling parched. "You said you're not here for your design skills, but did you design the Tarver addition?"

Bick took the pipe out of his mouth and howled with laughter. "Me? Design that?

Even *I* couldn't design something that ugly."

"You don't like it?"

He snorted out twin plumes of smoke; a small dragon in disgust. "Not me, not Browne, and definitely not Browne. That thing is a travesty."

My mouth opened and closed a few times before I found the traction to get going. "Your firm didn't design it?"

Another twin snort. "We provided three preliminary designs, but Agnes rejected them all. She had her own ideas."

I smiled. Sounded like Agnes.

"We told her we'd design anything she wanted, but who knew she'd want something that atrocious? Couldn't change her mind an inch." He shrugged. "But who's going to turn away a paying client? A school job with no bond issue to pass? Project sent from heaven." He made a face. "And except for the execrable taste of one particular person, it would have been."

"Where were the invoices sent?" I asked.

"No, no." Bick shook his head. "He who doesn't pay the bills doesn't get that information. And it wouldn't do you any good, anyway."

I turned that over in my mind, but I couldn't make sense of it. "You asked if I knew whether or not the project was a go-ahead."

Though Bick didn't twitch, I could see invisible antenna springing forward at full attention. "Yes?" he asked.

"Actually, I have no idea." Take that, Mr. Won't-Share-Information.

He froze, then pointed the pipe stem at me. "How about lunch?"

Mack Vogel, superintendent of the Rynwood School District, was an imposing presence. As a church elder, he often read the Scriptures, his wide voice filling the sanctuary, long arms waving with emotion. More than one small Rynwoodite grew up with the vague notion that Mr. Vogel was the image of our Heavenly Father.

Fallen leaves swirled around my ankles with a noisy rattle as I trod up wooden porch steps and knocked on a front door that had been opened by Vogels for more than a century. The wind had shifted from a warmish south breeze to northwest gusts that were sneaking down my neck and up my pant legs. I stuck my hands in my pockets and shivered. It was time to get out winter coats and warm hats and fat boots the kids wouldn't want to wear.

I knocked a second time, then looked

around at the home Mack and Joanna and their four children had taken over when his parents had moved to Florida. After they'd finished roofing, replumbing, rewiring, plastering, and painting, they rested for two weeks and then started landscaping.

In peak season, roses climbed arbors, day-lilies bloomed against picket fences, and creeping thyme planted between the bricks of the walkways perfumed the air. It was a showpiece, and Mack and Joanna gladly opened their house and grounds for fund-raising events, small concerts, and weddings.

Today, though, withering stems and spent flowers were turning the landscape into a forlorn wasteland. A few hardy mums were trying to perk things up, but leaves were floating down even now to cover them.

The front door opened and the early-evening sun lit Mack's face. "Oh. Hello, Beth." His normally resonant voice was flat. "What can I do for you?"

"Hi, Mack." I frowned. "Are you okay?"

"I'm fine. Would you like to come in?"

He didn't look fine — fatigue was written in the dark bags under his eyes and in the set of his mouth — but who was I to disagree with the school superintendent?

Mack led me inside, and he stood in the

middle of the living room, looking at the piles of newspapers and magazines and mail that covered every flat surface. His breathy sigh was full of weariness. "Just toss something on the floor. It doesn't matter."

Those last three words told me that something was truly, deeply wrong. Before today, I'd assumed the Vogels' house repelled disorder with some sort of magical power. Never once in the multitude of functions I'd attended there had I ever seen a speck of anything even resembling dirt. "Um, is Joanna here?"

His eyes looked glassy, then wet, and then, to my shock, he started crying. His shoulders shook in great heaving sobs, and he covered his face.

I stood stock-still. It wasn't a simple wink-out-a-few-tears kind of cry; it was a full-blown bawl. His face was red and twisted and old. "Jo-Jo-anna," he kept repeating, her name coming out in small gulps. "Jo-Jo-anna."

The cowardly parts that made up the majority of my body desperately wanted to flee. They wanted to pat Mack on the shoulder, say I'd come back at a better time, and run away fast.

The silvery ring of a handbell trickled down the stairs. Mack groaned. "I can't do this anymore." He swayed, a tall tree beginning its slow topple to the forest floor.

I took a fast step forward and shoved a chair behind his knees. "Sit." I pushed down on his shoulders, and he sank fast onto the velvet upholstery.

The bell tinkled again. "You sit," I said. "I'll go up."

Faster than a striking snake, he reached up to grab my hand. "Thank you," he said. I squeezed back and slid out of his grasp. At the bottom of the stairway, I put my hand on the acorn newel post and looked across the room. Mack sat loosely, looking as if he'd forgotten how to use his muscles.

I was getting a very bad feeling about this.

The small tinkling bell sounded again. I took a deep breath for courage and went up. At the top of the stairs a six-paneled oak door stood slightly ajar. I sucked in another breath and knocked. "Joanna? It's Beth Kennedy. May I come in?"

"Beth?" Her voice sounded strong and vibrant. "What are you doing here? Come the heck in. If I have to spend one more day in this bed without seeing anyone other than Mack, I'm going to go stark raving mad." She laughed. "If I'm not already."

From a Garden Club tour I remembered a brass bed covered with quilts and brightly colored pillows, lace sheer curtains at the bay window, a watercolor landscape of a country garden, a wood floor cushioned with an Aubusson rug. All that was gone. In their place were a hospital bed, stark white shades, and a wide collection of medical charts and graphs.

I stared at Joanna, at the naked windows and floors, at the charts littered with images that told me exactly what was going on. "You're . . ." I couldn't say the word. Maybe I was wrong. Maybe I was inferring an incorrect conclusion. Maybe I was —

"Pregnant," Joanna said cheerfully. "That's me."

"But . . ." The words crowding into my mouth couldn't be said out loud.

"But I'm forty-nine years old." She grinned. "Yah. Who would have guessed?"

"Um . . ." It felt like years since I'd finished a sentence.

"I felt weird, but I figured it was hormonal stuff. Menopause, whatever. I finally went to the doctor because I was throwing up in the mornings." Joanne giggled. "She took one look at me and asked, 'Have you been taking your birth control pills?' Lo and behold, I'd run out for a few weeks, busy hosting three weddings this summer and seven concerts. Never once thought about getting pregnant. I'm almost fifty years old, for heaven's sake!"

I dragged over a chair and sat down. "What do your children think?" One of the girls and both boys were married, and the younger girl was away at college. I tried to imagine my own mother getting pregnant when I was in my twenties and couldn't do it.

"Haven't told them yet. Been too busy with bed rest."

"From now until the end?"

"You bet. My doctor is worried about a miscarriage. Guess the rate goes way up when the mommy is more than forty. I'm stuck here for the duration." Smiling, she flung out her arms. "Nothing to do for months and months."

My knees knocked together, and I put my hands on them to keep them still. I'd felt old giving birth to Oliver when I was thirty-three. Joanna would be fifty when the baby was born. Fifty!

"Poor Mack is frantic." She chuckled. "He's got a bug about keeping this room germ-free. I'm surprised he didn't make you put on a gown and mask before coming up."

"How far along are you?"

"Two weeks into the second trimester. The morning sickness is already gone, thank goodness. That gives me only five and a half months of lolling around in bed." She looked sad for a moment, then perked up. "But that's five and a half months I don't have to polish Vogel furniture, dust Vogel knickknacks, vacuum old Vogel floors, or wash the glass on the front of Vogel pictures. Have you ever taken a close look at Mack's great-grandmother?" She shuddered. "With a face like that, I'm amazed there were any more Vogels at all."

"I'll try and remember to look."

"Don't get me wrong." She pleated the white sheet that lay across her chest. "I love this house. Keeping it in the family is important to me. But you know something?" She looked up at me, her face earnest. "It consumes me. I could do with a break."

Having a baby seemed like an extreme way to get out of housekeeping, but I kept that thought to myself.

"Honey?" Mack knocked on the door. "Joanna? Are you all right?"

Joanna grinned at me. "Mack?" she called in a faint voice. "Is that you?"

The door creaked open, and Mack's mostly white head of hair came inside. "Dinner's almost ready." He spoke with a sickroom voice. "Broiled chicken, rice, and a spinach salad. I'll have the tray here in ten minutes."

She held up a trembling hand. "Could I have noodles instead of rice?"

His frown came and went in an instant. "You can have anything you want. It'll take a few extra minutes, though."

She sighed and turned her head away. "Never mind. It's too much trouble."

"No!" His voice bounced off the room's many hard surfaces. "No," he said more quietly. "It's not too much trouble." He came to the bed, kissed her forehead, and left.

"I'd like rice just fine," Joanna whispered. "But I like the idea of Mack washing extra dishes even better." She gave an exaggerated wink.

After I'd said good-bye, I went down to the kitchen. The room, which I'd always seen with shiny copper kettles hanging from hooks and decorated with flower-filled earthenware vases, was a disaster. Dirty pots filled the sink, dirty dishes cluttered half the counters, and lumpy grocery bags crowded the other half.

Mack was standing at the sink, trying to fill a pot with water. Since the sink was overflowing with dishes, he was filling a glass with hot water and dumping it into the pasta pot, over and over and over.

"I'll have to cook another chicken breast," he said dully. "This one will be dried to leather by the time the pasta is done." He dumped a last glassful into the pot and lugged it over to the cooktop.

I looked at him, at the kitchen, at him, at the kitchen. Then I rolled up my sleeves and started running hot water into the sink. "Sit down," I said. "Eat that chicken and rice while the water is heating."

"I can't do that."

"Why not?" I opened the cupboard door and rummaged around for dish soap.

"Joanna hasn't had dinner yet."

"It's silly to let food go to waste," I said. "And how long has it been since you've eaten? Did you have lunch?"

"I'm not sure."

"Eat something. You're not going to be any help to your wife if you keel over in a dead faint."

Irresolute, he stood, the pot top in one hand. The other hand, without anything to do, wandered around aimlessly, plucking at a shirt button, tugging on a belt loop, finally coming to rest at his side. "She needs to eat," he said.

I tried to match this battle-fatigued husband with the decisive school superintendent I'd known for years. Again my imagina-

tion came up short. "You need to eat, too."
I found a dish mop behind a tottering stack
of glasses. "I'll wash; you eat."

"The dishwasher is broken," he said.

"Eat," I commanded.

The top went on the pasta pot with a clat-
ter. "I should eat something," he said.
"Maybe I'll have that chicken in the broiler
and the rice Jo didn't want."

I closed my eyes for a moment and
counted to ten. Which wasn't enough, so I
counted to twenty.

The ostensible head of the house took a
clean plate out of my hand, dried it, and
filled it with food. Still standing, he started
to eat. I left him alone and went on with
washing dishes. By the time I'd filled the
dish strainer, he'd polished off the entire
meal. I found a dish towel. "Joanna says the
kids don't know about sibling number five."
I held out a dry cookie sheet.

"Really?" He took the offering. "Oh. Well,
I suppose they don't. Maybe I should have
them over for Sunday dinner."

Past Sunday dinners would have included
a roast, mashed potatoes, a vegetable, fresh
rolls, a Jell-O salad, and some sort of home-
baked dessert — all cooked by Joanna.
"Maybe," I said, "you could have them over
on Saturday. Order pizza."

"Saturday?" A look of revolted surprise crossed his face. "But it's always Sunday dinner. Joanna makes —" He stopped, seeing the impossibilities inherent in his assumptions.

"It's going to be different," I said softly.

He stared at the frying pan I'd just handed over. The shiny bottom reflected a warped view of Mack's face. "I'm going to be a daddy again," he said. "At my age. Just think of it." A slow smile spread across his craggy features.

I smiled back at him. "Congratulations, Mack."

"A daddy," he said in wonder. He laughed, and I decided to stop worrying about the Vogels. Joanna would eventually tire of being waited on hand and foot, and their children would take one look at the wreck of the house and make sure Mack got some assistance.

"So," Mack said, "how can I help you?"

I carefully dried a wire whisk. Right. I hadn't stopped by to wash Vogel dishes. I thought back to what Bick had said. "I was wondering if the school board had made any decision about Tarver's addition."

"Is it still going to happen, is the question, correct?" Mack took the whisk. "The board was scheduled to meet yesterday." He waved the whisk around like a conductor's baton, convening meetings left, right, and center. "Joanna's situation delayed the meeting. It is rescheduled for next Tuesday. As a Tarver parent and the secretary for the Tarver PTA, you will no doubt be notified when the decision is made."

Yup, Mack was feeling better. Pontification galore. "Do you have any feel for how the vote is going to go?"

"As superintendent, I am obliged to keep meeting proceedings confidential until the votes have been cast and tallied."

A plethora of pontification, but those were just warm-up questions. "Who's funding the addition?" I asked. "All I ever heard was that it's an anonymous donor."

"Ah." Mack held the whisk at attention. "That question I *can* answer. The Ezekiel G. Tarver Foundation has agreed to pay for the entire project."

The paring knives I was drying rattled against each other. "Who," I wondered out loud, "is Ezekiel G. Tarver?"

Mack looked at me pityingly. "Dear Beth. It's the proper name of Tarver Elementary. Look at the sign near the front door next time you drop your children off at school."

Maybe I didn't know who Ezekiel was, but I did know it would be silly to insult anyone holding sharp objects. I felt the heft of a wooden handle and thought that maybe Joanna would play the Helpless Pregnant Wife for quite some time.

CHAPTER 16

Lois hummed as she realphabetized the picture books. The songs being hummed had bounced between "Stars and Stripes Forever" and "Take Me Home, Country Roads" for twenty minutes. "Why," she asked, "do we have five copies of *If You Give a Moose a Muffin?* Two I can see, even three, but five? Is Marcia doing the ordering again?"

"No." I adjusted my legal pad. No sense in letting the sharp gaze of my manager see the list.

"Have you thought about Christmas books yet?"

I looked at the crossed-off names. One single solitary name was left. "Not really." There had to be more names. There just had to be.

"Are you okay?" Lois squinted at me. "You seem even more distracted than usual. The kids okay?"

"Fine."

"Have you introduced them to that handsome hunk of maleness yet?"

"No."

"Are you sick?"

"Not since last winter," I said vaguely. More names. We needed more names. I only wished I knew how to get them. What came next when an investigation was at a dead end? Maybe I should page through some Nancy Drews for some ideas.

"Lois, do you know who Ezekiel G. Tarver was?"

"Sure. The school is named after him."

"But *why* is it named after him?" I'd developed all sorts of theories. Maybe he'd been a small-town bad boy but dragged himself out of the slop thanks to a dedicated teacher. Or maybe he was a World War I hero who died while saving his comrades-in-arms. Or maybe —

"He donated the property."

The prosaic reply deflated me. Once again, real life paled in comparison with my imagination.

"How's Marina these days?" Lois asked. "I haven't seen her in ages."

"She's been . . . busy." The night before we'd talked on the phone about what we should do next. I'd told her that Cindy,

Harry, and Joe Sabatini were off the list, I'd told her about the Tarver Foundation putting up the money for the addition, and I had wondered aloud what to do next.

"Money," she'd said. "It's always about money. We need to find out where all Agnes's money was going. She made good money, but didn't live like it. Maybe she was being blackmailed. If we got a look at her checkbook, I bet we could figure it out."

At that point Spot had bumped his head against my knee, his own personal signal for take-me-out-now-or-I'll-make-a-mess, and I'd had to hang up.

Now I was doodling dollar signs on the list and Lois was starting to hum "Oh, What a Beautiful Morning" at two in the afternoon.

Money. Did it make sense that Agnes was killed for money? School principals couldn't exactly afford charter planes and personal chefs. Not that some people wouldn't kill for a pair of shoes, but nothing had been taken from her house or the school during the break-in.

Again, I saw the stain on the living room floor. And again I remembered how Marina had noticed my reaction and pushed me out of the room until she'd done the cleaning herself. No one could ask for a better friend.

Lois dropped the mail on my desk. "Are you crying?"

"Don't be silly." I sniffed and rubbed my face. "An eyelash fell into my eye."

"Of course it did." She moved away, humming Fleetwood Mac's "Little Lies."

Erica couldn't have killed Agnes. She just couldn't. I started circling dollar signs. If money was the reason for Agnes's murder, what had happened to it? I didn't see how money from a foundation could have anything to do with her death.

An anonymous donor was going to fund the addition, but the donor was the Tarver Foundation. Hmm . . .

I went to the counter, pulled out the phone book, and dialed.

"Lakeview Animal Shelter, how may I help you?" a woman asked.

I introduced myself and asked about the donor who had funded their new building.

"It was an anonymous donation," she said. "No one knows who was behind it."

"Yes, I understand. But the checks had to come from somewhere." I tried to sound reasonable. Jovial, even. "Were the checks written by the Tarver Foundation?"

There was a long pause. "How did you know?"

I gave a broad and vague answer, then

hung up.

So. Two big projects, one foundation. I didn't know much about foundations, but I was pretty sure they could be funded by a large group or they could be created by a single person.

Somehow Agnes had been involved with the Tarver Foundation. Maybe the money-as-motive theory was workable. I might as well try it out because I didn't have diddly else to work with. Marina's blackmail theory seemed about as unlikely as her short-lived theory that Agnes was an embedded FBI agent. No, the only money involved was held by the Tarver (Ezekiel G.) Foundation, and the next step was clear.

Ick.

Lois noted my change of expression. "You look pale. Are you sure you're feeling okay? I know you normally only get sick in January, but I hear the new flu that's going around is a tough bugger."

I felt my cheeks with the back of my hand and was surprised at the chill. "Just hungry." Which was probably true, but any appetite was gone, because today was Wednesday. Tonight the kids would be with Richard, and I'd be free to do stuff.

The evening moonlight cast long, creepy

shadows. Dry leaves skittered across lawns and down sidewalks. The noise was loud enough to cover my footsteps and, I hoped, had covered the thunk of my car door shutting. Late October; a perfect night to do stupid things and scare myself out of my silly wits.

With cold, bare fingers I inserted the key into Agnes's back door. I stepped inside, shut the door, and stood in the kitchen, waiting for my eyes to adjust to the gloom. Turning on lights didn't seem like a good idea. The last thing I wanted was Marina to barge on over here, pound me with questions, then broadcast the answers all over her blog.

The house smelled stale and empty. I wondered who would live here next. Would the pink bathroom or the Minnesota Wild basement be the first thing to go?

After a few minutes of imagining new color schemes — warm earth tones in the bathroom, with the obvious choice for the basement being the green and gold of the Green Bay Packers — I could make out the dim outline of kitchen cabinets. Arms spread wide in the dark, I grandpa-shuffled across the linoleum and tripped when the flooring switched to carpet. Rats. Nancy Drew never seemed to run into problems like this. Of course, Nancy never had to go to the bathroom, either.

I went into the study and shut the door. Agnes had a tall wooden fence in the backyard that would hide any light that escaped around the thick curtains. Wouldn't it?

Shuffling again, I went across the hallway, grabbed a blanket that was folded across the guest bed, then spent an awkward couple of minutes in the dark, jamming it over and around the study's curtain rod.

When I flicked on the overhead light, the sudden brightness stung my eyes. There was a gap underneath the door, but I decided that not even eagle-eyed Marina could detect that small amount of light from across the street.

Even so, I turned on the desk light and flicked off the overhead fixture. I put my hand on the back of Agnes's desk chair, then paused. If there were ghosts, if Agnes was a ghost, would she haunt me for sitting here? I tried to imagine solid, no-nonsense Agnes as a ghost. She looked the same; just transparent.

I held out my hand, palm up. "Do you mind?" I asked. The imaginary ghost shook her head. Her lips, thin and colorless, moved, but I heard no sound.

"What's that?" I tipped my head. Lipreading was not one of my strong suits. Once again she spoke, and again I had no idea what she said. Most people wouldn't have imagined a ghost they couldn't manage to communicate with, but then again, most people would never have tried to make a go of a children's bookstore in a town with a population under ten thousand.

The imaginary Agnes ghost didn't look threatening, so I went ahead and sat in the wooden chair. As soon as I landed, the casters rolled fast across the hard plastic chair mat. "Whoops!" I grabbed the edge of the desk.

In her gravelly voice, my ghost Agnes said, *"Just oiled those wheels last month."*

Agnes had a sense of humor. Who knew? "Gee, thanks." My voice startled me. There I was, sitting at the desk of a murdered woman, hearing her imaginary ghost, and talking back to it.

I shook my head. "Get a grip," I said. There was a reason I'd sneaked back into this house, and frightening myself with made-up ectoplasm wasn't helping. I was here to snoop.

The desktop held a few books: two dictionaries; a thesaurus; a world almanac; two foreign-language translation dictionaries — English-Finnish and English-Czech. I puzzled over the foreign dictionaries until I remembered the hockey team's roster.

Other than the lamp and books, the only other thing on the desk was a worn leather desk blotter complete with calendar. I hunched down and looked for any indentations in the paper. In old movies, investigators were always finding clues via forceful penmanship, but I didn't see a thing. I ran my hand flat across the blotter. Still nothing.

The calendar was tucked into the blotter's triangular corners. My grandfather had often slid notes into corners like that. I flipped out October back through January.

Nothing.

I retucked the calendar corners. So much for doing stuff the easy way. I stared at the desk. The desk stared back. Maybe Agnes's ghost would help me out. "Don't suppose you want to just, you know, *tell* me about the Tarver Foundation?" I asked. "Simple things. I'm sure you have the answers. How old the foundation is, who sits on the board, where the money came from. Any of that would be great."

My lunchtime had been spent trolling the Internet, looking for information on the Ezekiel G. Tarver Foundation. Old Ezekiel popped up on a few genealogy Web sites —

he was quite the seed-sowing patriarch, and the G stood for Gunther — but I discovered absolutely zero about the foundation. Hence, my bizarre conversation with an Agnes I didn't believe in.

"How about it, Agnes?"

The ghost didn't reply.

"Well, how about an office location? That shouldn't be a secret."

Nothing.

"Did you hear the joke about the Dutchman and the canoe?"

Either she had and didn't think it was funny, or she didn't want to hear it. Not that she was there at all, but if she was . . .

"Get on *with it."*

"Fine," I snapped, and yanked open the skinny middle drawer. All the normal supplies were there, collected in tiny cups and lined up in rows — pencils, erasers, pens, paper clips, stapler, stamps. I looked at it with a small heap of jealousy on my shoulder. The closest I came to an orderly desk these days was when I visited the local office-supply store.

I pulled the drawer out as far as it would go, but the only interesting thing I found was a slide rule. Its leather case opened so easily, I wondered if Agnes actually used the thing. Which made sense — Glass Wax, powdered laundry detergent, slide rule.

Onward and downward.

The top drawer on the right held note cards, greeting cards, and stationery. Other right-hand drawers held mailing supplies, packaging tape, and maps of various states and cities.

It was in the left-hand drawer, the very bottom-left-hand drawer, that I finally found something. In retrospect, I should have looked there first. The only twenty-twenty vision I had was hindsight.

The bottom-left-hand drawer was a file drawer, crowded with colored folders and black ink with handwritten block letters labeling each one.

I started reading labels. Red folders were for telephone, water, electricity, garbage. Behind those were yellow folders — plumber, dry cleaning, newspaper, health insurance, life insurance.

Behind the yellow folders was a set of green ones. I skipped over the listings of checking account and savings account folders and went straight to the pay dirt folder with its hand-printed label, "Tarver Foundation."

"Should have looked there first," Agnes said. Even her ghost was on the outside edge of tactless.

Imaginary ghost, I amended in my head. The fact gave me courage enough to talk back, something I wouldn't have done in a million years to the real Agnes.

I pulled out the Tarver Foundation folder and slapped it on the desk. "Your snide comments aren't helping, thank you very much." I flipped open the folder as I talked. "Did you ever think that maybe your attitude is what got you killed? If you'd been a nicer person, maybe I wouldn't be pawing through your desk tonight."

The top paper was an invoice from Browne and Browne for an eye-popping sum. "What was wrong with you, anyway? Okay, your husband dumped you after a year. So what? You had half a lifetime to get over it." The second paper was from Bick and outlined the proposed construction schedule. "Are these the papers that are going to tell me who the killer is? I certainly hope so, because —"

Darkness descended. Before I could think much beyond "Hey!" the dark was followed by a warm, heavy weight. A wide band circled my neck; I couldn't talk, couldn't breathe, couldn't think. I reached through the blanket to grab away the pressure and felt hands — large and strong ones.

"Do what I say and you live," said a low

whisper.

Another option would have been nice, but I didn't think it was going to be offered.

"You going to fight?"

My instincts warred between the atavistic urge to claw at the hands that held me and fear for Jenna and Oliver. If I was killed, what would happen to them?

"No," I said aloud, though it sounded more like a croak. The tight collar around my neck made it hard to say anything. "No," I said again. "No fighting." I let go of his thick hands.

"Up," he commanded.

Fear banged around in me, knotting my stomach, and shortening my breath. I was used to fear; we mothers know all about how that emotion weasels into the fabric of our life, coloring every action and decision with a rim of red. We're afraid of getting our kids vaccinated; we're afraid of not getting them vaccinated. We're afraid of pushing them too hard, afraid of not pushing them hard enough. We're afraid of car accidents, bicycle accidents, skateboard accidents. We're afraid of colds, flu, and every type of cancer that hits the news.

"What are you going to do?" I asked.

Going to do with me, is what I really meant. Where was he taking me? Was it going to be unpleasant, painful, and/or cold? Was I going to be shoved into Agnes's refrigerator and have the door shut on me? "She was alive last time I saw her," he'd be able to say truthfully.

"Shut up." His fierce whisper carried a threat that lifted the hair on my arms. He meant what he said.

I nodded. "Up," he said again, and this time I stood. So much for all those articles that cautioned against following the orders of an attacker. Point B was always more dangerous than Point A, but in this case Point A wasn't exactly a place of safety and sunshine.

We moved out of the study and started an awkward walk down the hall. With one of his hands on my neck like a firm collar and his other hand tight on my upper arm, our feet kept banging into each other.

For a short moment I debated tripping him intentionally. The scenario played out in front of me like a movie. Potential victim is marched down a hallway, sees an opportunity, trips the evildoer. Evildoer does not release grip on victim as he falls, but he hangs on to the frail neck and uses victim to cushion his crash to the floor. Evildoer's elbow jabs into victim's abdomen, knocking the wind out of her.

Without breath, she cannot run. Without breath, she cannot even scream as Evildoer, in a rage at her efforts to escape, squeezes her throat until there are no more breaths.

So much for that plan.

"Keep moving."

He pushed me, and I moved forward. It seemed unlikely that he'd lead me straight into a wall, but my experience with bad guys was minimal. The closest I'd come to witnessing a felonious assault was in a parking lot after a Northwestern vs. Wisconsin football game.

"Oh . . ." I stumbled forward a step and was jerked back upright by Iron Grip. Choking and gasping, I regained my footing and realized the flooring had changed from carpet to linoleum. We'd made it to the dining area, and I'd tripped over the little piece of trim that kept the carpet in place.

Don't kill me, I pleaded silently. My children needed me. My bookstore needed me. My siblings needed me — or they might one of these days. My mother would be disappointed at having to plan a funeral for a single daughter. My cat would miss me, the dog will be sent back to the animal shelter, and who would volunteer to be the PTA's secretary?

Inside my blanket, which was getting

warm and steamy from too many of my breaths, I looked at my last thought. Did the role really mean that much to me? I'd taken it on, thinking I could retire permanently after a year, but there was so much to do. The afternoon Erica had stopped by to give gardening advice, we'd come up with a dozen projects. A year wasn't enough; two years wouldn't be enough. If I wasn't careful, I'd end up like Randy, a lifer on Tarver's PTA committee.

If I had a life.

I stood up a tiny bit straighter. He pinched my neck hard, and I sank back down again. Okay, if I couldn't act brave, I'd try to think brave. Be smart. Pay attention. Pick up clues. Do something useful. All those mysteries and thrillers I'd read must have some practical application. Jack Reacher would have overpowered Iron Grip in an instant, so he wasn't much use as my role model. Best to stick to my own gender. What would V. I. Warshawski have done in my situation? Sharon McCone, Tess Monaghan, Anna Pigeon? Harriet Vane? Even Miss Marple would be doing *something*.

That was it: Miss Marple. She'd be noticing things. I could do that. And why hadn't I already?

I wasted half a step in self-recrimination,

then tried to pay attention. Was he wearing any cologne? Washed with a scented soap, used a perfumed deodorant, had garlic for dinner? I sniffed quietly. Nothing.

Sight was no good with a blanket over my head, so what was left? Taste, but all I could get was the metallic and slightly bloody taste of adrenaline.

"Stop," he whispered.

Sound. I could hear. And touch. Maybe I'd be able to sneak a feel of his clothing or even him. How long was his hair? Did he have a beard or mustache?

A door creaked open. "Down the stairs," he said. The last *s* slid into a hiss. I was sure that *s* would haunt my dreams for years — assuming that I had years left to me.

"Down," he whispered.

I edged forward until the front ends of my shoes curled down over air. Through the blanket I felt for the handrail. The grip was slippery, but I gained a small sense of comfort from the rail's existence.

Down one stair. Down another. When I had both feet on the third stair, the door slammed shut behind me. I whirled around and almost fell down the rest of the stairs. I started to shout, but the memory of his threat kept me from calling out. Maybe he hadn't meant it, but maybe he had.

I heard the screech of heavy furniture being slid across linoleum. It screeched closer and closer until it thumped against the basement door. I was blocked in.

Now what?

I went up a step, then retreated a step. What could I do when I was virtually blind? The blanket over my head was so thick —

There are those rare days when a stroke of genius strikes you like a bolt out of the blue and you bask in the glow of smartness. This wasn't one of those days.

I pulled the blanket off my head.

But even blanket-free, I was still surrounded by mostly dark. I felt around for the light switch, and brightness burst around me. Instantly, I felt better.

I listened to Iron Grip move around the house, opening and closing doors, and tried to figure out what he was doing. His movements didn't make any sense — not at first, anyway. He had a mission; I was just too dumb to understand.

He'd been looking for the electrical panel. One loud click and I was plunged back into a deep and endless darkness.

CHAPTER 17

I went all the way downstairs, found a chair, and spent some time scolding myself. If I'd worn spike heels, maybe I'd have had the presence of mind to do a rapid double-stamp backward on Iron Grip's insteps, send him into fetal-position pain, and run as fast as I could to Marina's house.

For a moment I let myself dream that dream. Brave Beth, using her wits to escape her captor, bring a killer to justice, and return peace of mind to Rynwood.

Hah. Maybe men could maintain fantasies like that. Most women had a firmer grasp on reality. I recalled a bit from a long-forgotten comedian. Girls read superhero comic books as the stories they are; boys read comic books and consider the superhero's job a career option.

I wondered what Iron Grip had in mind for me. Then, and only then, did I start wondering why he was here in the first place. As an amateur sleuth, I was making an excellent divorced mother of two.

If I made the mental leap that Iron Grip had killed Agnes, why on earth would he have come back to the scene of the crime three weeks later?

If he'd wanted to steal something, surely he would have done his thieving the night he'd killed Agnes. He wouldn't have been trying to retrieve something he'd accidentally left behind at this late date, would he? What could he have been looking for? Or in the grammatically correct version of my thoughts, for what could he have been looking?

Heavy footsteps thudded over my head, and I was suddenly and fiercely glad I'd cleaned out the kitchen. He wasn't going to be drinking or eating anything Agnes had bought. I made a mental note to call Gloria about turning off the water and electricity, assuming I got out of the basement, of course.

I spent a few unhappy moments speculating on Iron Grip's plans. I imagined a flowchart. The oval at the top of the chart was the question, "Is he going to kill me?" The "yes" arrow went to the right to a diamond-shaped object around the question, "Tonight?" There should have been more diamonds and arrows leading away from the Tonight box, but even in my head I lacked the courage to draw them.

Going back up to the "Is he going to kill me?" oval, I drew a "no" arrow.

I liked this arrow a lot better.

It ran into a diamond with the question, "Is he going to let me go?" The "yes" arrow went to "When is he going to let me go? Like, tonight, before 8:30? Because the kids always call me before they go to bed." A yes answer to that seemed unlikely, so I returned reluctantly to the other path leading away from "Is he going to let me go?"

Because, really, why would he set me loose? No one would think to look for me in Agnes Mephisto's basement — not until it was much too late. I hadn't left a note labeled "In case I don't return by Thursday morning, look for me at Agnes's." If I were a character in a movie, viewers would have long ago labeled me as TSTL — Too Stupid to Live.

"Am not," I said quietly, sounding like a nine-year-old.

Above my head and to the left, I heard the thumps and slams of drawers slamming and objects dropping. It sounded as if he were doing what I'd been doing — going through Agnes's files. I almost wished

Agnes's ghost weren't imaginary. I nearly smiled thinking of the tongue-lashing Agnes would have given the man who'd killed her.

After an eternity and a half, Iron Grip's footsteps thumped into the dining area. I followed his path around the table and chairs; past the kitchen counter; through the kitchen; past the door to the basement; out the back door. After a small click as the door shut, there was silence.

Or, rather, relative silence. In the sudden stillness, my panting, frightened breaths sounded louder than Oliver's raspy breathing the winter he'd had a bad case of the flu.

Was Mr. Grip gone? Or had he stepped out to his car for a weapon?

A shiver started deep in my bones. My teeth chattered as if the basement's temperature had dropped below freezing.

"Being scared isn't going to help you one bit."

Agnes — she was back in her ghost form to taunt me. "The suggestion box is open. All ideas are welcome."

"You have a brain, don't you? Use it."

"Not much of a suggestion," I muttered, but the spasms of shivering diminished to mild rattles, and I started thinking.

He wasn't coming back with a weapon;

with a grip like that, he didn't need anything else. If he wanted me gone, I would have been dead long since. Since I hadn't seen his face and hadn't heard his real voice, I was no threat to him.

Was he going to let me out of this basement?

"Why would he?" Agnes asked. *"Any additional contact with you increases the chances of your being able to identify him."*

Even Agnes's make-believe ghost was annoying. Everyone would be nice after death, wouldn't they? I pondered this for a moment, thinking about mean Mr. Orton from my childhood. He'd been a cranky old man who yelled at the neighborhood kids if they so much as looked in the direction of his pristine lawn. What would he be like in the afterlife? If he wasn't still mean, he wouldn't be Mr. Orton any longer, would he?

I abandoned that path of thought as too philosophical for my tiny little brain. My time would have been much better spent trying to get out of here. Why had I hidden my car so well? If I'd parked in a more visible location, Marina would have seen it and ridden to my rescue.

I wouldn't die here, would I?

And there it was again: the fear that made my breaths come fast and my stomach hurt, and undoubtedly shortened my life span.

Of course, I lived in constant fear. This was just on a higher plane. Once upon a time, Richard had started a list of the things that frightened me. He soon ran out of room on the kitchen notepad and went to the computer. I'd started with typical mother fears: that our children would meet with random accidents; that they'd be stricken with deadly disease; that a food I fed them would contain a toxic substance and cause irreparable damage, etc., etc.

Then I'd moved on to being afraid of tornadoes, of ice storms, of driving in heavy rain, of high winds, of global warming, of random asteroids ramming into our planet. Then came my fears of losing my children's love, of being crippled by arthritis, of breast cancer, of macular degeneration, of dying alone, of heart disease, of diabetes.

Richard had looked at me with concern. "Do you have a family history of diabetes?"

"Well, no."

He'd sighed, and I continued with the anxieties. That the Middle East would never know peace, that our country would be attacked by fanatics who'd cobbled together a hearty supply of nuclear warheads, that our children would inherit a world in which violence was the only realistic response.

Then there were the little nagging fears. That the car would break down and I'd be late dropping the kids off at school. That I'd forget one of Jenna's soccer games or swim meets or softball games. That by owning the bookstore I was damaging my children's psyches by not welcoming them with open arms and warm cookies when they came home from school.

I'd started mentioning my fears of dentist drills and stubbing my toe in the dark when Richard had rolled his eyes and turned off the computer. "How can you look so normal on the outside but be such a mess on the inside?" he asked. "Have you ever considered therapy?"

I'd tried to tell him that all women worried like this. It was part and parcel of being female. The estrogen made us do it, Officer.

Agnes made a snorting noise.

"Well, maybe not *all* women," I said.

A shiver climbed through my body, and I wrapped the blanket tighter around me. I deeply regretted that Marina and I had turned down the thermostat.

Somewhere out in the darkness lurked a murderer. He'd killed once, and though I didn't think he planned to kill me, how did I know? Any happy ending I'd hypothesized could easily be attributed to wishful thinking.

Somewhere out there my children were waiting to call their mother for a bedtime phone-kiss.

Oh, my sweet Jenna.

Oh, my darling Oliver.

"Now what do I do?" I asked the empty air.

"What do you think?"

I could wait and hope for rescue. It would come, eventually, but when? Or I could shout and scream and yell in hope that someone would hear me. But who? And even if someone heard something, would they think to call the police?

Maybe, just maybe, it was time to stop being afraid. An excellent idea. Why hadn't I though of it earlier? I said it out loud. "It's time to stop being afraid." Though I waited for Agnes to make a comment, she was quiet this time around.

But I still felt the fear licking at my ankles and threatening to run up my legs and into my heart where it would take hold forever.

Okay. If I couldn't stop being afraid, I could at least do *something*. If I were busy, maybe I wouldn't have time to be afraid. But before I did anything, I had to wait a little longer. Time played tricks on people.

My father had once collapsed at home from what turned out to be his first heart attack. Mom called 911 immediately and for weeks went on and on that it had taken the EMTs "at least half an hour!" to arrive. My sister Kathy finally called to check. The first responders had arrived in four minutes and thirty-eight seconds.

Since Mom had provided half my genetic material, the possibility of similar time expansion was strong. Even though it felt like hours since Iron Grip had left, maybe it was only five minutes. Maybe he was outside, waiting for Marina's neighbor to finish walking the dog.

Once again, I considered my options. Once again, I didn't come up with anything good.

I counted seconds in my head. One one thousand, two one thousand. Ten times I counted to sixty thousand. Ten minutes. The steady rhythm calmed me and cleared my mind. I counted out another ten minutes, then another ten. He'd been gone for at least half an hour — long enough. First things first, I decided.

"Help!" I yelled. "Hellllp!"

My shrieks brought no assistance. The night was too cold, the basement too soundproof, my screams the wrong frequency — for whatever reason, I was on my own.

"You had to try," Agnes said.

I nodded in the dark. "Would have been silly not to." It was nice to have some support, even if it wasn't real. "Do you have any ideas you'd like to share?"

But here she was silent.

Ah, well. It was probably best that I stopped talking to myself, anyway.

Once upon a time I'd carried a small pocketknife. Then one day, a small Jenna reached into my purse, dug out the knife, and pried out the knife's short, sharp blade. I'd immediately taken it away from her, thrown the knife in the wastebasket, and carried the wastebasket into the garage.

Too bad. Even a small knife would have been handy right now.

I banged on the door with my knuckles. Banged on it with the heels of my hands. Kicked at it with my toes. Kicked at it with my heels. Banged on it with my fists. All I got for my efforts was a nice collection of wood splinters.

That was when I started to cry.

I don't know how long I cried. I'd like to say it wasn't very long. I'd like to say only a tiny tear escaped before courage reasserted itself. I'd like to say the intrepid spirit of my homesteading ancestors surged forth and brought me strength and innovative ideas for escape.

What actually happened was that I sobbed long and hard enough to exhaust myself. Right there at the top of Agnes's basement stairs, leaning against the door, I fell asleep.

When I woke up, disoriented and with a stiff neck, I heard something. No, not something, but someone.

Iron Grip — he was back.

As quickly and as silently as I could, I tiptoed down the stairs. Faint moonlight washed through the windows — enough light to let me pick my way across the room. My breaths were rapid and shallow.

He was back. He'd come back to finish me off. What was I going to do? I had to defend myself somehow. There had to be a way.

I made my way to the workbench. Surely there'd be something here I could use. Too bad the workbench was in the darkest corner of this dark room. I need to find something sharp, something heavy, something . . . anything. . . .

Furniture screeched.

Wildly, I felt for something that would save me. And I had the element of surprise on my side, didn't I? He didn't know there were tools down here. Not that I was finding anything bigger than a screwdriver, but there must be something. . . .

More screeching. The door opened. Light bounced down the stairwell and onto the far side of Agnes's hockey memorabilia.

"Hello?" called a male voice. "Is anyone down there?"

I rushed across the room and my hands wrapped familiarly around the best weapon possible. I stationed myself on the darkest side of the stairs. When he came all the way down, I'd give him a good slash, then run up and out across the street to Marina's house and safety.

"Hello?" A heavy tread squeaked the top stair. "Is anyone here?" He came down one stair at a time.

His legs came into view. From my position I could see his leather belt, then his jacket, then his shoulders, and finally the back of his head. My hands tightened on my weapon. Head up, eyes intent on the goal, I swung the stick fast and high.

At the last second he turned, and I watched with horror as the curved blade of Agnes's autographed hockey stick sailed straight into the side of the unsuspecting head of Don the dry cleaner.

CHAPTER 18

"Beth!" Marina forced her way around two law-enforcement officers, jumped over a case of medical equipment, and ran to my side. "Beth! Are you okay? Tell me you're okay." The rotating lights of the ambulance and two police cars came through the living room windows and washed over us all, giving the scene a bizarre disco feel.

"I'm fine." I blessed Gloria for being lax in having Agnes's utilities turned off. My cell phone was in my purse, which was in my car. Luckily, Don had ducked away from the hockey stick and I'd barely landed a glancing blow. After he'd assured me that he wasn't hurt, I'd called 911, then called Richard's condo and talked to the children, getting a lecture from Richard beforehand on my irresponsibility of not being available when they'd called earlier and did I really expect him to wake them so I could say good night (to which the answer was, of course, yes). Then, as sirens broke the suburban quiet, I'd called Marina.

"What happened?" Marina's red freckles stood out sharp on skin turned white. "Don, what are you doing here?"

"Finally got those drapes done." Don nodded at the plastic-encased drapes hanging on a dining chair. "I've had them in the van for a couple days. I was driving past and I saw a light on, so I knocked. The door was unlocked, and there was Beth in the basement, swinging a mean high stick."

"What?" Marina looked at me blankly.

"I'll tell you tomorrow. One of Gus's young men" — I nodded at the officer in blue standing nearby — "is going to take me to the hospital."

"The hospital?" She put shaking fingers over her mouth.

"For a tetanus shot," I said patiently. "And to take out a few splinters. But who knows how long that will take, so I need a favor."

She dropped to her knees. "Anything. Just say the word."

I squinted at her. All I needed was a little shot. She was acting as if I'd had a near-death experience. "My car is behind the school. Can you drive it to the hospital and get your DH to pick you up?"

"No. I'll wait for you. I won't abandon

you in your time of need. I'll sleep in the waiting room if I have to. I'll sleep on the floor. I'll —"

"Ma'am, are you ready?" The EMTs helped me to my feet. A sudden and blinding headache reminded me of the damage Iron Grip had done to the back of my neck. There was no need to mention that tidbit to Marina.

"Beth." Marina moved to my side and touched my leg.

"I know. This place is a mess." Iron Grip had sliced open pillows, emptied bookshelves and cabinets, and strewn papers everywhere. "I'll take care of it later. You'll move my car, right?" I asked as the officer guided me toward the door. "Just drop the keys off at the front desk."

"But I don't *have* your keys," she wailed.

"I left them on the dining table."

"Beth . . ."

Whatever she wanted to say, she wasn't saying it fast enough. "I'll see you tomorrow," I called.

Then I was out in air cold enough for heavy frost. I looked up at the clearing sky and couldn't stop shivering as the officer opened the sedan door for me.

"It'll be warm in a minute," he said. "I'll have you toasty before you know it."

"Thanks." But I hadn't been shivering from the cold.

Both Gus and Deputy Sharon Wheeler interviewed me in the hospital. I'm sure they grew as tired of hearing my two standard answers as I did of saying them.

GUS: "Was there anything missing from the house?"

"I'm not sure."

DEPUTY WHEELER: "Can you think of anything about your attacker that would help us identify him?"

"Sorry, no."

DEPUTY WHEELER: "What time were you attacked?"

"I'm not sure."

GUS: "Did he leave in a vehicle? Did you hear a car start?"

"Sorry, no."

And so on and so forth. The Rynwood police department had jurisdiction over the break-in, but the sheriff's department was investigating anything connected with Agnes's murder. Why at least one of them couldn't wait until the next day to talk to me, I didn't know.

I was dirty, I was hungry, and I was growing immensely tired of the emergency room doctor's humming as he pulled tiny hunks of wood from my skin. It was barely past Halloween, but all the songs this impossibly young doctor hummed sounded like "Frosty the Snowman."

DEPUTY WHEELER: "Did your attacker say anything that led you to believe he killed Agnes Mephisto?"

"Sorry, no."

DEPUTY WHEELER: "Do you have any idea what he was looking for?"

"Sorry, no."

GUS: "Why were you there, Beth?"

"Sorry . . . oh." This was a question I should have been able to answer. "Um, well, Gloria — that's Agnes's sister — asked me to clean up the house. Marina and I did most of the work a couple of weeks ago, but there was some paperwork to do. I had a free night since the kids are with their dad on Wednesdays, so I took the opportunity and . . ." I was doing that babbling thing again. "And that's about it."

Gus and the deputy both made notations on their notepads.

Taking down the facts was all they were doing. I wasn't being arrested, and I hadn't done anything wrong. So why did watching them jot down my words make me feel guilty?

"I might be in contact for some follow-up

questions, Mrs. Kennedy," Deputy Wheeler said. "Thanks for your help." She nodded at us, then left.

"Help?" I crossed my eyes. "If I was helpful, I'd hate to see someone who wasn't."

Gus chuckled and slid his own pad into his coat pocket. "You were polite at least." He looked at the doctor. "How much longer?"

Still humming about Frosty, the doctor pulled out another splinter and dropped it onto a metal tray. "Ten minutes."

"Have you had any dinner?" Gus asked me.

"Not really, but —"

"I'll go down to the cafeteria and get you a sandwich. Then I'll drive you home." I started to object, but he overrode me. "No arguing. You try to drive like that and you'll be sorry tomorrow."

"Sure will," the doctor said cheerfully. "Tomorrow morning she'll be okay, but I hope you have an automatic transmission."

We ignored him. Long ago, in the back of the choir stalls, Gus and I had come to an agreement about Christmas carols before Thanksgiving: Anyone who forced them upon an unwilling world should be ignored as much as possible. "I'm driving you home," Gus said. "And I'll get one of the guys to drive your car back to your house."

"But I'm —"

"You're not fine," Gus interrupted. "For once, let someone help you."

Tears stung my eyes. I must have been more tired than I thought. "Okay," I whispered. "Okay."

The next morning personal hygiene was an exercise in frustration. The doctor had slapped gauze pads on the worst of the splinters. "Keep those dry for twenty-four hours," he'd said. What he hadn't said was how to manage that simple-sounding task. With gauze on both hands, I couldn't take a shower and I couldn't take a bath.

I ended up using a washcloth and kitchen gloves. I washed my hair in the sink, and by the time I put it up wet in a ponytail, I wanted to go back to bed. Who knew that a few splinters could make you so tired?

With one thing and another, I was half an hour late getting to the store. I came in the back door and hung up the coat I'd draped over my shoulders. "Sorry I'm late, Lois."

"Oh! My! Lord!" Lois dropped the armload of books she was carrying. "What happened? Did you — ? Are you — ?" She put her hands to her mouth.

"It's nothing. An accident." Kind of.

387

"Accident?"

"Yes," I said. "I was doing some cleaning at Agnes's house and you know how klutzy I can be. A picture fell off the wall and onto my hands, and the glass broke." I looked at the masses of gauze. The story had sounded better last night.

The front door burst open. Marina flew in, her red hair sticking out in a dozen directions. "Beth, it's all my fault you're hurt. I am so, so sorry." She flung herself onto me and drew me to her bosom. "How can I make it up to you?"

Lois looked from Marina to me and back again, then lifted her eyebrows. "Accident?"

My best friend snorted into my hair. "If you call someone overpowering Beth and tossing her into a basement an accident. If you call Beth using her wits to escape certain death an accident."

The future unfolded before me. Marina would spread the story hither and yon. A parade of people would traipse through the store, gawking at my wounds, begging me to tell the story over and over again. No one would buy a single book, and I wouldn't get a thing done.

I extracted myself from Marina's clutches. "Lois, can you watch the store?" I dragged Marina to my office and shut the door. "Tell me you didn't blog about last night."

"Not yet." She pursed her lips. "I'm trying to think of the best way to start it. How does this sound? 'Local business owner defies death.' Or how about 'Courageous Rynwood woman lives to fight another day.' Or —"

"Don't you dare post anything about this."

"Of course I won't. But just think if I did." Her cheeks glowed with color.

There was a knock, and Lois popped her head in. "Beth, there's a gentleman to see you."

Before I could tell her to send whoever it was away, Evan Garrett came in. "Good morning, Beth. Oh, sorry. I didn't realize you were in a meeting."

His gaze fell on my hands. "Oh, my God. Beth." He took hold of my shoulders and looked into my upturned face. "Are you all right?" He kissed my forehead, then pulled back and searched my eyes. "You're in pain, I can tell. Here." He hooked his foot around the leg of a chair and drew it near. "Sit."

"I'm fine," I said, pulling free of him. "Marina, this is Evan Garrett. Evan, Marina Neff."

They nodded, and Marina shot me a you've-been-holding-out-on-me look. "Evan and I," I said, "went to kindergarten together. He bought the hardware a few weeks ago."

"Kindergarten?" Marina's eyes narrowed to small slits, and I knew I'd be grilled later on.

Evan paid no attention to the feminine undercurrents swirling about. He was gently turning my hands this way and that. "How on earth did this happen? A car accident?"

Excellent idea. A car crash could explain all sorts of bizarre injuries. Anyone would believe a car crash story. This would work. All I had to do was convince Lois I'd been in a car accident, work on getting Marina to spread a car-crash story, and make sure Gus and Deputy Wheeler didn't release my name to the press. Piece of cake.

"Hah." Marina tossed her hair back. "This young lady was almost murdered last night."

"What?" Evan went still.

"Don't be ridiculous." Maybe sitting down wouldn't be such a bad idea. I groped for the back of the chair and sat. "If he'd wanted to kill me, I wouldn't be here now."

"What!" Evan's voice rose. "Who? Your ex-husband? Have you told the police? You'll need a restraining order." His former profession was rearing its legal head. "Let's go. The paperwork takes a while, but you'll be safer in the long run."

I wanted to drop my head into my hands, but I didn't want to undo the carefully taped gauze. Instead, I closed my eyes and wished they'd both disappear.

"It wasn't her husband," Marina said. "It was the guy who killed Agnes Mephisto."

"The school principal?" Evan looked from Marina to an unresponsive me, then back to Marina. "What's going on here?"

Marina launched into an extravagant version of what I'd done last night. Every time I tried to get her to stop, she overrode me. After three attempts, I quit trying. It was like trying to fight a tidal wave.

She concluded, "Beth made her way to a telephone and called 911."

I opened one eye. Evan was crouched in front of me, his mouth firmed into a straight line. "Why were you in Agnes's house?"

Trust a lawyer to get to the crux of the matter. "Cleaning up," I said lamely.

"No, you weren't." Evan touched one of my earlobes. It was burning hot. "What were you doing?"

I didn't say anything. Marina, for a change, didn't say anything, either.

"Are you two investigating the murder?" he asked.

I closed the open eye.

"You are, aren't you? Leave this to the

police," he ordered. "They're trained for it. They get paid for it. It's why we *have* police. Investigations into murder aren't for amateurs. You could get hurt."

No kidding.

"Beth." His courtroom-hard voice was suddenly soft. "Don't you see? I don't want you in danger. I care about you. Please leave this to the police." He cupped my cheek with his palm. "Please." His lips brushed my hair, and he left.

I opened my eyes in time to see Marina fold her arms. "Well, well, well," she said. "Isn't he the handsome one?"

"Don't start. All I've done is go to lunch with him a couple of times. He hasn't even met the kids yet."

"Really?" She put ten pounds of doubt into the two syllables. "He's acting awfully possessive for someone you barely know."

In some ways I barely knew him; in other ways I'd known him most of my life.

"For *uno momento*," Marina said, "he sounded like Richard."

I frowned. "He did, didn't he?" Matter of fact, he'd treated me like a bubbleheaded female who didn't have the sense to kick off her shoes if she fell into deep water.

"Um, you're not going to give up, are you?" Marina sounded unsure, scared, and small, and I longed to have my confident friend back.

Evan had assumed he could tell me what to do. And why? Because he was bigger and stronger and a lawyer? Hah. There was nothing lawyers could do that children's bookstore owners couldn't do better.

Give up? I looked at Marina. "Not a chance."

The doorbell of Agnes's house chimed. Spot leaped up from the living room floor and burst into a flurry of barking. "Nice job," I told him. "If Mr. Grip comes back and rings the doorbell, we'll have plenty of time to hide."

Standing on the front stoop was a stocky balding man. "Hi," he said. "I'm Pete Peterson of Cleaner Than Pete. You're Beth?"

At the hospital, Gus had given me the name of a Madison cleaning company that did forensic work. I'd called Gloria, squirmed as I'd told her most of the truth, and gotten her okay to hire someone to clean up the mess. "Sure, what do I care?" she'd said morosely. "Have them send the bill up here. It'll get paid when the lawyers get done lawyering."

"Yes." I stood aside and waved Pete in.

"Thanks for coming out on a Thursday night."

"No problem," he said. "Hey there, pup." He leaned over and ruffled Spot's ears. "What's your name, big guy?"

"Spot," I said.

Pete gave me a startled look, then laughed. "About time someone named a dog Spot. Don't suppose you have a Rover, too?"

"Just a cat. George."

"Good cat name." He gave Spot one last pat and straightened. If he'd stood as tall as he could, he might have been an inch taller than my five foot five. His gaze flicked to my hands, then back to my face. "What do you need help with?"

I gave him a bonus point for not asking any questions and showed him around the house. "It all needs cleaning, and I just don't have the time." Or the energy. "How long do you think it will take?"

He ran a critical gaze over the mess. "Three hours, tops. I can do it tonight, if you want."

"Will that cost extra?" I didn't want to spend any more of Gloria's money than I could help.

"Nah." He smiled easily, and I found myself smiling back. It was the first time I'd smiled all day.

"Sounds great," I said. "I'll be in the master bedroom if you have any questions."

My former splinters were aching as I tied up a garbage bag. "Almost done," I said to Spot. "One more room and we can pick up the kids." Despite their pleas to see Agnes's messy house, I'd left them with Marina and a new bag of gourmet popcorn.

"Ooo ave ids?"

I jumped, turned, and shrieked. In the door of the guest room stood a monster. White from head to toe, the lower half of its face was covered with —

Pete lifted off his hood and pulled down the respirator. "Sorry about that."

I put my hand to my chest. Heart still working, adrenaline still flowing — I was, in fact, alive.

"I always wear the hazmat — hazardous materials — suit when I'm working."

"Sure." I tried not to be offended that he was scared of my germs. "Safety first."

He flashed me a boyish grin. "Just wanted to tell you I'm all done out there." He jerked his thumb in the direction of the living room and kitchen.

"Great. Thanks."

He shuffled from one foot to the other. "I was surprised to hear you say something about kids."

My tired brain made a small leap. "This isn't my house," I said. "It's a friend's." Somewhere in the back of my head I heard a dry chuckle.

"Oh." Pete looked puzzled, and I realized that, though I'd given him one answer, I'd created a whole list of new questions.

"Do you want some help with that?" Pete gestured at the bulging garbage bag.

Reflexively, I started to refuse the offer, but then I thought of Gus's comment. "That'd be great. Thanks."

He took the bag. "I'll dump it in my van. No, not a problem. I rent a big Dumpster, and it's not even half full." With no obvious effort he lifted the bag, a weight I would have had to drag.

I took one last look around the bedroom and went into the study. Spot lay down in the doorway with a sigh. I waded through the mess, sat in the desk chair, and started flattening papers. A faint whistling grew louder and louder, turning into an off-key rendition of "I've Been Working on the Railroad."

Pete poked his head inside. "Whoa. You've still got quite a mess in here." He'd stripped off his white coverall and was back to khaki pants and denim shirt. "Do you . . . Um, I mean . . . would you like some help?"

I looked at him. He must have been sorely in need of business. Though I knew what that felt like, spending more of Gloria's money didn't seem right. "Well . . ."

"Off the clock, I mean," he said hurriedly.

"Oh." Now I was the puzzled one. Why on earth would he want to spend what was left of his evening helping a stranger tidy a room that wasn't even hers?

He interpreted the look on my face correctly. "I just like to clean things," he said, shrugging. "And if it's helping you or watching the Wild lose another hockey game, well, lead me to an empty garbage bag."

"We could do both." I nodded at a small television tucked into the end of a bookshelf. "And who says the Wild will lose? Their new goalie is hot right now."

Pete's face lit up. "A fan! Now I'm staying for sure."

With Pete's help and garbage-hauling expertise, we straightened up the room before the end of the first intermission. We parted amicably at the curb, with his climbing into his van and my crossing the street and walking up to Marina's house.

My children, up past their bedtime, were whiny. I gathered up their belongings while Marina pestered me for details. "Are you okay? Are you sure? How tall do you think that guy was last night? Do you remember anything? Did he take anything?"

Guiding a sleepy Oliver out the door, I told her I'd call her the next day. Once the kids were in the car and buckled in, I patted my coat pocket and felt the reassuring crackle of paper. I didn't know if Mr. Grip had taken anything or not. But I had.

After dropping the kids off at Ezekiel G. the next morning, I rushed back home. Some things are best done in privacy. "Please open at eight," I said, dialing the phone. "Please."

The phone rang two, three, four times. I looked at the paper I'd taken from Agnes's house and double-checked the number. No, I'd dialed correctly. I was about to hang up, when there was a click.

"Hunter Clinic, this is Brooke. How may I direct your call?"

"Um." The pat little speech I'd prepared vanished out of my head, gone away as if it had never existed. I knew I should have written it down. "Good morning, Brooke. My name is, uh, Gloria Kuri."

"Yes?" When I didn't instantly respond, she went on. "Are you a patient here, ma'am?"

"Oh." She started to say something, but I

jumped ahead. "No, I'm not a patient. My sister was."

"I see."

"My sister was Agnes Mephisto. She died more than three weeks ago."

"She did? I'm so sorry."

"Thank you." It dawned on me that Brooke had no clue Agnes had been murdered. "It's been hard on all of us." I made a sniffling noise. "I was wondering . . ."

"Yes?"

I detected sympathy, and my rehearsed speech swam back. "Agnes didn't want to trouble anyone with the details of her illness. She was so brave."

"I'm sure she was. The patients here amaze me."

When I'd come across an invoice in Agnes's files from the Hunter Center, a little buzz had set off in the back of my brain. The Hunter Center. The Hunter Center . . . At home, a Google search had yielded the information I'd expected, but not wanted, to see. Due to privacy laws, I knew Brooke wouldn't tell me anything specific, but maybe I'd find out enough. "We'd like to make a donation," I said, "and we want it to go to research."

"Lots of people donate to the American Cancer Society," Brooke said.

"We were hoping to send a check to a more specific organization." Agnes had been living with cancer. No wonder she'd been pushing so hard on the addition.

"Oh, I see what you mean. Let me see a minute." I heard the sound of a keyboard tap-tapping away. "Mephisto, Agnes?" Her voice went quiet. "I probably shouldn't say — you know how that HIPAA stuff goes — but I don't see how this could hurt."

"I won't tell a soul where I got the information. Cross my heart." And hope not to die.

"If I were you," she whispered, "I'd send my money to the American Brain Tumor Association. And I'm really sorry about your sister. I know she didn't have long, but this was really fast. She seemed like a nice lady."

Brain cancer. Poor Agnes.

I sat at my desk and stared out at the golden autumn morning. A few leaves hung tight to tree branches, swaying slightly to and fro. They were bright orange leaves, more brilliant by far than any leaves I'd ever seen.

Oh, Agnes.

There were places to go and people to see, but I sat there for a long while, mourning a woman I'd never known.

CHAPTER 19

"Are you seeing him or what?"

"Shhh!" I tried to hush Marina. We were sitting at the kitchen table, and Jenna and Oliver were with Zach in the Neff family room watching Saturday cartoons, but if so inclined, little pitchers did indeed have big ears.

"Why?" Marina continued at normal volume. "Is he some big secret?"

"Of course not."

"Then what's the problem?"

"There isn't one."

"Dear, dear Beth." Her voice took on a Southern drawl. "Ah can always tell when you're lying."

My fingers shot up to feel my earlobes.

Still in belle mode, Marina said, "He is remahkably handsome — yes, indeed, he is. But your brainy little head doesn't turn at mere good looks. Or does it?" Her eyebrows arched.

"I knew him in kindergarten."

"Yes, mah dear, you said so."

"Quit with the Scarlett O'Hara bit, will you?"

"Ooo, Beth is a little uptight this morning." Marina put her feet up on the chair next to her, an act she knew was guaranteed to make me edgy. "Problems sleeping? Maybe your pretty boy will come in handy, because I bet I know what you need. How long has it been?"

Some days it was best to ignore everything Marina said. "I owe you one for taking the kids." Thanks to Richard's unpredictable boss, I suddenly had my children two weekends in a row. Any other time I would have been delighted, but this weekend was different. "I'll call tonight at bedtime. Come give me a kiss, you two!" I called, pulling on my coat and picking up my purse. There was a long drive ahead, and time was ticking away.

"Don't go, Beth." Marina's face was serious. "Let me go instead. This is all because of me, and I shouldn't be letting you fight my battles."

In some ways she was right, but in other ways she was very wrong. It wasn't because of Marina's death threats that I was abandoning Jenna and Oliver for half the weekend; it was because of Agnes.

"I'll see you tomorrow." Then I kissed my children and left.

Two hundred miles later, my cell phone rang. Normally I didn't talk on the phone while driving, but since there were exactly zero cars to be seen on this particular stretch of U.S. 53, I decided to risk taking the call.

"Beth? This is Evan." Static punctuated his words.

"If I hang up on you," I said, "I didn't hang up on you. There aren't a lot of towers out here."

"Where are you? Never mind," he added quickly. "It doesn't matter. I called because I want to apologize for the other day."

"Apologize for what?"

"For acting as if I had any right to tell you what to do."

"Ah." Take that, Marina.

"You're angry at me and I don't blame you. We barely know each other, and I assumed control and did those guy things that make strong women want to swear off men forever."

If he thought I was strong, he really didn't know me at all.

"Let me make it up to you. How about

dinner?" He named one of the fanciest restaurants in Madison. "Soft lights, a piano playing in the background, a bottle of wine. Just the two of us. What do you say?"

Or maybe it was time for the big test. "How about dinner at my house, instead?" I smiled, and warmth filled me from head to toe. "Just us — and my two children?"

Six hours after leaving Marina's house, I was sitting in Gloria Kuri's living room and sipping a mug of coffee strong enough to curl my toes — not my hair, though. Nothing was strong enough to curl those stick-straight tresses.

Gloria caught my glance at her living room decor. "I need to do something about them. Last week I got a new Oklahoma one and it's messing up everything."

None of Gloria's furniture was placed against a wall; the couch, the overstuffed chairs, the coffee table, and the console television floated in the middle of the room. With the single exception of a wood fireplace burning bright, every bit of flat wall space was consumed by vintage postcards, and each one was mounted in the exact same type of frame.

"Got started collecting when I was a kid." Gloria looked around. "That one there. The

Wisconsin Dells ducks in 1954. You know about the ducks, right?"

I nodded. Once upon a time, my parents had trundled the whole family across Lake Michigan in a car ferry. My older teenaged sisters had been ostentatiously bored the entire trip, but my brother and I had loved the resort area and riding on the old army land-and-water vehicles.

"After the Dells, you branched out?" I asked.

Gloria laughed, a throaty smoker's laugh. Her house didn't smell a whit like cigarette smoke, though. Maybe she didn't smoke in her house for the sake of the postcards. "You could say so," she said. "If you're buying Wisconsin cards, why not Minnesota?"

"Why not?" I agreed.

"Then Michigan, then Illinois, and then I figured I should get one from every state. Then I started for two for every state. I'm on seven." She frowned. "But now I got this Oklahoma one. I gotta decide if I want to get rid of one of the old Oklahomas or start into the eights. And they don't make these frames no more. I'd have to buy new ones. Eight times fifty of even a cheap frame is a lot of bucks."

"What about putting one set in another room?" I suggested. "Then you'd have to buy only fifty frames."

She stared at me. "They have to stay together."

It occurred to me that Gloria and Agnes weren't as different as I'd first thought. Whether from nature or nurture, both had the gift of making people feel stupid. With both hands I held out the cardboard box that had been sitting on my lap. "This is for you. From Agnes's house."

"Yeah?" Gloria put down her coffee and took the box from me. "Oof, that's heavier than I thought. What's in here, rocks?" She held it close to her ear and shook it back and forth.

"They were in her guest room."

"Bet that got used a lot." Gloria rolled her eyes. "Can't imagine Aggie had a whole lot of friends staying over."

Or relatives, I thought.

Gloria unstuck the tape and pulled back the flaps. "Books," she said. "You brought me books." She poked at them with her index finger. "Not even new ones."

I was starting to understand why Agnes hadn't often traveled to Superior. "No, they're quite old — from the 1920s and 1930s. That's one of the reasons I brought them up. Books that old should be in a regulated environment. And most of them are inscribed inside the front cover by Agnes Kuri."

"These are Aunt Agnes's books?" Gloria's face hardened into stone. She picked the top book, *Alice in Wonderland,* from the box. "And my sister kept them all these years." Gloria put the box on the table, picked up two books, and stood.

"You're not going to —"

"You bet I am." Gloria pushed the fireplace screen aside with her foot and pitched *Alice* into the flames, *Fahrenheit 451* in heat and glowing life. In went *Anne of Avonlea.*

"If I were a nicer person," she said, "I'd let my brothers and sisters take a turn." *A Girl of the Limberlost* was committed to the flames. *The Wonderful Wizard of Oz* followed. "But I ain't that nice." Book after book went in. "There." She dusted her hands and replaced the screen, then sat down and put her feet up on the coffee table, a wide grin on her face. "I ain't had that much fun in years. Thanks."

"You're, um, welcome." The fumes of burning glue stung my eyes.

Gloria laughed. "Let me tell you about my dear departed sister. My parents named her Agnes after my dad's aunt. Dad loved his auntie Agnes. She lived with us for years, the old bat. Only one to have her own room, and we always had to run whenever she rang this dang bell."

I wondered if Joanna was still ringing her bell to summon Mack.

"Anyway," Gloria went on, "we waited on her hand and foot, and when she finally died, turns out she had enough money to buy this whole town ten times over. She'd hung on to her stocks during the Depression, and ended up making a killing. How did that old biddy know to pick up Xerox and IBM early? Coca-Cola, too, can you believe it?" Gloria's cheeks were blotched with red indignation.

With the inevitability of an incipient train wreck observed from afar, I knew where this was going.

"Agnes ended up with everything." She slouched low into the couch, shoulders slumping. "Who'd have thought a name would mean so much? It's not like Agnes was going to carry on the family name. We had plenty of boys around to do that.

"Anyone else in the family would've shared." Gloria's face was etched with hostility. "Not my sister. She said she had things to do with that money." Spittle flew out of Gloria's mouth at every overpronounced consonant. "What could have been better than taking care of family? She had millions! It's not like we asked for much. A nice house, a little income. Wouldn't have made a dent in what she had."

"How old was Agnes when your aunt died?" I asked.

She didn't answer for a moment, mired in an ancient battle. "College," she finally said. "The one in Eau Claire."

There it was. The timing explained the first, very short marriage. Poor Agnes. I wondered how much money he'd taken from her. No wonder she hadn't married again. No wonder she kept her distance from people.

And then, with the certainty of a celestial voice from on high, I knew that Agnes herself had donated the money for the school addition. The Tarver Foundation was Agnes.

"Did you know she was sick?" I asked.

"What do you mean?"

"She was a patient at a cancer clinic. The prognosis wasn't good."

Gloria stared at the flames. "Seems a good time to give her sisters and brothers some of Aunt's money. But all she cared about was that stupid foundation. That's all she's cared about for years. Who the heck is Ezekiel Tarver, anyway?"

"Maybe she intended to give something

to her family," I said, "but was killed first."

Gloria watched the fire. "Maybe."

I got up, touched her shoulder, and left. Before I'd backed all the way out of the driveway, I'd started punching buttons on my cell phone.

"Hey, pest," my sister Darlene said. "What's up?"

"Just wanted to hear your dulcet tones." Though I spoke lightly, I meant it as sincerely as I'd ever meant anything I'd ever said.

"Aren't you the funny one? Have I told you about the stunt your oldest nephew pulled the other day? You'd think he'd have more sense at age twenty-five." She went on, telling a tale of pumpkins and white sheets and toilet paper. I pushed the phone against my ear until the skin burned, pulling the comfort of my sister's amused voice into my heart.

Early the next afternoon, I parked in Marina's sunny driveway. The day was as warm as mid-September. After leaving Gloria's house, I'd driven south until just before Oliver's bedtime; then I'd stopped and found a place to sleep. In the motel room's weak light, I'd spoken to the kids, then told Marina about my afternoon.

410

"Wow," Marina had said. "So Agnes was loaded. Who would have guessed? And it was bucks from Agnes that were paying for the addition. No wonder she was pushing it so hard."

"We don't know for sure," I'd cautioned. "It's just a guess."

"Guess, schmess," she'd said. "The puzzle pieces are fitting together. I can feel it."

Now I knocked on her back door and walked in. Maybe Marina could feel things fitting together, but what I felt was a gnawing sense of failure. I didn't feel any closer to identifying the killer than I had the night Marina had sat in my kitchen, pleading for help.

"Mom's here!" Oliver thudded into me, his small arms wrapping around my waist.

I kissed the top of his head. "Hi, handsome. Are you and Jenna ready to go?"

"Hi, Mom." Jenna sauntered into the kitchen, too cool to hug me. "Mrs. Neff made us pack an hour ago." She kicked the bottom of her backpack, which lay near the door.

"Beth!" Marina swept into the room, carrying her laptop like a platter, her hands palm up. "Your timing is impeccable." She thrust the computer at me.

A crawling sense of dread wiggled its way

411

into my stomach. She wouldn't have, would she? I read the title on the screen.

"Jenna? Oliver?" I asked quietly. "Please get your coats, get the dog, take your bags, and wait for me in the car."

"But, Mom —"

"Now," I said, and they went.

Marina, however, was oblivious. "I posted this about nine this morning, and just look at the comments!" She plopped the laptop on the counter and scrolled down. "Almost fifty already. Okay, some of them are mine, but there must be at least forty."

"What's the original post?" My voice was still quiet.

"Well, duh. What you told me last night, about Agnes. Here." Marina scrolled to the top of the page. Again I saw the title: "A Secret Life Revealed?"

My hands turned into dry fists and my throat grew tight. I made one brief attempt to think calm thoughts, then let myself go. "Are you nuts?" I yelled. "That was private information. I didn't go up there so you could blog about it."

She frowned. "You didn't?"

"No, I did it to help you. To find out who killed Agnes. To find out who sent you death threats."

"That doesn't mean I can't use it on WisconSINs."

My whole body felt hot. "I didn't spend my weekend driving to Superior and back so you could get fifty comments on your blog."

A small ding diverted Marina's attention. "Fifty-one," she said, smiling.

"Listen to me!" I pounded my fist on the table. "Some things should stay private. Not everything needs to be broadcast to the world. I gave you that information in confidence."

"You didn't say so." Marina crossed her arms.

I stared at her. "What is wrong with you? Should I get a flag to hold up when something I tell you is off-blog? Put a flower in my lapel?"

She tapped her lips with her index finger. "Not a bad idea."

Cold anger flowed through me. "I have an even better idea — one that would be even easier. How about I never tell you anything ever again?"

She laughed, but her laugh fell away when I picked up my purse. "Beth, come on. Don't be so sensitive, okay? Maybe I went a little far, but there's no harm done. We're trying to find the killer, right? This has to help. I'm sure of it."

I put my hand on the kitchen doorknob, as I had countless times before. "I'd say good-bye, but it might show up on your blog." I shut the door behind me with a quiet thump.

"Are we going home, Mom?" Jenna asked from the backseat. Her arms were full of wriggling dog.

I dragged my thoughts away from *I just had a huge fight with Marina; I just had a huge fight with my best friend* and concentrated on my children. "What do you two want to do?"

"Play!" Oliver giggled.

The sun was shining bright, and I had no compulsion to go home and do housework. "Play it is." In a short minute, we were parked at the school and I was opening the trunk to get out the Frisbee I hadn't put away since our last summer trip to the lake.

"Think we can teach Spot to catch this?" I waggled the plastic disc in front of the dog, and he bounced up and down like a kid on a pogo stick.

"Throw it!" Jenna ran into the empty playground, brother and dog chasing after her.

For a laughing, breathless hour, we were a family, bound together by those invisible cords that can be thinned and loosened, but never broken. "Throw it to me!" Oliver shouted, his small body leaping into the air with wild abandon, the dog at his feet barking with the joy of being able to bark.

"Here!" Jenna held up her arms.

I threw the Frisbee halfway between them. They ran pell-mell toward each other, their gazes locked on the spinning disc, but before either one reached it, a brown streak of dog snatched it out of the air.

"Hey!" Jenna started laughing. "He really can catch them! Look at him go!"

Frisbee in teeth, Spot was galloping into the wild blue yonder.

"Don't let him run off," I called, and the three of us started chasing the dog. He thought it a great game, and we chased the canine from one side of the playground to the other. I grew tired, the kids grew tired, but Spot ran on.

"He's getting away!" Oliver shrieked as the dog darted under a post-and-rail fence that delineated a backyard.

"We'll catch him," I said soothingly, deciding that never again would I let the dog off a leash. "Jenna, don't —"

But she was already climbing through the fence. "Here, boy," she called.

Spot, his doggy grin not quite hidden by the Frisbee, darted out of her reach and scrambled under the side fence and into the next yard. We repeated the sequence through half a dozen backyards, and my patience was long gone when Spot squirreled under a rusty chain-link fence.

"You two stay here." Harkening back to my youth, I put my toes in the open diamonds of the fence and climbed over. "Here, Spot."

The dog actually looked droopy. Without too much effort, I walked him into a corner of the fence, arms outspread. "That's a good boy, pretty boy," I crooned. "You'll never run free again. Nope, never, ever again. That's a good boy." I snatched his collar. "There's a good dog." I leaned down to pick him up, grateful that we'd chosen a dog under thirty pounds, when I noticed a collection of bicycles leaning against the fence.

I stole a glance at the house — dark, with drawn curtains — and edged closer. It was Paoze's ancient bike. It had to be. There weren't many white, scabrous bikes with large metal baskets on the front. It was tempting to take it, right then and there, but I couldn't do that with the kids around. I'd call Gus later.

Thoughtfully, I carried Spot to the fence and deposited him on the other side. "Don't let him go," I told Jenna. When I was halfway over, I looked back at the bike. It had been here in plain sight all the time. All I'd needed to do was look in the right place.

I lowered myself to the ground next to a wagging dog and two chattering children, but I didn't hear a word they said. I looked at the bike, then at the school. At the bike, then the school.

It had been right here all the time.

CHAPTER 20

"You want property information?" The Rynwood deputy clerk peppered me with questions. "What kind? Deeds? Liens? Taxation information? Tax maps? A plat book?"

The brilliant idea that had hit me Sunday afternoon while I was straddling the fence was lacking in specifics. "Property ownership," I said. "That's public information, right?"

"Sure. Do you have the parcel number or an address?"

I shook my head, shifted from one foot to the other, and tried not to feel intimidated. Rynwood's city hall was one of those old municipal buildings with high ceilings, elaborate crown molding, and the scent of an aged patriarchal history. That the thirty-something assistant, Kristen, didn't seem fazed by the environment intimidated me even more.

"Town, range, and section? Subdivision?"

The friendly gaze with which Kristen had begun our conversation was turning into that polite look.

"No, sorry." Up on that fence, I had been struck by the idea that maybe Agnes's murder *was* related to the building addition, but maybe the reason didn't have anything to do with money or even the design from the Black Lagoon.

Maybe the reason was in plain sight; I just had to look at things the right way.

I glanced at my watch. If the city couldn't provide, maybe Dane County could, and I was itchy to see how this idea panned out. Due to long-overdue holiday planning and a busy store, I'd had to wait until Wednesday, when Marcia came in to work afternoons, to get this far. "Well, thanks anyway." I reached into my purse for the car keys.

"Hang on," Kristen said. "There are ways and there are ways. I'm guessing you don't have an AccessDane account?"

"A what?"

"From the Dane County Land Information Office. It's part of their GIS system."

"Gee eye ess?" Down the rabbit hole, once again.

"Geographic Information System. It captures, manages, analyzes, and displays geographically referenced information."

"I see."

She noticed the glazed look on my face and switched to the lay explanation. "Through a GIS you can see where utilities run, see population density, and" — she tapped the computer monitor at her elbow — "you can use online maps of Rynwood to figure out who owns what property."

"I see." And this time, I did.

"Have you ever used a program like this? No? Then you're going to run into a learning curve. Come on in and I'll show you the basics." Kristen tipped her head sideways, indicating a metal door with a sign, AUTHORIZED ADMITTANCE ONLY.

Faster than the White Rabbit on his way to that important date, I found myself seated in a castered chair facing a computer screen full of mysterious things to click.

"This here?" Kristen pointed. "That starts the informational query. Just zoom into the area you're interested in, click on that button there, and the basic parcel info will pop up over here." More pointing. "If you want to see more detail, click this button here."

Information overload. I squinched my eyes shut and reopened them, hoping to see something that made sense. "This one will show me the owner?"

"No. That opens the infrastructure palette.

420

You can turn on and off the water main, gas lines, sanitary sewer, storm sewer. Electrical, if you're lucky. Sometimes cable, but I'm not sure I'd trust that layer. You know how cable guys are."

I was afraid to ask any more questions. If I asked, she'd tell me, and my brain was already too full. I thanked her for her time.

"No problem," she said cheerfully. "I love this program. Intuitive, really. Let me know if you have any trouble."

Half an hour later, I'd had enough of the easy, intuitive, best-thing-since-sliced-bread program. After the third time I'd locked up the computer, Kristen had given me blanket permission to reboot as necessary and shut her door firmly.

"Stupid computers," I said. "Why didn't we stick to paper and pencil? Is this really so much better?" I clicked the mouse on a property next to the school. Nothing. Whacked at the keyboard. Still nothing. "You stink."

"Hey, I showered this morning."

I whirled around. Pete Peterson was leaning against a filing cabinet, the label on his shirt pocket telling the world he was CLEANER THAN PETE.

"What are you doing here?" It came out snippy, but for once I didn't apologize. I hated being watched.

"Trolling for work. City clerks know everyone." He grinned, and I smiled back. I couldn't help it; the man's cheerful mien was infectious.

"Having problems?" He waved at the computer.

I glared at the hateful thing. "I'll figure it out."

"Sure?"

"Sure." I told myself to straighten my shoulders, square my jaw, and focus. Instead, I sighed.

"Tell you what." Pete grabbed a nearby chair. "I'll sit over here and study the latest update from OSHA." The stack of paper in his hand was thicker than Jenna's math book. "If you have any questions, just holler." He sat guy-style, crossing his ankle over the opposite knee.

"You don't have to do this."

" 'OSHA Regional News Release,' " Pete said in a monotone. " 'Legion five. The U.S. Department of Labor's Occupational Safety and Health Administration (OSHA) has cited MHJ Packaging with alleged serious, repeat, and willful failure to abate citations of federal workplace safety and health standards. Proposed fines . . .' "

I turned my attention back to the computer and started concentrating.

"You looking for ownership?" Pete had inched closer. I nodded. "Fastest way," he said, "is to double-click on the parcel number."

I tried it, and lo and behold, up came the ownership information without any need to decipher the meaning of mysterious hieroglyphics. "Hey, that's slick. Thanks!"

"No problem." He went back to his boring news release.

A nice man, that was what Pete Peterson was. He wasn't drop-dead handsome, he wasn't a man to set your pulse racing, and he wasn't the stuff of which dreams were made, but he was nice. Not a bad way to be.

I clicked on things and wrote down things, and soon the blank paper I'd brought with me was filled up with a rough sketch of property lines and the names of who owned what around Tarver Elementary.

Most were people's names; a few of the properties were held by banks, a few by businesses. All the business properties were on a small industrial park directly behind the school. Rynwood Auto Parts, Lakeside Dry Cleaning, Glass Enterprises, and Otto's Heating and Cooling all had properties that abutted Tarver's. But so did thirty-two residences.

My fence-sitting stroke of brilliance had persuaded me that when I saw this list, my brain would make an electric leap. I'd suddenly know — just *know* — who'd killed Agnes.

"This was a dumb idea," I muttered.

"Sorry?" Pete asked.

"And a complete waste of time." I pushed the mouse around. Where was the GET OUT OF HERE button? I started clicking anything that looked remotely appropriate. Why did they make these things so complicated, anyway?

"Hey, slow down," Pete said. "That's a good way to lock it up."

Locking up was good. Then I'd reboot and go away. Click. The dark gray background turned to an aerial image. Click. Thin curvy lines appeared everywhere. Click. Another menu popped up. Click. Red lines appeared.

"Water main." Pete indicated a red line. "Is this what you wanted?"

I stared. A thick red line cut across the school property, close to the school itself, and went into the industrial park. My brain started making little leaps. "Is there a way to find out when this was put in?" I asked slowly.

"Sure." Pete reached for the mouse, made

a long series of clicks, and a list popped up on the screen. "Here we go. Twelve-inch cast iron . . ."

A memory niggled at me, and I tugged around until it pulled loose. The kids and I had been standing in Oliver's favorite part of the playground, back before Agnes had been killed, looking at stakes that had "12″ WM" scrawled on them in thick black marker.

Pete was still talking. "Blah, blah, blah, inspected by whoever, here it is. That main went in three years ago. Laid in August."

Three years ago in August . . . I sat up straight, my brain jumping in great leaps and bounds. Three years ago we'd taken a summer trip to Colorado. No wonder I didn't remember. No wonder I hadn't made the connection before. Dot to dot to dot and none of the dots involved Erica.

Open utility trenches deep enough to bury small children. Or, more pertinent in this case, a full-sized adult.

A disappearing wife.

Interval of a few years.

A surprise construction project.

Certain exposure and imprisonment.

Another murder.

Dot to dot to dot. The clues had been there all along, I just hadn't seen them clearly. But now I knew who had killed Agnes. And I knew why.

"Thanks a million, Pete." I jumped up and gathered my purse and papers.

"Hey, no problem. Glad to help."

He really was a nice guy. I bent down and kissed him on the cheek. "I owe you one." I walked out and, out of the corner of my eye, saw his hand go up to his face.

My cell phone rang as I hurried outside. "Hello?"

"Beth, it's Richard. I can't keep the children tonight." He spoke loudly over an odd assortment of background noises.

I unlocked the car and slid in. "It's Wednesday."

"Yes, I know, and I'm sorry, but my mom is having heart surgery tomorrow. She went in for a checkup, and now she's in the hospital. They wouldn't even let her go home."

"Richard, I'm so sorry."

"Thanks." His voice was rough. "I'm sure she'll be fine, but . . ."

"You have to go. Of course you do. Give her my best."

"I will. How soon can you get here? My flight leaves in an hour and a half."

"You're at the airport?" Suddenly, the noises made sense. He was rolling his suitcase, and disembodied voices were calling flights.

"The kids are right here with me. We'll be waiting at the front entrance."

"I'll be there as —" But he'd already hung up.

"You two stay here." After stuffing the car keys in my coat pocket, I half turned to address both children at the same time — Jenna in the backseat, Oliver in the front. "I'll only be a minute," I said.

"But I haven't seen Mrs. Neff all day." Oliver's lower lip stuck out. "I want to show her my new drawing." He kicked his backpack.

"Show her tomorrow." What I had to tell Marina wasn't for the consumption of small children, and since Marina's DH always took Zach to karate lessons on Wednesday nights, I knew she'd be alone. I was still angry with her, of course, but I could ignore that for as long as it took to deliver this news. "Be back in a flash."

A whoosh of cold, wet air flew in. I got out quickly and shut the door behind me. Inside the car, the kids were already arguing about something. I rapped on the window. "Be nice to each other," I said loudly.

Before I'd moved two steps from the car,

the argument started anew. I shook my head and hurried around the side of the house. For once the gate opened easily; I took it as a good omen. Like I always did, I knocked on the back door as I turned the doorknob. "Marina, it's me." But the door was locked. I rattled the knob and knocked again. "Hey! Let me in!"

A ruffled curtain covered the lower two-thirds of the door's window. I got up on my tiptoes. Marina was at the kitchen table, hands on her lap, staring at the calendar on the far wall.

I banged my knuckles on the glass. "Marina, it's Beth! I need to talk to you!" Marina was first; then I had to call Deputy Wheeler and then Gus. "Hey, c'mon. Open up!"

Marina shook her head and continued her stare-down with November.

Sunday afternoon's spat came back with a rush. "Oh, please." Rain was coming down my neck. The kids were in a car that was growing colder by the minute, and Marina was playing a thirteen-year-old princess.

I hurried off the back stoop and went across the wet lawn. A few months ago when Marina and I returned late from a Friday night movie in Madison, we came back to a locked door. Her DH had bolted it before he went up to bed, and since I'd driven, Marina hadn't brought her keys. "Not a problem," Marina had said as she reached for a hidden key. "Swear you won't tell, okay? The DH doesn't know." Now I waded through soggy shrubbery, crouched, and reached under the wooden deck for a key hanging on a nail.

Water slicked onto me as I backed out of the yews. More water soaked through my shoes and into my socks as I crossed the lawn again. Princess Marina was going to have to lend me some footgear before I went home.

Back on the stoop, I banged on the door one more time. "Hey! Are you going to let me in or what?"

Marina, still at the table and still looking at the wall, shook her head.

I slid the key into the lock, turned the dead bolt, and went in. "What's wrong with you?" Wind came inside with me, and I turned around to push the door shut. "Geez, it's like December out there. Anyway, you wouldn't believe what I found out. I know who killed —"

I faced Marina and suddenly nothing I had to say mattered.

"Beth." Her voice was strained.

It made sense that her voice was tight.

Mine would sound like that, too, if a long and very sharp knife were being held against my throat.

CHAPTER 21

There I was, standing in Marina's kitchen, as I had hundreds of times before. We'd baked cookies, roasted turkeys, and broiled fish in this kitchen. I could almost smell the sugar we'd burned last winter when we'd tried to make caramel. A killer with a knife couldn't possibly have been in this room. Could he?

"Women!" Don Hatcher said. "Why can't you leave well enough alone?"

Much too late, I remembered seeing a white van parked in the driveway next door — Don's, with the magnetic signs for Lakeside Dry Cleaners peeled off.

"Because men keep messing things up," Marina said.

Panic shot through me. I was still standing by the door, at least fifteen feet away from the tip of the ten-inch chef's knife. No way was I going to be able to move fast enough to save Marina from that sharp edge. I shut my eyes.

"Only reason men mess things up is women are always nagging at them. Do this, do that." Don pitched his voice high. "Why did you put the margarine on the left side of the fridge? Why don't you ever take me anywhere? Why haven't you painted the living room yet? Nag, nag, nag." He returned his voice to normal. "You're all the same."

Slowly, I opened my eyes.

"I'm the same as Catherine Zeta-Jones?" Marina put her hand to her chest and fluttered her eyelashes. "How very nice of you to think so."

Don't make him mad, I begged silently. My dear sweet silly best friend, don't, don't, don't make him mad.

"Don't be an idiot," Don snarled. "You're about as like Catherine Zeta-Jones as I am."

Marina cast off a heavy sigh and slid a glance in my direction. "Dashing my hopes and dreams, Don. Just dashing them to bits."

I licked my lips. The fear I'd felt in the basement was nothing next to the fear that was now shredding my heart. Somehow I had to distract Don long enough for Marina to get away from that knife, long enough for us both to get away.

"You didn't mean to kill Agnes, did you?" I asked.

"Another woman who couldn't leave well enough alone. Like this one here." He made a slight move. Marina gasped, and a slow trickle of red started running down her neck. "And you, too, Miss Bookstore. Why were you in Agnes's house the other night? All I wanted was to figure out a way to stop that school addition. Why did you have to get in the way?"

My breaths sounded loud in my ears. "Like your wife?"

"Tanya." The knife sagged away from Marina's pale skin. "It wasn't supposed to happen. She kept on and on about moving to Florida. If it hadn't been during the Packers game, I might have listened." He sounded as if he believed it. "But, no, she had to stand in front of the TV right in the middle of a beautiful pass. Okay, it was a preseason game, but still, I had to shove her out of the way; I *had* to. Wasn't my fault she fell and hit her head on the corner of the coffee table. All those years I thought she had a hard head, and turns out it was soft."

"And the digging for that new water main was right there," I said.

"Yeah. Like an omen or something. They'd just laid the pipe next to the school, and the dirt was nice and easy to dig. After, I told people she took off for Florida. Everyone believed me. No one would have known except that Agnes Mephisto had to get a bug in her head to build an addition. Couldn't leave well enough alone, see? I went there that night to talk some sense into her. I mean no one wanted that addition, no one. But she wouldn't listen." He swore. "I got a little mad and tapped her on the head. Had no idea there were so many people with soft skulls."

"Then here I come with WisconSINs!" Marina sang out.

I made urgent shushing gestures, but she paid no attention. Why was she doing this? If she kept this up, we'd both die. I'd never see Jenna or Oliver again. Or Marina. Or my mother and my sisters. Or Evan.

"Yeah, that stupid blog," he said. "Most of your suspects were dumb. Randy Jarvis? How stupid."

"It could have been Randy." Marina narrowed her eyes. "His car was in her driveway lots of nights."

"Because he was driving her to hockey games in Minnesota. What'd you think — they were a couple?" He laughed. "Women are so dumb. So dumb that you're making me do this. Sooner or later you were going to get too close to the truth."

"I was?" Marina turned a blank look into a smile. "Of course I was. But how did you know the WisconSINista was me? I'm dying to know."

I winced at her word choice.

"Everybody knows." He leered down at her. " 'Daahling.' You're the only one in Rynwood who says that. 'Daaahling,' " he mimicked. "It was all over WisconSINs. You're the worst anonymous blogger in the history of blogdom."

Marina sat straight. "I am not!"

"Shut up." Don grabbed her hair and yanked her to her feet. "You're both coming with me."

"Don't be ridiculous." Marina crossed her arms. "We're not going anywhere."

"No?" Don pulled her head back and inserted the tip of the knife into her ear. "I bet you do exactly what I tell you," he said in a low, quiet tone. It was the scariest thing I'd ever heard. "Beth, I need string."

"Beth, don't you dare." Marina's tone brooked no argument, but I wasn't going to argue. I just ignored her.

"She keeps string here in the kitchen," I said. "Right of the dishwasher, third drawer down."

"Get it."

"Beth," Marina said, reason at the forefront. "It's best to keep a kidnapper from taking victims away from the original scene. If we let him move us to a location of his choosing, there's —"

"Shut up!" Don Hatcher and I said simultaneously.

I held my hands out in front of me — palms up, no threat to anyone — as I went to the cabinet. Don, with the knife blade back at Marina's throat, came behind me.

She was right about the moving thing, but there was one very good reason to get as far away as possible from this house — two reasons, actually, two small, child-sized reasons.

I opened the drawer and took out the ball of string.

"Hands behind your back," Don ordered Marina.

"I would rather not," she said, and for the first time, she sounded scared. Up until now, she obviously hadn't taken the situation seriously. Don Hatcher, balding, bowlegged, and teller of knock-knock jokes, was no one's idea of a vicious killer. But putting your hands behind your back was a kind of surrender, and Marina wasn't ready to give up. "Surely we can work something out."

Her Southern belle accent was weak, but

436

still charming. Tears stung my eyes. Marina was doing all she could. Why couldn't I come up with —

"Tie her hands," Don barked. "Good and tight. Maybe the pain will get her to stop talking."

"Sorry, Marina," I said. "This is all my fault."

"Your fault?" She hung her head. "Don't be ridiculous. I'm the one who talked you into running for secretary of the PTA. I'm the one who started the blog. You told me to stop posting, but did I? No. I had to keep going and going and —"

"Shut up!" Don roared. The knife blade moved, and Marina squeaked in pain. "Tie her. Now!"

Marina's hands, shaking with the palsy of fear, went behind her back. I gripped her fingers briefly, trying in one brief instant to transmit courage and grit and a shared determination to get out of this alive.

"Faster," Don snapped.

My own hands were shaking as I started to wind string around Marina's wrists. There had to be a way out of this. There had to be. We'd find one, and we'd come up with a plan.

Those hopeful thoughts were interrupted when the back door banged open.

And everything changed.

"Mom! What's taking so long?" Jenna ran into the kitchen.

"Yeah, we're freezing!" Oliver dodged his sister and came to an abrupt halt. He looked up at Don Hatcher. "Oh. Uh, hi."

If I'd thought I'd been scared before, I'd been greatly mistaken. Great gulps of panic overtook every part of my body. My hands shook, my teeth chattered, my heart pounded, and the single breath I sucked in seared my lungs with horror.

"No!" To whom I was shrieking, I had no idea. To my children, as a shorthand way of telling them to run? To Don, as a begging plea? To the heavens above, as a prayer? "Don't!" But whoever it was I'd called upon, he didn't respond.

Don's expression of surprise turned crafty and sly. "Perfect," he said. The knife left Marina's neck and she stumbled back, sending us both bumping against the kitchen range.

"Two for the price of one." Don wrapped one arm around Jenna's slender neck and the other arm around Oliver's. "Just do what I say, kids, and no one will get hurt."

It was a lie. The man had already killed twice. What were a few more bodies? All he had to do was stuff us in that white van, then find some rope and a few concrete blocks. There was plenty of deep water in Wisconsin for him to dump us. Pain flared raw in my chest, followed quickly by spasms of guilt. All this was my fault my fault my fault. . . .

"Now we're going to be real quiet, right?" Don tightened his grip around the necks of my children. "Any noise and this is going to get cut off." The knife's point waved in front of Oliver's pale nose.

Jenna's eyes stretched wide. She opened her mouth.

And screamed.

The rage that had been building inside me — anger at Agnes's murder, anger at the way money had ruined her life, anger at my entrapment in the basement, anger at the drips of blood on Marina's neck — erupted as my daughter screamed. The sound electrified my body and catapulted me into action.

Jenna's scream had made Don wince. The knife dropped away from Oliver. I hurled myself forward and grabbed Don's wrist, digging with my nails into his skin and twisting with all the strength a mother could summon. "Drop it!" I yelled. "Drop it *now!*"

The knife clattered to the floor.

"Hiii-yah!"

There was a dull clunk, and Don sagged against me. I sidestepped his weight, and he sank to his knees. Another clunk, and he fell all the way to the floor. Marina stood over him, brandishing the cast-iron pan that lived on the range top.

Instantly, I dropped down, jamming my knees into the small of his back. I grabbed Don's wrists, pulling them up behind him. "Marina," I commanded, "sit on his legs. Oliver, get me the ball of string. It's there on the floor. Jenna, open the tool drawer and get the duct tape. The wide silver tape. And a pair of scissors."

In moments, Don Hatcher was bound and gagged. Oliver brought Marina her cell phone, and she dialed 911. While we waited on our lumpy and struggling sofa for the dispatcher to send cars and trucks and lights and sirens, Marina looked me up and down. "Wow, Beth. I didn't know you had that in you."

Smiling shakily, I held Jenna and Oliver close.

"I knew you'd save us," Jenna said into my shoulder.

"Yeah," Oliver said. "You promised."

"I did?"

"Yeah, every night, when you kiss me good

440

night. You say, 'Sweet dreams, and may tomorrow be your Beth day forever.' Your name is Beth. It's like a promise, right?"

"That's not what she says." Jenna said. "It's 'May tomorrow be your best day ever.'"

"Oh." Oliver drooped, then brightened. "Well, it's like the same thing, isn't it?"

Marina was beaming at me, and my arms were full of living, squiggling children. All was right with the world. "Yes," I said, "it most certainly is."

ONE YEAR LATER

"Can everyone hear me?" Mack Vogel's voice boomed out across the crowd. Our esteemed school superintendent tapped the microphone, and everyone flinched at the loud popping noise.

"We're here today," Mack said, "to open what Agnes Mephisto began so many months ago."

I tried to listen but couldn't quite manage to do so. The absurdly warm weather was too nice to spend listening to run-on sentences. Besides, somewhere in this mass of people was the man I'd recently started to call my boyfriend. Evan was joining Jenna and Oliver and me for a Saturday afternoon of cautious togetherness, and I was trying not to be nervous.

Joanna Vogel, a burbling infant in her arms, stood near me, alternately smiling at the baby and smiling at her husband. Debra O'Conner was almost unrecognizable as a natural brunette. She looked relaxed and content. The two of us had gravitated toward a monthly lunch date, and it was strange not to feel incompetent around her. Maybe someday I'd tell her so.

Julie Reed, the PTA's vice president, held on to a small twin-sized stroller as her husband held the hands of two seven-year-olds. Two parents, four children — Mom and Dad would have to work on a zone defense instead of man-to-man. They looked tired already, and it wasn't even noon.

Erica, representing the PTA, stood at Mack's shoulder. Randy was sitting on a handy bench, wiping his forehead with a handkerchief. Teachers and staff stood in clusters, and small children tugged on parents' hands.

"If Agnes were here today," Mack was intoning, "she'd be proud of what we've done in her memory."

I smiled, thinking back to the day after Don Hatcher was arrested. I'd called a special meeting of the PTA committee and proposed an idea. Erica, Randy, and an extremely pregnant Julie readily agreed. The PTA as a whole leaped on the plan. Erica and I passed the idea up to Mack, Mack passed it to the school board, and the school board talked to the attorneys who guarded the Tarver Foundation. Bick Lewis welcomed the idea, and twelve months later, here we were, standing in the sun.

Mack hefted a pair of hedge clippers and held them at the ready. "Ladies and gentlemen, the Agnes Mephisto Memorial Ice Arena is officially open!"

He snipped the wide ribbon, and the red edges curled high, floating in the light breeze. A stampede of youngsters surged past, and Mack staggered back, bumped by bag after bag of skating equipment.

"I'd like to see him *on skates,"* said a voice in my head.

"Agnes?"

"What did you say, Mom?" Oliver asked. Two inches taller than he'd been a year ago, my son had left behind all his stuffed animals, a few of his poor study habits, and found a new best friend. Robert and his family had left Rynwood one snowy weekend, leaving behind an empty house and a garage full of bicycles.

I put one arm around him and another around Jenna. "Nothing, sweetheart."

"It's not bad," Agnes said. *"I gather Bick's office chose the color scheme? You should have done it yourself."*

"Probably," I agreed.

"Mom?" Jenna asked.

444

"Thank you, Beth. For everything."

And Agnes was gone.

Jenna tugged on my sleeve. "Mom? Did you hear me? Mom? Hello, Earth to Mom. Can I get some goalie pads?"

My daughter, on the other hand, had not abandoned Bailey as a best friend. But two other girls were competing for Second Best Friend, and the expansion was welcome.

"Your dad bought new pads in August." I frowned. "Did you lose them?"

"Not soccer goalie pads." She rolled her eyes. "Hockey goalie pads."

Hockey? It was okay if I wanted to play hockey, but my precious daughter? "Let me talk to your father about that."

"Okay." She grinned up at me. "Cool."

Her smile made my heart almost burst with love. I pulled my children tight, wanting nothing more than to hold them forever and ever.

"Aw, Mom," Oliver said. "Not in public!"

One by one, they shrugged off my embrace and headed into the arena. "We'll be inside," Jenna tossed over her shoulder.

"Daahling." Marina appeared, an orange scarf wrapped loosely around her neck. As a scarf it would have been unremarkable except for the bright pink circles that dotted it. Neither the orange nor the pink went

445

well with either her red hair or her pale peach coat. She noted my look. "Don't you recognize the scheme, mah dear? It's the colors of the girls' bathroom in your new building."

"I didn't have anything to do with the colors." And after a tally of thirty-seven, I'd stopped keeping track of the times I'd said so.

"Silly you," Marina said.

We stood side by side, watching a small river of people head into the arena. A warm glow enveloped me. Thanks largely to my role in the Tarver PTA, I'd helped get this much-needed facility built. I, Beth Kennedy, had done something substantial and worthwhile. My name was on a brass plaque that thousands of people would pass by every year. None of them would read it, but Jenna and Oliver had, and they were the only ones who counted.

Now I was in my second year as PTA secretary, and I had lots of project ideas — a father-daughter dance; then maybe the start-up of a mentor program; after that, a video about the Tarver Foundation.

"Hey, Beth." Marina had snapped out of Southern belle mode.

"What?"

"Now that Don Hatcher's trial is over, and

he's in prison and all, what do you say —"

"No."

"You're going to reject my latest brain-storm out of hand?" She put her hands on her hips. "What happened to the intrepid Beth Kennedy who trudged on with her murder investigation through defeat after defeat? What happened to the brave Beth Kennedy who risked life and limb to save her children and best friend?"

"She decided to retire her superhero costume and live a quiet civilian life."

"Oh, pooh. Aren't you the teensiest bit bored these days?"

"No." But I'd hesitated, and a twitch on her face told me she'd heard the pause. Because she was right. After the excitement of tracking down a murderer, after appearing as a witness in a murder trial, after hearing the guilty verdict, and feeling the satisfaction that no one would suffer from Don Hatcher's temper ever again, I had to admit that life did seem a trifle flat.

"Ah-hah!" Marina grinned. "Bored silly! I knew it!"

Not that I wished anyone dead, of course — not ever, not in a hundred million years. But if something happened, well . . . a *little* murder might be interesting.

We hope you have enjoyed this Large Print book. Other Thorndike, Wheeler, Kennebec, and Chivers Press Large Print books are available at your library or directly from the publishers.

For information about current and upcoming titles, please call or write, without obligation, to:

Publisher
Thorndike Press
10 Water St., Suite 310
Waterville, ME 04901
Tel. (800) 223-1244

or visit our Web site at:

http://gale.cengage.com/thorndike

OR

Chivers Large Print
published by AudioGO Ltd
St James House, The Square
Lower Bristol Road
Bath BA2 3BH
England
Tel. +44(0) 800 136919
info@audiogo.co.uk
www.audiogo.co.uk

All our Large Print titles are designed for easy reading, and all our books are made to last.